RED WIDOW

RED WIDOW

A NOVEL

ALMA KATSU

G. P. PUTNAM'S SONS
NEW YORK

G. P. PUTNAM'S SONS
Publishers Since 1838
An imprint of Penguin Random House LLC
penguinrandomhouse.com

Copyright © 2021 by Alma Katsu
Penguin supports copyright. Copyright fuels creativity, encourages diverse voices,
promotes free speech, and creates a vibrant culture. Thank you for buying an authorized
edition of this book and for complying with copyright laws by not reproducing, scanning,
or distributing any part of it in any form without permission. You are supporting writers
and allowing Penguin to continue to publish books for every reader.

Library of Congress Cataloging-in-Publication Data

Names: Katsu, Alma, author.
Title: Red widow : a novel / Alma Katsu.
Description: New York : G. P. Putnam's Sons, [2021] | Summary: "An
exhilarating spy thriller about two women CIA agents who become
intertwined around a threat to the Russia Division—one that's coming
from inside the agency"—Provided by publisher.
Identifiers: LCCN 2020049599 (print) | LCCN 2020049600 (ebook) |
ISBN 9780525539414 (hardcover) | ISBN 9780525539438 (ebook)
Subjects: GSAFD: Suspense fiction.
Classification: LCC PS3611.A7886 R44 2021 (print) | LCC PS3611.A7886
(ebook) | DDC 813/.6—dc23
LC record available at https://lccn.loc.gov/2020049599
LC ebook record available at https://lccn.loc.gov/2020049600

Printed in the United States of America
1   3   5   7   9   10   8   6   4   2

Book design by Kristin del Rosario

To Anthony Olcott

Colleague and friend, missed by all who knew him

RED WIDOW

ONE

The gentleman in seat 2D was in medical distress when he boarded, the flight attendant is sure of it.

He was the first on the plane, leading the rush of premium club members. She noticed he was already having trouble, stumbling in the narrow aisle, sweat visible on his face. He shoved his overnight bag into her arms to stow for him and asked for a drink right away, a vodka neat. She is used to this kind of treatment from business class passengers, especially on this hop from JFK to Reagan National, which is often full of VIPs, senators and businessmen. He looks to her like a politician, the worst of all. She knows better than to argue with him.

She brings him a glass of water, too, even though he didn't ask for it, in case he needs to cool off or take medication. He's not in great shape—three hundred pounds easy, squeezed into a suit at least two sizes too small. His face is pale, but there's a deep flush creeping up from under his collar.

He grumbles to himself throughout the boarding process, but is otherwise quiet. His cell phone is clutched in one hand as the rest of the passengers squeeze by, his face turned to the tiny window, shunning any possibility of contact. He pays no attention through the safety demonstration but then again no one does anymore, and the flight attendant stopped taking offense long ago.

As the plane taxis onto the runway, she checks the manifest. His name is Yaromir Popov and he came to JFK via an Aeroflot flight from Heathrow. A Russian businessman, then.

No sooner has the Airbus A330 lifted into the night sky than the Russian starts having problems. From the jump seat in the galley, the flight attendant sees his face has turned bright pink and that he's having difficulty breathing. Could he be choking on something? He hasn't pressed the call button so it might just be garden variety anxiety. Takeoffs are the worst for many passengers. She counts the minutes until the fasten seat belt signs go off.

The flight to Washington, D.C., will be quick. Because the plane is barely one-third full, the airline cut back on flight attendants. Tonight, it's just her and another woman, the bare minimum. Still, there's plenty for them to take care of and she doesn't think about Popov again until it's time to take drink orders. By then, he's gotten worse. He is shaking in his seat and on the verge of convulsions. His eyes bulge, and his bright red face is shiny from sweat.

She is glad the cabin is dark and the plane practically empty. She doesn't want to alarm the rest of the passengers. Most have their heads down anyway, trying to catch a quick nap on the ninety-minute trip.

She leans over him, bringing her face close to his so she can check for the smell of alcohol. "Are you okay, sir? Is there something I can do for you?"

He opens his mouth but no words come out, only a gurgling, choking noise.

Something's seriously wrong. Her pulse immediately quickens. She's never had to give emergency medical aid on a plane and she frantically tries to recall what she's supposed to do next. Loosen his tie? Check his airway for obstructions? Signal for the other flight attendant to come help her?

Bubbles form in the saliva that coats his lips, like a rabid dog. She darts into the galley for another plastic cup of water which he gulps down greedily but it does nothing to help him to speak. The shaking increases; it is like he is riding his own personal wave of turbulence. There is a strangled look of panic in his eyes—he knows something is very wrong—but stubbornly keeps trying to speak, as though he is determined to give a message to her.

Spooked, she leaps to her feet and sprints for the cockpit. She knocks on the door and waits for the click of the lock as it disengages before popping her head in. The pilot and copilot look up at her at the same time without even a hint of curiosity as to why she needs to see them. Maybe they think she is bringing coffee.

"We've got a passenger in medical distress. In business class," she adds, knowing that sometimes makes a difference.

A look of annoyance flits across the pilot's face. "How bad is he?"

"I don't know. He seems pretty bad."

The pilot twists in his seat to look directly at her, like this is her fault. "Do we need to turn back?"

"We're almost over Trenton," the copilot says, looking at the instruments. "Even if we turn around, we'd have to circle at JFK for an hour before we could land. It's only another forty minutes to D.C. We can ask for priority landing and for a medical team to be waiting at the gate."

She can tell by the glassy look in the pilot's eyes that his mind is made up. "Yeah, sure, that's what we'll do. You"—he turns to the flight attendant, not having bothered to remember her name—"keep him as comfortable as possible. See if he can give you anything we can radio on ahead to Washington—the name of a doctor, what medications he's on, anything."

She hesitates. "Could you see if there's a doctor on the flight?"

Both pilot and copilot exchange glances; it's the kind of thing they hate to do. It makes the passengers nervous. Ask over the intercom if there's a doctor on the plane and some passengers immediately assume that Ebola has broken out and start freaking out. But the pilot gives a quick nod.

By the time she gets back, Popov is having a full-blown seizure. Luckily, after the announcement on the intercom, the flight attendant from economy class came forward to help. She has the confidence of the very young and—thank goodness—remembers first aid training from her time as a lifeguard at the town pool. She's brought the plane's automated defibrillator with her. The two women huddle over Popov. Given his size, putting him on his side is out of the question, even in the more spacious business class seat. The attendant tucks one of the small, thin pillows under his head and spreads a blanket over him. He's not cold—his clothes are soaked through with sweat—but she does it for privacy more than anything else.

The flight attendant notices a man has crept forward from economy class, watching from a couple seats back. He didn't announce himself to the attendants so he's probably not a doctor. He's just morbidly curious. He is middle-aged but tough looking, like he's former military. She holds out hope for a second that he's an air marshal—she will take all the help she can get at this point—but knows they wouldn't put an air marshal on this flight, not a midnight run.

There is a cold curiosity in his eyes. "Are you a doctor, sir?" she asks.

He says nothing, just gives a curt shake of his head.

"Then would you return to your seat, please?" she asks with only a hint of irritation. People can be unthinkingly rude; she has learned this in her ten years on the job. "We need to give him air."

After one more look at the sick man over the attendant's shoulder, the passenger retreats down the aisle.

The attendant turns her attention back to the Russian. She pats his hand. "Mr. Popov, is there someone we can contact for you? Someone waiting for you in D.C.?" She wishes she had thought of this earlier as the Russian is now nearly unconscious. His eyes are rolled back in his head, his face freezing in a rictus of fright and surprise. He is unresponsive to their questions. His hands are balled tightly, his arms and legs rigid and shaking. Worst of all, foam is coming out of his mouth in waves, like a washing machine gone out of control, like something you might see on a television show. She can't imagine what's wrong with him; she's had passengers with food poisoning and one heart attack, but it was mild. She's never seen anything like this. She is nearly paralyzed from fright.

She glances at her watch. Twenty more minutes. "Hang on, we're almost there," she tells him, though she doesn't think he can hear her.

That's when she sees the note. A scrap of napkin. She can't make out what he's written. It could be a name, but the ink has bled into the napkin's porous fibers. If he was trying to tell her something, she's at a loss.

The rest of the trip goes by in a blur. When she sees that he's slipped into unconsciousness, she and her colleague in economy do as they were trained. One strips the clothing from his upper torso while the other readies a defibrillator. She breathes a silent prayer of thanks for the muscle memory of the classes; it makes what they're doing now seem less unreal. This is something she *can* do. She attaches the pads to the man's chest and side as indicated, sits back on her heels as the machine searches for his pulse. *No heartbeat detected.* It delivers a shock. The other flight attendant begins CPR and she waits impatiently for her turn as the machine counts off two minutes before it will check again. The pair take turns doing CPR, two cycles, four cycles . . . Before long she is damp with sweat and shaky from nerves as each time the machine says *No heartbeat detected* and shocks him again . . .

By the time the first wheel touches the ground—the bounce and sudden deceleration as rubber catches on the second touch—she is ready to accept that he is gone. If not dead then so far gone that it doesn't matter.

They will not be able to keep the other passengers on the plane while waiting for the medical crew to remove the body—they are like thirsty cattle that smell water in the distance—and so she does her best. The other flight attendant ran down the aisle just before landing to get her cabin ready, leaving her alone with the Russian. She takes a second blanket from the overhead bin and drapes it over Popov so his entire body is covered. She stands in the next seat to block the view as passengers disembark, her knees trembling. They shuffle by quickly, eyes averted, even Mr. Curious, who can't get off the plane fast enough.

It's not until the last passenger is gone that the medical crew comes down the jet bridge with a gurney. The crew is nudged aside as the EMTs congregate around the body. The flight attendant stands in the galley, craning her neck to see what's going on, but the EMTs' body language is clear: the passenger is gone. The way they handle the body, there can be no doubt, pulling it out from the tight space like a beached whale and then—drafting in a member of the cleaning crew for assistance—lugging it over to the gurney. The flight attendant takes one last look at the dead man's face as they struggle past her. Poor man.

Then she remembers the note. She had left it next to the passenger, thinking that it might come in handy at the hospital. But it's gone. Disappeared.

Maybe the EMTs took it with them.

Whatever he was trying to tell her, she will never know.

TWO

The phone rings, a jangle of notes that cuts through an Ambien-induced fog and drags Lyndsey Duncan up through the depths of sleep, near but not quite all the way to consciousness. As she fumbles for the cell phone, her hand runs up hard against a lamp, knocking it off the nightstand. In the dark, everything is a puzzle. She moved in two weeks ago, but the apartment still feels like a hotel. Maybe because it came furnished, an impersonal apartment for business travelers.

Large white numbers glow from the screen: *3:22*. It's tough to force yourself awake when you've only been asleep for a couple hours. Or maybe it's jet lag—do you still get jet lag after two weeks?

Then again, she's learned to expect calls in the middle of the night.

"This is Sergeant Mitchell from the SOC." In the back of her mind, she remembers that SOC stands for Security Operations Center, the operational watch at CIA. "I'm calling for Lyndsey Duncan."

"You've found her." *And woke her up.*

"I'm sorry to be calling at this hour, but we need you to cut your leave short and report to work today."

Lyndsey pushes back the bed things—the sheets stiff, blanket heavy, none of it hers, everything unfamiliar. "What?"

The voice remains patient. "I was told that you are currently on home leave and were not expected to report for work until"—a piece of paper rustles in the background—"January twentieth, but there's been a situation and your presence has been requested."

A situation. It could be only one thing, the reason she was put on administrative leave. Her throat is dry from the medication. A glass of ice-cold water would help her to wake up.

"You will need to report to room . . ." As he recites a short string of numbers and letters, Lyndsey has the presence of mind to reach for the cheap pen-and-pad set next to the phone and write it down in the dark. She's been trained to remember things on the fly (telephone numbers, license plates, addresses) but with the Ambien, why risk it?

As she writes, her mind starts to clear. This is not good. There's no reason for them to call her in unless a decision has been made, and a decision this quick is likely to not be in her favor. She came home hoping for a second chance, but apparently that's not going to happen. *We've reviewed the facts of your case and I'm afraid that we have no option but to revoke your clearance and terminate your employment with the Central Intelligence Agency.*

For the millionth time, she thinks of the things she'd done for her job, things she didn't think herself capable of as a young girl growing up fatherless in a small town in Pennsylvania. The Agency picked her up right out of college and changed the course of her life.

She can still remember the presentation that she gave to the recruiters. The slides she'd prepared based on her psychology studies in college, the index cards she'd held in her damp hands. *Ninety percent of all people will lie consistently. The average person will tell three lies every ten minutes. I can predict when someone is lying with greater accuracy than a polygraph.* Not that polygraphs were very accurate, but she knew that was what the Agency used. She thought they'd laugh at her, but the recruiter loved her research. Turned out CIA was very interested in knowing when someone was lying to them.

She thought she'd spend her days in a lab but the Agency had other plans for her.

But now her career is over. Ten years after it started.

"They'd like you to report by eight a.m., ma'am, if that would work for you," the security officer goes on to say. She almost asks if there will be a hearing, if she'll get a chance to tell her side of the story or if she's only coming in to turn in her badge.

But then, the sergeant adds one last thing. One thing that stops the angry conversation in her head and brings her safely back down to earth.

"Oh, and one more thing: you're to report to Eric Newman."

There will be no going back to sleep now.

Lyndsey retrieves the lamp from the floor and clambers out of bed. She can't find her bathrobe. It's as though a spiteful servant packed her bags when she left Lebanon. She's been living out of two suitcases filled with a crazy assortment of odds and ends. Unsuitable shoes, not one decent dress, mismatched jewelry. She is constantly reaching for something that isn't there, a possession that's in a box making its way to the United States on a very slow boat. Since she was the one who did the packing, she has no one to blame but herself.

Even though the apartment is fully furnished down to the sheets and towels, pots and pans, she can't mentally adjust to the space. It's like trying to ride a bicycle in high heels and an evening gown; she seems to constantly be running into things (an awkwardly placed coffee table, a wall where a door should be). Unable to find what she needs in any given moment, nothing ever at hand.

She rubs her face. She should have used the past couple weeks to search for a place to live. She was supposed to have two months of home leave, the term for annual leave you aren't able to burn while you're stationed overseas. Leave that piles up while you're busy being invaluable to the nation's security. Some people come back with six months of paid vacation. Lyndsey offered to forfeit hers if they would let her go right back to work. She wasn't trying to be a hero; it would take her mind off her troubles. But they insisted she take the time.

Trust me, the OHESS doctor had said during the customary checkup on her return. She never liked dealing with the Occupational Heath, Environmental and Safety Services office, it seemed intrusive for your doctor to work for your employer. *Everybody needs to de-stress after an overseas tour. You need to get used to being in the States again.* He had been instructed to say that, she was pretty sure. They needed time to decide what to do with her.

Lyndsey wanders through the apartment in the oversized T-shirt she wears for sleeping, turning on lights as she goes. Because of the Ambien, she rules out another drink. Something hot? Herbal tea, cocoa? But there's next to nothing in the place, only one-cup bags of ground coffee brought daily by the housekeeper, because she has been avoiding the grocery store. She really should go shopping.

She can hardly believe her luck. She hasn't been fired; she knew as soon as she heard Eric Newman's name. He was her first boss at the CIA. Their paths have crossed innumerable times since then, which is to be expected since they work the same target. He'd been made Chief of Russia Division a few years ago, a powerful position. Whatever's happened, the reason for the call, has something to do with Russia. But CIA has lots of

Russia hands, many of them with more years on target than her. It's a little odd that he would ask for her by name. She wonders what he might know about her time in Lebanon—and her return.

She sits on the couch, tucking her cold, bare feet beneath her. She tries to remember how she left things with Eric the last time she'd seen him. She'd always thought him a good guy, a boss who wanted to do the right thing for his people, but there had been grumbles. Weren't there always grumbles about the boss? *Show me one manager who is loved by* everyone.

Eric Newman asked for her by name.

She finds the remote and turns on the television, flipping quickly to CNN. The news is all reheated from earlier, not a clue as to what could be behind Eric's request. Wrangling over financial reforms in Congress, another round of peace talks in the Middle East, and baseball's team owners about to meet in Florida. The reality is that whatever is behind the SOC's call, it hasn't hit the news. It's something bad that the rest of the world doesn't know about yet.

But, in four hours, she'll find out.

THREE

CIA has not changed in the five years Lyndsey has been gone.

The next morning, the headquarters building makes no attempt to charm, only to impress. White walls like a glacial field. Wide terrazzo floors. The main hallway hung with oil paintings of former Directors, their solemn faces (knowing, judgmental) staring down on the passing streams of employees. While it has felt stifling at times, Lyndsey also finds something reassuring about the sameness, a promise that despite the rolling crises, where the job is meeting one impossible challenge after another, this place will endure because it must.

She sees as soon as she steps through the door to Russia Division that not much has changed here, either, a fairy kingdom that went into hibernation the moment she left, awaiting her return. The same drab colors, the dated furniture. The same binders of case studies and training materials collecting dust, that no one has looked at since they were first shelved. And the window dressing to remind visitors where you are: a row of *matryoshka,* Russian nesting dolls, line up on the receptionist's desk.

A Soviet-era flag that's seen better days hanging on a wall, greeting visitors as they enter the vault. *Welcome to the Evil Empire. Abandon all hope ye who enter here.*

As she waits for the office manager to fetch Eric Newman, she looks over the rows of cubicles. At this hour, the room is only half-full, but most heads remain hunched over computers. Only a few swivel in her direction and she doesn't recognize any of them. The old hands, the people who would know her, have worked their way into the corners, out of sight.

Eric Newman emerges from his office, his right hand outstretched. He shakes hers like a politician who needs her vote. He hasn't changed much, either, since the last time she saw him. They like guys like Eric at Langley, tall and lean and reasonably good looking. Works out every morning in the gym in the Agency's basement, dresses well but not too expensively, charges around with a seemingly endless supply of energy. He's always calm and competent and in control.

"Good to see you, Lyndsey. Thanks for coming in. How—" He almost asks about Lebanon but catches himself. It would be a perfectly normal thing to ask someone who's just returned—unless that person has been recalled pending evaluation.

Lyndsey pretends not to notice. Instead, he asks, "How long have you been back?"

"Two weeks."

"That's barely time to unpack. I'm sorry to have to cut your home leave short."

He leads her down the hall to his office. It's nicer than she remembers. They're treating him well. Large by headquarters' standards, with enough room for a couch and armchair to one side, a conference table and six swivel chairs to the other. A cluster of three tall windows looks out on the trees, the scene so idyllic and peaceful that it resembles a college campus.

His desk sits toward the back of the room, facing out like a captain's bridge. Unlike many managers at Langley, Eric doesn't decorate his office with mementos, no "me wall" of awards and commendations doing their best to impress you. Uncluttered and focused, Eric's office projects that he's stronger than that.

Lyndsey's mind flits back to when she and Eric first met. He was a branch chief then, two rungs down the ladder from where he is now, with his circle of responsibility commensurately smaller. He was her first boss in the clandestine service when she finished the trainee program and wrapped up her assignment in the Directorate of Science and Technology, building on the paper she'd worked on at the University of Pennsylvania, the one that got all the attention, brought the job offer in the first place. Eric had been interested in her work in the DST, even the paper she'd written, though she'd been out of school for years at that point and college seemed like another life. He undoubtedly had something to do with the decision to send her to Moscow for her first overseas assignment. It was rare to get such a plum assignment right off the bat. "Don't make us regret sending you," he'd said with a chuckle as he toasted her at the going-away party.

Then she brought in Yaromir Popov as a major asset and her future seemed assured, all their trust in her validated.

Now she is on administrative leave pending adjudication. What a difference a couple of years can make.

Eric takes the armchair with the easy command of a king on his throne, but his face is troubled. "I'll cut right to the chase: I called you in because we have a crisis on our hands. In the past couple weeks, we lost two of our assets in Moscow. They disappeared. Vanished."

When two of your recruited spies disappear in such a short a time, you have to assume the worst. Discovery by Russian internal security, arrest. Prison, or worse. She can't remember this happening since she's been at the Agency. Sure, assets stopped performing and took themselves out of the game, or you stopped expecting anything from them. But they'd never lost one to the enemy, not in her time.

"These were two of our most promising assets," Eric continues. "The first is a colonel in the Russian Ground Forces, Gennady Nesterov. He'd been working for us for a few years. He'd just been assigned to a new unit, an elite cyber force. The unit was supplementing its ranks with hackers. They'd arrest guys selling malware on the dark web, you know, garden variety criminal activity, and give them the option to either work for the government or go to jail. It was the only way for the military to get the skills it needed." Lyndsey is familiar with the story. Russian army recruits were bottom of the barrel, country boys with no prospects, most of them dropouts from school. "Nesterov had just warned us that his unit got the call: something big was about to happen. Then he disappeared."

"You think they were on to him?"

"Moscow Station was just starting to look into it when the second disappearance happened. A scientist, Anatoly Kulakov. He's part of a very small but very important program. The Office of Tactical Solutions. They look for ways to apply new technologies to ground warfare. Most of what he's passed to us hasn't been immediately useful. Developmental stuff, basic research. Still, we get insight into the strategic direction of research over there. He disappeared a few days ago."

One in the military, one in research. Two different departments. You might lose one to a routine counterintelligence sweep. Lyndsey knows there are reasons why an asset might get rolled up. It could be entirely self-inflicted: he may have made a mistake that led to his arrest. He might have been arrested for reasons that had nothing to do with spying—a domestic squabble, a lawsuit gone bad. It happened. But two assets, from two different walks of life? The odds against it are astronomical. No, this is textbook: when arrests start, chances are that you've got a spy in your midst. A traitor handing over your secrets to the adversary.

There could be a spy in CIA.

Eric shifts unhappily in his chair. "I want you to handle the investigation. Obviously, I can't turn to anyone inside the Division. You have experience both with Moscow Station and Russia Division. You know how both operate and we're going to need that. I knew you'd be the right person for the job. When I heard you were back from overseas, I couldn't believe my luck."

Lyndsey hesitates. It will embarrass Eric if he puts her in charge and then finds out that she's being investigated. As much as she would like the opportunity—she feels strongly about the mission, having worked the Russia target nearly her entire career. And it would help rehabilitate her reputation. But she owes it to Eric to tell him. Though the thought of recounting what she's done makes her sick to her stomach. It's like admitting he was wrong to trust her all those years ago, to have any faith in her whatsoever.

Her palms have gone sweaty and she rubs them against the legs of her pants. "I appreciate the vote of confidence, Eric, I really do. But there's something you should know first—"

He waves her off. *He already knows.* She can tell by the way he looks at her, the hint of disappointment he struggles to hide. "If it's about what happened in Beirut, you don't have to tell me."

She's not sure if she's irreparably embarrassed or grateful that she doesn't have to explain. "Well, I don't know the *details,*" he clarifies quickly. "Security is pretty strict about that stuff. When I raised your name up to the seventh floor, that's when they told me you were sent home early from Lebanon."

She wishes she could walk out and spare herself this shame, but the feeling passes. You learn early in this job that it's going to require an uncomfortable degree of candor. That you must admit your every trespass, your every failing, to complete strangers. You're expected to lie to your spouse and your children in the line of duty, but you can't lie to the Agency. It's your confessor and parent and spouse.

She fixes her gaze on him. Steady. "You want me to tell you the whole story?"

"It's your call. If it makes you feel better."

Who knows, maybe it will. Aside from Security, she's talked to no one about it. Left the Chief of Station's office in Beirut so utterly embarrassed, she'd wished the earth would open up and swallow her. Her shame was red-hot, like she'd been on fire. What she needs is someone with a bucket of water. And here is Eric Newman, volunteer fireman. "Maybe sometime. Soon. I'm not ready to talk about it yet."

He seems disappointed but nods.

"If I'm cleared to work on this, I can only assume they don't consider me a security threat." She's only a danger to herself.

Eric shifts again in his seat. "Well, they had their reservations, but I told them there were extenuating circumstances. There was no runner-up. It had to be you. Because there's one more thing—something I haven't told you yet." The tentativeness falls away and suddenly he looks like the saddest man in the world. "Have you seen the *Post* this morning?" He is watching her face. "I'm sorry to have to tell you. So, so sorry."

Enough with the apologies—tell me already. Her skin is crawling. How much bad news can one person take?

Eric takes a deep breath. "Yaromir Popov is dead."

Her heart does a stutter step. Her first asset. *Impossible. This cannot be.*

Eric continues, talking over her shocked silence. "It happened last night. He was flying to D.C. From everything we've been able to gather, he had no reason to make the trip. It came out of nowhere. State Department didn't have him scheduled for meetings, no 'official duties.' It could've been some other business or a personal reason, of course, but . . ." Eric trails off; they both know that this isn't likely. "Are you okay? It's got to be an awful shock. Can I get you some water?"

Lyndsey can only blink at him. To the rest of the world, Yaromir Popov looked like a mid-level diplomat in the Russian foreign ministry, a man who filled out the table during negotiations, chatted up visiting foreign delegations, and attended endless rounds of diplomatic functions.

But behind the quiet façade and accommodating demeanor, he was really a high-ranking officer in the Russian Foreign Intelligence Service. A man with thirty years in Russian intelligence.

A man who had been a double agent for CIA.

Lyndsey knows this because Yaromir Popov was her first triumph as a case officer. But there was more to their relationship. She could admit to some people—no one at CIA, of course, but the people who were really close to her—that Yaromir Popov was like a father to her.

And she'd already lost one father. Losing two might be too much to bear.

Time has slowed. Seconds pass like minutes. The sunlight falling across the conference table is so bright, it stings Lyndsey's eyes. Sound is muffled, like the world has been wrapped in cotton batting, quietly ushered away.

She pictures Popov's face. The way he smiled for her, like a delighted parent. Always happy to see her, even when the business at hand was bad. They met in that shabby safe house off Arbat Square or in rented cars parked along quiet Moscow streets. He always carried himself with dignity, but there had been sadness, too. He had been somewhat tortured, ending his career working with the enemy. But his disgust for what had happened to his country under the oligarchs ate away at his belief that the enemy was *external*. The more patriotic thing to do was to try to rid his country of the parasites.

He had managed to turn his sadness aside, and even seemed to enjoy working with his American handler. To channel his energy into teaching the tricks of the trade—*his* side of the trade, that is. He had come to see her, over time, as his protégée.

But now, he was dead.

She had been his recruiter, his handler. Yaromir Popov wouldn't have been a target if it wasn't for her.

Eric has the office manager bring coffee, dark as pitch from sitting too long on the burner. It unblocks her ears and focuses her eyes.

Her hands are unsteady on the cup, making the coffee tremble. "How did it happen?"

"It looks like a heart attack. He was on the last leg of the Moscow trip, JFK to Reagan National. It departed JFK at eleven p.m., arrived at Reagan about midnight. The attendant said he started showing signs of distress shortly after he boarded. That's all we know. No surprise, the Russians are demanding the body back right away. We got the D.C. health department to hold on to it, saying he might've died of some communicable disease, but they could only do so much. It's got to go back today. We're waiting on the report."

How did they kill him? Russian intelligence is known to love its poisons. They have a long history of political assassination by poison, quirky and cruel at once. Something about the delayed effects and painful drama at the end that appeals to the Russian nature. Lyndsey thinks of Popov dying alone on the plane, panicking as his airways swell shut. Realizing that help is 33,000 feet below. Recognizing what is happening to him, knowing that his choices have caught up to him.

Was he running for his freedom? He wouldn't flee without his wife,

Masha, and daughters, Polina and Varya. She is sure of that—pretty sure. Even though the Russia of today is not Cold War Russia. The spouses and children of traitors aren't automatically thrown in prison. If he were running, then poisoning him on the plane would send a message to other would-be traitors—and the big middle finger to America at the same time. *We knew he was your man and you were not able to save him.*

Now that the shock has eased, she sees pain on Eric's face. Of course, Eric must be taking Popov's death hard, too. He knew the man—not as well as Lyndsey, but the Russian asset had been one of Eric's coups. He owed much to Popov. Nearly as much as Lyndsey.

Eric won't want consoling, however, so she presses on. "Do we think his cover was blown?"

"He should've gone to Moscow Station if that was the case. We have procedures for this."

And, in this case, there is only one person for Popov to turn to. The person Popov was *told* to report to. "Who's his handler now?" Lyndsey asks. When she left Moscow Station, there had been a near complete turnover in personnel. This is not uncommon; the bureaucratic changing of the guard had a rhythm to it. Popov's new handler hadn't been decided by the time she left for her next assignment. There had been no overlap, no handoff.

But Eric doesn't answer her question. Instead, an eyebrow shoots up: *don't go there.* "No one was going to have the same success with Popov that you did. You can't blame the handler." Things will undoubtedly get ugly, political. Moscow Station will feel threatened and defensive. His subtext is clear: *don't start attacking Moscow Station and turn this into a war between headquarters and the field.*

Yaromir Popov. The thought of him pushes all other concerns out of her head. She will always be defined in part by the man. She never told him what he meant to her. That for two years, he was the mentor she never had at CIA. The one person, ironically, she felt she could trust.

Eric stands: this meeting is over. He starts to ease her to the door. "The Director told me to set up a task force to get to the bottom of this. It needs to be small, given the circumstances. We're not lifting the compartment, for obvious reasons. I need you to work quickly on this. He would like an answer as soon as possible. If the Russians knew about Popov, all of our assets there could be in jeopardy. Lives are at stake."

Lyndsey rests her hand on the doorknob and turns to him. "One last question . . . You've had some time to think about it . . . If there is a mole, chances are it's either here or in Moscow Station. Do you have a sense . . . ?"

"I'd rather it was in the Station, of course," he says quickly. "And Moscow Station will insist that the mole is here. That's another reason why I asked for you: both offices will see you as neutral. And for Popov's sake, I knew you'd want to be involved. So you see, Lyndsey, it has to be you."

FOUR

Eric calls the office manager, Maggie Kimball, a tall, no-nonsense woman, and asks her to help Lyndsey get settled. To Lyndsey, he apologizes: she'll need privacy for her work but it will take a day or two to clear one of the private offices. In the meantime, she must make do with one of the empty cubicles.

Every office at Langley, it seems, has a Maggie, a take-charge woman whom everyone turns to when they need something done. Organize the office holiday party, accommodate all the dietary restrictions to make sure that no one is offended or poisoned. Figure out a way to seat three summer interns and two new hires when there are only two empty desks. And, most important, wrangle the boss and make sure he gets his to-do list done each day. One look at Maggie and Lyndsey is sure the woman—a little younger than Lyndsey, highlighted hair piled on top of her head, dark green polish on her dragon-lady nails, tight smile—is more than up to the task.

Maggie finds Lyndsey a desk in a quiet corner of the floor, half-hidden behind a pillar and a row of safes, the reinforced file cabinets with combination locks that are as big as Sherman tanks. It feels like exile, though for the job Lyndsey is about to undertake, that's not necessarily a bad thing.

The woman in the next cubicle looks strangely familiar. Lyndsey feels she might know her, though not in a personal way. More like someone you might recognize from a TV commercial. She is fortyish, a few years older than Lyndsey. She is elegant, with narrow shoulders and hips. Her russet-red hair is cut in an old-fashioned bob that goes perfectly with her chic black dress. She looks like the kind of woman you find in the New York Sunday society pages, very white and very thin, the product of one of those aristocratic families who believe in eugenics.

The woman shows no interest in Lyndsey, continuing to peck at her keyboard as though Lyndsey isn't standing five feet behind her. It's odd behavior, but Langley is full of odd ducks.

Lyndsey steps into the woman's field of vision and sticks her hand out. "Hello. I'm Lyndsey Duncan."

They shake. The woman's hand is like doeskin wrapped around a mouse's skeleton, small and soft and crushable. "Theresa Warner."

Theresa Warner. Theresa Warner was a junior officer who'd already distinguished herself when Lyndsey first came to Russia Division. Five years ahead and she made the most of every one of them. She looks so different from how Lyndsey remembers her.

"I actually worked here previously. I think we met, briefly."

Theresa's head tilts like a terrier's as she puts the pieces together. "Oh yes, *Lyndsey.* Of course, I remember you." She must be pretending: there is no reason for Theresa Warner to remember her. They were in different circles then. Lyndsey, fresh out of training and Theresa part of the elite. Worlds apart. "Welcome back."

Lyndsey checks out the desk as she waits for the computer to boot up. A steno pad with half the pages ripped out. Two old pens, tooth marks in the plastic shells. A handful of paper clips. Does anyone even use paper clips anymore? "I won't be staying long. I'm here for the investigation," she says absently.

A thin, perfect eyebrow arches. "The incident from last night, you mean? The Russian on the plane? They haven't told us anything about it yet. It's all close hold."

That's right, the compartment. You don't know who has been read in and who hasn't. She shouldn't have said anything. "Yes, I suppose you're right."

Theresa Warner turns back to the monitor. Next to her computer is one and only one family photo, a picture of a young boy with dark hair and the biggest eyes Lyndsey has ever seen. No pictures of a husband anywhere.

That's because Theresa's husband had been killed in an Agency operation gone wrong. The pieces come back to Lyndsey now. Theresa Warner is The Widow. They had made a big deal when they put her husband's star up on the Wall of Honor, splashed around a photo of Theresa from the ceremony. Skeptics snarked it was because she looked like Jackie Kennedy and would remind people of the tragic romance of dying for your country. Lyndsey heard about the incident shortly after she arrived in Lebanon and she never heard any details of what had happened. Close hold, no need-to-know. Like everyone else, she only heard that Richard Warner had died.

Richard Warner had been a branch chief in Russia Division when she first came on board. Not that she'd ever worked with him. She only knew him in passing. He and Eric had both been branch chiefs then—though he surpassed Eric at some point.

It is kind of strange to find Theresa still working at Langley. How awful it must be, to spend your days in a place where everything reminds you of your lost spouse. Most people would've quit. Of course, everyone's circumstances are different. Perhaps Theresa can't afford to leave, or doesn't want to look for a new job. There is the son, obviously. Perhaps she stays out of loyalty, or the possibility of avenging her husband's death.

Suddenly Eric is walking toward her. He looks like he's on his way to something important, a stand-up over a late-breaking crisis, a meeting with the Director on the seventh floor. He is rushed but puts on a good face.

"Good, you two have met. I was coming to introduce you. Don't you know each other already? Didn't you work together in the early days?"

"No," Lyndsey says.

"Well, if you need anything, I'm sure Theresa would be happy to help you get settled." Then he heads off to fight his next battle.

Theresa narrows her eyes, studying Lyndsey. "Weren't you at Moscow Station recently?"

Lyndsey thinks she knows where Theresa is going with this but she wasn't there when Theresa's husband died. Lyndsey opens her mouth to say how sorry she was to hear about Richard, but Theresa cuts her off. "I'd love to catch up, but I don't have time to talk right now. I have a report to finish. Maybe later?" And with that, she turns her back on Lyndsey and goes back to her keyboard, keys clacking away.

Dismissed. Lyndsey pokes around the empty desk for a few minutes and then heads to Maggie's station. The office manager looks up as she approaches.

"Is there another empty desk I could use? I feel like I'm—imposing on her space."

"Oh, don't mind her. She can be a little chilly." Maggie drops her voice and leans forward, a curl dropping onto her forehead. "You know who she is, right?"

Lyndsey nods.

Maggie glances over her shoulder to see if someone might be listening but there's no one around. "They call her the Red Widow around here. Because of, you know." She gestures to her mouth. Theresa's fire-engine-red lipstick. Not something a widow would wear, is the implication. "Then there's the sports car. It's a Jaguar, that really famous model. Bright red. It was Richard's. She drives it once in a while, when the weather is really nice. Parks it in Richard's old spot. So everyone will remember him, I guess."

"That's very—loyal of her." Lyndsey struggles for words.

Maggie shrugs and turns back to the monitor, to whatever she was doing before Lyndsey came up. "I'm afraid we're full up, no other desks at the moment. But don't worry, it'll just be a day or two. I'm working on getting you a private office. You won't have to put up with her for very long."

Lyndsey walks back to her desk, sobered. She would've liked to reconnect with Theresa, but this is not the woman she knew. She has been upended by loss and changed irrevocably. No longer a person harboring the usual hopes and beset by normal tribulations. She has been transformed by tragedy into The Widow.

FIVE

yndsey has just returned from the vending machine in the hall—vending machine coffee has to be better than the tree pitch in the office's coffeemaker—when Maggie stops by her desk.

"There's someone in the conference room to see you. From CI."

Counterintelligence. It's not the worst news: if it had to do with Lebanon, they'd have sent someone from the Office of Security. The men in Security are humorless, unsmiling and unblinking. After the events of the past month, the accusations and threats, she's had enough of Security to last her a good long while, thank you.

There is something unexciting about the man she finds in the small conference room. Counterintelligence are the people who look for in-house spies. In many ways, it's a small world unto itself, chasing leads that rarely pan out. A dull job for dull, suspicious people. As opposed to the Clandestine Service, her service. The glamourous work, the stuff of legends.

"Raymond Murphy," the man says as he rises to shake her hand. His dishwater-colored eyes give her a once-over. She studies his face in return.

Wary. Something he's trying to hide, that he doesn't want me to see. He's the kind of man who mows the lawn every Saturday morning whether it needs it or not, shines his shoes every Sunday, always buys the same brand of cereal. "I've been assigned to work with you on the task force."

It makes sense that Eric would get someone from CI to assist on this. They have access to information that she wouldn't, from financial disclosure statements to background checks. And computer logs. Still, she can't help but feel slightly uncomfortable, as though he's looking over her shoulder, too. All Agency people feel that way about them, she figures. They're like internal affairs in a police department.

"I've been told that you're just back from overseas, getting your feet on the ground," he continues. How much has he been told about her specific situation, she wonders, before admonishing herself to *STOP THINKING ABOUT THE THING* that hangs over her head like the Sword of Damocles. Her lapse of judgment. Her relationship with a foreign national, an agent of another intelligence service to boot. Davis Ranford, a British citizen . . . and a member of a rival service. *The rules are there for a reason,* Chief of Station Beirut had said when he sent her back to D.C.

Rules that others have broken and gone unpunished, but who does the breaking is as important as which rule was broken.

Murphy gives no indication that he's aware of the debate raging in her head. He swivels his chair lazily. "I thought maybe we could start with some background, get you set up. Have you ever been involved in an investigation like this before?" He leans back, but she senses he's not as relaxed as he'd like her to think. "This is probably an insider threat. We like to say Counterintelligence is like an iceberg. The part we can see is probably less than ten percent of what's really going on. You usually don't have a clue until something like this happens."

He means a double agent. Someone on your team selling secrets to the enemy. It's not entirely a surprise to Lyndsey. The Agency teaches its employees about treason. They sit in classes devoted to the case histories of famous traitors: Robert Hanssen, Aldrich Ames, Ana Montes. They are made to learn the particulars of their treachery. They are taught the warning signs—unexplained wealth, sudden and unaccountable foreign travel, spurts of sudden chumminess alternating with prickly distance—so they'll know when to be suspicious if they see these signs in a coworker. So you'll be able to tell when the person sitting beside you might be selling secrets to foreign masters.

And yet it seems surreal to Lyndsey. Impossible. The kind of thing that never happens in real life. That only happens in movies.

"It's more common than we think," Raymond says, as though reading her mind. "You should know that going in. We're going to have to look *hard* at some of your colleagues and it's going to feel uncomfortable. You're not going to want to believe what you're seeing." His dishwater-brown eyes don't seem so vague now. "Chances are good that someone inside this building has committed treason. Maybe even someone you know."

She already feels funny. She doesn't want to judge her coworkers; she knows what it's like to be judged. "Isn't it possible that it *isn't* someone on the inside? Couldn't the Russians have found out on their own?"

He smiles like he feels sorry for her, clinging to a fairy tale. "Well, sure, there's always a *possibility*. And if that is what happened, it'll be your job to prove it. But it's far more likely that it was someone inside. Someone who knew these guys were working for us."

"But it could be Moscow Station. Could you look into the people there, see if there are any possibilities . . ." *See if there are any weak links,* she means but cannot say. Disciplinary cases, case officers who've fallen behind in child support or started drinking.

"That's a good division of effort. I'll look at the Station and you cover Russia Division. I'd like you to start by finding out which officers in

Russia Division were working on those cases. Kulakov, Nesterov, and Popov. Check their reactions, how they're taking it, see if any of them act defensive. You pass those names on to me. I have access to their files, so I can check out their stories, look for unusual activity." That means financial disclosure forms, security paperwork, requests for unofficial foreign travel. A CIA officer's personal life is well documented. It's hard to keep secrets from Uncle Sam.

"We should check the access lists, too," Raymond continues. "Who knew these guys' true identities in the first place? See how many people we're talking about. We've already started the paperwork to get you approved for the compartments. Get in touch with your Security office."

"Okay." And again, she sees something funny in his expression. A razor-thin but shell-hard veneer. Suspicion.

He can't seriously think she had anything to do with this. That's the thing about dealing with CI: they have a way of making you worry even though there's nothing to find.

It's not Davis Ranford. Raymond Murphy might know about Beirut—let's face it, he probably knows—but she suspects it's something else, something that's been around longer. Maybe he's heard the stories about her, stories that will haunt her for the rest of her career.

Because Popov had been a legendary Russian spymaster and she had been his first handler, and they had been close. Lyndsey had gotten the old SVR spymaster to give up more on the Russian spy machine than anyone else in CIA's history. With that success came suspicion. How had a young officer on her first big assignment been able to succeed where no one else had? Was it because she was merely lucky, or had there been some quid pro quo, some double-dealing? There were some—officers with many years of service with nowhere near the same success—who were sure something bad had gone down, that Lyndsey could not have been that good or that lucky. Men who were as sure of it as they were of anything.

They had investigated—and found nothing. Because there was nothing to find.

They can't seriously think she has been working for Moscow all this time. That she and Popov fed Langley a string of lies to establish her bona fides, to make her look like a wunderkind. In their twisted logic, Popov's death would make sense: Moscow could've killed him to protect her story, if he was the only one who knew the truth . . .

Now there's Lebanon. Actual proof that she is a bad egg.

Anxiety blooms in her chest like heartburn. She knows there is no link between Yaromir Popov and what happened in Beirut, just as she knows they will look, because that is what the job calls for, chasing ghosts. Hoping to catch something that you can't see.

This eternal suspicion, which some would call vigilance.

How sad to always be suspicious, she thinks as she looks at Raymond. To never be able to trust anyone you work with, not one hundred percent. What that must do to a person over time, filled with mistrust as corrosive as acid. Stay in the job too long and one day, you're hiring a private investigator to follow your spouse and having the kids microchipped and installing keylogging software on their computers.

How much does he know about Davis Ranford, about what she did? Everything, probably. No, not everything. He can't know her feelings. He may know that she and Davis often met at a bar on Armenia Street, even though they avoided nightclubs and going out in general because the threat of being seen together—he was MI6—was too great. But sitting on a restaurant terrace on a Wednesday night to watch the last streaks of light evaporate from the sky seemed safe enough.

She couldn't date anyone in the Station. It didn't take a week after she'd arrived to know there was something off about Beirut Station, a toxic boys' club led by a sadistic Chief of Station. She'd known when she agreed to the assignment that going from the Russia target to the Middle

East would be what they liked to call a "challenge," needing to prove herself all over again to people who'd just as soon not have the competition. She just didn't know how bad a decision it had been until she walked through the door. That the old guard in the Clandestine Service clearly had it in for her.

She couldn't be friends with coworkers: she couldn't trust them, that was clear. She'd reconciled herself to a lonely two-year tour when she met Davis at an embassy function. She sensed right away that he was also an outcast, even if she couldn't tell what personal failing or mortal sin had made him so. Why his colleagues at the British embassy ostracized him—except maybe jealousy, but she was partial to him. She liked his dry wit.

So many evenings spent on the terrace of the bar on Armenia Street, neither of them saying a word to each other. They'd done a few touristy things—visited the Cedars of God in Kadisha Valley, explored the Jeita Grotto—but more often than not, if they went out in public, they ended up at this terrace bar, sipping gin and listening to bickering rise up from the street below. Davis was in his mid-forties and she'd never dated someone that much older, but it only seemed to amuse him. "It'll be a huge boost to your ego, you'll see," he said with a smile. "You're so much quicker and nimbler than I am, and know everything that's popular—books, movies, celebrities—while I will know absolutely nothing. Before long you'll be wondering what you ever saw in me."

It wouldn't last forever, she knew, but she had been in no rush to end it. She liked that he never stumbled by mentioning their world outside of Beirut: saying that she'd have to visit when he went back on home leave, or offering to join her in America at Christmas. Their two worlds had to remain separate. It was why they didn't venture outside one or the other's apartment on the weekend: too great a risk of being seen together. Officers from different intelligence services should not date one another.

"I don't see the harm. You're British," she'd said once. "You're practically American."

"Is that supposed to be a compliment?" He'd made a face. "Don't believe that 'cousins' talk people like to toss around. MI6 is well aware that Langley hates us, and you'll find your lovely ass in serious trouble if they find out."

Davis was the only thing that made Beirut bearable. He was always honest with her, perhaps the only one in the entire strange city. He'd been in MI6 for over twenty years and had come by his jadedness honestly. "I'm in it for the travel. I'm afraid England's not big enough for me and my family and my ex."

Sitting in this stuffy room with Murphy, she can still picture Davis on the terrace of the bar, the warm night breeze riffling his hair. Can hear the sounds wafting up from the street below, the honking of taxis and occasional catcall from a shopkeeper, as they sit side by side without speaking, wholly given over to the sultry languor. One time she'd complained about Lebanon, some trifling thing she could no longer remember, telling him she preferred Moscow.

His glance was kind but not apologetic. "Moscow will always be your first love because it was your first assignment. Fret not, you'll go back one day." Then he said the words that echoed in her head to this day. "In the meantime, though, you must learn to love the one you're with." Is that what she was to him? Nothing more than an opportunity to him, a convenience? She never asked. She would've stayed in Beirut, toxic office and all, if she'd been able to stay with Davis.

Lyndsey snaps back to the moment, breaking the pleasant trance she let herself fall into. There is no loving this assignment, possibly the worst possible job of all the difficult, unpleasant jobs at Langley. But she will do it for Yaromir Popov, because he is dead and she owes him.

It is then she realizes her mistake. Raymond Murphy is not a dull man trapped in a dull job. That is a façade he has built to lull her into complacency, so she will let down her guard. He wants to ask her about Popov (and probably Davis, too), she can feel it, but he can't. That's not how you do the job, running headfirst at it. They are to work together on the disappearance of the Russian assets, yes, but she will be Raymond's target, too. He will watch her as closely as everyone else.

She can't afford to forget that.

SIX

Lyndsey arrives early to work the next day, determined to follow her old routine. Predawn alarm, hair pulled back in a ponytail, a protein powder smoothie on the drive to the gym. This is what she wanted, wasn't it, to slide back into her old life?

As she slips through the door to Russia Division, Maggie stops her as she heads for the desk in the corner. "We found an office for you. Eric said you should have privacy."

Maggie leads the way, carrying a cheerful coffee cup that reads *This may be wine* next to a drawing of a poodle in a beret hoisting a goblet. The private office is small and out of the way, next to the copy room, but that will do fine. Lyndsey doesn't want to be in a high-traffic area, anyway. The rest of the people in the Division will be curious about the investigation, once word gets out. Maybe this will reduce the drive-by snooping.

The office is barely larger than the desk itself, and has obviously been vacated hastily. There are out-of-date books on some of the shelves (*World Factbook 2002*; inexplicably, an ancient *Janes All the World's Tanks* from 1982 in a tattered blue dust jacket). Cheap ballpoint pens and paper clips scattered about like bread crumbs. The chair is tired and worn. At least the desk drawers seem to have been emptied of any classified papers.

Maggie leans in the doorway. "I'll get you the keys"—to the door, the desk, the file cabinets—"once the previous occupant finds them all."

After Maggie leaves, Lyndsey begins tidying up. It's going to remain a Spartan cell. There's no reason to settle in, to bring in photos from home or any other personal touches. It would send the wrong message. She's not here for the long haul. She's here to do a specific job.

She's just locked away all of the detritus when she notices someone hovering in the door. It's The Widow.

Theresa shows the faintest hint of a smile, shy and apologetic. "Maggie told me I'd find you in here. I want to apologize for my brusqueness yesterday. I was crashing a report for Eric and I guess my mind was elsewhere."

"I understand completely. No need to apologize."

"It looks like we won't be neighbors anymore. They got you your own space." Then she cocks her head, hair falling across her face and momentarily obscuring her eyes. "Say, have you had any coffee yet? I was just about to head down—would you like to join me? We could catch up."

I t still happens, even after all this time. A head will turn after Theresa has passed. A whisper behind a hand. Only the most brazen gawk openly, eyes widening. Theresa has to know they're looking at her. And yet she doesn't react at all.

They cross the ceremonial entrance to the building, a cavern of white marble and glass. It's where all the icons are kept. The life-sized statue of Wild Bill Donovan, who led the organization in the OSS days. The Agency seal inlaid into the terrazzo floor, where important visitors are unfailingly positioned for a souvenir photograph. But the most famous feature is surely the Memorial Wall, commemorating the Agency's fallen, a field of five-point stars, each one solemn and distinct, carved into white Alabama marble. Below, on a little shelf, is the register that bears the name of the Agency employees killed in the line of duty.

Which one is Richard's star? Lyndsey wonders.

Theresa seems to sense what Lyndsey is thinking. "Do you want to see it? Richard's star?" Before Lyndsey can answer—there can be only one answer, *yes, of course*—Theresa is off, heels clattering against the terrazzo floor.

Luckily, there are no groups of visitors lingering in the hallway today. There are tours most days, visiting officials or families allowed in for an award ceremony. But today, except for the guards, they have the alcove to themselves. Theresa stops in front of the big marble wall. "Here it is." She points quickly at it. The last one, the chiseled edges fresh and crisp.

She traces the edge with her finger. "Looks rather lonely, doesn't it?"

After a respectful minute, Theresa leads the way to the cafeteria. The first pit stop is for coffee, steam rising from the coffee urn as she draws a cup. They pick a table set next to the towering glass wall overlooking a grassy courtyard. They head to the farthest corner, so they will have a buffer of empty space around them.

It's amazing how much Theresa has changed from the woman Lyndsey remembers, but it's understandable given what she's gone through. Theresa always was thin but in a healthy way, fashionably so. Now she is positively gaunt. Frightening, what grief can do to you.

Theresa watches steam rise from her cup. "I'm so sorry about yesterday. I'm not normally like that. I try to be friendlier. It's been hard since Richard's disappearance. Especially at work." Theresa lets out an ironic laugh. "I blame the Director, I really do. They broadcast the service for Richard at the Memorial Wall. The Director did it for ratings. He was new at the time, a political appointee. Nobody liked him, so he did it to score points with the workforce." Her smile is grim. "That was two years ago and still everyone knows my face. You'd think there are wanted posters of me in the restrooms."

She isn't exaggerating. Even though they are hidden away in the corner, Lyndsey notices the stares. What must it be like to have whispers follow you everywhere? *That's her. The Widow.*

Theresa seems to withdraw into herself, not wanting to be noticed. "This isn't how I thought it would be. There are days when I want to quit. After the incident, they told me to take as much time as I needed. But after a while it felt like I was hiding. I was only forty. I had to figure out how to live in the world again."

Lyndsey won't be forty for some time, but her reckoning has come earlier. There are times when she wants to hide, too, to go back to the way things were. To pretend that things haven't changed.

Theresa pushes a pair of narrow gold bangles over her bird-boned wrists. "I had a son to take care of. Brian was only five at the time. He was watching me to make sense of his world. That's when I realized I didn't have the luxury of feeling sorry for myself or being mad at Richard for putting duty before his obligation to his family. So, after two months, I asked Eric if I could come back. He said I could if that's what I wanted. I found a woman to take care of Brian after school, and here I am. It hasn't been easy. But the counselor said the return to normalcy would be good for Brian. And for me."

"You've come a long way," Lyndsey says, trying to sound cheerful.

"There are still days when it feels like yesterday."

"I remember Richard. I had just started in the office. I couldn't get on his team because everyone wanted to work for him."

"He had a great reputation. They thought he'd be running this place one day." Theresa turns the paper cup of coffee in her hands as she turns her thoughts. "Richard and I met here. It was still common, then, to meet our future spouses at the office. He was nine years older than me. I had a schoolgirl crush on the boss." She buries her face in her hands in mock embarrassment.

Plenty of women in the office had crushes on Richard, Lyndsey remembers. At first glance, you wouldn't think he was the kind of guy women fell for. He was on the slight side. He wasn't what you call handsome; he had a craggy face, lines etched into it too early. He could be stern. But he was fair, and he always wanted to see the right thing done. He was one of those rare managers who were loved and respected by everyone who worked for them.

Theresa tosses her head. "I found our attraction rather thrilling, but as things started getting serious between us, Richard insisted I transfer to Eric's branch. 'If we're going to do this, we're going to do it by the rules,' he said." Lyndsey is impressed; there are plenty of supervisors who openly dated subordinates, thinking no one would dare to challenge them.

She couldn't think of Richard without thinking of Eric, too. Everyone knew they had come up in the system together, their careers mirror images. Yet they had been opposites in many ways. Eric was good looking in the conventional sense, like a prep school boy, with a thick head of hair and square jaw. He was the appeaser, the one who knew how to cajole and negotiate. Who knew how to tell a joke to ease the tension and could make everyone who worked for him feel good.

In some ways, Eric seems the more natural choice for a woman like Theresa. She had been the "it" girl in the office at the time. Still, she chose Richard. Perhaps she had been drawn to his intellect: he was easily the smartest man Lyndsey had met at the Agency at that point. If you were asked to predict who would be running things in a decade's time, everyone would've said Richard. Eric would be the deputy, the one who smoothed feathers Richard had ruffled.

Theresa's eyes glow. "He was just so different from the men my age.

Do you know what we did on our first date? We hiked up Old Rag in Shenandoah National Park. Another man probably would've booked a table at L'Auberge Chez François, but there we were in the Virginia countryside on a fall day, getting to know each other during the hours it took to climb up and back. It was glorious, and typical Richard."

The good times are seductive, Lyndsey thinks. You believe they're going to last forever.

Theresa picks up her debris, packing crumpled napkins into the empty cup. "More than anything, I wish Brian could've known what his father had been like here, at the Agency. He had a brilliant mind for our line of work. He made amazing deductions, saw possibilities that no one else did. He engineered these really smart exploits that led to great coups, and ultimately provided for the security of the nation. But Brian will never know—unless he gets a security clearance of his own one day, but I am dead set against that."

"Really?" Lyndsey is surprised. Most parents who work at CIA or other intelligence agencies usually hope their children will follow them into the business—or, at least, they wouldn't be vehemently against it.

Theresa turns away but not before Lyndsey sees her press her mouth into a firm line. "Not after what I've been through."

They walk back to the office without speaking much. Lyndsey's not sure what to say. Their conversation in the cafeteria seems to have ended on an awkward note. At one point, Theresa apologizes for dominating the conversation, though Lyndsey is happy not to dodge questions about herself. She's not ready to open up yet.

But a few steps before the door to the office, Theresa finally breaks the silence. "Strange, isn't it, what happened yesterday?" She can only be talking about Popov. A flash cable had gone around, announcing his death. "Had you heard of him?"

"Heard of him, yes." While word of the investigation will come out sooner or later, for now Lyndsey is sure she should play it cool. To honor the compartment that protects the knowledge that Popov was a double agent.

"He must've been one of ours: the Division wouldn't go on alert like that for just any Russian official."

True enough. Still, Lyndsey is careful not to confirm or deny.

"You said you were conducting an investigation. It's got to be about this death, isn't it?"

Now Lyndsey feels doubly wrong for letting it slip out yesterday. "I'm not free to say."

"Of course. I didn't mean to pry." Theresa smiles apologetically. "Still . . . you're getting settled in. It's all got to be disorienting, topsy-turvy. Let me know if I can do anything to help." And they slip back into the office, parting silently, Lyndsey feeling slightly better about her return. The prodigal daughter.

SEVEN

B ack in her tiny office, Lyndsey closes the door. It's time to put aside
interruptions and get started with this investigation.

There had been an email earlier from Raymond Murphy. He'd
started looking into Moscow Station for bad apples and hinted that he'd
found a possible suspect. It wouldn't be the Station Chief Hank Bremer,
Lyndsey could anticipate that much. She hadn't worked with him—Hank
had come in as she'd been leaving—but he had a reputation for being rule-
bound and old-school, and it is hard to picture a guy like that selling out
to the enemy.

Raymond had only hinted at the cards in his hand, but it sounds like
one of the case officers. Someone who was known to be having money
problems and had been caught fudging about the situation in paperwork.
Raymond wants to poke around a bit more before sharing a name with
her, so that's all she has for now. Enough to know that Moscow Station
couldn't be ruled out at this point.

It's time to get started on the tasks Raymond outlined. The first step
is to get the access records for Popov, Nesterov, and Kulakov. The informa-

tion that an asset provides to the Agency might be widely reported, but those reports wouldn't reveal the true identity of the source. To get on the access list, you would've had to prove a need to know the asset's true identity—usually in order to validate the truthfulness or usefulness of the information. That access list would include policymakers, which means there's a chance, albeit a slim one, that a U.S. diplomatic or military attaché could've accidentally let slip a true name during a negotiation or meeting. There are other ways the Russians might've found out, too, but it's highly unlikely they would've found three assets on their own. And for Popov, a consummate professional, to trip himself up? It seems almost impossible. The most likely reason, far more likely than any other, is that someone on the access lists told the Russians.

She also needs to read all the reports issued by Popov's new handler Tom Cassidy, the CIA officer who took over when Lyndsey left Moscow. It will be the first time she's able to see them, since her access was taken away when she left Moscow Station, a standard security procedure. She no longer had need-to-know.

Her first move is to call Russia Division's chief security officer. "I need to know who's on the access list for Genghis, Skipjack, and Lighthouse." The code names for Popov, Nesterov, and Kulakov. "And I need it asap."

The security officer hems. "It's going to take some time. I can't promise that I'll get back to you today."

With this investigation her only responsibility, Lyndsey has time in abundance. "Let me into the files and I'll go through the records myself and connect the dots."

Ten minutes later, she's got entry into the records she needs. She starts going through the access lists, beginning with Kulakov. The number of people who would need to know the true identity of a scientist would be small. Senior managers wouldn't bother to be read in. The information that Kulakov provided might've been widely disseminated in classified reports, but most readers wouldn't need to know the true name of the person who provided that information in order to understand it.

More people would be given access to Nesterov's true identity because of the subject: every agency in the federal government seems to be working Russian cyber operations right now. Still, the list for Nesterov is shockingly long. Lyndsey makes a mental note to raise this with Eric. It seems an unnecessary risk.

She goes back and sifts through the list of names under Kulakov's file, only about thirty. Then, she checks each one against Nesterov's list, which numbers almost two hundred. After eliminating some false matches—common names that turn out to be different people—Lyndsey arrives at the conclusion she was afraid of: no single person appears on both Nesterov's and Kulakov's access lists. Which means, aside from a handful of senior managers who get included pro forma, no one person would know of both men's true identities.

Whoever gave these names to the FSB—Federal Security Service of the Russian Federation—got them through other means.

Next, Lyndsey compares both Kulakov's and Nesterov's access lists with the third list, Popov's. Just as she suspected, there are no matches against Kulakov's list and only a handful of matches against Nesterov's, and all are senior leaders at CIA—including Eric Newman. The idea that any of them could be an FSB mole is laughable.

Lyndsey starts on the next task she gave herself: going through all the reports featuring information that Popov provided to his new handler. On a yellow legal pad, she scribbles notes as she reads, a stream-of-consciousness grab bag of the things that have caught her attention. By now, she's burned through the morning and her body rebels at being yoked to that chair for so long. But she keeps at it, plodding through cables one by one.

Lyndsey skims over her handwritten notes one more time. Popov slowed down after she left Moscow Station, no question. A turnover in handlers sometimes changes things. Sometimes the asset will feel abandoned, will only trust the first handler. Sometimes personalities don't mesh. But Popov is a pro and he knew what to expect. There is nothing in Tom Cassidy's reports to suggest there was a serious problem. *Popov is being careful as usual,* Cassidy wrote. But Russia Division took issue, felt there was a change in the quality and value of the intelligence he was passing. Had there been a problem brewing that escaped everyone's notice?

She skips down to Cassidy's last report on Genghis dated two months ago. No contact with Popov, or no record of any, for the past sixty days. It is a frightening gap: anything could've happened in those sixty days to send Popov skittering to Washington. It would be criminal negligence if something had happened, but Moscow Station missed it.

Tom Cassidy has a lot of explaining to do.

Then Lyndsey comes to a line in a report that hits her like a concrete wall.

Popov's youngest daughter, Varya, is dead.

SUBJECT: GENGHIS

Asset reported that his youngest daughter had died three months earlier. She was age 16 at the time of death. Subject did not tell us at the time because of the circumstances: she died of a heroin overdose. He had not revealed to us earlier that his daughter was a drug addict, though he seemed to be aware of the fact.

Lyndsey remembers the girl in the picture Popov had shared with her years ago. Elfin, twelve years old at the time the photo was taken, with flyaway sandy hair and a crooked smile. She knows what this would have meant to Popov: his daughters came late to him and his wife. They had been totally unexpected. He said it changed their lives, made him think about how the elites were robbing the common Russian blind, made him angry at the oligarchs for hollowing out the country to stockpile obscene amounts of money in offshore accounts.

According to subject, the daughter drowned at the family's dacha while they were on vacation. The police investigation was inconclusive; it could've been either suicide or accidental. She was reportedly hanging out with friends in a boathouse and fell into the water. The friends claimed they were unable to get to her in time.

Asset has been traumatized by the event. Although the asset has not said so for himself, I get the impression that he would like to end his service to us. After his daughter's death, nothing seems to matter to him anymore.

Lyndsey feels like she's going to be sick. Popov had often worried that his girls were being shortchanged by having such old parents. The world had changed so much and he and his wife had not kept up with it. Varya's addiction would have been glaring proof of their failure. Her death would have gutted him. She wishes she could've spoken to him while he was still alive, to have consoled him.

And could this have had some bearing on what happened to him? In some way, she senses it could have. She just can't see it yet.

There is a rap on the door. Eric Newman, looking incredibly well put together in a gray suit and burnished silk tie. He's always tried to look polished, in her recollection, but this seems a new level of effort.

Eric follows Lyndsey's eye, smiles. He shoots his cuffs, perhaps in self-deprecation. "I have a meeting on the seventh floor." The Director's suite. No wonder he wants to impress.

"Popov?"

"And a few other things." He can't tell her, of course. Instead, they use these veiled references, insinuating other intrigues, intrigues within intrigues. "If things go well, I'll let you know. Meanwhile, do you have any good news for me?"

She tells him about the access lists. While she'll need to double-check her findings before coming to any conclusions, that's something she feels safe in sharing. But she doesn't mention Varya's death; she's not sure what that means yet, and she wants to dig more deeply before bringing up Moscow Station's drop in production.

Lyndsey takes a deep breath. There's one thing they can do to protect themselves, and now's her chance. "CI turned up something, too, on Moscow Station." Eric's brows shoot up; she hates to get his hopes up that Russia Division isn't to blame—as fortuitous as that would be. "Too soon to tell . . . It may be nothing. But do you think it's time to warn our other assets in Russia? Get them to go into hiding?" Two assets have disappeared in two weeks. Isn't that enough cause for alarm?

He's shaking his head before she's finished speaking. "If there's the possibility that the mole is in Moscow Station, we can't tip them off that we know. And we can't tell Moscow Station to stand down all operations without something concrete. Once you turn these things off, it's hard to get them back on track. Assets lose their nerve. Things might never be the same again. We can't look like we're jumping to conclusions. I need proof—which is why I brought you in."

He takes in her frown, her frustration. "I know you've only been on the case for a day, Lyndsey, but the Director is breathing down my neck. This meeting I'm going to? The Director has asked for an update *every day* until we have an answer. And he's not a patient man. If he doesn't like what he sees, he'll start calling the shots himself. I don't intend to be marginalized in my own office. Do whatever it takes to get answers, and if somebody stands in your way, you let me know. We need to figure out what's going on before the Russians pick up one more of our assets. I know you can do this, Lyndsey—I'm counting on you."

EIGHT

Closing the door behind Eric, Lyndsey's thoughts turn back to Varya. Reading that report was a punch to the gut.

She throws herself into her chair, letting it roll backward to hit the wall with a jarring thud. Too much is happening at once. Even though she hasn't seen Popov in years, losing him has shaken loose an old sadness inside her. She lost her own father when she was very young, but that loss has never gone away. It has merely been dormant, and now those emotions kick up like a sandstorm. Being left with her aunt while her mother rushed her father to the hospital. Her mother returning in the middle of the night—alone. The feeling that the floor has suddenly dropped out from beneath her. The sensation of being completely vulnerable. Of never being whole.

Poor Masha. Losing her daughter and now her husband. Though Lyndsey never met them, she has always felt as though she knew Masha and the daughters, Polina and Varya. Popov had told her stories about how it was just the two of them, he and Masha, for a long time, before the girls came along. For a girl who had few memories of her own parents together, it was a balm to hear about their marriage. How he valued Masha's wisdom and had come to trust her judgment, even with his intelligence work. She remembered the photos he'd shown her of Masha from the early days, her round, serene face; the two in somber Soviet-era clothing, standing outside their grim, regimental apartment building. Later, Masha as a schoolteacher, her hair gray and piled on top of her head. Photos of the girls, too, of course: he was a proud father. Little girls in snow suits, teenagers in fur hats and lipstick.

Should she try to reach Masha, offer condolences? It would be risky to try to contact them directly right after Popov's suspicious death. The authorities undoubtedly would be watching the family, particularly if they knew he was a double agent.

Lyndsey doesn't have a way to contact Masha, anyway. There was no protocol for covert communications with the family, only with the asset. Strictly speaking, families were not supposed to be witting; it would endanger both them and the asset.

Thank goodness for modern technology. The spy's friend. For backup, she'd had them both set up special accounts on a secure messaging app. It wasn't even one of the popular ones; reputedly, it was used almost exclusively by teenagers. Popov had balked, saying he felt ridiculous having it on his phone, even if no one knew, but she had pressed and eventually they were both glad she had.

She'll have to wait until after work to use the app. Cell phones aren't allowed in secure spaces at CIA, for obvious reasons. Her phone sits out in her car, waiting patiently, like the family dog. Some people at Langley take a break to go out to their cars if they need to use their phones, but even that is frowned on. Lyndsey can be patient. She has plenty of work to keep her distracted.

———

As soon as Lyndsey is back in her cheerless apartment that evening, she leaves her purse and coat at the door and heads straight to her couch, cell phone in hand.

She stares at the black glass of her smartphone. She hasn't used this secret channel since she left Moscow. Lyndsey swipes through the screens, looking for the app. She's not a big smartphone user, not like some people she knows who download every hot app they hear about—use it a couple times and then forget about it. She can't remember the name of the app but she remembers its icon: a square pink telephone sporting a cartoonish human face, one eye winking. On second thought, she can see why Popov didn't like it. She finds it on the second to the last screen—she never used it in Beirut because she hadn't developed any assets during her short time there, no one who merited special back-channel communications. The app is like a guilty memory, a reminder of her willingness to flout the rules, now buried on her phone.

It opens with a tap. Her account name is Mindreader, plucked out of thin air at the time but so silly now, so naïve, it makes her cringe.

There's a red flag next to it. An unread message.

There was only one person she corresponded with on that app: Yaromir Popov.

Her stomach goes into free fall. She had turned off notifications after she'd been in Beirut for a few months, determined to put her old life behind her. The handoff to a new handler was where an asset could stumble; they both knew it. She and Popov had agreed he'd give the new handler a chance. Then, too, her life had been in such a state of flux: being pushed off the Russian target, told to prove herself by doing something completely different. *See if you can make lightning strike a second time,* COS Beirut had said with a touch of bitterness. It had been time to get back on track. To prove, if only to herself, that she could abide by the rules.

She squints at the tiny print. The message is dated the day before Popov's Aeroflot flight.

Taking a deep breath, she opens it.

I need to talk to you. Something has happened, and I don't know who to trust.

Guilt washes through her like acid. She wills herself to calm down, but the same thought keeps swamping her: *he tried to reach me before he died.* Before he made that fatal flight to Washington. He had come to try to find her because she hadn't answered him. Because she had forgotten all about him.

She resists the urge to throw the phone across the room, frustrated by that cryptic message. Why didn't he explain in his text what had happened? But it's useless to ask questions that can't be answered. She can only guess. Maybe it was because he didn't think it was safe, even though the app encrypts the messages.

Whatever he had to tell her must've been exceptionally sensitive.

She stares at the phone's screen for a long time before she starts to type.

What she writes is pure wishful thinking. It's like stuffing a message in a bottle and throwing it in the ocean. A bottle adrift in a vast sea. Chances are it will never be found, never read. But she does it anyway, because it's all she has.

M or P, if you're watching this, please reply. A friend of Y.

Then she goes on a run to clear her head.

Lyndsey can't wait to get back to her apartment so she can check her phone. Superstitiously, she didn't bring it with her on her run—*a watched pot never boils*—but she heads straight to it as soon as she unlocks the door. She snatches the phone off the coffee table, squints at the screen, and holds her breath as she scrolls, frantically looking for a message.

This is M. Y said you would help us. Is that why you've texted?

Her heart first explodes with glee—success—then clenches like a fist. Tom Cassidy should've reached out to them as soon as they learned Popov was dead. But it's obvious this hasn't happened.

She's about to tap a response but pauses. There is a momentary, passing instinct to suspect interference. That response was awfully fast. Maybe it's not Masha, maybe it's an FSB tech operative. But no: she and Popov used this channel for two years and were never found out, by either the FSB nor the CIA, so she feels certain that she is talking to Popov's wife and not an FSB operative pretending to be her.

She begins to type. *I'm so sorry for what happened. Are you okay? Has the FSB contacted you yet?*

The dialogue box fills slowly. *The authorities are still not certain what happened, I believe.*

She has to ask a question, a very important one. It can't wait, though she feels badly for trying to get information from Masha while she is grieving. She has no choice.

Y contacted me before he died saying something terrible had happened but didn't explain. Do you know what he meant?

She counts the seconds after she finishes typing. There's a long pause on Masha's end. Lyndsey prays that he shared this secret with his wife.

Y said the FSB knew about him. He went to the U.S. to find you.

The missed text. Another stab of regret, right in her heart.

There is her answer: the mole—whoever he is—gave them Popov, and he had no choice but to run. But the FSB went after him, his running might as well have been an admission of guilt, so they killed him.

Lyndsey tries to push the overwhelming grief away, though she feels like she's drowning. She needs to think clearly while she's able to communicate with Masha. There's more she needs to know.

Did Y tell his handler that the FSB was onto him?

The answer comes back quickly. Without hesitation. *He didn't trust Gerald.*

They use code names for handlers. Gerald is Tom Cassidy.

He didn't trust Tom Cassidy—or, by extension, Moscow Station. That was why he was flying to Washington.

The implications are staggering. For a second, Lyndsey can scarcely breathe. She needs to think through all of this coolly, deliberately. But time is ticking by, and it's dangerous to stay on any communications channel for too long. You want to be stealthy, to avoid drawing attention.

One last thing. *Do you need anything?*

The answer is not immediate, and Lyndsey feels the seconds tick by as Masha deliberates. *I do not think we will be safe here soon.*

She is asking, in so many words, for CIA to save her and her daughter. Her husband would've told her this was part of the deal. Lyndsey remembers sitting across the table from him in the safe house during one of their early meetings, hammering out the provisions of his cooperation. The payments and how they would be held in a special Swiss bank account (nothing outrageous; he'd been looking for security, not a payday). And the promise of extraction if things ever got tight. This was a promise made just to the big fish (rather cynically, Lyndsey always thought, knowing how few assets take it). Not to the small fry, and Popov knew this, too. He and his family would not be left to take the fall.

Only now, they are.

She wishes she could type *yes, of course,* because she knows that's what Masha needs to hear. She is a new widow with a daughter to protect. But Lyndsey doesn't want to lie to her. Russia Division won't do anything until they know what's going on. Someone is giving the names of CIA assets to the FSB and even though Yaromir Popov is dead, until he's completely cleared, Russia Division is not going to act—as callous as that sounds. The seventh floor is focused on finding the mole. The wife of a dead asset will not be their greatest concern at the moment.

Masha needs to feel heard and seen. There is no one else she can go to for help. It is Lyndsey's duty. *I'll get started on that right away,* she types. *Sit tight. If it becomes necessary, is there some place you can go where no one would think to look for you?*

A few more beats. *Yes. My sister's dacha.*

Keep watching this app. I will be in touch.

She is sorry she can't do more at this moment, that she has to leave Masha like this. She closes the app, a tremble of rage passing through her. How they've failed Yaromir Popov. He placed his faith in her—and the Agency, but mostly in her—and she let him down. Because she trusted the system.

Something has happened, and I don't know who to trust.

NINE

Begging your pardon, Dmitri Ivanovich, but there is a report in your queue that requires your immediate attention. It has to do with Kanareyka."

Kanareyka. Canary.

Dmitri Tarasenko's assistant stands in the doorway. She is afraid to come in and so she stands twisting a lock of hair like an anxious little girl. *I really should fire her,* he thinks for the hundredth time. And he would, if he hadn't been the one to encourage to her work for him in the first place, which he only did because she was so pretty. But she hasn't slept with him yet, and that was the whole point, wasn't it, why he's suffered through four months of her incompetence. She loses his phone messages. His calendar is a complete disaster. At this point, he feels she owes it to him. It's his due for putting up with her.

Tarasenko puts down what he is working on. "Very well, Teresa Niko-layevna, I will look at it right away, since you have interrupted my work." Perhaps she will be more compliant if she suspects he is displeased with her.

She immediately crumbles. "Oh, I am so sorry, Dmitri Ivanovich, I didn't mean to—"

He waves her away and looks for the email. Finds it, clicks on it.

MESSAGE RECEIVED FROM KANAREYKA. CIA HAS BEEN BLINDSIDED BY THE DEATH OF YAROMIR POPOV AND HAS LAUNCHED AN INQUIRY. INVESTIGATION BEING LED BY OFFICER BROUGHT IN FROM THE FIELD, FORMERLY STATIONED IN MOSCOW. KANAREYKA WILL PROVIDE MORE DETAILS AS THEY ARE KNOWN.

KANAREYKA IS UPSET BY LACK OF FOREWARNING ON POPOV. QUESTIONED WISDOM OF TERMINATION. KANAREYKA FEARS DISCOVERY AND DEMANDS EXTRACTION NOW. PLEASE ADVISE.

Tarasenko pushes back in his chair, chuckling to himself. First, it is ludicrous for an asset to make demands. The FSB holds all the cards and Kanareyka should have realized this when the deal was made.

Honestly, what does he care if Kanareyka is discovered? The FSB had gotten all they were likely to get from this asset. Kanareyka is balky and obviously has no intention of giving the FSB what it wants. What's more, Kanareyka is a traitor, and all traitors are by nature untrustworthy. They betray their masters, the hand that feeds; knowing this, you'd be a fool to trust them. Though it's protocol to make a fuss over them, to call them heroes and applaud their courage and the like. Dmitri Tarasenko never believed in that. They are self-serving liars. They cloak themselves in glory, pretending to be doing it for one noble reason or other, but in truth they serve no higher purpose; they only serve themselves.

Still.

No sense slaughtering the cow when it might have more milk to give. As much as it would please him to burn Kanareyka, he realizes to do so now would be premature.

Then there is this matter of Yaromir Popov. The office had received word of Popov's abrupt death; something about dying while on vacation, an obvious fabrication. A few of the old-timers were shaken up—you could still find one or two who liked the man—but it hadn't mattered to Tarasenko, not at all. Popov was an old dinosaur who hadn't done anything notable in years, one of these hangers-on who had no intention of retiring and seemed to want to die behind his desk. Well, he got his wish.

Still.

People don't die on airplanes every day, much less SVR officers. And why would CIA set up this investigation if there wasn't a reason? Obviously, Popov meant something to them. Who would've guessed that the old fox had been secretly betraying his masters?

Someone's head would roll for that and Dmitri Tarasenko would make sure he had a front-row seat for the beheading.

Kanareyka is Tarasenko's asset. Because of the sensitive nature of the situation, General Morozov put Tarasenko, his protégé, in charge from the beginning. Morozov trusted Tarasenko not to botch things up. It would be disastrous if things fell to pieces now.

Tarasenko looks back at the computer monitor, drumming his fingers on his desk.

Morozov has been restless lately, hinting that he might take a trip out of the country. Ten years he has been confined inside Russia. It is Morozov's own fault. No one told him to kill CIA's Chief of Station in Kiev. He had lost his temper. Usually, the stakes in the clandestine world are high for such folly. Morozov had gotten off lightly, all things considered. He could've been stripped of his position; he could've been jailed. Maybe the Hard Man had understood that the worst possible punishment was one meted out by CIA: a wanted man, Morozov risked being snatched up if he left the country. Dragged to the United States and put on trial.

Confined, Morozov is like a child in detention staring out the window at his classmates enjoying themselves in the playground. There are only so many times one could visit St. Petersburg or stay in the country in one's dacha. He misses getting up to mischief in Paris and Vienna, Bangkok and Singapore—but mostly he misses Washington. Oh, how the old man misses Washington. It calls to him like a mistress. The old friend is snoozing, past offenses forgotten, Morozov claims. He is rested and ready to get into trouble again.

But so far, the Hard Man has ignored his requests. He needs Morozov alive and safe.

Morozov has a soft spot for Kanareyka, though. Kanareyka could be his downfall.

From Tarasenko's point of view, that might not necessarily be a bad thing.

Many times, Tarasenko has protected his impetuous boss from his bad nature. Protected Morozov from himself, as it were. Morozov is his benefactor. Tarasenko, too, needs Morozov alive and safe.

But most men outgrow their benefactors, yes? A tree doesn't grow strong if it remains in the shadow of the forest. Besides, Morozov is not above throwing people to the wolves, subordinates as well as rivals; Tarasenko has seen the proof. He's learned to follow Morozov's lead: stepped over their corpses, moved into their offices, moved his way up the ladder.

Tarasenko continues drumming his fingers against his desk. An opportunity might present itself from this strange confluence of events. This is how men get ahead in this pestilent kingdom: seeing opportunity before anyone else, and seizing it.

The matter bore watching, very closely.

TEN

t is Saturday, a day for running errands. Lyndsey forces herself to tug on a pair of jeans, tie her hair up in a ponytail, and head over to the sprawling Tysons Corner mall. She only needs a few essentials and promises to get something good for lunch (Tacos? Sushi? Something she cannot make in the barren wasteland that is her kitchen) as enticement to get out of the apartment.

One purchase later (athletic socks), she is standing outside Macy's when she sees Theresa. Lyndsey is always surprised when she sees someone from work out in the wild, as though the two worlds make a combustible combination and should never, ever touch.

There is no mistaking Theresa. Chic as always, trench coat cinched tightly at the waist, sunglasses pushed on top of her head. She holds the hand of a small boy and has leaned over to whisper something in his ear. The boy stares as though hypnotized by the sprawling play space in front of them. Children brush by him to clamber onto the huge plastic structures. They are all laughing and shrieking except for little Brian. He stares at a neon set of monkey bars with something akin to reverence.

Should she leave them to their moment? But when will Lyndsey have the chance to meet Theresa's son? She walks over, tiny shopping bag swinging from her arm. "Hey, fancy meeting you here."

The smile on Theresa's face seems genuine. At his mother's prompting, Brian turns to face Lyndsey, his big eyes mapping her face. *He must take after Richard,* Lyndsey decides. Those wary, owlish eyes.

"This is mommy's friend. We work together," Theresa says. Brian blinks and shifts his weight. Theresa crouches to speak to her son. "Why don't you go play? Lyndsey and I will sit right over there and watch you. You'll be able to see us the whole time. I'm not going anywhere."

They sit on a plastic bench together and watch as Brian begins to hoist himself up the constellation of bars until he's above the heads of the other children. A hint of excitement betrays Brian's otherwise controlled expression, but his gaze stays glued to his mother, like a dog rescued from the pound.

"Two years Richard's been gone, and Brian still doesn't like to go anywhere without me," Theresa says. The shopping bags at her feet are all from children's stores. "The therapist says he'll outgrow it."

Lyndsey is aware that today will mark a change in her relationship with Theresa. Although they get together every day for coffee, their talks haven't been overly personal. Lyndsey talks about her widowed mother living alone in rural Pennsylvania, and Theresa mostly frets about how Brian is doing in school. Today feels different, however. Today, Theresa seems to be in a mood to open up.

Does Theresa have any friends? Lyndsey wonders. She seems to have dedicated herself to her son and her son alone. It seems crazy that this has happened to the wife of Richard Warner, once king of their insular kingdom, the pair a golden couple. Theresa Warner had had her circle of friends, a queen with her court, but it seems they've all deserted her now. All those people who knew and loved Richard Warner—why aren't they helping her? It seems Eric Newman is the only one left.

In an odd way, Lyndsey knows what Theresa is going through. They have both fallen from grace, their worlds turned upside down, and are now forced to build new ones. What happened to her in Beirut—that anyone felt threatened enough to want to see her fall—had been a surprise, but it also had taught her a valuable lesson about Langley. Most people keep their resentments hidden. Suddenly, she realizes that she probably understands Theresa better than she first thought.

Theresa watches children scamper agilely over the monkey bars. "I try not to dwell in the past, you know, but sometimes I think about how different everything would be if Richard was still alive."

Lyndsey's not sure how much to pry into such a sensitive topic, a man's death, but Theresa *seems* to want to talk about it. "You know, I never heard what happened to Richard. The details didn't reach Lebanon. We weren't told anything at all."

Theresa gives her a pained look. They're not supposed to talk about classified stuff out of the office but it happens all the time, whenever two or more Agency employees are by themselves, wherever there's a reasonable expectation that they won't be overheard. They will skirt around the edges, of course. Talk in code, leave out details. Avoid the secret stuff.

Theresa rises from the bench and jerks her head toward a little alcove, close enough so that Brian can still see her, but away from everyone else. They are by themselves, a bubble in a sea of mothers and teenagers, no one paying attention to them.

Theresa takes a deep breath, then lets it out slowly, ready to bare her soul. She drops her voice. "No one ever told me the whole story. I figured it out on my own from bits and pieces I heard over time. It started with a problem with an asset. The asset was a woman, one that Richard had been running from Langley. There was a case officer on the ground in Moscow, of course, but he only took care of the physical stuff, dead drops, stuff like that. Everyone at Langley knew that it was Richard's case—and that it was a success because of him." There is still pride in her voice for her husband, for what he did.. She glances over her shoulder to make sure there's still a wide buffer around them before continuing.

"But then Richard came home very late one evening, his face white. Brian had already gone to bed. Richard pulled out the bottle of Yamskaya, his favorite vodka, and poured us both a drink. They'd just learned the Russians were onto his asset. By sheer luck, she had not been home when the police came for her and managed to go into hiding. She wouldn't survive long on the street, though, now that she was blown. And Langley had no resources who could help her, no one they were willing to risk.

"Richard wouldn't let them desert his asset. It fell under Eric. Richard went to him and told him they *had* to get her out, no matter what. You know as well as I that extractions are complex operations. They take months to plan, not days. And dangerous, too. The whole thing seemed absurdly foolhardy, the gesture of a hard-core romantic—and for a moment I even questioned Richard's motives, wondered if there was something going on with this asset that I didn't know about." She stops, her expression a tangle of regret and unhappiness. So, she's wondered all this time, too, if Richard had been faithful, whether he had ulterior motives going to Moscow . . . The hurt this woman has been carrying is unimaginable.

"I wanted to ask him, 'What about us?' What about putting his family first? I wanted to throw it all in his face, but I couldn't. It's not that simple, is it? There's no equation to tell you how much loyalty you owe to an asset." She puts a hand over her eyes. *Hiding from the pain.* "He had to go, he argued. His asset had risked her life on his word. He couldn't let the Russians catch her. Besides, no intelligence professional ever thinks he's going to make a mistake. Richard didn't think for a split second that he wouldn't be coming home."

Theresa takes a deep breath. Fighting back tears. "Eric Newman was the one to tell me. He called me into his office . . . I sat on the couch like everything was normal, even though I knew something bad was coming. Even though every nerve in my body was telling me to get out of there. To *run*.

"The rescue operation had not gone well, he said. It was as though the Russians knew Richard was coming. He had been the one to go in for her. He had *insisted* on escorting her to the safe house. She was his responsibility, he would take the risk. That was the last anyone saw him."

Is this good, recalling all this? Lyndsey wonders. Is it cathartic? The woman had just admitted that she hasn't any friends; she probably hasn't talked to anyone about it, not in a good, long time.

Theresa continues. "Details came out over the next few months, bit by bit. It was like Chinese water torture. Eric claimed he was given permission to share it with me in fits and starts. The Russians refused to return Richard's body. Apparently, CIA had scored a serious coup with this asset and made the FSB look bad.

"But then the counterarguments started—you know how that is, how they love to twist and twist and *twist* a story, to see if there's some angle they can come up with, something no one's thought of before. And sure enough, someone got it into his head that the asset had been a plant, an elaborate trap by the FSB to redeem itself in Putin's eyes, and that Eric and Richard had been duped all along. There wasn't a shred of evidence to support it, but that didn't stop it from taking on a life of its own. The whole episode—the asset, Richard's death—became radioactive on the seventh floor." All the tension goes out of Theresa all at once. She is wrung out like a washcloth. "I was told to stop pushing the issue and to accept what had happened. There was nothing more I could do."

With that, the spell is broken. The sounds of the mall courtyard return, yelps and laughter of excited children. Lyndsey blinks, the story Theresa just told her evaporating like perfume on the air. Did Theresa really just share all that with her, here, in a crowded mall? Maybe she can only tell that story outside of Langley. As an act of defiance. Outside the Agency's domain, beyond their reach.

Brian runs up to them, a flush to his pale face. He has a few breathy words for his mother—"monkey bars for my little monkey" Theresa says as she ruffles his hair affectionately—before turning once again to Lyndsey with wide, curious eyes. Trying to make sense of her, her importance to his mother.

Something has happened just now: Theresa shared her burden with Lyndsey. Lyndsey now knows the complicated tale of loyalty and betrayal that has left a woman alone to care for a fatherless child. She suddenly feels close to Theresa and is sorry that this didn't happen earlier. Why didn't they become friends at the start? she wonders. Too dissimilar, probably: Theresa was already married, a young wife, whereas Lyndsey was just out of college and still green. Theresa was also the wife of a branch chief, in an entirely different social world. But circumstances have thrown them together now. Lyndsey realizes with a start, as Theresa gathers her shopping bags, that this is the most intimate conversation she's had with a woman in the last five years. Overseas stations are notoriously light on female officers. And one tends to let old friends and even family slip away during covert overseas assignments.

Theresa Warner, The Widow, is the closest thing she has to a friend.

"That's great, slugger," Theresa says to her son as she places a hand to his back, gently steering him away from the play space and into the throng of shoppers. "But now it's time for lunch. Where do you want to go? Do you want to get a hamburger? And a chocolate shake? And maybe if you're very good"—her eyes flit to Lyndsey, holding her gaze for a second—"Miss Lyndsey will agree to join us. And she can become your new friend, too, like she's mommy's friend. What do you say?"

ELEVEN

In the middle of a quiet afternoon, Lyndsey slogs through the stack of last year's reports, looking for clues. She's been unsettled all day, restless and prickly. She feels the pressure of Eric's warning—*the Director has asked for an update every day*—but also, it feels as though something is about to happen, as though there's a storm in the distance. It's the waiting: waiting for the missing assets to turn up, waiting for the other shoe to drop. She promises herself another coffee if she can keep at the reports until the top of the hour.

But then Maggie Kimball knocks on the door. She shifts her weight from foot to foot. "Eric wants you in the conference room for a teleconference with Moscow Station."

Why would Moscow Station request a teleconference at this hour? It's late in the evening, Moscow time. As Lyndsey weaves through the desks, she notices—or is she imagining it?—tense faces and rounded shoulders, twitchy and ready to bolt. At CIA, people are like gazelles at the watering hole, exquisitely attuned to the slightest change in the air. They know that something is up.

Eric is the only one in the room and he nods slightly at Lyndsey to close the door. On a monitor, two men sit hunched and scowling at a table, braced for contention. She recognizes Hank Bremer, bald and overweight, his unhandsome face flushed bright pink like he's just run up flights of stairs, though the monitor might be to blame. Next to him is a man she doesn't recognize, Hank's opposite physically, with thick, dark hair and a trace of a Mediterranean complexion.

Eric addresses the screen as she takes a seat. "This is Lyndsey Duncan. She's helping with the Genghis investigation. I want her to sit in." To her, he says, "You know Hank, I believe. That's Tom Cassidy."

It's all Lyndsey can do not to lash out at Cassidy. She hasn't brought up to Eric what she learned from Masha, not yet. She wants to work it out in her head first, make sure she's not overlooking something. Yaromir Popov didn't trust Moscow Station and it cost him his life.

Eric swivels to face the monitor. "Tell us what happened, Hank."

Bremer's hands are clasped in front of his face, hiding his mouth. *He has news he doesn't want to share.* "Kulakov's body was found today."

One of the missing assets, the scientist. The news is not unexpected but still it takes Lyndsey's breath away.

"It was all over the newspapers and television. They *wanted* us to hear about it." Is Bremer mad because he's embarrassed that one of his assets was killed under his nose? There seem to be only two types of Chiefs of Station: ones who keep their thoughts to themselves, or emotional types who lash out at the slightest provocation. Reese Munroe, Chief of Station during Lyndsey's time, had been the former, for which she was grateful. She never liked working for the volatile ones. No one did. "His body was found in a strange place, not near his home or his work. They're claiming it was a mugging, of course. The body was in bad shape when it was found. Broken bones, face a bloody mess."

Not a mugging, in other words. Extreme damage implies it was not impersonal. "Could it have been something else?" Lyndsey asks. A hate crime. There is no shortage of these in Moscow. Kulakov was Jewish.

"We've seen the police report. They're trying to insinuate that he was gay. They said his profile was found on a gay website that's seen trouble recently. Members lured out by homophobes and beaten up."

"Was he gay?" Eric asks. His tone is clipped; he isn't in the mood to beat around the bush. He wants answers, not speculation.

"No." Cassidy jumps in. "He was married. Had children."

"Married men have been known to have secret lives—"

"He was my asset. I knew the man. I say no," Cassidy snaps.

So, Cassidy was Kulakov's handler, too. Can this much bad luck be coincidental? Though to give up two of your own cases to the Russians would be the height of stupidity, to say the least. She tries to read his body English, but it's hard under the circumstances. He could be defensive. Or merely unhappy.

"Have any of the other victims from the website been killed?" Eric asks.

Bremer sucks in his cheeks as he thinks. "Not that I recall."

"It's a smoke screen. They killed him," Cassidy snaps. He means the FSB. "Maybe they figured out he was working for us. The timing is— suspicious." He looks sideways at his boss, a sheepish expression flitting by in the blink of an eye but she catches it, knowing where to look. "We were waiting for him to pass missile plans to us. The INF—it was going to be the main focus of the negotiations this summer."

"Oh?" Eric says. His voice is sharp with surprise.

"Yeah," Cassidy says. "He was finally going to pay off, after all the waiting . . . He told me last time we got together. He said he could get his hands on the plans. I was waiting for him to deliver."

Bremer leans toward the camera, his pink face glowing in the low light. "I think those assholes found out what he was up to and had him killed. Made it splashy, too, as a warning."

They are all quiet for a moment, turning over individual thoughts. The loss of those plans is a huge blow—the importance of the INF flaring up as both the U.S. and Russia hurl accusations of cheating on safeguards—and Kulakov's death suddenly takes on greater meaning. Finally, Eric clears his throat. "See what else you can find out, but until we find proof otherwise, we have to assume the state is behind this. We don't know how they found out about him, but they killed him."

Popov and Kulakov killed, Nesterov missing. The grim truth settles over the four of them. The evidence seems undeniable: Moscow is rolling up CIA's assets.

Eric clears his throat. The corners of his mouth twitch. What he's about to say next pains him. "Hank, I want you to stand down all operations for the time being." It's the same advice Lyndsey gave him, only now he's ready to act on it.

Bremer's pink face goes red, like his shirt collar has suddenly gone too tight. "You can't do that. We have things in the works—"

"It doesn't matter, Hank. You know that. Shut it down, all of it. Tell your people"—the assets, Eric means, their Russian spies—"to lie low until we get things under control. We can't afford to lose anyone else right now."

Bremer is clearly upset, but he knows not to say anything more. Instead, he strikes the table with a closed fist.

"I know you don't like it, Hank, but we have to think of our people." Eric's tone is more conciliatory but it's too late. Station Chiefs don't like to have their authority questioned in front of subordinates. He should've helped Hank come to this conclusion himself. "We'll figure out what's going on and stop it."

"It's not coming from here," Bremer booms. "Whoever's talking to the FSB, it's not someone in the Station. I know my people." He points a finger at the camera in accusation. "CI has been sniffing around lately—is that your doing? Trying to place the blame on us?"

"They're just doing their job," Eric says, pushing back from the table.

The finger jabs emphatically. "If there's a mole, it's in Langley. It's one of *your* people, Eric."

"We'll see," Eric says through gritted teeth.

"Yeah, we'll see all right." Big talk from Bremer; Lyndsey wonders if he knows something he's not telling.

"You'd warned me that we'd have to do this to protect our remaining assets . . . Happy?" Eric says to Lyndsey after the video connection is shut down.

"That you're shutting down the Station? It's the right thing. And there's something you should know: I heard from Popov's widow." It means admitting the backdoor channel, but Lyndsey tells Eric about the exchange with Masha.

"So, the problem is at Moscow Station," Eric says slowly. Floored, maybe, by the news.

"I can get CI to look into Cassidy—"

"No," Eric says. Too quickly. Lyndsey raises an eyebrow. "Let them conduct their own investigation. Let's see if they can corroborate what Masha told you. We shouldn't take anything at face value . . ."

Does he think there's a chance Masha might be lying to them?

Lyndsey's instincts tell her that's not the case, but Eric is the boss. And he's more experienced than she is. Lyndsey trusts Masha because she trusted her husband, but she's never met Masha. It's hard, but Lyndsey forces herself to see it from Eric's perspective. They have to remain objective. She says nothing, nods, and heads out the door.

As Lyndsey heads back to her tiny office, she sees a small group gathered around a cubicle, low murmuring passed back and forth as they console someone. A young woman at the center of the group dabs her eyes with a tissue. As Lyndsey approaches, the gathered melt away. Given Lyndsey's chumminess with Eric, they probably lump her in with management and don't want to be seen gabbing, shirking their jobs. The teary-eyed woman looks up as Lyndsey approaches.

"I'm sorry, I don't mean to interrupt, but were you working on Lighthouse?" Lyndsey is careful to use Kulakov's cover name. "I'm working on the investigation—you probably heard about it. You can talk to me."

The nameplate reads JAN WESTERLING. The woman nods as she reaches for her eyeglasses on the desk. "I'm the reports officer. I've been on Lighthouse's case for a couple years."

Exactly the person Lyndsey needs to speak to: the reports officer acts as the liaison between Langley and Moscow Station. Lyndsey rests her shoulder against a pillar, blocking the desk off from view to the rest of the office. She needs to ask a few questions and it would be better if they had even a shred of privacy. "This has got to be tough." You're not supposed to let yourself get too close to an asset, but you do if you're human. Even someone like this reports officer to whom Kulakov is little more than a name in a report. Who didn't have the kind of relationship Lyndsey had with Yaromir Popov.

The young woman nods. Still shaky, she taps a couple keys and then turns the monitor toward Lyndsey. What she sees on the screen is a punch to the gut. The image is of a man's face, but you'll get nothing about him from this picture. His age, his likely ethnic background, nothing. His entire face is distorted by swelling. The eyes are crusted shut with dried blood and the mouth is an open pit of glistening black, all his teeth gone. It *could* be a hate crime: the victim has been obliterated.

Shock washes over Lyndsey as reality hits her. *This* is what they're dealing with.

"That's from the police report," Westerling says, her voice thickening.

Lyndsey takes a deep breath before leaning over the keyboard to page through the rest of the images. There's one of the body on asphalt, arms and legs twisted unnaturally, like he fell from a distance. He wears a shirt and tie and a beige trench coat, the kind of clothes he'd have worn to work. "Did the report say when he was last seen?"

"He didn't return from work one evening, about three weeks ago."

"And who reported him missing?"

"His wife."

Lyndsey peers at the photos more closely, looking for signs of decomposition. "Does the police report say anything about the time of death, or the state of the body?"

"They're waiting on an autopsy for time of death, but they estimate that he's been dead about a week."

Which means whoever abducted him kept him alive for two weeks. Although you could make a case for torture from the state of his face, it didn't seem likely that a bunch of homophobes would kidnap a man and hold him for two weeks if they meant to kill him.

It did sound like an interrogation, however. "Could you forward that report to me?" Lyndsey asks, getting ready to head back to her office.

As Westerling reaches for the mouse, tears spill down her cheeks. "It's different now, you know, from when I started. They're playing rougher in Moscow." *Tell me about it,* Lyndsey wants to say, but she doesn't want to shut the young woman down, so she nods. "It's like the FSB feels they can take the gloves off. I can't believe they did this to—this asset. He was a nice guy. A scientist. Harmless." A few more tears. "He didn't sign up for *this.* This should never have happened. We can't take care of them . . . Something's wrong." She wipes at her tears, shaking her head. "Forget what I just said, I'm upset. I don't know what I'm saying."

Westerling meant every word and Lyndsey knows it. She's just afraid

Lyndsey will tell Eric. Lyndsey puts a hand on her shoulder. "Don't worry about it. I know what you mean."

The first thing Lyndsey does is forward the Russian police report to Raymond Murphy, sure that word hasn't traveled as fast to him down in Counterintel and wanting to keep him aware of the development. Then she sends it to a woman she worked with early in her career, Ruth Mallory, someone who has followed Russian internal security services for decades. She only wants Mallory's take on the killing; she won't be given the background on the case, won't betray any compartments.

Lyndsey looks up to find Maggie, the office manager, standing in the doorway to her office. She has a quizzical expression on his face, like she's just heard bad news. She steps inside and closes the door.

"I've noticed you're spending a lot of time with Theresa Warner." There's a warning in Maggie's tone, if you've ears to hear. "That's not a good idea."

This is not what Lyndsey expected, not at all. "What are you talking about?"

"There are things you don't know." How Lyndsey hates those words: they are used too often in the intelligence business. There's always someone happy to remind you that there's a deeper secret you're not privy to. After ten years, Lyndsey has learned that sometimes there's a secret, and sometimes there isn't.

Maggie tilts her head, weighing her words. "Theresa Warner . . . has a reputation. She's rubbed some people the wrong way."

Lyndsey parses this silently. *Some people* means senior managers. *Rubbed them the wrong way* means she's made enemies. Committed unforgiveable offenses.

Lyndsey feels a slow burn ignite in her chest. "The woman's husband died in a CIA operation. *Of course* she's angry and upset—"

"She's let her anger cloud her judgment. She's alienated people, people who have tried to help her. I'm only telling you what I've heard." Maggie takes a deep breath. "Be careful aligning yourself with Theresa. She's burned too many bridges."

How many times has Lyndsey heard these exact words whispered about a coworker? Someone could say the same thing about her. CIA can be a difficult place to work, politicized in unspoken ways. Failure isn't viewed well, no matter whose fault it is. Some people probably distanced themselves from Theresa after Richard's death, afraid that the taint would stick to them, too. It was a lesson she learned as a child, when some of her friends withdrew after her father's death. They were afraid, her mother had explained. *The death of a parent is scary and they're transferring that fear to you.* Her mother had always been good at seeing what was going on inside a person's mind, and she'd taught her daughter to be the same way. It was the reason she'd decided to major in psychology. Lyndsey didn't hold it against her young friends, but that's when she learned not to depend on them too much. She's surprised that she's grown so close to Theresa. Maybe it's because they're so alike. Two loners.

Lyndsey looks at the office manager, reading her expression and body language. She's sincere. She's only trying to help. She doesn't appear to be anyone's cat's-paw. Maybe there's something to what Maggie is saying, something that bears looking into. "Okay—thanks for the warning." For now, there's nothing else to say.

TWELVE

Time drags in Lyndsey's minuscule office. With no window, she judges time by the sounds outside her door. Lyndsey is about to head downstairs for another coffee, her third of the day—and stifles the urge to text Theresa to see if she wants to join her—when an email appears in her inbox.

Preliminary toxicology report on Genghis.

Popov. Her eyes skip down the page. She opens the attachment, a pdf of the report from the Office of the Chief Medical Examiner of the District of Columbia. While it is grainy it is also readable, but most of it is technical jargon and medical-speak that she doesn't understand. One page in, she sees that she needs someone to interpret it for her.

Although it is past Theresa's usual quitting time, she is still at her desk. She smiles at Lyndsey when she sees her approach.

Lyndsey looks over her shoulder for Maggie (does Maggie report this sort of thing to Eric? she wonders) before starting to speak. "Do you have a minute? I could use your help. Before I left to go overseas, there were a couple analysts who worked on medical issues. Do you know if they're still around?"

"Let me show you a way to find out." A couple taps on the keyboard and a website comes up on Theresa's monitor that reminds Lyndsey of Facebook. It shows a wall of posts from an assortment of individuals, some with photographs next to the name, some with avatars. "In the last couple years, everyone's started using collaborative tools more regularly. It really helps get things done. This is the latest. It makes it much easier to find who might be working on a target that's similar to yours, or if you need someone with a particular expertise," Theresa explains.

Lyndsey admires Theresa's ease with the tool. Theresa types "medical analysis" in the search bar and hits Return. A number of links come up to posts where a robust dialogue goes on between analysts and officers: an outbreak of avian flu in Vietnam, prevalence of malaria in Australia.

"That was easy," Lyndsey says. In the old days, it would take asking around until you found someone who could help you. This is much more efficient.

"Isn't it, though? So . . . any of these what you're looking for?"

Lyndsey hesitates. She shouldn't get specific. Theresa doesn't have need-to-know. "I've taken enough of your time. How about if I play around with it myself? What was the link again?"

Theresa scribbles it on a scrap of paper and hands it to Lyndsey.

Back in the privacy of her office, Lyndsey types "poison" into the search bar. She feels a twinge of guilt for not telling Theresa. It seems petty to hold her at arm's length. Surely the toxicology report will be the talk of the office by quitting time. But given the task she's been given, finding a potential double agent, Lyndsey of all people should obey the rules.

A handful of links come back and, after clicking through the first five, it's readily apparent that there is only one expert on poisons at the Agency: Randy Detwiler. All she can make out from the tiny thumbnail is that he has wiry, light brown hair and wears glasses.

Lyndsey finds Detwiler on the internal system's instant messaging service. Luckily, he's at his desk. He asks her to send the toxicology report to him, and within fifteen minutes, he's texted back. "Very interesting! But my response is too involved to type. Want to stop by my office?"

The trek to Randy Detwiler's office takes less than ten minutes, but it feels like another world. Detwiler is part of the Agency's collection of analysts who keep track of every matter of importance to policymakers. It's home to a hodgepodge of skills—political scientists, researchers, historians, linguists, and economists, to name a few. Lyndsey, like many case officers, is secretly intimidated anytime she's had to work with the specialists, but there's no denying their usefulness, especially when it comes to esoteric matters like this.

The small team of medical analysts are kept in a sleepy hallway in the basement. The basement is a twisty maze of corridors, home to offices with strange needs, equipment that makes belching sounds or emits bad smells, or is too large or heavy to go in a conventional space. Detwiler's office is in a lab, he's warned her. She finds the entrance by its sign: LABORATORY OF MEDICAL SCIENCES.

She passes the lab itself, something out of a sci-fi series. Through windows in the double doors, stainless steel countertops support an array of equipment whose functions Lyndsey can only guess at. Shelves are filled with trays of mysterious vials. A few of the stools are occupied by researchers in protective gear hunched over microscopes, lost in whatever they're examining: new strains of diseases, possible traces of nuclear material, blood samples from a crime scene? It seems wild to Lyndsey that something like this should exist in the Agency's basement.

Beyond the lab, Lyndsey is confronted by a row of small private offices, no open floor plan here, like in other offices, as befits a team that's made up of doctors and PhD researchers. She walks down the hall, checking the nameplates until she finds Detwiler. He towers over her when he stands to shake her hand. He must be at least six and a half feet, and looks to be in his mid-fifties. He has a benign, bookish appearance, like an accountant or librarian. His most distinctive feature, aside from his height, is a head of graying curls.

"That was quite an interesting report you sent," he says. His tone is almost amused.

"Can you tell me what it means?"

"The short answer is that the cause of death was alkaloid poisoning. In and of itself, it's not remarkable. It's the *source* of the alkaloid that's so interesting. Gelsemium. Have you heard of it?"

Lyndsey shakes her head. "Should I?"

"It's commonly used as a homeopathic remedy. Used to treat colds, sleeplessness, that sort of thing. Do you know if the victim used homeopathic medicines?"

Like many Russians, Popov was a skeptic. In Lyndsey's experience, he put his faith in very little. It might've been one reason why he enjoyed talking to her; he thought Americans were refreshing. "No, I don't think so. The only thing he took for colds was vodka."

"Compounds used in homeopathy can be tricky. Especially when the system isn't flooded with the compound, like you'd see in a deliberate overdose."

"So, you don't think he was murdered?"

The man smiles at her question. "I might have thought that if I hadn't been studying political assassinations for the past five years. Your run-of-the-mill police department would probably write this off as an accidental overdose. They might not even catch the exact chemical agent unless they had reason to look for it. Believe it or not, you sometimes see cases of alkaloid poisoning in people who've eaten too many green vegetables, though usually those people only get sick."

Lyndsey nods, encouraging him to continue.

"When I see that someone has died from alkaloid poisoning, I think assassination. Both the Russians and the Chinese are known to use gelsemium in political murders. Let me show you." Detwiler swivels the monitor around in Lyndsey's direction so she can see the report up on the screen: a Russian name, a black-and-white photo of a man, forty-ish. "That's Alexander Perepelichny. He was involved in the Magnitsky case— you know, the guy who uncovered the big swindle involving Putin. Because of his murder, the U.S. imposed sanctions on Russia."

"Perepelichny was killed by this same poison?" she asks. Detwiler nods. "So, it's something the killer can administer in one dose? Like a hit-and-run?"

"Exactly."

"And how long before it takes effect?"

"It depends on a number of factors: the amount used, the victim's condition, the usual variables . . . But it can be quite fast-acting. At the levels that were in his blood—thirty minutes, maybe."

That narrows the time down to the flight, or possibly just before boarding. Her chest tightens at the thought of Popov dying alone in an airplane. Because of his trust in her. "How would it have been administered?"

"It's usually done orally. Easy enough to slip into a drink, for instance. I'll check to see if it can be injected."

She looks at the monitor again, into the face of the dead man. "And who was responsible for Perepelichny's death?" Lyndsey asks, even though she's sure she knows the answer.

"Well, since the case involved elites in the Russian government laundering money overseas, it's assumed that the FSB was behind the murder, but of course it's never been solved."

Will Popov's murder go unsolved, too? What will happen to his wife and surviving daughter? Will the government take its ire out on them, harass them, cheat them, starve them? Lyndsey's mind swims with questions.

It seems there can be no denying that Popov was murdered by his own country. The only question that remains is why? It would be easy to assume the Russians discovered what he was doing, but this is Lyndsey's guilty knowledge talking. She shouldn't jump to conclusions. There could be another reason, something CIA didn't know about.

Whatever the reason, it won't be found in the toxicology report. She has work to do.

She stands to leave. "Thank you, this has been very helpful."

He walks to the door with her. "Sure, my pleasure. I read about this death in the papers. Unhealthy middle-aged men die every day, of course, including on planes, but when I heard he was a Russian official—well, it sounded awfully suspicious to me."

A word catches in Lyndsey's ear. "Unhealthy? Why do you say he was unhealthy?"

"It was in the toxicology report." Detwiler rummages through the papers on his desk until he finds the one he wants. He runs a finger down a column of numbers. "See here? They list the medications in his bloodstream. It says that he was on SSRIs—selective serotonin reuptake inhibitors. Antidepressants."

Varya. It's no surprise for a man whose daughter has just killed herself to be on antidepressants. Even for an old-school Russian, when the vodka wasn't enough.

She shakes her head for Detwiler: nothing to see there.

He taps the page again. "He was on a bunch of worrisome medications. Diovan; it's used to treat blood pressure, but it's commonly prescribed for someone who's just had a heart attack."

A heart attack? Lyndsey raises an eyebrow.

He reads from the paper. "Tissue plasminogen activators—that's for breaking up blood clots. You commonly see them administered after someone's had a stroke. Anticoagulants. At the levels found in his blood, I'd say this man had had a serious medical episode fairly recently."

Had Popov been ill? This case is one secret after another. What else doesn't she know about her old friend?

"If he was so sick, how can you be sure he didn't die from a heart attack?"

"No, it was the gelsemium, all right. You couldn't have those levels in your bloodstream and live. But in his condition, it probably didn't take much to get the body to shut down. It's all right here in the report," he says, rattling the sheet of paper, "though I'd be happier to run my own tests, you know, rather than go off someone else's numbers. Mistakes happen. They're rare, but they happen. Maybe I'll call the medical examiner's office and see if they have any material left."

Typical analyst, wants to button things up. She is grateful to Detwiler, but their talk has nonetheless saddened her. Popov had not been this sick when she left. His deterioration was rapid.

Still. The clues are aligning too perfectly. It makes her nervous. She's been trained to expect outliers. Sometimes it *is* a slam dunk, and everything lines up because the expected is exactly what happened. But other times . . .

"You've been very helpful. If you come across anything else of interest, even if you don't think it's significant, get in touch. Please." After another handshake, she starts back to her office with one answer and a lot of new questions.

THIRTEEN

Lyndsey is barely back at her desk when there's a large figure lurking in the doorway. Raymond Murphy stands just outside, hovering like a vampire waiting to be invited in. The thought amuses Lyndsey briefly, until she remembers that he might very well be there to tell her she's lost her clearance, to pack up and go.

But no, it seems she's been spared for another day. "We have a development at Moscow Station," he says as he drops into a chair. *Let it be Cassidy,* she says to herself, and doesn't even feel bad for it.

Murphy sounds pleased, though he tries to hide the satisfaction in his voice. "Turns out they flagged one of the case officers, Kate Franklin, as a potential concern. She's been at Moscow Station for a year, with the Agency about twenty years. The Chief of Station came to us a few weeks back after noticing something odd about her. We've turned up some irregularities in her finances. Money in a bank account not covered in her financial report."

Lyndsey's disappointed that it has nothing to do with Cassidy. Still—so much for Hank Bremer's complaining at the teleconference about Raymond Murphy's inquiry: he'd reported the employee himself. Which is part of a COS's job, after all. On the other hand, she knows what it's like to be questioned over what seems like a minor infraction.

"Hank's talked to her," Raymond continues. "Turns out it's a little gambling problem. The thing is, she didn't do the usual online thing because she was afraid of being discovered by us. So, she was doing it the old-fashioned way: with the locals. She'd been losing money steadily and then—voilà, she suddenly scores a jackpot."

"And you think it's a gift from the FSB?"

"It's not impossible, is it? They find out she's an intelligence officer, try to reel her in. Now she's in a blackmailable position, accepting bribes from an adversary. 'If you don't want CIA to find out about it, do this one small favor for us,'" he says in a bad Russian accent.

"A bit tenuous, isn't it? What's her relationship to the three cases?"

Resentment in the set of Raymond's shoulders: she's caught him. "That's yet to be determined. We don't have the whole story from Station yet. Franklin knew about Nesterov. She'd backed up the case officer on more than one occasion. But I'm not sure yet about Popov and Kulakov."

The whole thing makes Lyndsey nervous. If this gets out, everyone will think they found the mole. They'll be relieved to have a suspect, any suspect. Success will be assumed, and CI will slow the rest of the in-vestigation. But remembering Masha's texts—*the FSB knew about him, he didn't trust Gerald*—this sounds to Lyndsey like a distraction from the real culprit.

"I'm not sure . . ."

He rises from the chair, extracting himself from the awkward corner. "It's not something you need to be worried about, is it? I'm dealing with Moscow Station. That's the division of effort."

She's tempted to snap back at him but that won't help the situation. "I don't want anyone thinking we have the guilty party until we're sure."

Murphy sniffs like he's been insulted. "You're not calling the shots here, if you remember . . . CI has the lead. You're only here because Eric Newman insisted. Wouldn't take no for an answer."

He wants to make sure she knows her place. And to think she had almost told Murphy about Cassidy, hoped he could dig up something without Eric getting wind of it. Now she's glad she didn't. Murphy would only use it to get her into trouble if he saw a chance.

He rolls his eyes. "And it's not like our investigation against you has been dropped, you know. It's been put on hold. They'll open it up again as soon as this is over. And then we'll see."

The look on his face is petty and exulting, the face of the mob outside the jail, waiting for the hanging. He glares at her, as though she personally did something to hurt him. What she did was a minor bending of the rules, she reminds herself. It *should* be a minor infraction. It's only a big deal because someone has it in for her.

She turns her attention to the computer monitor. "Are you done? Because I need to get back to work." She waits until he's left to react. She pushes the keyboard away, pressing her hands into the desktop to stop them from trembling. She feels like she's been hit by a truck. This is getting a taste of what Franklin must've felt: that once you make a mistake at the Agency, there are some people who will never let it go. Who will make sure it haunts you for the rest of your career, if not your life.

Lyndsey doesn't return to the present until she realizes Theresa is standing in the same spot where Murphy was just a few seconds ago. Staring at her.

Her smile is tentative. "Something happen?" She nods in the direction of the front door, where Murphy undoubtedly has just left. "Want to get some coffee?"

The cafeteria is near-empty, for which Lyndsey is grateful. People stroll by in twos and threes on their way to the steam tables and cashiers, but she and Theresa have the seating area to themselves. Two steaming paper cups stand on the table between them.

She turns the cup gingerly in her hands. It's blisteringly hot but she barely feels it.

Theresa winces as she watches. "Do you want to talk about it? I assume it had something to do with the guy I saw leaving your office?"

Theresa is right: Lyndsey feels the need to talk about Davis pushing against her chest, but who can she talk to? It's not the kind of thing she can talk about with anyone outside the Agency, and it's not the sort of thing to confess to someone inside. The idea of calling Davis suddenly flits through her head but that would be the last wise thing to do, especially with the investigation still open. During the exit interview in Lebanon, she told Security it was over with him. It had hurt like hell to say that but now it hurt even more to make it stick.

If she tells her secret to Theresa, it will change everything between them. Or . . . maybe not. Maybe Theresa's not like that. She's been through a lot, after all. Suffered more than her share.

Theresa is throwing her a lifeline. Lyndsey decides to take it.

"I'm under investigation."

Silence. Theresa leans back in the plastic chair. "Wow. No offense, but you seem like the last person who'd break the rules."

"Am I that much of a goody-two-shoes?"

"It can't be too bad if they're letting you keep your badge."

A half smirk. "It's only because of Eric. For the investigation."

Theresa's eyebrows shoot up. She seems to start to say something, then hesitates. "You don't have to tell me what happened if you don't want to . . ."

Say it fast, like pulling off a bandage. "I dated a foreign intelligence officer while in Beirut." Theresa is working hard to suppress whatever thoughts she's having. Lyndsey can't tell if she's being judged at this moment.

"He's a Brit," she adds, knowing that will make a difference.

"Did you get any good intel from him? If you got any reportable information out of it, all would've been forgiven," Theresa cracks. She's trying to lighten the situation but it's not entirely untrue.

"It wasn't like that. We didn't talk about work." That is never true, not in this line of work. Now Lyndsey doesn't want to say anything more, doesn't want to relive it all over again. The wound doesn't smart as sharply as it did this morning. Finally telling someone about it has loosened its power over her.

Except now Theresa knows something bad about her. Something she could hold over Lyndsey's head if she chose to. She has given The Widow leverage.

But a true friend wouldn't do that, would she?

"So, he was just a fling, this guy?" Theresa asks. "That's too bad . . . It's good, you know, being with someone in the business. They understand what you're going through."

Lyndsey's heard this said before. But she's not sure this isn't just a way for Agency folks to excuse themselves. *My wife doesn't understand me.* Then hop into bed with a coworker.

"It would be a shame to lose this guy if you really like him. It's hard to find the right one. It would be too bad if you had to let him slip away." Theresa takes a long draw on her coffee. "There's another way to look at this, of course. Without a man in your life, you're free to do what you want. Ask for an assignment in Paris, or Timbuktu, any place that takes your fancy. Take that plum assignment, volunteer to be the Director's executive assistant. You can do the long hours now."

Lyndsey chuckles. "You're not going to tell me I need a husband?"

"God, no." Theresa turns somber. They are treading on sensitive ground. "Marriage is a big deal. A commitment. I truly believe that. It's a test of who you are as a person. You have to be sure that you're ready."

For a while, they sit in silence. The most important thing in Theresa's life, it seems, was her marriage. Now that Richard is gone, what does that mean for Theresa? What is she if she's not Richard Warner's wife?

Lyndsey puts down her cup. "Thanks for being my talk therapy. I liked Davis—this man—a lot." Referring to him in the past tense rankles, but Davis Ranford is part of her past now. She can't see any way to get back together with him, not as long as she's still working.

"The only advice I have is to do what feels right," Theresa says. "If that's fighting to keep this man, then fight. Or if you know in your heart that it was a mistake, let him go. Only you know the answer to that."

Lyndsey walks out to the parking lot with Theresa. The women say their goodbyes and Theresa heads off to where she's parked her Volvo as Lyndsey sits behind the wheel of her rental. She's been unable to stop thinking about Davis since the conversation in the cafeteria. Was it a mistake to let him go, is this what's been troubling her? There's nothing she'd like to do more, at that moment, than lean against his long, rangy frame and feel his arm slip around her shoulder, drawing her close. To feel him nuzzle her hair and remind her that life is too short for regrets.

Taking a deep breath, she turns the key in the ignition and drives away.

FOURTEEN

The mornings begin to fall into a steady rhythm. Powering up her computer and spinning the dial on the combination lock to her safe. Shutting the door to mute the sounds of life outside, the murmur of voices and thump of footsteps approaching and receding. To put herself into the necessary mind-set to hunt a traitor.

She needs to be sure about Kulakov, that the official cause of death isn't plausible. So, she calls Ruth Mallory, one of the old Russia hands. One of the few who has worked the target since the Soviet days, but Lyndsey hears she is about to retire. "Did you get that report I sent you?" Lyndsey asks as soon as Mallory answers the phone.

"Sure did. Those were some pictures."

"Whose handiwork, if you had to guess?"

"Oh, it's FSB, no doubt about it. Maybe the *politsiya* were involved, too. They've been known to go overboard if the FSB lets them in on the fun."

"I'm disappointed they didn't do a better job covering their tracks."

"They have no reason to hide. It's better, for intimidation purposes, for everyone to know what they're capable of."

When Lyndsey asks Mallory—who knows everyone who's walked through the doors of Russia Division for the last forty years—what she knows about Kate Franklin, Mallory gives a brusque laugh. "It's a fool's game, trying to guess. I've been through that once, you know. Aldrich Ames. I was a junior officer. It's a miserable ordeal to go through. Absolutely miserable. They turn the office inside out, question everyone. They investigate you to within an inch of your life. It destroys morale. Here, your whole identity is built around *trustworthiness.* You're given access to secrets because they trust you, and—not for anything you did, poof, it's all taken away from you. That's when you see things for how they really are: they don't trust us, not really."

Lyndsey feels a flutter of recognition. Being pushed out of Beirut Station, sent home.

"Then you find out that one of you *was* a traitor, that it wasn't a wild-goose chase like you hoped, and it's worse. Infinitely worse. You remember all the conversations you had with him. You remember all the sketchy things about him, how no one really liked him, how it was so obvious that something wasn't right and yet they let him continue . . . Why is that? Have you ever wondered? You want to give them the benefit of the doubt, but why is it that they're always so slow to move on the bad eggs and so quick when it comes to the innocent? I've never really understood that . . . It seems a kind of cowardice, to me. And a disappointment to those who trusted the system."

While everything Mallory has just said is true, it doesn't help the situation at hand. As Lyndsey's about to say goodbye, however, Mallory adds, "If I remember correctly, there may have been something a few years back involving Franklin . . . I can't remember the details. But you might talk to Reese Munroe. I think he was her supervisor at the time."

Reese was Lyndsey's boss in Moscow. While some time has passed since they'd last been in touch, she'd like the opportunity to speak to him again. "Where is Reese now?"

"In Belarus. He must've made someone very angry to get sent there," Mallory says with a laugh.

Lyndsey makes a mental note to send Reese an email.

She turns her attention to the files Raymond Murphy sent yesterday. They arrived late, just as she was packing up. He pulled the access logs for all three compartments, Lighthouse, Skipjack, and Genghis. If anyone tried to access these electronic files, which reside behind a firewall, it would be noted in these logs. Raymond has already warned her that no one looks through the logs for anomalies in real time; they're only there for backup, to check after an event has taken place. The files are nothing but rows and rows of numbers and punctuation marks and fragments of words that mean something to a computer but nothing to her. You're looking for patterns and nothing more, which is why Raymond punted this task over to Lyndsey. *I don't have time to go through the logs,* he'd written in his email. *And I've set up a time for you to interview Kate Franklin this afternoon.*

They really should have a programmer do this but there aren't enough programmers to go around, and besides, most programmers would consider this beneath their dignity, which means she would wait for days, if not weeks, for one of them to get around to it.

She pores over the lines until her eyes sting. Eventually she identifies the code that means an attempt was made to access a file, but access was denied. Then she figures out which string of numbers is the computer ID. Most of the time she sees a computer's ID only once, meaning that a hit on a restricted file was probably a mistake, a typo. But repeated hits from the same computer ID: that's someone consciously trying to access restricted files.

Before long, she has a short list of IDs.

She sends the list to Raymond, asking him to pinpoint the computers with these IDs. He writes back that this will only give her the location of the computer, which doesn't necessarily equate to a person. Someone could deliberately use another person's computer, waiting until the unwitting person has stepped away without locking their computer: it's a known way to try to hide your identity. It's why most of the computers are set to lock automatically after a short while.

That's why it's so hard to catch these guys, he types as an afterthought.

The logs Raymond sent cover the last three months. After all her sifting, she found only a handful of suspicious activity, which surprises her but would probably make Security happy. She's afraid the chances of the mole being one of the numbers are pretty slim. Three months may be too recent. The mole may have gone after information months ago, but the Russians only decided to act now. Perhaps she should ask Raymond to pull the logs from a year ago . . .

And then it hits her: the number of attempts to access the files, even from authorized users, is small. That means no one is reading the reports— electronically. But what about paper copies? Officers are discouraged from keeping paper copies for various reasons. It's less secure, and then there's the problem of storing and disposing of them. She knows, however, that it's still done. Everyone prints copies of important reports, the ones they refer to frequently. Could the mole be getting paper copies?

Jan Westerling is the reports officer for Lighthouse. Lyndsey remembers talking to the woman the day Kulakov's body was found, how upset she was. Her impression of Westerling is that she is inexperienced but earnest and not especially careless.

Lyndsey wanders over to Westerling's desk. One of many gray cubicles, it takes Lyndsey a minute to remember where it sits, but at last she finds it. There are the discarded walking shoes under the desk, a stainless steel water bottle. Thumbtacked to the fabric panel is a picture of Westerling in hiking clothes, a down vest, and sunglasses, her straight black hair pulled back in a ponytail, her head bowed next to another woman of about the same age.

The cubicle is empty. The reports officer is probably away at a meeting. Without appearing too obvious, Lyndsey glances around. The computer monitor is locked, just as it should be, but there are papers in the open. A two-drawer safe sits at a right angle to the desk, and it's clearly open, the drawers pulled out to keep it from automatically locking. People leave their safes open though they're not supposed to, like leaving your car running while you go to the ATM. It's convenient. You don't believe anything is going to happen. You open them in the morning and leave them open all day, never expecting that someone would go through them when you're not there.

She looks around. The vault is a big, open cavern made up of cubicles with partitions five feet tall. You can see into Westerling's area from at least three other cubicles, though it would be a partial view and that's if the neighbors happen to look up from the computer. Lyndsey could reach down and rifle through the reports in the safe, and while she might be noticed, she doubts anyone would call her on it.

She has what she needs for Lighthouse. To follow up on Skipjack, she needs to ask Maggie where she can find Kyle Kincaid, the reports officer. As it turns out, he's in another part of the building, sitting with a team that follows cyber targets. As they make the short walk, Maggie asks how Lyndsey is settling in.

"Oh, fine," Lyndsey says, wary about saying too much about the investigation, not sure what Eric has told Maggie. Some managers treat their office managers like secretaries, but others include them in just about everything.

"Eric's glad you're here. I don't know that there was anyone else he could turn to."

It's nice of Maggie to say, but could it be true? Lyndsey knows there are plenty of other former officers from Russia Division who could also handle the investigation—some more experienced. Then there's Beirut hanging over her head. She wonders if Maggie knows anything about that. If anything, it's Lyndsey who is indebted to Eric: this could go a long way toward making the problem go away.

Kyle Kincaid is found in another vast, open, dimly lit office. The men in the cubicles around him are all younger, and he holds court with a stream of chatter about a paintball outing this past weekend. From his buzz haircut to his erect posture and beefy build, Kyle Kincaid comes across as former military, most likely leaving the service as a junior officer to join the Agency. He wears a white shirt with the sleeves rolled haphazardly to his elbows, and an ugly tie, the kind picked by a man who hasn't had to buy many. A battered canvas briefcase sits by his feet.

"Kyle?" She interrupts his chatter to introduce herself and tell him why she's sought him out. "Is there somewhere private we can talk?"

They walk down the hall to a conference room. He slides into a chair. He doesn't bother to try to hide his skepticism. It's not that he doesn't believe what she told him, but he clearly doesn't like that she is going to be judging how he has done his job, if he might've done something that got his asset apprehended. "We're just trying to figure out what happened," she says even though she knows it won't set his mind at ease.

"How did the Russians find out about Nesterov?" Kincaid asks.

"That's what we hope to find out. I need you to answer a few questions."

He smirks. "You sound like a cop. Do I need a lawyer?"

She should've brought Raymond Murphy with her, then at least they could play good cop, bad cop. "I'm not with CI. I'm sure they'll talk to you soon enough. I'm trying to figure out if someone got access to Nesterov's files who shouldn't have. Have you noticed anything off lately? People asking questions who weren't read into the access, asking to see his reports?"

"No . . . But there's a lot of interest in Skipjack's reports now. He's been turning in some good information, though that wasn't always the case. The number of people who know his true identity, though—that's small. Most people don't care who the source is as long as the information is good. Once they're satisfied that he's not lying, they don't think about it again."

"And there's nothing out of the ordinary you can remember?"

"Nothing." He frowns like a petulant schoolboy. "Why would a mole turn in Skipjack? That's the part I don't get. Moscow wouldn't care about small potatoes like him. I think Station was ready to write him off. He was lucky to get reassigned to that cyber unit. Things were about to turn around for him."

Lyndsey's ears prick up. He's touched on something that's been nagging her: how did the mole decide to hand over these three assets? They're lopsided: Lighthouse and Skipjack hadn't been big producers, as Kincaid said. But Genghis, Popov, was a crown jewel. Genghis alone would be more than the Russians could hope for.

For another thing, they are as diverse as can be, from three different programs: science, military, and a highly placed security asset. You'd think that the mole would have access to one program only. The mole is either showing off his ability to break through firewalls or . . . there's another reason at play here, one that Lyndsey hasn't thought of yet.

On her way out, Lyndsey gives Kincaid's desk a once-over. He sits with his back to three other officers, their four cubicles forming a square with a shared table in the middle. It seems a lively place, the four men talking among themselves constantly. She notices Kincaid's safe, too: the drawers are open, manila folders peeking out, tempting anyone to pluck them up. But most likely, at least one of these four guys would be around at any given time. It would be hard to get to those files without being seen.

Unless the mole sits nearby. Or Kincaid is stupider than he seems. There's a path through all these bits and pieces that leads to an answer, but at the moment she can't see it.

That afternoon comes an appointment Lyndsey hasn't been looking forward to: the interview with Kate Franklin. Lyndsey told Raymond Murphy she wanted to talk to her alone, rather than participate in CI's questioning. Beirut is still fresh in her mind: her own interrogation by the Chief of Station, hammered with questions even though they were uninterested in her answers, their minds already made up. The shame and regret and fear. It's too raw for her to sit on the other side of the table, to watch someone else go through the same ordeal.

She feels for this woman across the table, made to confess her failings in front of strangers. Franklin sits at the table, shoulders hunched, eyes downcast. An ugly patch of psoriasis has broken out on her face. Her hair is barely combed, her clothes don't seem to sit right on her body, as though she's misaligned buttons or put on things a size too small. Everything about her posture and demeanor says she has given up already. She probably wishes the floor would open up beneath her, that she could hand in her badge and kiss her pension goodbye if only they would let her walk out the door. They've threatened her with jail time, though, rattling her into submission. Lyndsey's stomach clenches to look at her.

The questioning will need to be indirect. CI was clear on that. Lyndsey can't ask any leading questions, nothing that would reveal there's a mole hunt going on. If Franklin is involved, it should come out under questioning, revealing threads that lead back to spying activity. Unless she is an expert and determined liar.

She extends her hand. "Hello, I'm Lyndsey Duncan from Russia Division. I have a few questions for you."

Kate's eyes lift briefly to meet Lyndsey's, then dart away. "Is this really necessary? I've already talked to CI and Security several times—"

Can this be over, please? I'd like to go home, crawl into bed, pull the covers over my head and never come out. Lyndsey understands only too well. "Absolutely necessary, yes. I'll try to be as brief as possible. Why don't you tell me when the, uh, problem started?"

Franklin sighs, collapsing further into herself, like a falling soufflé. She knows she has to talk about this, but she's ashamed. Revealing your weakness to strangers is part of the job, however. You lay yourself bare, over and over.

When she speaks, her voice is small and helpless. "About a year ago. Right before I was posted to Moscow. I hadn't gambled in a long time. At least five years, I think. Nothing, except the occasional lottery ticket. I started taking weekend trips to Charlestown, or Arundel Mills in Maryland. It was no big deal, just something to do with my girlfriends. A little excitement. But it was never a problem. Things might've been a little tight from time to time, but it wasn't anything I couldn't handle."

"What happened in Russia?"

Russia. The bleak nights, the wet cold that suffuses everything. The loneliness that all single women suffer at an overseas post, probably worse for someone Franklin's age. Franklin looks at her red, chapped hands as though they are responsible for her lapse. "I don't know how it got out of control over there, I really don't. I told myself I'd only do it once in a while, a treat when I'd had a rough day."

"You ended up placing bets with the locals? But gambling is illegal in Moscow."

Her first smile for Lyndsey is a half grimace. "It's easy to find a bookie to take a bet on sports . . . a football match, boxing match. Everyone does it."

"How much did you lose?"

She hesitates. "Twenty thousand. More than I ever thought . . . I don't know how it got out of control—" She sniffles, reaches into a pocket for a wadded tissue, and dabs her nose. "The bookie, he knew I was an American, he figured I'd be good for it . . . But he let me know he expected to collect—or there would be consequences."

"Did he make an offer for you to work off your debt?"

"Work for the Russians, you mean?" Her look is beyond contempt. "I would never do that. It was only twenty thousand. I don't have that kind of money lying around, but I could get my hands on it. Take it out of my retirement fund. Borrow from relatives. I wouldn't agree to spy—no way." She stops to compose herself. "It didn't come to that. He let me make one more bet—and that one came in." Franklin pulls back slightly as though waiting to see how Lyndsey will react. *Even she knows it was too good to be true.* "Sure, I thought it was suspicious . . . But he said I won it. It would wipe out my debt. I wasn't about to turn it down."

"But you didn't tell the Station about it, any of it . . ."

"I was hoping for a miracle. That it would all blow over and everything would be okay . . ." She starts shredding the tissue. "CI has made it clear they think I was being set up. That the Russians were going to start pressuring me after I'd accepted the money, when I didn't have any choice because they'd have proof I was dirty."

"You understood the risk."

"But that's not what happened, I swear."

Lyndsey says nothing, absorbing every flick of her eyes, twitch of her mouth, every nervous fidget of her hands. CI says they'd caught Franklin before the Russians had a chance: there'd been a little money left over after paying off her debt, a few thousand dollars, which she put in her bank account. It wasn't necessarily sloppy tradecraft: such a small amount could be overlooked or explained away if anyone asked. It was just her bad luck that this happened as the mole hunt kicked off, and Security pressed harder than they normally would. She crumbled under questioning.

"I admit I haven't used the best judgment. Have I done things I wish I hadn't? Sure, hasn't everyone? I haven't committed a crime." The tears subside as anger rises to the surface. "I'm not stupid. I know what's going on: something bad happened and they're looking to pin it on someone. If they can't find out who did it, they're going to pin it on me." Her eyes frantically search Lyndsey's face for confirmation.

"We want the guilty party. We're not looking for a scapegoat." Lyndsey tries to sound authoritative, but Franklin glares at her. *She thinks I'm being naïve.* "Look, your best bet is to cooperate fully with the investigation. If you're innocent, you'll be exonerated."

Franklin turns away from her in exasperation. She's shaking visibly from head to toe. Her strange behavior worries Lyndsey: could it be a sign of guilt? Does the heightened emotion mean she's lying? Lyndsey's own recent scrape with Security doesn't help. It's hard to be objective.

Then she remembers what Ruth Mallory told her. A past incident? Maybe there's something in Franklin's past that would be relevant. Reese Munroe, the Station Chief, might know.

Lyndsey stands. "That's all I have—for now. Thanks for your time." She can't quite read the expression on Franklin's face, but it is worrying. Angry and sad and hopeless all in one. She gathers up shreds of tissue before leaving without another word.

Raymond Murphy is waiting in the next room. He sits on the edge of the table, arms crossed over his chest, chewing his bottom lip, but stands when Lyndsey enters.

His face shines with excitement, like a dog who has caught a hare.

"So—what do you think?" He wants the human lie detector to congratulate him.

"I couldn't tell if she's hiding something but . . . it *felt* like the truth."

He is crestfallen and stares at her with displeasure. "And you were able to come to this conclusion after just a couple minutes with her?"

"I'm not done yet. Let me ask you—have there been other incidents in the past? Have you spoken to her former supervisors?" She doesn't want to bother Reese if Murphy's already spoken to him.

The Counterintelligence officer squirms. "I've spoken to some of them—but I'm not done with my investigation, either." *Defensive.* She's caught him in a lie. "But I think you're wrong. I say where there's smoke, there's fire. People aren't just a *little* bad, Lyndsey. There's something else going on here, I know it." She catches the subtext here. He's talking about *her.*

It's early days in the investigation and Raymond is undoubtedly under pressure by his management to find the guilty party fast, just as Eric is under pressure from the Director. She understands why he wants her to agree with him, but she feels in her bones that he's wrong.

Franklin is not the mole.

Should she argue with him? It would be pointless, she decides. He needs to figure this out for himself. "Fine—you do that. In the meantime, I'll continue with my end of the investigation." It was inevitable that she would clash with Raymond but she doesn't like the way things are going with him. She throws the door open and exits before she can say anything worse.

FIFTEEN

L yndsey checks her watch once, twice, three times in five minutes. She hasn't spoken to Reese Munroe, the Chief of Station when she was posted to Moscow, since she'd left a few years ago. Chiefs of Station were important, busy positions. Lyndsey regretted losing touch with her former boss but had expected no different. That was how it went with people shuttling off to positions in other parts of the world, Beirut for Lyndsey, Minsk for Munroe. She'd emailed him a few days earlier, mentioning Kate Franklin's name and asking if he could find the time to talk. An officer at Minsk Station got in touch right away to arrange a time, not a good sign.

She sits at her desk, drumming her fingers as she waits for the call. Why has she let so much time pass since talking to Reese? Of all the bosses she's had, he has been the best, even better than Eric. He believed in her when she was a rookie in his Station. A father figure to a girl who barely remembered having one.

She needs someone to believe in her now.

Lyndsey remembers the night that changed her life: Yaromir Popov had made contact and asked her to meet him in secret. She was a rookie then, knew just enough to know she might be misreading the encounter, that it might not be the godsend, the once-in-a-lifetime opportunity that case officers dreamed about. She was so excited that she couldn't wait for morning, and she had called Reese, Moscow Chief of Station, right away.

They met in a coffee shop that night, a block away from his home in the neighborhood of Barrikadnaya, not far from the U.S. embassy compound, Reese still in the suit he'd worn all day, stirring his coffee as Lyndsey told him what had happened at the party. "He wants to meet tomorrow." Even though she'd only been working for Reese a few months, she felt they had a good relationship. He'd already given her more autonomy than the rest of his case officers—though that could all be over after tonight.

The ring of the metal spoon as Reese tapped it against the thick mug. "It could be a trap."

But when she had looked Popov in the eye, she thought she had seen something there. She held on to that. "If the SVR only wanted to go on a fishing expedition, they would have sent a lower-level officer, someone more plausible."

The restaurant's overhead light had cast Reese in a harsh shadow, deepening the lines on his face. He looked like a man who'd spent a lifetime in a prison cell. "He wants to meet in less than twenty-four hours. We won't have time to take the proper precautions. That's just what they'd do if they wanted to test us. See what our weaknesses are."

"Or he might be rushing so his people won't have time to get him under surveillance."

They both had known at the time that the Agency was struggling in Moscow. Russian internal security seemingly had doubled down on them, and in two years, the Station had picked up no new assets. "When was the last time we had someone with this kind of inside access? Let's hear him out, at least. What have we got to lose?"

He'd given her a sober look. "They could arrest you. Throw you in jail."

It could happen. They were trained for it: a little rough treatment, a couple nights in jail. But the SVR tended to throw disgraced intelligence officers out of the country quickly, persona non grata, rather than hold on to them.

The long-term implications were huge. If Lyndsey were caught, her career probably wouldn't survive. It had just started to look up with the early posting to Moscow: most of her friends were slogging away at backwater posts in far-flung corners of the globe, hoping someone back at Langley read their reports. She could be throwing all that away. She had to pick her battles.

Her gut told her that this was the battle to pick.

"This whole thing doesn't feel right," Reese warned her at the time. "They would try something like this if they wanted to get rid of you, but you haven't had time to piss them off. These things are usually tit-for-tat, but they have no reason to throw one of us out now. There hasn't been a recent scandal. It just doesn't make sense."

Lyndsey had leaned across the battered tabletop, straining to get through to her boss. "Let me do it, Reese. I'm willing to take the risk. That's why I'm here. If we don't take chances, we might as well go home." Then there was the part she couldn't say aloud: Moscow Station is failing on your watch. Let me help.

He'd stared back at her for so long, his expression unreadable, that she was sure she'd lost. But then he cracked the tiniest smile. "I knew Josh Kleinman, you know. I have great respect for his judgment. He gave me that paper you wrote, the one on microexpressions."

Lyndsey had tried not to look surprised, or too pleased. Kleinman had been her psych advisor in college. He'd been impressed with the work she did with a pair of computer vision specialists to come up with a program that picked out tiny changes in video subjects' facial expressions. It enabled computers to tell when people were lying or even thinking about lying more accurately than with a polygraph. It had brought a flood of attention from police departments and casinos and—unexpectedly—the CIA, too. It wasn't until later than she figured out her professor had encouraged Langley to get in touch with her about a job.

But in Moscow, there would be no video camera taping Popov, no program scouring his image for near-invisible twitches and tells, no advisor whispering in her ear.

Reese had sighed. "So far, from your time here, I haven't seen you do one thing to refute Josh's opinion of you, Lyndsey. Your instincts have been spot-on. If you think Popov is on the up-and-up, I'm on board. Okay, let's do."

She still cannot imagine why she had been so lucky. What Popov had seen in her, why Reese had believed in her.

The phone rings, jarring her out of her memories and bringing her back to the present day. "Lyndsey?" It's the same friendly but firm voice she remembers.

They exchange pleasantries and chat for a minute about Reese's time in Minsk. The cold, the fog, the preponderance of grim Soviet-era architecture. He asks nothing about Beirut, which makes her think he's heard about the trouble over Davis. She simmers with an embarrassment that can't be discussed.

There's no need for preliminaries. She mentioned a task force in her email so Reese knows exactly why she's called. "You want to know about Kate Franklin," he says as they settle down to business.

"I was told she worked for you at one time."

"Yes. A few years back, in Dushanbe." Tajikistan, a tough post for anyone. "She had some trouble with gambling, as I recall."

So much for this being a recent problem.

"She was counseled. Claimed she had it under control. But then something happened." Reese's voice gets quieter. "One of the case officers swore he saw her talking to Tajik liaison. Well, technically he didn't see her with them, but caught her walking away from a couple guys he recognized as Tajik internal security."

"So, you couldn't prove it?"

"I interviewed her. She swore up and down there was no meeting and accused the case officer of having it in for her."

"Did he?" Competition can be fierce at stations.

Reese grunts. "I didn't see it that way. I didn't feel I'd gotten to the truth of it and had her assignment curtailed. Frankly, I'm surprised she got posted to Moscow. She must've been able to convince Security that it was all a big misunderstanding."

The CI people will tell you it usually takes several attempts for a traitor to go through with the offer. That they'll try one avenue, chicken out, try again. Dushanbe may have been Kate Franklin's dry run.

She may have finally succeeded in Moscow.

"Thanks, Reese. And it's good to hear your voice."

"Yours, too, Lyndsey." It is warm again, and full of unspoken emotions. "Look—this career you've chosen, it's not an easy one. That may be the understatement of the year."

He knows. This can only mean he knows about Davis, about Beirut. About her shame and failing. What must he think about her being the one to investigate a fellow officer? It's the height of hypocrisy. She wishes she could disappear in a puff of smoke.

"What you're going through now, it'll blow over. They're making it a big deal. It isn't. I know Davis Ranford"—he interrupts himself with a chuckle—"and while your taste in men may be questionable, I wouldn't say he's a security risk."

He knows Davis. After not being able to talk to anyone about him, even to acknowledge him, this is like a drink of water after a long spell in the desert. She longs to talk about Davis with Reese. A thousand questions leap to mind—How did you meet him? When? Where were you posted?—but this is not the time for chitchat.

Reese continues with his fatherly advice. "If I were you, I'd be more concerned about who is pushing the matter with Security. You've made an enemy, Lyndsey. Someone with clout."

"I've been asking myself that same question."

"Security wouldn't be dogging it otherwise: there's no merit in the case. I *know* you, I know they're barking up the wrong tree. Have faith in yourself. Hang in there." Reese has more integrity than anyone she has met at the Agency. Her bottom lip wobbles a little; his faith in her means so much, especially at this moment.

"Thank you, Reese. I'll try." A thought comes to her. Reese, like Ruth Mallory, has been with the Agency a long time. He's probably worked with just about everyone who's currently working on the Russian target.

"One more thing, Reese . . . Have you ever worked with Tom Cassidy?"

There's a sharp intake of breath on the other end. "Why—is he a suspect, too?"

Lyndsey doesn't know if Reese has a relationship with Cassidy. They could be old friends. She could've just made a big mistake. "Masha said her husband didn't trust Cassidy."

"You know as well as I that assets don't always get along with their handlers. 'Trust' can mean a lot of things."

She weighs how much she should share. "Reese, I think Popov was on his way to Washington because he had something he wanted to tell me."

"Even if that was the case, you can't be sure it had anything to do with

Cassidy. Here's my opinion. You may not want to hear it, but . . . Tom Cassidy doesn't seem the type to sell out to the Russians. Not to me. The guy's main problem is that he's ambitious. *Very* ambitious. He wants to succeed, but inside the system. He doesn't want to burn the whole thing down."

Is Reese right? Lyndsey has no way of knowing without meeting Cassidy for herself. In the meanwhile, she's always known Reese's judgment to be sound. She should trust him—for now.

"Thanks, Reese." As she hangs up, it hits her how much she wishes it was Reese here at Langley. How much she trusts him. How exposed she feels at headquarters, near-friendless and alone.

SIXTEEN

A flicker from the computer screen catches Lyndsey's eye. Her chat window blinks at her. She squints: there's a message from Randy Detwiler, the poison expert. *I have a thought about the toxicology report. Come see me. I am at a conference the rest of today but will be back in the office tomorrow . . .*

She makes a mental note to contact Detwiler in the morning.

In the meantime, she thinks about how she found Detwiler. The tool that helps you find experts scattered across the Agency. Perhaps she can use it to find someone who could advise her on this investigation, weigh in on what she's done and tell her what she needs to do next. She feels like she's missing a lot.

Instead of searching on some term—unsure of what term to try—Lyndsey goes to the forum home page. There's an index of groups by topics. She marvels as she scans pages and pages of topics, a map of parts of the Agency she never knew about. Who would've thought there were experts here on desert agriculture and renewable energy and econometrics? It seems endless, this river of expertise.

She comes to the section on Russia. It is huge, bigger than all the other categories—of course. It is one of the oldest and most important targets. She is transfixed as she pages through the subgroups and threads of discussion. No wonder Russia Division is so quiet: the office chatter has gone underground. They quietly ask questions of one another in this forum, everything from the mundane (*Is there a problem with the printers this morning?*) to the profound (*Who will rise to lead the All-Russia People's Front if Putin were to die suddenly?*). Lyndsey tiptoes through the threads, feeling as though she has stumbled on a secret cocktail party, eavesdropping on conversations and no one realizes she's there.

You could use this to spy on the office. It doesn't provide everything you need to know, but it would be a start. It would point you in the right direction, provide clues.

She works her way methodically through the sub-forums, noting who is working on which targets and who chimes in on their threads. She watches the communities forum. The names start to repeat themselves: here's the guy who always has an opinion on Russian weapons, here's the guy who knows everything about Russian troll farms. The names rarely cross between groups and the ones that do are either the sage hands who have worked in the Division forever or the burnouts with too much time on their hands.

She fleshes out a diagram on a piece of paper. In the middle of each group are the people who ask the most questions on a subject or seem to be at the center of discussions on that topic. Next, she lists the people who chime in or occasionally post their own questions. She fills a page, then three, then five. Two hours later, she has pieced together a skeleton of a network diagram of the office. The curious thing, she sees, is that it provides a level of detail that isn't generally known, the precise targets or cases—or assets—that are only known to supervisors.

Lyndsey runs her finger along the spokes in the diagram. There is Jan

Westerling, the reports officer for Lighthouse, the scientist, surrounded by all things Russian research and development. She asks questions about metamaterials and nanotubes and 3D printing. The number of people in her circle are few. The names Lyndsey doesn't recognize she assumes are in the Directorate of Science and Technology but there are some from Russia Division, people she knows.

Kyle Kincaid sits at the intersection of military targets and cyber. The group that follows his posts is made of military and cyber experts and they mix it up freely. Though she notices Kincaid doesn't post many questions himself; probably doesn't want to be seen needing help. Mostly he chimes in on other officers' posts or gives his opinion on a breaking piece of news. She smiles when she sees one of the old Russia hands smack down one of his naïve assumptions. It stings when it happens but it's how you get better in this business, being schooled gently in public.

Still, Lyndsey hasn't found any posts explicitly about Lighthouse or Skipjack, the military officer. You could infer a few things from the posts she's seen, but nothing about a specific asset and certainly no true names.

Lyndsey stands and stretches. She looks at the clock on her monitor: it's nearly one p.m. No wonder she's stiff: she's been sitting motionless for hours.

Her eye falls back to her notes, lingering over the crude network diagram. It's like she's got a whole new way of thinking about the people in the Division, like she can see an invisible spider's web that connects them. Ruth Mallory tends all the discussions about Russian internal security like a busy mother hen (which begs the question, who will take over when she retires?). Zach Gelfman, the other officer still working from the Soviet era, is there whenever a question comes up about the Red Square days.

Lyndsey notices that Zach Gelfman comes and goes. Always watching, apparently, only decloaking when a topic comes up that he's interested in.

Always watching.

Which gives her an idea.

She runs a finger over the sheets, looking for the names that dip in and out of conversations. She recalls vaguely that there is only a small handful of these gadflies, alighting in the strangest places, with no apparent consistency. They'll comment on anything, from Russian performance in the World Cup to food prices in the outer oblasts to the depletion of old-growth forests in Siberia. The names she finds confirm her suspicions: these are the kooks, people with axes to grind and grievances whom no one listens to anymore.

And, curiously, Theresa Warner.

Lyndsey double-checks her diagram but there is Theresa's name popping up here and there like a hummingbird. From what she recalls of Theresa's posts, the ones she read, they're never anything substantive. Theresa usually just surfaces in the conversation, drops a tidbit of something useful.

The IM window in the corner of her screen flashes: it's Theresa. Like a genie or a demon, seemingly summoned by the mere thought of her. Lyndsey is so startled that, for a few seconds, she can only blink at her monitor.

Want to grab lunch? Theresa asks.

Sure, Lyndsey types after another second's hesitation. To turn her down might seem suspicious. Not that there's any reason to be suspicious.

She locks her screen before heading out the door. She looks out at the big, open office, the physical representation of the diagram she's just made, the invisible spider's web of links hanging in the ether. She makes a mental note to find out who is in the corner cubicle: many double agents favored secretive spaces to reduce the chance of being seen doing something they weren't supposed to be doing.

She looks in the direction of Theresa's cube, and then Eric's office.

Should she tell him what she's discovered even though she's not sure what it means? It would be good to have him weigh in on her deductions. She needs perspective. Maybe it all means nothing. It's easy to get lost in a forest of shadows.

Lunch first, she decides. What's the harm in that?

Lunch is salad and more coffee and Theresa's story of how Brian has started asking for a dog. "A puppy, to be precise. How do you tell a little boy that he can't have a puppy? That mommy has no time to take care of a puppy? I blame our neighbors—their Labrador just gave birth. The wife offers one to Brian every time we see her. Am I a bad mother? I feel like I'm robbing him of his one chance to grow up with a dog . . ."

Lyndsey listens, stabbing listlessly at lettuce, but all the while her mind is on what she left behind at her desk. She can't help but wonder, *What were you doing in the network chats, Theresa?* Of course, she broaches nothing with her friend. Eventually, they amble back to the office, and Lyndsey can't wait to head to her little office.

There's a bombshell waiting for Lyndsey when she gets back to her computer. An email from Murphy:

Katherine Franklin was found dead in her townhouse in Springfield this morning. Security was dispatched to her house when she did not report for duty at her normal time and did not respond to supervisor's phone calls. EMTs found her unresponsive and she was taken to the nearest hospital, where she was pronounced dead. An autopsy will be conducted but preliminary diagnosis is suicide by overdose. A note was found at the scene and, after review by Security, the contents will be shared with you. While not admitting guilt, she does express remorse for her mistakes in judgment.

Lyndsey clutches at her chest. She spoke to Franklin just yesterday. Now the woman is dead.

Before she can absorb the news, however, there's a briefing to attend, and she gets pulled into another meeting. Hours pass, during which she turns the news about Franklin over in her mind until she is almost numb to it. *I can't process this right now. There was something else I needed to do . . .*

That's right. The forum.

It's the end of the day before she can go back to the forum and search on Theresa's posts. Luckily, it's easy to find them, just a couple clicks and she can pick up where she left off.

What have you been up to, Theresa? Who have you been talking to?

Theresa replied to Jan Westerling. And Kyle Kincaid.

Friendly little connections made to both reports officers.

Suspicion flares up like acid reflux. Lyndsey tamps it down, blaming the lateness and hours spent poring over tiny bits of information that are now all cloudy in her mind. There's an innocent explanation for it, she assures herself.

Get a good night's sleep and take another look in the morning. Don't stew on it now.

Lyndsey flips the light switch and hurries past Eric's office. She definitely won't bring this up to him now. For something like this, you need to be sure.

Theresa leans in the doorway to her son's bedroom, watching him sleep. It's one of her favorite things to do. He's so peaceful—not that he's not peaceful most of the time. He's such a quiet kid, it worries her sometimes. He can sit completely still for hours, you can barely tell he's breathing. Not many kids can do that.

Why did she bring up Brian when she spoke to Lyndsey at lunch? She hates to do that; she doesn't want Brian involved in this horrible business at all. Though it's impossible: he's at the very heart of it. She's doing it *for* Brian. Though she would never, ever resent Brian for it. It's her own choice.

She would love to let him take one of the neighbors' puppies. She can picture the two of them in the yard, Brian running and laughing and calling to the dog, the puppy nipping and jumping. Brian acting like a seven-year-old boy instead of like a ninety-year-old man, always so careful because he knows the earth can open up and swallow you whole at any time. It happened to his father, didn't it?

But: no puppies. It wouldn't be fair to the dog. Where they're going, they'd only have to leave it behind.

SEVENTEEN

Theresa Warner always disliked hospitals. For one thing, there was the air, so sour. The antiseptic tang of it turned her stomach. And then there was all that uncertainty, long hours of waiting. She never was good at being patient. This hospital, Sibley Memorial, reminded her of past visits: days spent in the ICU when her father was dying, or that time Brian fell from a tree. Four hours in the emergency room for ten stitches to close a gash on his forehead. Fretting over whether it would leave a scar.

She came straight from work, feeling out of place in her navy suit and heels. Everyone else was dressed in comfortable clothes, ready for a long day in the waiting room or at a loved one's bedside. Then there were the nurses and cleaning staff dressed in well-worn scrubs, but also latex disposable gloves and aprons. That settled it: she wouldn't touch *anything*. She wasn't going to bring some god-awful germ home to her son. Antibiotic-resistant germs were out of control, new ones found every day, ones that ate the flesh from your bones, could kill you before the week was out. And they all lived at the hospital.

Under ordinary circumstances, Theresa would not be visiting Jack

Clemens. But Eric Newman had told her that Jack had asked especially for her. Jack was not someone she knew well; he belonged to her past, a former colleague of Richard's. She was not about to deny a dying man (pancreatic cancer, no less, no coming back from that) but she wasn't happy about it. Sibley was in the District, not an easy drive from McLean. It meant leaving work early to beat rush hour traffic but worse, it meant time away from Brian. It was bad enough that they were apart the entire day because of work and school, which couldn't be helped but she resented anyway. She *doubly* resented any imposition on her time outside the office. Even for a dying man. Her throat closed as she imagined the terrible things that could happen to Brian if she wasn't there to protect him. A home invasion. A tree falling on the house. She never had this crippling anxiety before Richard's death, of course. She kept waiting for it to fade but it only got worse with time.

She scurried through the maze of hospital corridors, wondering what Brian was doing at that moment without her. Probably sitting on the love seat in the den with the cushions stacked around him like his own little bunker. The National Geographic channel, his favorite, would be on—it was always on, like white noise—but he would have one eye on the clock, watching for her return. He would be deaf to the sitter, listening only for the sound of his mother's car pulling into the driveway.

Theresa hesitated outside Clemens's room, gathering her resolve. *You're here, just get it over with. For Richard's sake.* The hospital bed was surrounded by high-tech equipment. Lit-up boxes, adorned with red LED numbers, beeped. A monitor displayed vitals in lines and numbers. Tubes and wires hung from the ceiling and twisted around the bed rails like vines in a jungle. A nurse stood to one side, squinting at the monitor as she typed at a portable stand.

And in the center of the bed, completely dwarfed by all the equipment, was the shrunken figure of Jack Clemens. He had once been a good-looking guy, secretly admired by more than one woman in Russia Division, but was now practically child-sized and bald from chemo. It made him seem like an old, old man but—Theresa did the math in her head—he should be in his early fifties. A breathing apparatus sat on his face like a creature from an *Alien* movie. There were dangling tubes everywhere; he looked like a frail white spider at the center of a very large web.

Theresa didn't notice Jack's wife at first. She was a chunky, sturdy midwestern sort with dyed blond hair, disproportionately large next to her withered husband. She rose from a chair, a balled-up tissue clenched in her hand. Theresa felt sorry for her. She was faced with a horrible reality: her husband would not be with her much longer. That was inarguably terrible, yes, but it was a blessing Theresa had never had. To see her husband's death coming. To have time to make that emotional adjustment. To *be* with her husband at the end. *You think this is the worst thing that could happen to you but it's not. This is a luxury,* she wanted to say to Clemens's wife. *At least you get to say goodbye.*

She knew she was a bad person for thinking this, but she didn't care.

On seeing Theresa, Jack Clemens's dim eyes lit up. A desiccated hand clawed at the breathing mask.

Theresa felt a rush of alarm at the sight. She turned to the nurse. "Should he be doing that? Shouldn't that stay on?"

But the nurse only pulled the mask off the man's face matter-of-factly. "Oh no, he doesn't need this, strictly speaking. It just makes breathing easier," she explained.

"Theresa. Beautiful as ever." Jack's voice was barely audible. "Thank you. For coming."

Theresa stood by Jack's bed, determined not to touch anything. *Germs.* "I'm sorry that it has to be under these circumstances."

He nodded toward the foot of the bed. "My wife. Helen. I don't think. You've met," he said, laboring for breath like an asthmatic.

"I don't believe so." She extended a hand. "Theresa Warner. Jack and my husband were old friends." Theresa wasn't going to explain about Richard or share her personal story with Jack's wife. If the two men had been close—and Theresa had no evidence of that, Jack's name rarely coming up in all the time she was married—then Helen would already know what had happened. If not, then, there was no need to rehash it, not with Richard gone and Jack with so little time.

The wife shook Theresa's hand limply. The grip of a woman in shock.

Jack looked at his wife. "Give us. A minute alone," he said. How many times had he asked that of her, a CIA spouse? She didn't seem surprised, not in the least. Secrets, right up to the end.

Clemens waited as the wife and the nurse shuffled out, his eyes trained on Theresa. There was something ominous in his stare, his silence. What in the world could this be about? Suddenly, she wished she hadn't come. She wanted to leave before he could say whatever it was he wanted to tell her.

"Jack—" She looked longingly to the door.

He held up a hand to stop her. "Theresa, I have something to tell you. I'm sorry. I didn't tell you sooner." Then he stopped abruptly, coughing, then reached toward a pink plastic jug on a counter, a bendable straw jutting out of it. She held the jug for him as he drank. It reminded her of the early days with Brian, the sippy cups.

He nodded to indicate he was finished and fell back against the pillows, sweat on his brow. "Pancreatic cancer. Was stage three when . . . they found it. Nothing worked. Only a matter of time, they said." Why was he telling her this? she wondered. He sounded sorry for himself, but he must have come to terms with his imminent death by now. She knew, instinctively, that he was telling her for a reason: so she would feel sorry for him. So she would excuse him for what he was about to say.

He dropped a hand onto Theresa's forearm. "I was in Richard's office . . . when it happened. I was Eric's deputy."

"I know, Jack." She didn't want to cut him off, but she couldn't do this again. Couldn't accept one more person's tribute to her dead husband. Couldn't hear *I'm sorry* one more time. "We all loved Richard. We all regret what happened. But whatever it is you want to get off your chest . . . please, don't. You don't owe Richard anything. Let it go."

But he kept shaking his head, his skull frail and weightless like a dried seedpod, trembling on the end of its stem. He set his bloodless lips stubbornly. "No. I *do* owe Richard. I know what happened. To your husband. It's time *you* know."

He pulled at her arm, trying to draw her closer. This time, she didn't resist.

"Richard is not. Dead. Richard. Was captured and held."

Somehow, Theresa made it to her car. She stumbled out of Jack's room, past the nurses' station. Down a dizzying maze of corridors. The walls were spinning so she felt her way, inch by inch. Staggered across the parking lot to her Volvo wagon, where she sat behind the wheel, shaking from head to toe. Blood thrummed in her ears. She couldn't breathe. White spots flashed before her eyes. She was afraid she was going to pass out.

It couldn't be true, what Jack told her. And yet she knew in her heart that it was.

Her husband was still alive.

CIA lied to her.

Everything she had gone through these past two years, her suffering, Brian's suffering . . .

Never mind that, what about Richard's suffering? What has he gone through, locked away in a Russian prison?

Was he still alive? Jack didn't know. He only knew that Richard hadn't been killed in the operation.

Richard is alive. She had to believe that. The Russians wouldn't kill him, not if there was a chance of getting anything out of him—or getting something in exchange for him. She knew that much about the Russians.

She gripped the steering wheel with white knuckles, wishing she could wrench it off the pillar, throw it through the window. She wanted to destroy something, to shatter glass, kick, scream. The betrayal hurt like a dagger plunged in her heart. Why had they lied to her? Was there more that Jack hadn't told her, because he didn't know?

There *had* to be.

The treachery was breathtaking.

We got a report a month later that the FSB had an American spy in prison, Jack had told her. *But the Clandestine Service didn't want to pursue it. They wanted to pretend the whole thing. Never happened. Because it made them look bad. How could they admit. To Congress. That the Chief of Russia Division. Authorized a rogue operation? It made them look weak. Out of touch.*

Jack had sworn that Eric didn't know, that the seventh floor had decided to keep the secret from him since they blamed him—and Richard—for the whole fiasco in the first place. *Brought trouble down on themselves,* was how Jack had put it. *Left us to clean up the mess.*

No, Eric had to have believed Richard was gone, like everyone else. The way he'd made her life easier in a hundred little ways, it had to have been out of guilt and regret. Did she need time off to chaperone Brian's class on a field trip? No problem. She wanted to leave early to take Brian to see the doctor? She didn't even need to ask. He had looked after them—looked after *her.*

She choked back a sob and dropped her head until it rested on the steering wheel. How could the Agency betray her like this—betray Richard? This was a wake-up call, a hard slap to the face. Work was a twisty place, halls of funhouse mirrors that reflected back only a distorted, partial view and hid a multitude of sins. Nothing was as it seemed. She winced to recall other, far more minor incidents of casual betrayal. Colleagues who had bettered themselves in their boss's eye at her expense, petty comments made for no reason other than to assuage the speaker's ego. It was easy to forget that there were bigger betrayals hiding beneath a civilized veneer. It was time she learned that lesson in earnest.

She twisted the key in the ignition, even though she could barely see the road through her white-hot anger. She would drive to Langley *now* to talk to Eric. To see what could be done, to find out if Richard was still alive.

Theresa was halfway to Virginia before she realized Jack Clemens's deathbed confession would do her little good. Sure, he had told her the truth—a precious thing among spooks—but it would give her no leverage over the seventh floor. The men who ran CIA were masters of manipulation. That was how things worked at Langley. The deck was stacked. Running at things headfirst didn't work: you had to come at them sideways. That was why Theresa had never gone into management or reached for more responsibility. She'd always found it too distasteful and—if truth be told—had been afraid she would be eaten alive.

She looked at the speedometer. Seventy-one. Trees streaked by in a blur on both sides. With a startled gasp, she lifted her foot from the pedal: getting a ticket—hell, getting killed in a fiery crash—would not help her or Brian. She had to *calm down.*

She eased onto Chain Bridge Road, brightening at the thought of heading home to Brian. Langley could wait. She needed to see her son. Time to think. To plan.

She would step up to the challenge. She would outmaneuver the seventh floor, with or without Eric Newman's help—because, let's face it, to take on the seventh floor would take an extraordinary level of courage. Courage Eric Newman might not possess.

But she would do it. She would beat them at their own game. She would prove herself worthy of being Richard Warner's wife.

She couldn't let her husband down.

EIGHTEEN

Another weekday morning at Langley. Men and women streamed across the parking lots—past the towering parabolic antennas, the Blackbird spy plane made into a monument—to converge on a set of doors placed into a wall so discreetly that they could be secret doors, known only to the initiated.

It was a cold morning. In raincoats and windbreakers, they moved with mindless determination, like ants following the scent of sugar, minds already on the coming day, chores left undone from the day before, a confrontation anticipated with a boss or coworker. Or they were brooding over what they'd just left behind, an argument at the breakfast table, the last thing a child said before running for the school bus. Not one of them was thinking about what it meant to cross the threshold of the most secretive building in America.

Theresa Warner wended through the parking lot in a black raincoat, sturdy walking shoes on her feet, a pair of sensible heels in her tote. The day was no different from every day before it, and yet this morning *felt* different. She felt as though she was in disguise. That she was only pretending to be the woman she was yesterday.

Jack Clemens had changed everything.

Last night, she managed to drive home and act normally in front of her son. They ate dinner together and afterward, she helped him with his homework. Watched him brush his teeth and climb into bed. Kissed him on his head and fingered the familiar silky, dark brown hair while suppressing the urge to share this new secret with him. *Brian, your father is alive!*

But that would be unfair until she knew, *really* knew that she could get Richard back. Then she sat on the sofa and planned how she would enlist Eric Newman, get his help in taking on the men who ran the most powerful agency in the U.S. government.

Now she crossed the threshold into the building, going over her plan. Repeated the steps to herself as she waved her badge over the scanner and punched in her PIN. She avoided the guard's gaze and the gaze of other people because if anyone looked into her eyes, *really looked,* they would be able to tell something was wrong. So instead, she followed the coagulating stream of people as they headed for the elevators. Stood as unobtrusively as possible in the crowd until the doors opened at her floor.

It would do no good to approach Eric first thing. Mornings were for meetings with the next level of management. Managing up was very important for bosses so it would be better to wait until the busyness of the morning played itself out. There was usually a lull around eleven a.m. when it might be possible to catch him, but Eric sometimes used the opportunity to slip down to the gym. Better to wait until after lunch, around two thirty, when things got sleepy. He'd be the most approachable. And she would be able to get him alone.

Though Theresa wasn't sure how she would manage to get through her day. Every minute was agony. She kept looking for Eric, afraid that he might disappear, take off suddenly for a doctor's visit or be called to some interminable meeting. She didn't think she could wait another twenty-four hours to confront him.

At 2:20, Theresa peeked through the maze of partitions toward Eric's office. She could just see him behind his desk, settled so low in his chair that he looked like he'd fallen asleep. She rose and wove quickly through the cubicles, eyes down on the carpet. She kept her mind blank; if she thought too much about what she was about to do, she was going to chicken out.

She leaned in the open doorway. "Say, Eric, do you have a minute?"

He looked up. For a second—just a second—she thought she saw a pained look on his face, but no, that was the face he always gave her. She just never noticed before that his warmth was offset with just a hint of pity. "Of course, Theresa. For you, anytime."

She closed the door softly behind her and took the chair opposite his desk, clasping her hands in her lap to hide the shaking. She cleared her mind, so the conversation she practiced over and over last night would come naturally to the fore.

"I saw Jack Clemens yesterday."

Eric crossed his legs and leaned back in his chair, a picture of unease. "Yeah, I visited him on Tuesday. Looks terrible, doesn't he? Won't be long now. It's a shame—"

She closed her eyes. Her patience had been used up. "He told me Richard is alive. *Alive.*"

Eric froze. A dozen emotions seemed to pass over his face at once. Finally, he took a deep breath. "I wish that were true, Theresa, but we both know it isn't."

"He said there was a report that said Richard had been captured alive. They didn't share it with you. You were never told." As he listened, frozen as a statue in a Minnesota winter, Theresa recounted what Jack had told her. The report from Moscow Station, the seventh floor's decision to keep it from him as well as her.

He gripped the armrest of his chair like a man in shock. "Ever since that day, I've been persona non grata on the seventh floor. They didn't fire me, or remove me from this position, but I know that I'll never go any higher. No one in the DO approved the op, but I gave Richard authorization. I only gave him what he wanted, a chance to save his asset."

Jack had revealed this much, between gasps for air: that Eric, knowing the top men in the DO would never agree to take the risk, didn't ask for permission. That he did the whole thing on the sly. And that, to keep it secret, no CIA resources—aside from Richard—were used. No tech ops officers, no additional case officers. Only a handful of freelancers to help smuggle Boykova out of the country. They used untried mercenaries to watch her husband's back.

It was a fiasco from the start, Jack had told her, his papery voice thickened with remorse. With no CIA eyes on the scene, it was a full week before Eric and Jack found out what happened. Rumors began trickling in from shaky CIA assets in Moscow: something big had gone down. Assets in Russia got nervous, made them start asking for more money or new lives in another country. Or, for the most dedicated, poison pills in case of capture.

Theresa looked icily at Eric Newman. "And you swear you didn't know? You didn't leave Richard to rot in prison for your mistakes?"

Now he jumped out of his chair like it was on fire. "I thought he was *dead,* Theresa. As far as I knew, there was nothing coming out of Moscow, nothing." His words were like a dagger plunged in her chest. Knowing that he had been left in the dark the same as she did nothing to relieve her agony. "Do you think for one minute that if I knew Richard was still alive, I wouldn't do everything in my power to save him? That I wouldn't get on a plane myself, with or without Agency support, to find him and bring him home? He was my friend, too, Theresa. My oldest friend."

She watched him storm back and forth, angrier than she'd ever seen him. She hadn't expected him to yell at her, almost turning on her. Embarrassment for having been tricked? "Does that mean I can count on your support?"

He came up short. "Support in what? What do you plan to do?"

She was momentarily stunned. Wasn't it obvious? "I'm going to confront them—"

He rushed toward her. "No, no, no. . . . You can't, Theresa. It would be worse than futile, it would be suicide. You're not going to like this but . . ." She closed her eyes, as though that would stop her from hearing the rest. "We have to accept what's happened." He spoke firmly. Sharply. *He's thought about this.* Had he known? "Two years have passed and nothing's changed. What are you going to ask the seventh floor to do—approach the Russians for a swap? They've been clear about it, freezing out you and me. As far as they're concerned, the case is closed."

She looked him at him levelly, searching for the slightest indication that he was hiding something. A wavering gaze, a twitch of the lips. Something to tell her that there was a chance, a hope however faint . . .

Nothing.

She was having trouble breathing, fought for air. "You mean you expect me to do nothing? When I know there's a chance my husband is still alive?"

"I . . . I don't know what else to say. This is for your own good. Otherwise you'll just go crazy . . ."

She slapped him. So hard that her palm stung, before she had time to think about it. She had secretly worried that he didn't have the guts to stand up to the merciless men who ran this place. He'd taken his punishment two years ago docilely enough, gone off to lick his wounds, hadn't he?

Now he proved it: Eric Newman wasn't the man she'd hoped.

Well, fuck Eric Newman. Fuck all of them. She'd be damned if she would join him in the corner. She would show them what came of perfidy. When you betrayed the people who had placed their trust in you. They thought they could get away with it because the men who run spy agencies thought they had the world on a string. That the rest of the world would only know what they wanted it to know.

These egotistical men thought they could keep something of this magnitude a secret.

She brushed by Eric as she hurried out the door. She walked down the halls, down the miles of Agency corridors to cool off, to calm her jangling nerves and focus her thoughts.

She kept her eyes down, not wanting to see the glimmer of recognition in anyone's eyes—*ah, that's The Widow.* She wanted to be alone with her thoughts.

There was a tiny, distant voice questioning whether she should listen to Eric's advice. A survivor's voice. After years of suffering, she was finally gaining some distance. Healing. She was able to see a future for herself and for Brian. This had reawakened all the old feelings, ripped her hard-earned peace away like a bandage off a wound. Taking Eric's advice might be the smartest thing she could do.

Except she couldn't. Eric Newman was not their friend, not hers, not Richard's. This was proof.

She knew that she couldn't go to Eric's bosses in the Clandestine Service, the ones who had opposed Eric's scheme in the first place. Eric was right there: as far as they were concerned, it was over. They would never change their minds to side with her. They cut their teeth on the spy business during the Cold War. They were craven old men, notoriously conservative with a high instinct for self-preservation. *What's done is done,* they'd say. *Let sleeping dogs lie.* Richard Warner would not be the first CIA officer sacrificed to preserve the Agency's honor or to cover up another man's mistakes.

Theresa turned a corner and headed into a little-used hall, turning thoughts in her head the whole time. Should she go to her congressman? She snorted at the idea: CIA would play the national security card and stonewall any official who pressed for an inquiry—*if* she could get anyone to believe her. They'd say she'd become unhinged by grief. Their word against hers. This never, ever worked. It was a dead end.

She sighed, a heavy weight in her chest. They wanted to think they held all the cards and that she was powerless, nothing more than a helpless little widow. They wanted her to go away, go sit in the corner, be trotted out at ceremonies. Smile, wave, be a brave little trouper.

But that wasn't the case. No, she knew the answer. It had been with her all along.

Richard could be saved, and it was up to Theresa to do it.

NINETEEN

It's been less than twelve hours since Lyndsey was last in the office and even with the sunlight streaming through the windows and the bustle of people coming in to start their day, she can't shake the feeling that she never left.

Because she didn't sleep a wink. She spent the night drifting through her cheerless apartment like a ghost, unable to rest, her mind still in the office. She is haunted by two thoughts. First, that lingering shadow of a doubt about Theresa . . .

Second—and more immediate—Kate Franklin's suicide. She hasn't been able to stop thinking about it, not for a minute. To feel guilty for her part in it, for she certainly was a factor. The woman killed herself shortly after their interview. Lyndsey studied psychology and so she knows there had to be other factors, that their conversation alone didn't drive Franklin to do it. Still, she can't shake the guilt.

Was Kate Franklin the mole? Lyndsey is ninety-nine percent certain that she wasn't.

Will Raymond Murphy agree with her? She is almost as certain that he will *not*. That he will use the suicide to declare Franklin's guilt and to pack up his investigation.

Which would be disastrous. It would enable the real mole to continue, and what's more, the mole would know that CIA is on the alert and so would be more careful than ever.

Lyndsey can't let that happen. She might not be able to convince Murphy to keep his investigation open, but she vows not to let him make Franklin the scapegoat.

Even if the evidence takes her someplace she doesn't want to go.

Lyndsey stops at Jan Westerling's desk. The young woman doesn't notice her at first; she's too busy taking off the walking shoes she wore in from the parking lot and slipping on high heels, black pumps with four-inch stilettos. Her head jerks up when she sees she has a visitor.

"How are you doing, Jan? Feeling better?"

"I'm fine," she responds curtly. Westerling is defensive about crying in the office. She doesn't want Lyndsey or anyone else thinking less of her for it. They can smell weakness in the air here.

"That's tough for anyone to go through," Lyndsey hurries to say, thinking of the ugly photos of Kulakov's broken body filling Westerling's screen. It was hard enough reading Popov's toxicology report; she's grateful there were no autopsy pictures. "I have a question for you, but it's one that needs to stay between us"—Westerling nods quickly—"Has anyone shown an unusual interest in Kulakov? I'm not talking about recently. This would be before his death."

The young analyst's brow furrows. It might be that she doesn't understand the question, but Lyndsey thinks she's reluctant to give out names.

Her natural instinct would be to protect a coworker by assuming she misunderstood the coworker's actions.

Lyndsey studies Westerling's face, looking for clues that the young woman is suppressing a suspicion. And she is. There's something there—she's just not ready to talk about it. Yet. Doesn't want to betray someone she sees as a friend—not to Lyndsey, who is still an unknown quantity. An outsider.

Westerling shakes her head. "No. Nothing comes to mind."

"That's fine, but if you think of anything, no matter how trivial, come see me, okay?" She has to trust that duty will prevail and Westerling will break the traditional veil of silence.

Westerling nods quickly, and Lyndsey takes her cue to leave.

Lyndsey waits until after the morning team meetings to approach Kyle Kincaid. His face drops slightly when he sees her: this man will never be good at poker.

As a matter of fact, a change has come over Kincaid since the last time Lyndsey saw him. Something is going on, but she can't put her finger on what it might be. He's more guarded than the first time, but isn't that perfectly natural? Now that he knows what she's interested in?

Kincaid follows her out of the office, Lyndsey leading him to the vending machines at the end of the corridor where they won't be overheard. He rattles coins in his pocket as he looks over the assortment of snacks behind the Plexiglas. "I thought we were done. You forget something?" He sounds like a man who expects bad news.

Lyndsey folds her arms over her chest. "I forgot to ask who may have approached you about Skipjack. Anyone with an unexpected interest in cyber?"

"I've been thinking about that." He nods in agreement. Raymond Murphy will be happy to hear the mandatory CI training is having an effect. "It's cockamamie if you ask me . . . What are the chances that someone inside is responsible for his disappearance?"

She doesn't mention Lighthouse or Genghis. If he's unaware of the other cases, so much the better. "You think there's another reason?"

Kincaid shrugs. "He was an unhappy man. I think it's more likely that it's something we don't know about. Like he owed the wrong people money, or his wife was getting on his case."

We tend to assume other people's problems are like our own, she learned from the two behavioral researchers she worked with at Penn. In which case, there may be more to Kyle Kincaid than meets the eye. Still, he might be right about Skipjack.

He rattles the coins again, like they are burning a hole in his pockets. "Skipjack had just turned in some really good information, and a report was getting a lot of attention from new people, offices that hadn't bothered with his earlier reports . . . So, it's hard to say for sure whether there was someone bad in there. But there was one in particular . . ." Jiggles coins. He's stalling. "It struck me as odd, that she would be interested. She doesn't work in cyber."

"She?"

Kincaid casts a glance over his shoulder before continuing. "Her name is Evelyn Wang. In Russia Division. You know who I'm talking about?"

Lyndsey nods, but she's not sure if she knows the woman. Easy enough to find out.

"She gave me some story how she thought Skipjack might have something to do with a problem she was working on. She asked a million questions about him."

"And did you tell her?"

He swallows. He knows he is caught. "Yeah, I thought where's the harm? She has a blue badge hanging around her neck the same as me . . ." By the way he feigns and stammers, he knows he did wrong. "I didn't think about it at the time, but a couple weeks later I was taking that mandatory training course, the one where they talk about spies caught here, and they were talking about Aldrich Ames and it hit me, it was just like that. *Just like that.*" Now the bravado has gone out of him. Skipjack is gone and he could be responsible.

"Did you tell anyone about your suspicions at the time?"

"No. Because at the time, it didn't seem . . . It didn't make sense. There was nothing going on." His face turns red.

"You can't tell anyone about this, got that?" Lyndsey says. "This is an ongoing investigation. Not a word."

He nods. Funny thing is, Lyndsey thinks she sees a flash of resentment pass over his face—then triumph.

There's an IM flashing on her screen when she returns to her office. It's Theresa: *Coffee?* Lyndsey would like to, maybe probe discreetly about Theresa's use of that bulletin board tool, but there's one meeting she's been putting off that she can stall no longer. *Sorry, maybe later?* she types, then hits Send.

She has to see Genghis's reports officer.

The reports officer for Genghis hasn't changed since Lyndsey was Popov's handler. Lyndsey has known Evert Northrop for most of her career, ever since she came to Russia Division as a trainee. Northrop is past retirement age, with a reputation for being a martinet. They had a prickly long-distance relationship when Lyndsey was in Moscow and she's been avoiding him since she's been back, though she feels guilty about it. Northrop stays in his corner of the office, she has noticed, not talking much to anyone or participating in team meetings, a fussy old man making pots of tea with the electric kettle he doesn't let anyone else use.

He's still tucked off in a corner, forcing you to wend through a maze of safes and file cabinets if you want to see him. The light dims, giving you the sensation of descending into a library's long-forgotten stacks. There are old Soviet-era propaganda posters on the walls, probably salvaged from the trash thirty years ago, and bits of Russian kitsch: a pink babushka draped decoratively over a side table, and on a nearby shelf, a set of *matryoshka* dolls painted to resemble Russian ballerinas. The overall impression is a cross between a crazed Muscovite diva's parlor and Soviet party headquarters. He's carved out his own little corner, made a place for himself among the more predatory types, the Hank Bremers and Richard Warners and even the Eric Newmans of Russia Division.

His expression is unreadable as she approaches, though he seems to grip the report in his hands a little tighter. Seeing her would remind him of Yaromir Popov. She isn't the only one who lost Yaromir Popov. Lyndsey kicks herself for not coming to see him earlier.

Northrop avoids looking at her as he pours tea into his cup. "Hello, Lyndsey. I'd heard you were back."

As the reports officer for Genghis, Northrop would know about the investigation so he knows why she has come to see him. Still, there are niceties to observe. "How are you?"

"They're still waiting for me to retire. They want to replace us with younger models. You'd do well to remember that. You may be one of the younger models now, but it'll be your turn one day." His eyes are sharp as needles.

His desk is piled with stacks of reports, a wild hedge of white paper and manila file folders. Paper overflows from his two-drawer safe. Some officers never learn to trust a computer or claim they can't absorb what they read on a screen. They rail against passwords on the computer and using a PIN to cross a threshold into the vault, and grumble about the mandatory training they're asked to take. They stick to the old ways—and yet they complain about being eased out the door.

Will she become a dinosaur, too, one day? She doubts she'll last that long.

Lyndsey asks him the same questions she asked Westerling and Kincaid. "It's not like it was during your day, Lyndsey. Popov stopped producing after you'd gone. He gave us only tidbits. It might be that he got circumspect . . . After the episode with Richard Warner, things were very bad over there. You had left for Lebanon. The FSB made it impossible for Moscow Station. Morozov, the big man, that shit, made life hell. He was probably being spiteful—you know, because we had him pinned to Moscow after the affair in Kiev. He was always sending his goons to harass our officers, sending people over to rifle through apartments and leave little messages so we'd know they'd been there. Move things around, unplug refrigerators, take a shit on a bed. One officer came home to find his cat had been poisoned."

The Russians' love of poisons apparently extended to house pets. Was it the same one they'd used on Popov? And Morozov—the name roused old memories. He had just been elevated to chief of the counterintelligence department in the FSB when Lyndsey was in Moscow, a cagey old man who, like Northrop, had hung on since the Yeltsin era. He was rumored to have orchestrated the hit on the Chief of Station in Kiev many years back, before Lyndsey's time, and it earned him a place on CIA's most-wanted list. General Morozov—the rank was honorary, everyone working for Russian security services technically were members of the Russian army—was like a ghost, never seen but whispered about, not too loudly lest he be summoned by the mere mention of his name.

"Maybe he was lying low. Trying to avoid a dragnet . . ."

Northrop does a sly one-shouldered shrug. "Or it could be that he loathed Tom Cassidy. That was pretty clear."

"Why do you think that was?"

"I guess you haven't met Cassidy yet. He's one of those guys who only respects the people above him on the chain. Assets are commodities to be used up and discarded." Northrop puts down his cup and saucer with a rattle of china. "He's not an easy man to like."

Yaromir Popov would've despised him, Lyndsey guesses. "If Popov hadn't been providing information, does that mean no one came looking to get on the access list?"

"No, no one."

Then how did the mole learn about Popov? This doesn't fit the pattern for Skipjack and Lighthouse—if it can even be called a pattern. It's thin as tissue paper, and uncertainty starts to gnaw on Lyndsey again.

The time for directness has come. "Evert, I need you to be frank with me, but you have to promise me you'll be discreet."

Northrop smirks. "No one talks to me anymore, Lyndsey. Anything you tell me is not going anywhere."

He's a little hungry for gossip, though. She can tell by the way the corners of his mouth turn up, the slight twitch of his lips. She'll have to trust him, even though he's an old hand and likely to have certain alliances to the old guard. To Richard Warner.

"Did Theresa Warner ever ask you about Popov?"

Surprise registers on his face for only a second, but it's genuine. His gaze flicks in the direction of Theresa's desk. He can guess why she's asked.

"Theresa? No. Never."

"What about Evelyn Wang?"

He purses his lips. "Evelyn's a friendly girl . . . and a pleasure to talk to. But about Genghis?" He shakes his head.

Which leaves one suspect.

TWENTY

Lyndsey is back at her desk, mulling over her conversation with Northrop, when she notices the chat window on her monitor is flashing. Raymond Murphy sent a message while she was away: *You've got access to Pennantrace.* Pennantrace is the cover term for Olga Boykova, the asset Richard Warner was trying to save when he was killed.

There's more to the message. *Physical records have been destroyed.*

Irritation flares in her brain. It does seem suspicious, even though accidents have been known to happen to archived documents. But for a case this controversial, under such scrutiny?

It appears all is not lost, however. Murphy has one piece of advice: *Suggest you speak to Edward Sheridan, the reports officer at the time. He's on a detail to National Defense University.*

The drive to Fort McNair isn't pleasant but the campus makes up for it. It is hard to believe something this open and green could exist within the boundaries of Washington, D.C. Lyndsey is early for her appointment, so she takes a lap of the campus for the view. A few soldiers jog by in gray athletic uniforms, while a young officer appears to be showing his family around the monuments on the green. How tempting it must be to take one of these details out of the building, if you're with the Agency. To get out of the cross fire, where there's no target on your back.

She finds Sheridan outside the library, where he suggested they meet. He's an older gentleman with thinning brown hair and glasses, with the bland look of a man who is already retired in his mind. He shakes her hand. "I thought maybe we could take a walk. It's such a lovely day."

They have the sidewalk to themselves as they stroll the promenade. She keeps pace with Sheridan's unhurried meander. "I'm not sure I can answer your questions about Russia. I've tried to put that episode behind me," Sheridan says. Of course: it didn't end well and there are unhappy memories. That's probably why he ended up here, to finish out his career quietly.

She didn't drive all the way out here to fold easily. "With the records lost, anything you can remember would be of help . . ."

Sheridan sighs, thinking for the span of a few strides. "I remember that Boykova was a complete surprise. We couldn't believe it when we got the first drops. It was solid gold. Putin's talking points for upcoming negotiations. Background papers. Decision memos. It was like having keys to Putin's inner sanctum. We knew exactly what Russian leadership was thinking."

His joy is still apparent, even after all this time. Lyndsey remains silent, waiting for him to continue.

"Naturally, we thought that the asset must be very, very senior. It had to be someone close to Putin, perhaps an oligarch who had grown rich from Putin's patronage but had developed a conscience and could no longer stand by while the country was being plundered. Or a top aide who knew all of Putin's appointments and made sure the right papers were read in advance." Sheridan turns and gives Lyndsey a sheepish smile.

Nearly apologetic. "But Olga Boykova was none of those things. Olga Boykova was a housekeeper."

Lyndsey can scarcely believe what she's hearing as Sheridan lays it out. It sounds like a strange, political version of Cinderella. Boykova started at Novo-Ogaryovo, Putin's official residence just outside of Moscow proper, polishing the floors and working her way up in the household staff. Soon, she was assigned to the small team in the office wing. She had risen quickly despite her youth and lack of seniority—the older members, with a great sense of entitlement, guarded their standing jealously—because she had proven herself an exceptionally hard worker. In a society where initiative and competency were viewed with suspicion, it seemed President Putin appreciated having one person who could find a book when it had been misplaced or turn down sheets exactly the way he liked.

She had been working in Putin's household for five years when she decided to spy for America.

"It's not uncommon for foreign intelligence services to recruit household staff as paid informants, but these assets tended to provide little more than tactical information," Sheridan says. "They could tell you if a principal was drinking more heavily than normal, or who in the inner circle might be open to approach, but often lacked the know-how to go after really good stuff."

Sheridan walks slowly, hands shoved in the pockets of his jacket. Olga Boykova, he says, appeared to have no such reservations. Richard's reports documented her deep, irrevocable disappointment in the Russian president. She saw how the elites lived while knowing, intimately, the hopelessness that the average Russian faced. It was no longer the wild, frontier days of her childhood, the time after Gorbachev and later Yeltsin when the Soviet system imploded, the economy tanked, and lawlessness threatened to destroy Russia. Order had been restored, but the badness had only gone underground, disguised itself with fancy new clothes. Now oligarchs siphoned off Russia's money and hid it in overseas bank accounts, Russia's wealth unaccountably gone like a once-healthy man suddenly drained of blood.

Vampiry. And she knew who was to blame.

A single, childless woman who had come to Moscow to find work, Boykova was fiercely devoted to the brothers and sisters, nieces and nephews she had left behind in the country. All of them were struggling, she had told Richard in a confession that had made its way into a report. Every day, the average Russian got further and further behind in debt, squeezed on every front to pay more, money that found its way into the pocket of some Putin crony. While people like Boykova drank themselves to death to forget that there was no hope of escape, that they would always be a serf to a self-appointed tsar.

She could not stand by and let him steal her country.

"We were amazed to see what a lowly housekeeper had been able to do. She photographed hundreds of documents. She planted mics and cameras in the most off-limits areas in the palace. She was one of the most daring operatives we'd ever seen, with no regard for her personal safety. Richard"—Sheridan stumbles at the name, choking up—"admired her. He used to say Olga Boykova gave us more in her two years spying for CIA than more highly placed assets managed in their entire careers. Many assets string their handlers along with promises and excuses, you know, hand over dribs and drabs of near-useless information that could've easily been had through less dangerous means, and ask for a lot of money. Olga Boykova made them look like fools. Greedy, fearful fools."

He reaches into his breast pocket and hands Lyndsey a photo of Boykova, obviously taken by a member of a surveillance team during the vetting period. She is a little bird, just sturdy enough to move furniture and spend long days polishing woodwork. Her face is small and triangular with a tiny pursed mouth, serious eyes, and a sober expression. You can see her uniform under a winter coat, sturdy shoes with crepe soles, heavy tights like something a much older woman would wear. In many ways she is the opposite of Theresa, and it makes Lyndsey smile to think of Theresa's suspicion: surely this wasn't the sort of woman Richard would fall in love with.

Lyndsey understands why the FSB covered up the whole thing. Normally, if they'd found a traitor and caught the Americans red-handed, they would crow from the rooftops, splash pictures all over the internet, and make the most of it. But they were afraid. Olga Boykova would become a cult hero, a Robin Hood to the Russian people. It would embolden copycats and there weren't enough FSB officers in Russia to spy on all the disgruntled cooks and nannies in every oligarch's or corrupt official's household—if they were allowed to find out about her. So, the FSB swept the whole thing under the carpet. "They even refused to return Richard's body, because it would be evidence," Sheridan says. A gust of wind lifts strands of his hair over his head, revealing the shape of the skull beneath. "That's how afraid they were."

Lyndsey thanks Edward Sheridan with a handshake and heads back to her car, her mind whirling with each step. Knowing what Theresa thinks—what she's shared, anyway—Lyndsey has to believe these reports would give Theresa some comfort. She'd see the valuable information Boykova gave them, and while she might never agree with what Richard did, she might begrudge his sacrifice a little bit less.

It might give her some peace.

She thinks back to the crude network diagram and how Theresa's name kept popping up. *A mistake, surely.* There has to be an explanation.

The two thoughts rattle around in the back of her mind during the drive back.

Lyndsey has just taken off her coat and settled back at her desk when there's a knock at the door. Jan Westerling stands in the doorway, wobbling uncertainly on those four-inch heels. "I thought of something. Someone, actually."

Westerling sits in the chair opposite Lyndsey's desk like a reluctant witness at a police station. The reports officer is visually nervous, her fingers intertwined to keep them occupied, thumbs wrestling. Whatever she's got to say, she doesn't want to say it, would prefer to keep it bottled up inside. But duty prevents her.

Lyndsey listens patiently as the words come spilling out. How it didn't seem strange to her at first when Theresa Warner came to talk to her. They work in the same office on the same team, after all, The Widow's desk just fifty feet away. After the second visit, however, Westerling wondered why Theresa Warner was being friendly *now* when she'd been in the office for over a year and Theresa hadn't shown any interest in her in all that time. She dismissed this as being paranoid. Westerling had gotten kudos for a recent project: sometimes that thawed out the old-timers. They would suddenly notice you, as though you hadn't been toiling away in obscurity under their noses. She decided at the time to be happy about it, not bitter. She hadn't thought to be suspicious.

Until now.

"Did she try to find out Lighthouse's identity?" Lyndsey asks.

Westerling narrows her eyes as she thinks. "I'd say yes, definitely, but in a roundabout way. Not asking directly, so my radar wouldn't go up."

"When was this?"

Squints, again. "About four months ago, maybe? No, four months for sure, because it happened right around the time of the annual conference with the Brits and she made a point of saying she'd recommend that I got to go this year."

"But you didn't give her Lighthouse's true name or where he worked?"

Westerling pulls back as though hurt. "Of course not."

Then would Theresa—if she is the mole; Lyndsey chides herself for the mental slip—have found it? "Do you have this information written down anywhere . . . paper copies of reports?"

Westerling knits her brow. "Of course. But I keep that stuff in my safe."

"Could you do me a favor? Could you get all those reports from your safe and bring them to me? But try not to touch them, and put them in a folder or envelope before you bring them to me." It's a long shot, but perhaps they can get fingerprints off them. She's not even sure there's someone at the Agency who can dust for prints, or if it's possible to get fingerprints off paper, but it's worth a try.

Westerling gives her a perplexed look, but she nods, and leaves.

Once Lyndsey is by herself, she rifles through a drawer until she finds what she's looking for: the network diagram from the other day. Theresa's name is all over it.

But so is Evelyn Wang's. The name Kincaid had mentioned.

She spends another few minutes studying it more closely, then logs in to the forum, searching out Wang's profile. She has a ridiculously high number of posts, far above average. Lyndsey starts reading through them, in reverse order, and finds it's just as Evert Northrop said: Evelyn Wang is a friendly girl. She sprinkles pleasantries on every thread. Maybe she's trying to make friends—or more accurately, keep from making enemies. Or maybe she's trying to win Miss Congeniality. Could she be the mole? It doesn't seem likely.

Then there's Theresa. Lyndsey remembers her first day back in the office, the coolness.

Not Miss Congeniality. Unless it serves a purpose. Still—is that fair? Since then, Theresa has been good to her. The warmth feels genuine: stopping by to say hello every morning, dropping off homemade banana bread wrapped in foil (*I made too much and thought you might like some . . . I don't suppose you're much of a baker*).

Banana bread? *Don't be a sap.*

Lyndsey lets out a long breath. Finally, the clues are starting to come together.

The only problem is, she's not sure she likes the direction they're headed.

TWENTY-ONE

After Jack Clemens's confession, every minute of Theresa's day, it seemed, was an exercise in anger management. Seemingly every minute at work, she had to keep from breaking out in a screaming rage. Snapping at the neighbors or her mother on the phone, keep from bursting into tears in front of her son. (Tears were saved for evening, after she'd gone to bed and had closed the door on the world.)

She had to confirm what Jack had told her, to see with her own eyes how badly she'd been betrayed. Getting her hands on the report was out of the question, however. It would be highly compartmented. There wouldn't be a copy in the office, not if even Eric wasn't aware of its existence. The only place she could be sure of finding it would be a vault hidden away in the bowels of the building, a place where paper copies were kept of all sensitive reporting. Paper because many of these were historical records, written before the digital age. Paper, too, so they would survive an electromagnetic pulse or other type of twenty-first-century disaster.

The vault was a lonely little outpost manned during the day by a retiree hired back specifically for this assignment. She'd gotten to know him shortly after Richard's disastrous operation, hoping to bully her way into seeing all the privileged records. The old man had proven impervious to her charms as well as her threats. His name was Jimmy Purvis, a case officer retired over twenty years now and had undoubtedly been well past retirement age when he was finally forced out. Unmarried and childless, with nothing to fill his days, he'd dunned the Agency into giving him a position so he'd be able to continue walking through the security turnstiles in the morning and getting lunch from the cafeteria.

When she came for him this time, however, he already knew her. And she knew him, had heard all his stories from the old days and knew that he liked the crumb cake they sold upstairs in the coffee shop. So, she brought a square with her, tidy in its cling wrap jacket, and watched him eat it with his cold coffee as she sat in the battered old chair next to his desk.

"You're the only one around here who's nice to an old man," Purvis said as he chased the remaining clumps of sugar with his plastic fork. "Everyone else is too important." Behind them were rows and rows of shelves, on each shelf archival boxes filled with reports. A label on each box bore the dates and subjects and cover terms of the reports inside. She had a good idea where the records for Richard's case were, knew the general ballpark.

She smiled at him, but in the back of her mind, she was calculating. He had to be close to eighty. What could he possibly want, what could she offer him that would be worth fifteen minutes alone in the vault? Not her body: he barely looked at her. He might be insulted if she offered money. Or tried to trick him.

She leaned forward, touched a hand to his arm. He raised an eyebrow.

"Jimmy, I have a favor to ask of you—"

He drew back—but barely. "Not this again. You know I can't—"

"This is different. I'm only interested in one report. Just one." She slid a scrap of paper to him. On it was the date, cover terms—everything Jack Clemens could remember about the report. "I just want to see what it says. For my own peace of mind. Tell me what you want for it. Name your price."

She was thankful that he didn't erupt in fury, didn't try to throw her out. It meant he was considering it. His mouth twitched, eyes narrowed. Silently, he pushed back from the desk, picked up the scrap of paper and read it as he shuffled to the shelves. She listened to the sound of heavy boxes being pulled down, put back. Papers rustled.

Finally, five minutes later he was back with a thin folder bearing a triple red stripe along its border. He held it up, showing it to her like a boy who'd captured the flag.

"You still got Richard's car?"

The XKE. So beautiful, it was like the Mona Lisa on wheels. Purvis was a sports car nut and had long admired Richard's vintage Jaguar, had pored over the photo she'd shown him once. But the car was worth a fortune. That was like an insurance policy for Brian. She couldn't just give it to him, not in exchange for one single report.

She felt blood drain from her face. "You want me to *give* you the car?"

"What? No—I'm not greedy. Just a drive. Let me take it for a drive, someplace nice."

This seemed like a terrible idea. Jimmy Purvis was an old man, so old that he had shrunk too small for his clothes. He wore Coke-bottle glasses and his hands shook. Should he even be driving at all? Did he still have his license?

Still, on the list of things he could've asked for, this was benign. What the hell—he was doing her a bigger favor than he could imagine, and . . . he was an old man. This might be his last thrill.

She nodded. "Sure. I'll give you the keys for the whole weekend. Do we have a deal?"

He handed the report to her.

For two days after reading it, Theresa was in a fog. She managed to get by on autopilot, making sack lunches for her son and seeing him off at the bus stop. At work, she sat at her desk seething with resentment, her brain on fire. She wasn't herself and she knew it. She was giddy in the company of others, dangerously so, the truth pressing from inside, desperate to be free. It was all she could do not to run down the halls, telling the whole bloody story to anyone who'd listen. *You have no idea what your precious Agency is capable of. Our lives mean nothing to them, we're nothing but pawns, and not one of us is safe.*

As she sat at her desk, struggling with the urge to set the place on fire, to burn the whole house of cards to the ground, she began to grasp the terrible truth.

It had all been there in the few lines of that cable from Moscow, just like Jack had said. One of their assets, a most reliable one, had heard the FSB had captured an American agent in a botched exfiltration. The asset didn't know that captured man's name, but who else could it be? Everyone else involved in the mission had already been named dead.

Richard had been alive—and was still alive. She had to believe that.

And they'd kept it from her this whole time. Brought her back in to work—of course! So they could keep an eye on her, make sure she didn't get any funny ideas, would be able to control her if she did.

Could they control her? They shouldn't be too sure, she smirked.

She wasn't dumb. Quite to the contrary. And she was resourceful.

If the seventh floor wasn't going to help Richard, there was only one option open to her.

Russia.

Only the Russians could free her husband.

This went against everything she knew. Russia was the enemy, the target: this had been ingrained in her in eleven years of service. To go to them, hat in hand, and propose to work together—the very idea was heresy. Disdain roiled inside her like poison.

And yet, it was the only solution. Her last hope.

If Theresa was to become a traitor, it wasn't her fault. No, this was all on the Agency. They'd left her no choice. They'd lied to her face for two years, kept her cocooned in ignorance, and now held her down, sought to keep her helpless. Well, she was helpless no more. The Agency was responsible for the hatred now coursing through her veins. She would have her revenge. *The enemy of my enemy is my friend.*

But how to approach them? This was the conundrum. She couldn't stop thinking about it, turning it over and over in her mind as she went through the motions of a regular day. New employees were told during orientation about agents who'd turned traitor. Their cases were dissected in painful detail, the traitors' mistakes paraded before their eyes. The upshot was that new hires were made to believe it was impossible to contact a foreign service. Usually, would-be traitors approached the enemy's representatives closest to hand: foreign embassies. But Langley and the FBI had the embassies and consulates in D.C. covered, or so CIA officers were told. How they did this was never explained, but Theresa imagined they held stakeouts near the entrances. You could be fired for visiting a foreign embassy without express permission. Theresa was understandably nervous. She didn't want to be found out, caught, and arrested, before she'd even begun.

She read up on the ways that spies before her—Aldrich Ames, Robert Hanssen, Ronald Pelton—had made contact. Disappointingly, most happened overseas, where security was weaker and it wasn't possible for U.S.

authorities to watch their people all the time. Luckily for Theresa, it would be easy for her to find out about the Russians working at the embassy: it was there in the office files, the information needed to surveil the adversary. It was all at her fingertips: where Russian embassy employees lived, which schools their children went to, the bars and restaurants they liked to frequent. She was careful not to spend too much time at file cabinets to avoid drawing attention. Nonetheless, her heart raced and her palms sweated the whole time, as if she expected to be discovered. For a security officer to appear at her desk any minute with a curt, "Please come with me, ma'am." But each time she thought about stepping away and forgetting the whole thing, she was haunted by the thought of Richard in a Russian jail, wasting away. Anything he had suffered was a thousand times worse than what she faced. And she would return to the files.

Before long, her research led her time and again to the same man. Evgeni Constantinov seemed the best candidate; listed as a low-ranking officer in the embassy's cultural section, there was no doubt he was really an SVR officer using the position as cover. He lived in a good-sized house in Great Falls—no low-ranking Russian diplomat could afford to live there—and the clincher was his proximity to McLean. Surveillance would be a breeze. Being closer to home, there'd be less traffic to deal with. Less time away from Brian.

Having picked her target, she moved on to the next step: learning his route. It meant leaving her son with a sitter in the evenings but a necessary sacrifice, she told herself as she kissed his head and climbed into a rental car she'd left in a church parking lot near her house. After driving an elaborate surveillance detection route through northern Virginia, she headed to the Russian embassy on Wisconsin Avenue. The location had been quite a coup for the Russians, not far from the Naval Observatory where the vice president and his family lived, a lovely part of town. Every night, she parked or circled the block until she saw Constantinov's car leave the compound, then followed at a discreet distance as he drove home. The more she saw of him, the more she was convinced Constantinov was not just an attaché in the foreign ministry. He was a little too alert and attentive behind the wheel of a splashy SUV. A little too fit, he looked like Russian military. She followed him every night for a week until she was satisfied with his consistency. He left the building at approximately the same time each night, took the same route. Apparently, he didn't think he was being tailed by the Americans or didn't care. There would be times when he would work late or be called away on duty, but for her purposes, she felt pretty sure that he would fit the bill.

She found one spot in particular good for an approach: there was a bottleneck on Constantinov's route, where he had to maneuver his car from MacArthur Boulevard to the Clara Barton Parkway, around Ericsson Road. It was still city there and pedestrians milled on the street corners, waiting at bus stops and popping in and out of shops. She could do a brush pass by his car and it wouldn't be noticeable, if it turned out the FBI had someone watching him.

Another lucky break was that Constantinov smoked, a habit that was slow to die out among Russians. He often drove with his windows down, plumes of smoke rising above his car as he sat in traffic. He drove a massive SUV, surely an embassy vehicle, and it sat high on the road. She practiced making passes in her garage where no one would see her, walking by and aiming for a high shelf approximately the height of the SUV's door, until they were perfectly smooth. Undetectable.

Her hands shook as she wrote the note: *I am a CIA officer with information that will be of interest to you.* Followed by instructions for a rendezvous if they wanted to meet. The chances of follow-through, she knew, were almost nil. They would suspect the whole thing was a trap, albeit a clumsy one. It meant the possibility of multiple attempts passing notes to Constantinov to persuade them. And even if they were intrigued, it might be a long time before they decided to act. They'd need to identify her and then they would follow her and study her, until they were satisfied that she wasn't setting them up.

She folded the note so it would stay closed if she should somehow miss the window and it fell to the gutter or sidewalk, and kept it hidden in the rental car under a floor mat, but even this tenuous connection back to her made her nervous. It was proof of her perfidy in block lettering on yellow legal paper, tangible evidence of her intent to betray her country.

The country that had betrayed her first.

Every day, she did the same thing. She went home after work and made dinner for Brian, leaving him with the sitter. Then she drove the rental car to a sleepy branch library where she donned a wig and glasses, a different coat and handbag. After that, she went to MacArthur Boulevard, parked the car, and walked to the intersection where Constantinov would be in about an hour, stuck in traffic. She made many dry runs, practiced spotting his car and doing brushes. Calculating how far from the curb she'd need to be to slide the tightly folded note through the open window on the passenger's side—without being noticed. An entire week passed before she was satisfied that he wasn't being followed or watched by the FBI.

The second week, however, Constantinov disappeared. She watched the traffic at MacArthur Boulevard but didn't see his SUV. Whether his absence was due to late nights in the office or a sudden trip out of town, she didn't know. It was so maddening that, back in the office, she dared to check his file, but there were no updates, no new notes. While it meant she had no idea where he'd gone, the only upside was that he didn't appear to be on anyone's radar.

And then the third week, he reappeared, falling back into his normal routine. The amount of relief she felt was enormous, unexpectedly so. It was as though fate was reassuring her that this was meant to be. The plan was back on. She would proceed.

She did her run the first three days that week but chickened out at the last minute each time. She'd get the feeling she was being followed or didn't like the look of a man lingering on the corner, afraid he might be FBI even though she knew that he wasn't. Nobody cared about Constantinov, the out-of-date file in the office backed that fact up. She wasn't being followed. It was jitters, pure and simple. *Get a grip on yourself. Either you're going to do this or you're not.* So, on Thursday, she steeled herself and walked toward Constantinov's car as it idled in traffic. She veered to the curb. He had no idea what was happening, she could tell by the bored expression on his face, the way he looked through the windshield like a law enforcement officer, at nothing and everything at once. The effortless flick of ash from the end of his cigarette. She slid the folded note into his cab so efficiently that she almost could believe she hadn't done it, walking away with blood pounding in her ears. No one on the street had noticed, not even the people beside her on the sidewalk. Maybe even Constantinov—either that or he'd had the presence of mind not to react. Either way, he wouldn't do anything until he'd pulled into the two-car garage at home and leaned over for his briefcase and saw the yellow triangle of paper resting on the seat. A simple note waiting for him like a time bomb.

They were to meet at four p.m. on Sunday afternoon at the National Cathedral, three long days away. Theresa wasn't sure how she'd get through work on Friday without breaking down and blurting it all out in one long confession. She considered calling in sick but if they suspected her in any way, she'd only confirm those suspicions by taking a day off. She spent the first half of the day in a cold sweat, listening for the sound of unfamiliar footsteps behind her as men from Security made their way to her desk. But it didn't happen, and by lunchtime, she felt better. Mere hours to go before she was clear.

And after all this anxiety, she almost didn't go to the rendezvous. Her mind worked up insidious schemes. After all the propaganda she'd been fed in CI classes, it seemed impossible that Constantinov wouldn't have a tail on him, that the FBI hadn't questioned him and knew what she was up to. It was too quiet, too easy. *You are walking into a trap,* her brain hissed. But then a funny thing happened a couple hours before the appointed meeting: she saw on the news that there was a bust at the Chinese embassy. She didn't get the whole story—it had just broken and facts were scarce—but there, on the screen, FBI agents and police swarmed all over the Chinese compound. Blue lights, yellow tape, men in FBI windbreakers carrying out boxes of computers. Every FBI agent in D.C. had to be there. Minor routine duties, like routine surveillance of Russian officers, would be canceled for the day. She was sure of it.

She tried not to get her hopes up that Russians would actually be at the rendezvous. Even if they were curious, they would spend this first meeting playing it safe. They would go early to stake out the place. They would watch from afar to see if she showed up. They would look for FBI. They would give full rein to their suspicions. Offering yourself up for treason was inevitably a drawn-out affair. She'd have to be patient, play the long game.

She dropped Brian off at the house of a school friend, finally taking the woman up on her offer of a playdate, and spent the rest of the hour running a surveillance detection route. It was short, too short, but that was all she had time for.

She sat in the rental car two blocks from the National Cathedral and fought back the panic that now surged through her in waves. *Am I really going to go through with this? What if run into someone I know?* The wig wouldn't fool anyone for more than a minute. *This is madness.* But she knew that if the Russians showed up and she didn't, then it would be over. There would be no second chances. After the terror had subsided and she was awash in regret, she would wonder her entire life if she'd made a mistake. Every time she looked into Brian's face, she'd wonder if she could've given him his father back.

She took a deep breath and opened the car door.

She walked into the cathedral's gift shop prepared for disappointment, but there was Evgeni Constantinov by a rack of greeting cards. Up close, he looked just like his file picture, which was in itself a minor miracle, because spies never looked the same in person. The photos were usually years out of date, rarely updated. They always ended up looking older in real life than you expected, especially around the eyes. Exhausted and cynical.

A nervous-looking man in an ill-fitting suit on the other side of the shop was obviously with Constantinov, which meant there were undoubtedly several more she hadn't spotted out on the grounds watching for FBI. Theresa's brain crackled with conflicting emotions. Disbelief, that they had come as she'd asked, that they had taken her seriously. Worry, that despite her intense effort to lose any tail, she had been followed and FBI would swoop down on them any second. And, lastly, excitement, because she was doing something that had been long forbidden to her, like a schoolgirl finally trying her hand at shoplifting. *It's never as bad or scary as you think it will be.*

She headed to the herb garden after making sure Constantinov was following. The hedges on the paths were shoulder height, providing good cover, and the thick foliage would absorb sound. They wouldn't be overheard, accidentally or otherwise. The garden was usually popular with tourists but it was unseasonably chilly for June and the only other occupant was an elderly priest in a rumpled raincoat. He flicked a cigarette butt to the ground before disappearing into the main building.

It was important to set the tone, she knew, to let the Russians know that she could not be jerked around. They had to see that she wasn't the usual turncoat, deep in trouble and desperate for money. What she wanted was very, very specific. "I'm glad you took my note seriously. I don't have time to waste," she said to Constantinov in a low, even voice.

He made a scoffing sound in his throat. "It doesn't matter if you are in a hurry. There are still steps that must be taken, a protocol to follow." The Russian obviously wanted to take control of the situation. That's what any case officer would do, she knew, but she was through with letting someone else lead.

She turned to face him. "Let's cut to the chase. Your superiors are going to want to talk to me. Do you know who I am?" Constantinov looked uncomfortable, which pleased her. He was losing control and didn't like it, but at the same time he was afraid of making a mistake. "I'm Theresa Warner. Richard Warner's wife. He's a CIA officer sitting in one of your jails. You wouldn't have heard of him. It's a very sensitive case. There's been a big cover-up, both here and in Russia. Richard Warner—give that name to your bosses. They'll know who he is."

Constantinov edged away from her slightly as though she were mad. Did he not believe her? That was okay: he'd believe her soon enough. "And if this is true, what is it you think I can do for you?"

"I'm prepared to provide your organization with secrets in exchange for his release."

"You need to be more specific."

"I'm a CIA officer. I can get my hands on anything. I'll make it worthwhile. But this will be a one-time exchange. I will give you secrets, and you will release my husband, and then we'll disappear. Moscow will leave us alone—that's part of the bargain, too."

He thought for a moment. "Moscow perhaps, but what about Washington? Your own people will come after you."

"That's my concern." On this point, she'd be firm: she wanted nothing more to do with either side. She'd only trust herself from now on, her and Richard. "So, no disrespect to you, but I want to speak to someone high up at the next meeting, someone with authority."

He crooked an eyebrow. He wanted to tell her she was in no position to be making demands. They would decide who would deal with her. The Russians didn't run their assets like the Americans; they were more stick than carrot, a part of their authoritarian culture that ran through their psyches like a fat vein of ore. "I will see about setting up this meeting," he said finally, grudgingly. "But you must show us what you have to offer. You must give us a sample, prove that you can deliver." She nodded; she had expected this.

They set up a way for him to contact her when the meeting was set. He looked skeptical but now that they'd bitten, they'd follow through, she was sure of it. Chances like these didn't fall in their laps every day. Theresa went back to her rental car, shaking, unable to believe what she had done. She had gone toe-to-toe with a Russian officer. There was something primitive about it, like two animals squaring off in the forest, fang and claw. He had wanted to snap her up and gobble her down like some small, weak creature, but she had stood her ground. She had withstood him, and was only starting to realize it, to feel better and stop shaking. She flexed her hands before placing them on the steering wheel of the rental car.

For the first time, she allowed herself to believe that this was going to turn out okay.

TWENTY-TWO

I t had been three days since Theresa had met with the Russian and the guilt was only starting to fade. She tried not to think about what she had done, afraid it would show on her face while she was at work. In some ways it still didn't feel real, like she'd imagined it all. Constantinov's disbelieving face, the tightness in her chest, the breathless drive home. On Monday, she spent most of her day in a state of suspense, again waiting to be led away for a talk with investigators. It was only as the minutes ticked by and nothing happened that she grew more confident. She realized she could relax. They'd vastly underestimated her. She'd gotten away with it.

It was time to move on to the next step: find something to give to the Russians, something good enough to get them to agree to do as she asked.

It wasn't something to rush into. The Agency's computer system was a minefield, laden with traps—or so one heard. They were told so many stories, all meant to make employees afraid. Whether the traps existed or not, the seed of doubt was planted and did its job, keeping many of them from poking around where they shouldn't. If she was going to try to fool the system, she had to be smart. She couldn't leave behind a trail of crumbs.

She knew her limitations: she wasn't a computer wizard. Paper files would be the safest, but these would not be easy to get to, especially not for the compartmented, special access cases, the stuff the Russians were most likely to be interested in—these would be kept under lock and key by Maggie. Or down in the vault, but she couldn't go back to Jimmy Purvis; it would make him suspicious.

The only way she could think to explore without alerting anyone was through the collaboration tools on the Agency's internal network. The tools were meant to remedy the problem, raised after September 11, that intelligence analysts worked in silos. They were told they needed to share their puzzle pieces if they were going to avoid the next intelligence failure.

In her daily routine, Theresa rarely used these tools but, as she poked around the forums, she realized that you could find out a lot about what others were working on. And while an office somewhere in the bowels of the building might keep logs, the whole point was collaboration, so it wouldn't necessarily stand out if someone stuck their nose in subjects that technically weren't their business. She didn't think this would get her all the information she needed, but at least it was a start.

She sat at the computer, paging through the Russia forums. Officers and analysts were looking at every topic under the sun, and it seemed unbelievable that there were customers—policymakers, military commanders—interested in all that minutiae. She assumed it was a holdover from the Cold War days, when the Russians were doing so many crazy things that you couldn't be sure what might end up being important, so you studied it all.

She scrolled down the list of sub-forums, so comprehensive that it was practically a grocery list. Which of all these topics would the Russians be most interested in? What would be important enough to merit giving up her husband? What would tantalize them? It stood to reason that they'd be most interested in CIA's assets in Russia. You always wanted to know if you had spies in your midst, handing over your secrets, rendering your work useless. The identities of assets were closely guarded, however. It was unlikely she'd find names in the forums. But they might show her where to start.

After two days of carefully dipping in and out of discussion threads so she wouldn't raise any suspicions, Theresa had a short list of cases to look into. One was an asset code-named Lighthouse. Theresa thought Lighthouse might be a scientist working for the Russian government in some capacity. The reports officer for Lighthouse, Jan Westerling, was pretty cagey. She didn't provide details and so it was hard for Theresa to figure out where Lighthouse worked, exactly. But he seemed to know something about Russian missiles and the Russians would probably find that tantalizing, with recently renewed turmoil over the Intermediate-Range Nuclear Forces treaty.

The most important thing, Theresa decided, was not to give the Russians anything especially harmful. The thought of doing something that would hurt the country made Theresa's stomach turn. It was still anathema to her. She was mad at CIA but she still loved her country. She had to give Russia just enough information to get her husband released—and not one iota more.

After observing Westerling closely, Theresa realized that the young woman might be a new hire. That was both good and bad. New hires needed a lot of direction. Theresa remembered her early days, trying not to draw attention to herself so no one would realize how little she knew or understood, worried that if someone learned how incompetent she was they'd use it against her one day. She'd seen it happen, an old hand turning suddenly on a new hire to save his own neck or distract the boss from a mistake he'd made. She only saw now, from the distance of years, that being Richard Warner's girlfriend had saved her from all that backstabbing and henpecking. Nobody went after her. She had been protected—another debt she owed Richard.

But now it was her turn to take advantage of someone's inexperience. *Well, let this be a lesson to you,* she thought as she walked to Jan Westerling's desk. *Trust no one. I'm not your friend. I'm no one's friend.*

Westerling knew who Theresa was, of course. It didn't matter that they'd never spoken to each other before; the reports officer would be flattered that The Widow had sought her out. It was easy to get Westerling to talk about herself. Graduated from the Fletcher School of International Affairs at Tufts last May, passable Russian language skills, living with two roommates in an apartment in Tysons Corner, homesick for her family in Chicago. Still a bit dazed that she'd gotten a job at CIA and not fully aware of what it meant, the tremendous burden that it placed on her slender shoulders.

She proved it by giving Theresa everything she needed, without question.

Theresa started by giving something to Westerling. Something harmless, but it was recognition from someone more senior. Theresa pulled something from the back of her mind, a conference on changing Russian policy that the young woman probably hadn't heard of or, being so junior, been invited to. "You should talk to Eric about getting to go," she said, leaning against a pillar, casual and chummy. "Usually, they send Rodney to this sort of thing but he's getting ready to retire. They really should send someone else. New blood. One of the up-and-comers. I could bring it up to Eric, if you'd like." The look of gratitude that spread over Westerling's face was almost painful to see.

She left it at that. It was enough for the first touch. She'd nurture this budding relationship along and start asking questions about Lighthouse and before long the name would leak out. It was easy to forget among colleagues, people you knew had the same security clearance as you, that there was still need-to-know. Where was the harm?

After this, she had a few false starts. From what she could find out about a couple of the code names on her list, the assets were no longer active and it was impossible to ask questions about their identity without drawing suspicion. In one case she looked into, the reports officer seemed so security conscious that Theresa withdrew before she made the woman suspicious. Theresa started to worry that she'd need to take bigger risks than she felt comfortable with—not that any of this was comfortable, not by a stretch. By the end of the day, she'd crossed all but one case—in addition to Lighthouse—off her list.

That last case was code-named Skipjack. From all the online chatter, it had been easy to figure out that Skipjack was in the military and that he had something to do with cybersecurity. The topic was so hot that the members of this sub-forum were careless, discussing cases with far too much familiarity. Kyle Kincaid, the reports officer for Skipjack, was especially complacent. *My source is in the new Russian army cybersecurity unit and I'll believe what he tells me over your amateurish speculation any day,* he wrote in one post, striking back at someone who'd disagreed with his assessment of a situation. That caused some grumbling, a few people trying to remind him that a little skepticism was healthy when it came to assets who could lead you by the nose if you weren't careful, but he blew that off, too. He would learn the hard way, Theresa decided. Pride goes before a fall.

Kincaid proved to be easier than Westerling to crack. Former military and perhaps insecure in this new environment, he was only too happy to talk about his case. Everyone had heard of The Widow, after all, and Kincaid was eager to get in with the Russia experts. It made doing counterintelligence easy when people were eager to show off.

"Oh yeah, Skipjack is an officer in the Russian army. He's been in this new cyber unit since its inception. Anything he says, you can take to the bank," Kincaid said, leaning back in his chair and propping his feet up on his safe like he was relaxing in his living room.

"It must be great to have such a trusted source. Eric must think a lot of you to give you such an important asset." Theresa could feel him soak up the compliments like a sponge. Kincaid was likely lonely, perhaps having alienated himself from his teammates with his bragging and aggression. The man hadn't the first clue that he was being worked, that here at Langley you were always being worked. *It's not like the military here. It's not one big happy family. You have to control your own worst tendencies.* She told herself she was doing him a favor and one day he'd be grateful—when it was over and CIA had learned what she'd done, when she was someplace safe with Richard and Brian.

It took some wheedling, and a half hour in the cafeteria over coffee, smiling until her cheeks hurt, but she had Skipjack's true name by the end of their first chat. Gennady Nesterov, twenty-three years in the Russian army. Kincaid gave her every detail about him: he approached the U.S. after he'd grown disillusioned, sickened that his country had been taken over by greedy oligarchs. When he saw what the army was doing with his unit, making it into a powerful tool that would be used to further the oligarchs' interests, not those of the Russian people, he made up his mind about what he would do.

Skipjack had potential. Under the right conditions, he could be a gold mine. The cyber target was getting more important every day and Skipjack was in a position to give them a lot. She got the sense from Kincaid that up until now, Skipjack had been stalling on them, maybe ultimately ambivalent about betraying his country. That wasn't uncommon. Assets wanted money and a sympathetic ear but often got cold feet when it came to handing over the goods.

She had resolved that she would only give Russia unproductive assets, ones that wouldn't do much damage if they were lost, and so she didn't know what to do about Skipjack. Without him, she only had one name and a minnow at that: not enough to convince the Russians to work with her.

It was a gamble but . . . Maybe she could warn Skipjack before the Russians came to arrest him. They'd be happy to get the names and it would take time to evaluate them, but by then they'd have already released Richard. There would be damage, but she would try to minimize that.

Two potential names to give to the Russians. She turned both cases over in her mind, trying to be sure she wasn't overlooking anything, missing an important thread that could lead back to her. Thinking, too, of the consequences for others. For the two reports officers, Westerling and Kincaid, there would be fallout. She felt bad for Westerling, not so much for Kincaid—she had the feeling he'd been hitting on her. It would look bad for Westerling but she'd survive. She'd get a second chance. The assets, Lighthouse and Skipjack, would get it worse. They would bear the brunt. But they would only go to prison. This wasn't the bad old days of the Soviet Union. Spies weren't executed or sent to hard labor camps, left to freeze and starve in a Siberian gulag.

In any case, she wouldn't let it keep her up at night. This was part of the deal when you decided to spy for the enemy. If you didn't realize the danger, you were a fool. And whatever happened to them was nothing compared with what her husband had suffered. That made her feel better—or at least less bad—about what she had made up her mind to do.

TWENTY-THREE

A good summer day in Washington was like nowhere else in the world. The skies were the clearest blue, the air the perfect balance of cool and warm. Washington's infamous heat and humidity was nowhere to be seen.

It's a beautiful day. That's how I'll remember it, always, the day I sold out to the Russians.

For two weeks, she faithfully kept an eye out for the signal that would tell her the Russians were ready to meet. That happened yesterday. A chalk mark on the lamppost meant they met the next day at the prearranged time and place. She almost couldn't believe they had made a decision to proceed so quickly. It was so quick, almost irresponsible. It pleased and frightened her in nearly equal measure.

But it also peeved her, because it was a weekday morning. She had to call in sick to make the meet, even though she resented it. Being a parent, she'd used up too many sick days and vacation days as it was, but someone had to stay home when Brian got a cold or he had to go to the pediatrician. In a way, it was easier since Brian was with the sitter she'd found for the summer. And she was completely confident by now that the Agency wasn't watching her. Taking a sick day wouldn't be a trigger.

She noticed as she dressed for the meeting that she couldn't feel her fingers. It was as though she was having an out-of-body experience, or a stroke. Her mind floated like a helium balloon as she applied her lipstick—Chanel's Rouge Rebelle—and combed her hair. She'd have thought this would be easier since she'd met with the Russians once, the ice broken, but there was something different about this time. Edgier. Scarier. Like she was about to jump off a bridge.

They were to meet at the National Building Museum, a long brick building in the middle of bustling Gallery Place, with all its shops and restaurants and tourist attractions. Not that she was familiar with any of it. She'd been to the building museum once to see the Smithsonian's annual crafts show. Otherwise, she never spent time there; downtown D.C. was a swamp of traffic, too much road construction with too little parking. Suburbia was for mothers like her; D.C. was for hipsters and tourists, and never the twain shall meet.

Theresa thought the museum an odd place for a meeting until she stepped inside and saw that it was perfect: a big, open area, which made it easy to surveil, and multiple entrances and exits for an easy escape if needed. There were several exhibits going on, which provided a bustling crowd for cover. The exhibit in the main hall was a huge collection of paper models of famous buildings. The Reichstag, the Alhambra, the Bolshoi Theatre, the Empire State Building and the Flatiron, the Old North Church. Glass boxes filled with large, cumbersome paper skyscrapers and monuments made a maze of the space, ideal for avoiding detection. The people ambling about were mostly affluent-looking retirees, in the city for a day of sightseeing. A pair of young mothers sat at a table outside the tiny coffee shop, strollers at their sides, their children running between the tables, their laughter echoing off the vaulted ceiling. It all looked normal. Nothing set off her sixth sense for trouble.

After a few minutes, a man slipped into the exhibit area with a stack of files under his arm. There was a green folder on top, the signal they'd arranged. She followed him for a minute to satisfy herself that he was the one. Perhaps it was guilty knowledge, but Theresa thought he looked like a bad guy, possibly more so than anyone she'd ever met during her time at the Agency, and she'd met her share of dubious characters. He was in his mid-thirties and moved with the ease of an athlete. Better dressed than the average FSB or SVR agent, who tended to look like policemen in cheap suits. Beneath the polished veneer, however, there were rough bits. He had a scar next to his left eye, running back to the temple, as though someone had hit him there very hard, maybe even tried to kill him. There was a hint of desperation in the eyes and tight jaw. A striver, her friends might say. A bruiser who had muscled his way up the ladder and was trying to put it behind him now.

She stopped in front of a model of Westminster Abbey. It looked so flimsy, walls of paper, but still recognizable. She had been there with Richard early in their married life, a business trip, a week of meetings with MI6, but they took the weekend to play tourist. It had happened shortly after they'd wed, when she assumed they had a lifetime to travel the world together.

She'd thought it lost forever, but maybe this rough character was going to give her life back to her.

She sensed someone standing next to her and looked up to see his face reflected dimly in the glass. It was like seeing a ghost.

"I hear Metro will stop running at midnight." It was the phrase she had been told to expect. Silly and contrived, but they all were.

She turned to face him. There was not a shred of humanity there. A soulless monster walking around in a human suit. Something inside her—fear—spiked.

"Theresa Warner?"

She couldn't answer. She returned his steely-eyed stare. He nodded toward a bench in an alcove, away from the rest of the visitors.

He sat comfortably, as though he did this sort of thing every day. Maybe he did. He put the folders on the bench next to him, obviously glad to be rid of this subterfuge.

She found her voice. "What's your name? You know my name, it's only right that I know yours."

"I am Dmitri Tarasenko. I am with the Counterintelligence Division in the Federal Security Service of the Russian Federation." He gave her a smile that he probably imagined was charming. "I do not mind telling you that we were surprised to hear from you."

"I was surprised to be contacting you." But that was life, one surprise after another. *We're all capable of things we never thought we could do.*

"It's been two years. Why did you wait this long?"

The truth was galling but there was no other explanation. "I just found out that my husband is still alive."

He chuckled at that. "So, they kept it from you? That wasn't very nice of them, was it?"

"Never mind that—I know now, and I want to do something about it. But first, I want proof that he's still alive."

He reached into a coat pocket and pulled out a photograph.

It was Richard. Seeing his face knocked her for a loop, made her dizzy. He was thinner than the last time she'd seen him, and seemed to have aged twenty years, but it was him, no question. His head was tilted to one side fatalistically, almost like he was shrugging. One corner of his mouth kinked up as though he was trying to smile but had forgotten how. Had they told him the picture was for her? *Smile—this is for your wife.* She felt a sharp stabbing desire to hold him. She wasn't going to cry in front of the Russian.

"That picture was taken right before I left. You see he's in good condition. He hasn't been harmed."

She nodded, pressing the photo to her heart. He held out his hand for it but she was damned if she was going to give it back. She shoved it hurriedly in her purse. What was he going to do—wrestle it away from her in front of all these people?

The look on his face was threatening and grew darker by the second. *Case officers are the same the world over: manipulators. He's trying to get inside my head. Wait it out.* "This is not a good way to start our relationship, Mrs. Warner. You know how this works. You need to listen to me. To trust me." He relented after a moment, the thundercloud passing. "I'm thinking of your safety. What if someone were to find that on you? What about your son? He doesn't go through your purse?"

How dare you bring my son into this. "No, he doesn't," she said through gritted teeth. "I'm careful. No one will see it. You're just going to have to trust me."

"Let me be clear, Mrs. Warner, on where you stand. It may not be possible to get your husband released. There are important men who oppose it. We do not like spies in Russia. When your husband was caught, there were people who wanted him put to death. He is lucky to be alive."

At least part of that was a lie. Russia understood the need for spies: it was a country of spies, had made a cult out of spying. The population had been groomed to spy on one another, the tradecraft absorbed through osmosis from birth. The leader of the country was an unapologetic former KGB agent. The FSB may have been angry for what her husband had managed to accomplish at their expense, but on some level, they had to admire him, too.

Or perhaps she was over-romanticizing the situation because she believed in her husband so much. Believed the myth of Richard Warner that had only gotten richer with time.

He smiled again, all teeth, like the wolf in a bedtime story. *Tell me a story.* "But you are in luck. The Rezidentura at the embassy happened to contact my boss. General Evgeni Morozov. He is the head of counter-intelligence, a very powerful man in the FSB. General Morozov is the one who saved your husband, you know. When he had been captured. Talked the Hard Man out of killing him. The general told him it would be worth it one day, and the Hard Man listened." The Hard Man was Putin. Richard's asset had done something to Putin; it had been personal. The asset had died a terrible, torturous death, she'd been told. She once had imagined the same for Richard.

The Russian turned on the bench so that he blocked out the rest of the gallery. He was all she could see, all teeth and steely eye and hideous scar. "You see, Mrs. Warner, General Morozov is sympathetic to your plight. He does not think your Agency should have kept this secret from you. The FSB would not have done this to one of its officers. The FSB takes care of its own." *They are the good guys. Right.* "He wants to help you, but you must give him something to appease the Hard Man. To show that he was not wrong when he saved your husband's life."

She knew what they wanted: for her to stay at CIA and keep spying for them. But she knew she could never do it, couldn't face Eric Newman every day, wait to be discovered. Wait for the day they ripped Brian from her side. It would drive her mad.

She shook her head.

His smile sent a chill through her. "Ah, still you don't understand your position, Mrs. Warner. *You* do not set the terms. That is up to General Morozov to decide. You are asking us to bring a dead man back to life. So, you must ask yourself: what is the price of a miracle?"

The high, overhead lights seemed to flicker, fade in and out. It was all in her head. Panic. *What have I gotten myself into?*

It was too late to change her mind. They had her. If she got cold feet now, they could give her name to CIA. A hint, that's all it would take.

There was no going back.

She breathed heavily, in and out, in and out, trying to remain conscious. *Do not faint here. Do not cause a scene.*

What have I done?

He leaned back, observing her distress with no more concern than he would have for a dying moth. "I have given you a present, word of your husband—now it's your turn. You have something for me, no?"

She reached into her pocket for the envelope with the information on Lighthouse and Skipjack. She'd decided to give them two names to minimize the risk of being refused; she loathed the thought of the Russians dragging it out. It was all in there: names, where the men worked, what information they'd given over. As much information as she could find on them. She tried not to think of what would happen to them once the FSB got that envelope. They had taken a chance that CIA would protect them and here she was, betraying them.

Richard had trusted that CIA would protect him, too.

Remember Richard. You're doing this for him. It doesn't matter what happens to you. Or anyone else.

She thrust the envelope at Tarasenko.

He slipped it into his breast pocket. "Very good. That was not so hard, was it?" He was enjoying her misery, licking it up like cream.

He told her how she would know if they wanted to meet again: she was to look for a mark on a piece of equipment in a playground near her house. It was a little playground that Brian and his friends used regularly, and now the Russians would use it for their purposes.

The place would never be the same to her. Nothing would ever be the same.

He rose to leave, tapping the front of his coat where the envelope was hidden. "We will evaluate this and be in touch. I hope you have chosen wisely. Your husband's life depends on it. Good day, Mrs. Warner." She remained where she was, concentrating on breathing, willing herself not to faint, as she watched him walk away.

TWENTY-FOUR

Theresa returned to the office the next day, though she would've liked to stay home, to play hooky like a schoolchild. When she showed up pale and rattled, teammates asked if she was feeling better. "Fine, thanks," she mumbled. She remembered to cough occasionally to keep them at arm's length. *Let them think I'm contagious. Let them be mad at me, thinking I've brought some disease into the office.* She wasn't fine—she wouldn't be for a while—so she didn't want anyone looking too closely.

Her son, on the other hand, was not so easy to fool. She'd only been able to hide it from him for a couple hours. By evening, he knew something was wrong. "Are you scared, Mommy?" he'd asked at dinner. Unused to seeing his mother frightened, he was skittish, afraid to get close. "Nonsense, what would I be scared about?" she'd answered with false bravado. It was best to pretend around Brian. He was a sensitive boy, prone to worry.

The meeting with Tarasenko haunted her at work. She'd underestimated her conscience. Guilt coursed through her veins and swelled her throat shut. Going through the security turnstiles that morning, she'd felt like she would burst into flames, like a demon trying to enter a church. One of the damned trying to pass for normal. Nothing happened, of course, though she was still trembling by the time she got to her desk. The usual eyes were on her from the time she left her car to when she arrived at her office. *Look, it's The Widow.* Did those curious faces see that something was wrong? Was it written all over her face, etched in the lines around her eyes, hanging from the edge of her frown, engraved in the furrow in her brow? *That woman is a traitor.*

How long before she would hear from the Russians? A month, two? Never? Volunteer spies were generally problematic. CIA took a long time to decide whether to trust the embassy walk-ins who offered to turn over the secrets in their heads for money, or for a plane ticket to the U.S. and a new life. They were hot messes, unraveling mentally and emotionally, beset by financial troubles, alcoholism, difficult personalities that cost them family and friends. But Theresa's motive was pure as the driven snow: to free a loved one. She was blameless. How much more trustworthy could one be?

There was nothing she could do except wait. She felt helpless and vulnerable, and she didn't like it.

Her fingers moved by habit on the keyboard at work as she checked email, read through reports on her targets—not that she cared about her job anymore. The words didn't even register, falling on her and melting like snow. Her mind was back in the museum, the chill of fear on her afresh, Tarasenko's wolfish grin impossible to forget.

But she wasn't helpless. She had two names now—Dmitri Tarasenko and this General Morozov. She would get to work.

Tarasenko had probably been lying when he said Morozov had intervened with Putin to save her husband's life. If the Hard Man had a personal interest in the case, why get involved at all?

She needed to find out more about the two of them. Best to be prepared. But she had to do this cautiously. It was too easy to tip off Security by showing an abnormal level of interest in a subject that fell out of your purview. Even though she hadn't seen any sign of them yet, they could be hiding in the shadows, gathering more evidence against her. That meant she couldn't search on the names, even though that would be the most expeditious. She didn't want to give Security ammunition to later use against her.

It was tedious, but she started by reading through the reports on the Counterintelligence Division at the FSB. She had no idea how long this General Morozov had served there, but figured his name would turn up eventually. Hours passed before she saw the first mention of him and it was next to nothing, his name and title, one of the participants in a meeting where an important decision had been made. It was excruciatingly slow, like untangling a hopelessly knotted skein of yarn, and she itched to type his name in the search bar and get to the heart of the mystery. But she owed it to Richard and Brian to use her best tradecraft. Now was not the time to get sloppy.

She searched by dancing around the edges. Looked up other attendees at the meeting, hoping to see Morozov's name come up again. Backtracked when it didn't, tried another approach.

After lunch, she stumbled onto a second report, this one more sub-stantive.

She was confused at first. It was about Ukraine, not Russia, but the two countries had a long history together, so it wasn't exactly unexpected. Her eyes skipped down the screen, trying to absorb the story.

Something terrible had happened in Kiev. The Chief of Station had been shot. A wave of nausea passed through her as she remembered the incident, dimly. It had happened around the time she'd been hired so she'd never heard more than general rumor. He'd been shot on the street right outside his home, an apartment in a gated compound that housed

American officials. It had been so brisk and impersonal that they thought it was an execution. A man exited from a car as the Station Chief approached the gate, pulled out a gun and fired at him. There had been a security guard on duty at the time, but the assailant managed to flee the scene nonetheless. No one was ever caught. The Ukrainians told the Agency that it was a street crime with no political connotations but of course that wasn't true. The killer hadn't even tried to take the Station Chief's wallet or expensive watch. Theresa's lip curled as she read: the Russian way, to tell bald-faced lies even when you know you wouldn't be believed. Like it was a game.

When it happened, Theresa didn't grasp the significance; it would've been impossible for someone in her position, a new hire. Everyone in the office was angry and wanted to do something about it, but the anger was subdued. There were no histrionics, no chest-beating vows of revenge, only a little crying in public. When she wondered why everyone was so stoic, Richard took her aside and explained there was a code of honor at CIA. Whoever did this wouldn't get away with it. Look at Mir Kansi, the Pakistani who in 1993 had shot CIA employees outside the entrance on Route 123. It had taken four years, but eventually he was found, arrested, and stood trial. And was executed for what he'd done. *You kill a CIA agent, we'll find you. And you will pay.*

The horror of those days came back as Theresa read the cable. But what did it have to do with Evgeni Morozov, who seemed to be nothing more than an undistinguished colonel in those days?

An analyst in Kiev Station had figured it out, according to the report. They pulled out all the stops to gather more information. Bribed Ukrainian security, grilled liaison, put the thumbs screws to all their assets. This analyst had camped out in the Station without taking a break, not even going home to sleep, until he had solved the puzzle. He'd pored over every detail, but the picture didn't jell until he looked at travel data.

There'd been multiple reports putting a Russian colonel behind the hit, but it wasn't until the analyst found Morozov flying into Kiev a couple times before the hit that he was able to pull the story together.

Theresa was sure there was a report in the system with the full picture, tied Morozov to the assassination in certain terms, good and airtight. She just didn't dare search for it. More recent reports took Morozov's guilt as fait accompli. Right after the assassination, he was moved into an important position in the FSB and, a few years later, was promoted to general. It was enough to make Evgeni Morozov one of CIA's most wanted. He had managed to avoid capture or expedient dispatch by never leaving Russia, not after the hit. Always traveling with bodyguards, even inside Moscow city limits.

Theresa pushed back from her desk, stricken. She tried not to let her shock show on her face. The man who was pulling her strings was a mastermind. Her hands started to tremble again. It would be foolish to think she would be able to outmaneuver a man who'd managed to elude the CIA for a decade.

With great effort, she turned her attention to Tarasenko. This was going to be harder, she knew. There was bound to be less paper on him, given that he was younger and more junior in his career.

Theresa did not find the first report with Dmitri Tarasenko's name until the end of the next day. At this point, she'd looked at so many reports that she thought maybe she was hallucinating, seeing what she wanted to see. Surely it was a different Tarasenko. Her vision was blurry from staring at the screen for hours. She rubbed her eyes and forced herself to focus on the words. It was real; there was his photo, too. He was a few years younger, and there was no ugly scar, but she recognized the cagey set to his eyes, predation simmering just under the surface.

The report itself gave little insight into the man, just included him in a list of officers who were known to have recently moved from the army to the FSB. But it gave her an idea, something out of the ordinary. She decided to call Arthur Brown, the author of the report. He was a military analyst at DIA, the Defense Intelligence Agency. He might know about Tarasenko and it was less risky than speaking to the military analysts at CIA. And, an extra bonus: her name would mean nothing to him. He wouldn't know he was talking to The Widow.

His name and secure phone number appeared at the bottom of the report. The phone rang several times before going to voicemail. "I'm looking for information on a Dmitri Tarasenko, now with FSB, formerly with the Russian Ground Forces' Southern Military District. I'd be grateful if you could return my call." She left her secure phone number and wondered if she'd ever hear from him.

There was a message from Brown on her voicemail the next morning. She called him back right away.

He sounded like a smoker, raspy and out of breath. "I don't know if I can help you. Tarasenko left the service in 2010, like a lot of men, after the reforms. Everything I got on him is old."

"That would still be extremely helpful. That's what I'm looking for." A way to understand the man, that's what she wanted.

"I could send you a few reports."

"I'd appreciate it." There was something else bothering her. "For someone you haven't covered in a few years, Tarasenko's name seems to have jumped out at you."

A throaty sigh. "You don't forget the Butcher of Tskhinvali. He was in the South Ossetia campaign in 2008. You probably don't remember that— you sound kind of young—but it was a big deal. Relations between Georgia and Russia had been bad for a while, so Russia used South Ossetia as an excuse to push into Georgian territory. It was a pretty nasty campaign, bad on both sides, don't get me wrong, but the Ossetians wouldn't have done the damage they did without Russian support. In the end, the UN criticized Russia for its role."

"And Tarasenko was involved in this?"

Brown chuckled. "He was a lieutenant, eager to prove himself. He was the advisor attached to a South Ossetian unit that was guilty of the worst stuff. We're talking war-crime-level behavior. Razing towns, dragging grandfathers out to fields to shoot them, every woman in the village raped. Nasty stuff."

This was the man who sat next to her in the museum. A wolf in human clothing. She remembered the scar on his temple, the white teeth. A cold chill danced up her spine.

"He whipped the Ossetian troops into a frenzy and then he unleashed them. And the UN may have criticized Russia, but there was no punishment. The Russian military rewarded Tarasenko for this. After the Ground Forces were reorganized in 2010, he was moved to a cushy position in the FSB. Where they know what to do with a world-class asshole."

Arthur Brown's email appeared in Theresa's inbox an hour later, as promised, and she read through the reports, one by one. They traced a path of destruction, described air strikes raining bombs down on defenseless villages before the troops came through to finish the job, slaughtering villains who hadn't been smart enough to flee earlier. The Russians stole anything of value, even livestock, and burned farms behind them. Tarasenko's name was sprinkled through it all, urging the South Ossetians to give free rein to old grievances, pumping their ire, stoking their hate. All to prove to Georgia that it wasn't a good idea to stand up to Russia.

Theresa fell back into her chair, stunned. By now it was lunchtime, but she had no appetite. All she wanted to do was go home, crawl into bed, and pull the covers over her head but she was afraid of carrying this viciousness back with her.

This man. This fire-breathing ogre. She was bound to him now. How could she have been so naïve? For her plan to work, she needed to be in control. She would never be in control of either man. Not Morozov the spymaster, nor Tarasenko the bastard.

She pushed those thoughts away. No, she couldn't accept defeat from the start. She knew she was as smart as them. What she lacked was ruthlessness, but she'd learn. She'd find a way to succeed. She had to: there was no other choice. It wasn't just Richard's life at stake, or hers. There was Brian. You don't give your son over to a monster. It was her job to protect him, to stand between her precious boy and the monsters. Even the cold-blooded murderers and confirmed war criminals. She was only one woman, but she was his mother.

That's what mothers did.

TWENTY-FIVE

The little office is oppressive now. It's become Lyndsey's prison cell.

She doesn't want to make Theresa suspicious by going in and out too often. At the same time, she can barely stand to be in there, knowing Theresa is just beyond the door.

Is Theresa the mole? It's not as though she has much evidence to go on. Still, she remembers Jan Westerling's face when she told her Theresa had asked about Kulakov: she knew that was peculiar. And Kincaid . . . Lyndsey felt he wasn't being forthcoming with her.

Theresa. Despite the contradictory evidence, there's something there. She's sure of it.

You're the human lie detector, aren't you? You should be able to tell just by looking at her. Lyndsey flinches; she's always hated that nickname. Besides, it doesn't work that way and she knows it.

Lyndsey has gone for coffee twice this afternoon, even resorting to the office pot of tar because it gave her an excuse to walk by Theresa's desk. Half the time, Theresa isn't even there, and Lyndsey slinks around the office to see who she is speaking to. It could point to the next asset to disappear. Then when Theresa is at her desk, their eyes meet, and Lyndsey worries that Theresa might be able to tell that something is amiss. Lyndsey may know all the things that give you away but she's not capable of preventing them. She's not a hardened liar. How did she come to be in this strange situation, not one she ever expected, suspecting—knowing—one of her colleagues is a traitor?

The part she can't understand is *why*: why would Theresa betray CIA? There's no reason that she can see—unless it had something to do with Richard's untimely death. Still . . . It would take a lot for a professional intelligence officer to turn traitor.

First, she has to evaluate the other suspects. Wang—she's a long shot, and it's perplexing that Kincaid gave her name. Could he be confused?

She presses her hands to her forehead. With all the recent developments, she's pretty sure that *she's* the one who's confused. She could use someone to talk it over with.

Eric's office is steps away.

She raps gently on his door. "Do you have a minute?" she asks.

He nods. She closes the door and takes a chair opposite his desk.

"Have you found our mole?"

"I still need to do more research . . . there's conflicting information . . ."

"I get it, I get it, you retain the right to change your mind, but you wouldn't have come to me if you didn't have something. Out with it. Who do you think it is?"

This is her last chance to keep this to herself. In the pit of her stomach, however, she knows there's a chance she's right. She owes it to the Agency to speak out.

"I think . . . it might be Theresa Warner." She holds her breath, unable to believe she's said this terrible thing aloud. Accused her friend of the worst kind of betrayal. *Tell me I must be joking. Tell me it's not possible.*

But his expression remains carefully composed as he reaches for a pen lying abandoned on the desk. He starts tapping it against the blotter. "I'm not going to say you're crazy. You must have a reason for coming to this conclusion. Walk me through it."

She goes through the work she's done, every step of it. She tells him about the poison analysis, the conversations with Westerling. She lays out the conflicting information, too, and that CI seems ready to pin it on Kate Franklin.

"That was really unfortunate, about Kate . . ." Eric says. "But you're sure that you don't agree with CI? You're not just saying that out of pity?"

"If I thought she was the responsible party, I wouldn't hesitate to say so. But . . . CI is being overaggressive. I don't think Kate was the mole."

Eric sighs with relief. "I'm glad to hear you say that. I didn't think so, either. Not that I had any insight into this particular case; I'm saying that from what I know about Kate. But you wouldn't be so sure about Kate if you didn't have clues leading in another direction—am I right?"

When she comes to the part about examining the metadata, she hesitates. "I'm not finished with that. Depending on what I find . . . that could change everything. It could point to someone else. It could exonerate her."

"Or it could be the nail in the coffin," he says flatly.

This is what she has been afraid of, Eric jumping to conclusions. "But it makes no sense. The Russians killed her husband. Why would she help them?"

She's been counting on this being the moment when Eric agrees and says there's got to be some clue they haven't picked up on yet, a clue that will reveal the real traitor. *Stop me from turning in my friend.* But that's not what Eric is about to say, not judging by the grim set of his face.

"Losing Richard was hard on Theresa—who am I kidding? It was hard on everyone who was Richard's friend, but none of us can really know what that was like for *her*. It could be . . . that she's twisted the story around in her head, and instead of being mad at Richard for taking such an insane risk—because that's what it was, practically suicidal—she blames the Agency. After it happened, she waged an incredible crusade, trying to get the Director to look into it, when it was an open-and-shut case. What did she expect to find?"

Lyndsey opens her mouth but doesn't know what to say.

"She might think it's my fault, too. I wouldn't blame her. Maybe I should've stopped him. I could've put an end to it. But the asset was his big coup, you know. His claim to fame. If he could exfiltrate her from under the FSB's nose, well, it would be the stuff of legends. He wanted to try it and I didn't feel I could take that away from him. I didn't expect it to go so wrong—none of us did, obviously."

His regret is palpable. It's as though the ghosts from two years ago fill the room, all the anger and drama and regrets. "It's done. You learn from it—but you have to let it go." It's all she can think to say.

"As crazy as it sounds, if Theresa has gone to the Russians as a way to get back at us . . . I hate to say it, but I can see it. She's lost everything, and she wants us to suffer, too."

Can Lyndsey see that, too? She thinks of the conversations over coffee in the cafeteria. The bitter asides. The warning from Maggie. Yes, she can see it. It's a possibility.

"If this is true . . . If this is the case, Lyndsey, we have to bring her down. She can't get away with it."

"Of course." It goes without saying. She never thought that in her career she'd find a traitor in their midst, but now that she has she knows what her duty is.

Eric leans toward her. "Don't tell anyone else about this. Confirm your suspicions, then come to me first. We'll figure out the next steps—together."

He stands and paces away from his desk, strangely energized, like a fuse has been lit. "You should know . . . I have another operation going on right now with Moscow Station. It doesn't have anything to do with your investigation, but . . . If anything weird comes up on the Moscow end, before you spend too much time trying to figure out what it is, come to me."

She nods. This isn't too uncommon. Special operations are close-hold by nature, restricted to the handful of people directly involved. It could get messy to let one special operation, like her investigation, bleed into another. It could end up contaminating the cases, mislead you into thinking one had something to do with the other when there was no evidence to go on, nothing beyond your own suspicions. This is part of the clandestine life, being able to live with uncertainty, knowing you can never have all the pieces of the puzzle, knowing when you have enough of them.

"Speaking of the Station," she says, "I need to talk to Tom Cassidy, but he's not returning my messages. I was thinking of going to Hank—"

"You're not still on whatever it was that Masha Popov said to you?" Eric waves off the idea with his hands. "If there was anything to it, we would've found out by now . . . You probably haven't heard from Tom because he's helping me with this other operation. I'll ask him to get back to you—you don't have to get Hank involved." That decided, Eric settles back in his chair, a big smile on his face as he thinks about this other operation. "It has a lot of potential," he says, leaning back into the creaking chair. "Could be really big. I probably shouldn't talk about it, but . . . You heard about when COS Kiev was killed, right?"

"It was before my time, but yeah."

Eric swells with self-satisfaction. "Well, I think we're finally going to be able to bring the man behind the hit, Evgeni Morozov, to justice. That's a big deal to the seventh floor, you know. Something they've wanted for a long time."

"Aren't you a little bit daunted, to have to juggle so many potentially cataclysmic things?"

He chuckles. "No—it comes with being Chief of the Division. I guess I've gotten used to it. Life would be dull without it."

She's heard this about Eric, that he likes being the man on the flying trapeze. That he was this way before he moved up in management. Addicted to risk. There's a sign hanging above his desk in the office, like something a motivational speaker would say: NO RISK, NO REWARD.

"I think you're on the right track here, Lyndsey. It feels—right."

"I wish it weren't. You're not going to talk to anyone about this until I've had the chance to do more work, right?" Lyndsey isn't comfortable. There's something about Theresa's motives that seems incomplete, despite what Eric says. She wishes she felt more comfortable with what she's just done, admitting her suspicions about Theresa. Eric is technically responsible for this investigation. He has a right to be informed. And yet—as she walks out of his office—something doesn't feel right.

Lyndsey turns over her conversation with Eric as she drives home, still sick to her stomach for having voiced her suspicions about Theresa out loud.

Theresa has suffered. It doesn't feel right to have these suspicions about her. And now she's told Eric. She wants to trust him. She *should* trust him. He doesn't seem like others she'd known, eager to make a name for themselves and not caring who gets hurt in the process. Like the Chief of Station she'd worked for in Lebanon, or the managers in the Clandestine Service who sent her to Beirut hoping for the worst. She'd questioned it at the time—she was doing well with the Russian target, why move her to something different?—but she was told she needed to prove herself on unfamiliar ground. A real superstar will rise to the occasion, Chief of Station Beirut had told her with a glint in his eyes that she chose to ignore. She wanted to believe all the honey they poured in her ear.

Beirut. As it turned out, her enemies didn't have to lift a finger. She gave them all the ammo they needed to shoot her down.

Davis was the opposite of the men she'd tended toward in nearly every way: older, cynical, and worldly. She'd had no intention of getting serious with him. She had played it chaste in Moscow, not wanting to get a reputation, not with Reese looking over her shoulder, and besides, running Popov had kept her busy. As far as the Station knew when she arrived in Lebanon, she was a single woman. She was ready to have fun.

She figured wrong.

She had played into the hands of the people who wanted to see her fail. Not that she'd had a real nemesis. There was no one specific person out for her blood. No, the Clandestine Service brought her down for sport but also on principle: there would always be someone waiting to see you fall for no other reason than they thought you had succeeded too easily. And hadn't she gone and proved they were right? A smart woman wouldn't have taken up with Davis Ranford.

As Lyndsey walks up the steps to her apartment door, she wonders what Davis is doing at that very moment, wishes she could talk to him. He might not still be in Beirut: he might've been sent home, too. Consequences all around. She'd been kicked out of the country so fast that they'd had no chance to talk, and now it was wisest not to try to communicate. In the moment, she misses him fiercely.

It's not until she's kicked off her shoes that she thinks to check her phone and there it is: a little flag next to the pink secure messaging icon. From Masha. Lyndsey clicks it open hurriedly.

I think we are being followed. We need your help.

Can she be sure it's the FSB, Lyndsey wonders, then corrects herself. Of course, Masha would know: she grew up under the old Soviet regime, and her husband worked for internal security for decades.

Masha and her daughter are in danger. If they get pulled into the

FSB's net, being the wife and daughter of a traitor, who knows what might happen to them?

If it's Theresa who's put their lives at risk, all for some petty form of revenge . . . Lyndsey will never forgive her.

Go to your sister's dacha. Watch this app. I'll be in touch as soon as I can.

Lyndsey presses Send. She hopes it's a promise she can keep.

TWENTY-SIX

Theresa looks down at the notepad, the numbers swimming before her eyes. She is coding the message she needs to transmit to her handler, the ruthless Tarasenko, but she is getting lost in the rows and rows of numbers.

If she were being run by the book, she wouldn't be coding by hand. The Russians would've given her special equipment for burst transmissions or some other technical wizardry. Every time they try to communicate with each other it's a risk, the thread that tethers one to the other, damning if detected. Tremendous energy and cunning go into hiding those communications.

But because of the haste, she must make do: hand-coded messages sent through a messaging app, one that claims to be secure (end-to-end encryption, supposedly even the service provider can't read the messages and has no access to the encryption key) but Theresa is not sure she believes it. Her freedom and her husband's fate hang on it, after all.

She's been struggling with how much to tell Tarasenko. It's all calculations and risk. Tell the Russians no more than is absolutely necessary to achieve her ends. Hurt as few people as possible. She winces: she can't stop thinking about the man, Anton Kulakov, who was killed. She snuck a peek at the report, couldn't help herself though she knew she shouldn't. The twisted body, so much blood. It's all on her; there's no squirming out of that one. A few days have passed, the overwhelming guilt with it. Rationalizations creep into her head automatically: he knew the risks when he decided to sell secrets. It comes with the job. These seem hollow, even to her, but she clings to them. They are all she has to ward off the all-consuming guilt. Once she'd seen the pictures, she couldn't sleep, couldn't eat. It felt like she'd been punched in the gut. She was sick and wobbly all the time, feeling like the world had been turned upside down. They noticed around the office but she told them she felt under the weather, thought she might be coming down with a cold. She couldn't fool Brian, though. Exquisitely sensitive, he picked up her anxiety like a bloodhound. She had to get it together for his sake.

She taps the pen against the pad of paper. Tarasenko will want to know how CIA is reacting to Kulakov's death. You learn valuable things in the aftermath of the unexpected. Mistakes are made in the heat of confusion. If Theresa had been clear-headed, she would have used the moment for a better peek into the inner workings of the investigation. Pressed Westerling, maybe even risked asking Lyndsey a few questions.

Lyndsey. That's where Theresa feels the most guilt. She's grown to like her. It's too bad they hadn't been friends in the earlier days, when Lyndsey was one of the new, single girls looking for mentors to help them make sense of things. Lyndsey, she senses, would've been a good friend, someone who wouldn't have drifted away when the political fallout came after Richard's death. Now, being Theresa's friend is a career risk.

Theresa looks down at the rows of numbers, neatly printed out in her precise hand. She will have to run these sheets through the shredder, afterward. Leave no trace.

Tarasenko will be expecting a message. She left a blue ball in the playground, signaling that she'd be in touch soon—hating that they must involve her son's favorite playground, knowing it meant some Russian agent was watching it day in and out. Tarasenko would be enjoying her discomfort, eating it up.

What kind of sicko uses a playground in a covert operation?

She spent the day thinking about what she would write. It's not like there aren't things she could tell them. But she doesn't want to be invaluable, so the FSB will pressure her to remain in position. She doesn't want to be the FSB's star asset. The flames of her anger have died down and now there are only glowing embers. Her desire for revenge has shrunk; all she really wants is her husband's freedom.

Now that she's home, door to the bedroom pressed firmly behind her, she has pulled the codebook out from a shoebox on the floor of her closet and begun her task.

CIA NOT BUYING POLICE REPORT, BELIEVE FSB BEHIND KULAKOV'S DEATH. ADVISE GREATER DISCRETION WITH NESTEROV. SEARCH FOR DOUBLE AGENT CONTINUES.

REQUEST EXFILTRATION BE MOVED UP.

Her gaze flits over the words. Reading between the lines, it calls them idiots for making it too obvious. They've made it too hot for her to stay. They've put her at risk, but they know that, of course. Their pride and vanity are more important than any asset.

But she knew that going in. That's the way it's always been, the way the game has always been played.

That's why she trusts no one but herself. Depends on no one but herself.

She signs it, *Kanareyka*.

TWENTY-SEVEN

The next few days are difficult for Lyndsey.

She tells Eric about the latest message from Masha, hoping he'll agree it's their duty to help.

"I'm afraid there's nothing we can do for her right now," he says flatly.

Lyndsey's blood pressure spikes. "How can you say that? Her husband is dead and it's our fault—"

That seems to touch a nerve with Eric, and his face goes red. "We'll do something as soon as we can, but you've got to stall her. With my other operation about to go off, Moscow Station is stretched thin. I can't put anything else on their plate right now."

She doesn't know how to argue against that. She knows how important Morozov is to Eric, to the Agency.

"Keep her at the dacha. We'll come for her as soon as we can," he promises. It's not the answer she wanted, but it's the best she'll get at the moment. She bites her tongue. Sometimes the job is like juggling knives.

That afternoon, Lyndsey sits in on a briefing being done especially for

Eric. It's in the big, fancy conference room down the hall. It has tiers of seats along three of its walls, like an operating theater. In the center, on the floor, is the big conference table, overpowering the room like something out of *Dr. Strangelove*. People pick random seats as they drift in, looking first to see who has already arrived.

Eric is the last one, everyone else shifting restlessly in their seats as they're made to wait for him. His eyes lock onto hers momentarily as he enters the conference room but then he takes his chair at the head of the table, his back to her.

The briefers tell a fascinating story: analysts found a huge spike in FSB activity after the recent deaths and disappearances. "On the day of Genghis's death, all senior FSB staff out of the Moscow area were recalled back to headquarters," the briefer says as a fresh PowerPoint slide pops up showing a map of Russia dotted with thumbnails of various officials. "Communications between Moscow, Washington, D.C., and other world capitals—the channels we're aware of—have been noticeably higher than is usual for this time of year," the briefer says. Another map, this time of the world, with graphs over various cities showing rates of increase.

"Meaning what, exactly?" Eric twitches in his chair, trying to hide his impatience.

The briefer coolly adjusts her eyeglasses on the bridge of her nose. "They wouldn't break op sec"—operational security—"if it wasn't impor-tant. The increase in unanticipated communications shows that they were caught off guard."

"By Popov's death?" Eric forgets to use the cover term; Evert Northrop, sitting in a shadowy corner, winces.

"It's impossible to know the reason for the increase by the timing alone. As you know, we don't have access to these communications. Most are encrypted."

Eric nods as she speaks, processing. "Were there no other notable events on those days? Something else the Russians might've been talking about?"

"Only routine activity. Nothing that we judged likely to be the reason for the increase." Lyndsey leaves the room turning this over in her mind. *Moscow was surprised. They hadn't expected Popov's death.*

She has little time to think about it, however, as today there was an important visitor.

Shortly after Lyndsey told Eric of her suspicions about Theresa, he decided they had reached the limit of what they could learn from the resources they had at hand, computer logs and access lists and what coworkers were willing to say. They had a suspect now. CIA cannot run surveillance on U.S. persons. For that, you have to turn to the FBI.

The move rattled Lyndsey. Was it too soon? Will it turn out The Widow was innocent all along and make her look like a fool? But she will give this much to Eric: he knew how to make things happen. By the end of the day, the court order was ready to go before a FISA judge. They caught up with the judge at a dinner party in Georgetown, briefed him in the butler's pantry, and by midnight had authority to wiretap Theresa's phones.

Maggie swings by Lyndsey's tiny office, giving her a quick nod. It's time for the meeting. Everything is hush-hush, because no one in the office can know what the meeting is about. It still seems incredible to Lyndsey that they are meeting with the FBI when Theresa's desk is only a hundred feet away.

The woman at the table in Eric's office looks like she stepped right out of the Texas Hill Country. She's tall and lanky with an aw-shucks friendly smile but an undeniable quiet confidence in her gray eyes, just the kind of person you'd feel good about entrusting with the civil liberties of your friends and neighbors. She wears a navy pants suit and no jewelry except a wristwatch with a plain black band, and her hair is cut in a short, no-nonsense style. "Special Agent Sally Herbert," the woman says as she rises and extends a hand. She explains that she's a squad supervisor in the Washington Field Office and will be leading the team working on this case. "We've set up a joint task force with Foreign Counterintelligence Division Five in the National Security Branch. They're pulling in people from the U.S. Attorneys office to start work on the warrants for your Russian agent's arrest. Don't worry; we're pulling in the absolute minimum to work this case. We all appreciate the sensitivity." Herbert addresses Eric. "We executed the wiretaps and put a team on her house the morning after the court order was signed. She's under coverage twenty-four seven."

Lyndsey feels a twinge. It's hard to see this happen to someone you know and once liked, for a once-respected colleague to be treated like a criminal. To have law enforcement watching your house through binoculars and taping your phone calls. She fights to remember that Theresa has brought this on herself.

"Have you gotten anything yet?" Eric asks.

One curt nod. "That's why I'm here. We got extremely lucky. She got a suspicious call early this morning. We think it was in a code of some kind."

"And the caller?" Lyndsey asks.

"In the U.S. but it wasn't a number we've seen before. We're still tracking it down." Herbert takes a piece of paper out of her portfolio and pushes it across the table at them. "This is the transcript."

WARNER: Hello?

CALLER [MALE VOICE, NO DISCERNIBLE ACCENT]: This is a courtesy
    call from North Star Realtors.

WARNER: Uh—yes?

CALLER: We're holding a seminar on selling your house in the current market. It's Thursday night at eight o'clock at the Bethesda Marriott on Pooks Hill Road—

WARNER: I'm sorry, I'm not looking to sell my home right now. But thank you for your call.

[HANGS UP]

Newman pushes the paper back at Herbert with an undercurrent of irritation. "Doesn't look like anything to me. What makes you think it's the Russians?"

"We couldn't find any business listed as North Star Realtors in this area," Herbert says, her voice level and calm, "and the Marriott says there's no such seminar booked for that location at that time."

"Did you catch a lucky break or do you research *every* call like that?" Lyndsey asks.

Herbert smiles. "I'd like to say yes, but we've seen the Russians use this technique in other cases. One of our agents remembered hearing the FSB use North Star Realtors before."

Lazy tradecraft. It's the little things that trip you up and give you away. "Does that mean they're going to rendezvous next Thursday evening?" Lyndsey asks.

"I'd say something's going to happen, though it might just be a dead drop with information about the real meeting. You can be sure we'll be watching Warner on Thursday night," Herbert says.

Eric perks up considerably. "This is a great catch. The sooner we can get this wrapped up, the better." As he walks Herbert to the door, Eric adds, "I want you to contact me the minute you get anything else. I want to be kept in the loop."

Herbert gives him a patient smile. "I appreciate your enthusiasm

Mr. Newman, but from here out, the FBI is in control. We require your cooperation, but we are talking about a criminal investigation. I expect you to keep me informed of any changes in Warner's behavior. Anything— no matter how small." She hands them each a business card.

After Herbert leaves, Eric closes the door before Lyndsey can follow. "This is bothering you. I can tell by the look on your face," he says.

"Well, of course. I'd have to be an ogre not to feel bad about it."

"You were the one to figure this out. You should be pleased," he says.

"I'd be more pleased to be wrong."

"Look, if she's innocent, surveillance will exonerate her." A grin slips over his face. Is *he* the one who's pleased? "Though it doesn't sound like that's going to happen, does it?"

As Lyndsey heads back to her office, she realizes that she's shaking. After talking to Herbert, it suddenly feels very real. And yet, despite all the evidence she's found, the way the clues point . . . She doesn't know what it is, but something doesn't feel right.

TWENTY-EIGHT

Lyndsey pulls up outside the address Theresa has given her. It rained earlier, and the sky is still gray. The street debris looks as if it was just pulled out of the washing machine. Wet leaves and bits of twig strewn all over the road. The porch lights are starting to come on, and a warm lambent glow radiates from kitchen windows.

In the driveway, there's a car under a cover in the distinctive shape of an older-model sports car. Richard Warner's famous Jaguar, like it's waiting for him to come home. The cover is slightly askew, as though it's been removed recently. Considering that the car must be worth a fortune, it's surprising that she hasn't sold it already. Frankly, it's a sign Lyndsey realizes she should've caught earlier: a clear indication that Theresa cannot let go.

Theresa's house is in a nice old neighborhood in McLean, the kind of place that people hired early by the Agency bought to be close to work. Though they're all retired now and have sold out to doctors and lawyers and businessmen who've remodeled away their former charm. Theresa's gray-shingled Cape Cod is modestly sized, but even small houses in

McLean fetch a lot of money. A million dollars for a three- or four-bedroom Colonial on a postage stamp of land. Too expensive for government salaries, really, so it probably means either Richard or Theresa has family money. There is a set of people at CIA who don't need the salary but are patriotic and want the James Bond experience. If there is money, it came before there was any question whether Theresa is working for the Russians. There's that, at least.

The invitation came the day before, as Lyndsey and Theresa were having coffee in the cafeteria. "Why don't you come over tomorrow night for dinner?" Theresa asked, studiously offhand.

Curious, that offer. The timing was suspicious. Why make the offer now? Did Theresa suspect that Lyndsey was on to her? Had she messed up—left notes on her desk where Theresa could've seen them? Maybe someone in CI slipped up. Or maybe one of the reports officers blabbed to Theresa—despite Lyndsey's explicit instructions.

Should she turn Theresa down? Lyndsey wasn't sure. It would be the safest course of action . . . But it might make Theresa suspicious. And there was an opportunity here.

It was a minefield, but Lyndsey's pulse quickened.

There was only one way to know if Theresa's up to something, and that was to call her bluff.

"Sure," she'd said, stirring the cream in her coffee. "I'd love to."

Theresa answers the door, an apron over the dress she wore that day at work, Brian hugging her leg. He strikes Lyndsey again as too small to be seven. He's short and thin, with arms like sticks and those huge eyes. She hopes that he'll warm up to her—they've met once already, for goodness' sake—but he looks up at her shyly, not smiling, before breaking away from his mother to skitter back into the house.

Lyndsey hands Theresa a bottle of wine, her contribution. The house smells of garlic and oregano. She hangs her purse on a row of hooks by the front door, next to a child's yellow rain slicker. "Thanks for having me over. I can't remember when I last had a home-cooked meal, and I'm not exaggerating."

"It's going to be simple. Spaghetti and meatballs. Brian's favorite."

The inside of the house is more interesting than the outside. There's obviously been some remodeling done. The back opens into a great room, albeit with a few strategically placed columns so that the overall effect is of a cozy den. Two overstuffed couches with well-worn red slipcovers are flanked on one side by floor-to-ceiling bookshelves. Bins of toys, mostly action figures and Legos, are lined up in the corner. Across the back of the room is a wall of mullioned windows looking onto a dense wood. It reminds Lyndsey a little of her dream house, the one she thought she'd own once she married.

While Theresa finishes cooking—steam rising from the sink as she drains pasta, the rattle of china and cutlery—Lyndsey makes a slow lap of the family room. She tries to engage Brian, who sits on one of the sofas watching television, but he studiously ignores her, curled up around himself like a true introvert, a pillow in his lap like a shield.

"Can I look around the house? It's so lovely . . ." Lyndsey calls over her shoulder.

"Sure," Theresa replies from the kitchen. "Help yourself."

So, Lyndsey takes a little tour of the house. Glancing through open doorways, peeking into closets. What is she looking for? She's not sure . . . Signs that things have changed or that she's preparing for something, perhaps . . . Stockpiling, packing. Suitcases dragged out of storage, boxes marked for Goodwill. And the house does seem a bit at ends, like Theresa has been clearing things out of storage, but couldn't that be innocent, signs of a widow getting on with her life?

She pauses at an arrangement of framed photos in the hallway. So many pictures of Richard. It is indeed the man she remembers from her first years at the Agency. The same serious, intelligent expression. He wears glasses with small lenses, well proportioned for his face, and his brown hair is on the shaggy side and starting to gray. He could be a professor, or an accountant, but not a case officer. Not an action hero. No James Bond. Proof that still waters run deep.

Most are family photos, however. The three of them on a mountain top—family trip to Old Rag? Richard and Brian mugging together in front of the red Jaguar. Richard in an overcoat, the wind teasing hair over his eyes. Theresa and Richard in festive clothes, sitting in a pew—taken at someone's wedding? They look so happy together, so made for each other. She looks at the constellation of photos, meant to reassure somebody. She once would've assumed it's for Brian's benefit but now she knows better. It is a sign of Theresa's devotion.

She tiptoes upstairs. The first room she comes to is obviously Brian's: a single bed dressed in flannel sheets decorated with rocket ships, stars, and moons. A huge globe and a row of plastic dinosaurs sit on a shelf, posters of national parks on the walls. The second room is the master bedroom, so austere in grays and cream that it is a cipher. A tall mirror on a wooden easel stands in the corner, turned to an angle, reflecting nothing.

The door is ajar to the third room—the last room. Lyndsey stands back in the hall, straining to see in. The room looks unused, simple blinds on the windows, a bare bulb in the ceiling fixture. Cardboard boxes sit haphazardly in the middle of the floor. Lyndsey tiptoes in and peers into one of the boxes.

Clothing. Men's clothing. They have to be Richard's. At first, the sight makes Lyndsey sad. The Widow is packing up her husband's clothes, finally ready to get on with her life. But then, she thinks: *if she's packing them up to give away, why* now? *Can there be another reason?*

She touches the top item in the box. Is there a *tag* on that sweater? Could it be *new*?

She's about to pick it up when a voice rises from the kitchen. "Dinner's ready," Theresa calls. Feeling unfinished, Lyndsey heads back downstairs.

They start with salad and a plate of kid-friendly carrot sticks and grape tomatoes for Brian. Theresa draws her son out so that by the time they progress to the main course, he is talking to Lyndsey, telling her about his favorite subjects at school and what his day was like.

There are furtive glances in her direction as he toys with his noodles. Lyndsey can't help but want to ask him if his mother has been acting strangely. "So, Brian," she says as casually as possible. "What's new? Is there anything coming up that you're looking forward to?"

Theresa glances in her direction. Does she think that's a strange question? There is the slightest flash of something on her face, but she keeps eating. A nibble of pasta, a sip of wine.

Brian tilts his head like a bird. After consideration, he says, "We have a class trip coming up. We're going to look at moon rocks."

Is Theresa's faint smile one of triumph? Has she coached her son not to give away any secrets? "At the National Air and Space Museum. I'm going to be one of the chaperones."

Lyndsey puts on a smile. "That sounds like fun."

The conversation moves on to other topics, whether to enroll Brian in Cub Scouts or a science club and where they will go on summer vacation this year. The normal talk of normal families.

"I'm sorry he's so shy," Theresa says later, when her son has gone upstairs to do homework. She rinses dishes and stacks them in the dishwasher while Lyndsey scrapes leftovers into plastic containers. "He's had a hard time of it since he lost his father."

Lyndsey remembers the first few years after her own father died—was she that shy? Worse, probably. Then she thinks of a button to push, a way to see what's on Theresa's mind. "That's understandable," she finally says. "Maybe he needs a male figure in his life. You know, a father figure."

Theresa's eyes flash. Anger simmers below the surface. It's the first time Lyndsey's seen her like this. The air practically crackles. "What are you saying? That I owe it to my son to get married again?"

"I'm not saying marriage." She backtracks to more manageable territory but finds she wants to keep going. "You're still a young woman—don't you ever think about finding someone new? You could have children . . . Give Brian a brother or sister. That might help him . . ."

Her laugh is mirthless. "That doesn't seem like the best reason to bring another child into the world. Or to get married, for that matter." Her eyes narrow. She hefts up her wineglass a little too quickly. "Where is all this coming from? Why the sudden interest in seeing me married off?"

"I didn't say—"

Theresa cuts her off. "I'm not ready to move on. I can admit it. I still love Richard. This is not open for discussion."

Then she gives Lyndsey a small smile, a reconciliation. They retreat to the sofas, Theresa pouring the last of the wine into Lyndsey's glass. *Is she trying to get me drunk?* Lyndsey tries to remember how much wine Theresa has had.

Theresa runs a hand through her hair. "This is nice. I'm not used to having friends over. I can't remember the last time I got together with someone. Too busy worrying about Brian, I guess. And maybe I got to be too . . . oh, I don't know . . . notorious? Who wants to be friends with 'The Widow,' anyway?" Her smile is an invitation to talk. But what does Theresa want her to talk about?

They sip, wait each other out. It's a bit nerve-wracking but Lyndsey learned this at Penn: you can't rush the subject. They're going to speak when they're ready and rushing it will only ruin things, drive them in the directions you subconsciously want them to go. *Let them decide.* She takes the smallest sips possible, making the wine last. She doesn't want to drink too much, risk a slipup.

Finally, Theresa speaks, filling in the awkward silence. "So, how is the investigation going? Making any progress?"

It's the first time Theresa has asked, and as much as she's trying to play it cool, there's the slightest hint of interest in her voice. This is an opportunity to try for a reaction from Theresa, to try to get her to misstep, to wobble. It's not without risk: you don't want to push her too far, to spook her.

As Lyndsey is thinking it over, however, Theresa decides to press. "Who was that you were meeting with yesterday? In Eric's office? I didn't recognize her."

Bingo. She has to be talking about Sally Herbert. Lyndsey didn't think Theresa was at her desk when she and Eric had met with Sally. *She's more on top of things than I think.* "She's with the FBI." Will this make Theresa realize this could mean wiretaps and surveillance?

Theresa forges on anyway.

"Oh? So, you must have a suspect, then?" There is an unmistakable quaver in Theresa's voice. Lyndsey just shrugs. Maybe this admission will push Theresa, make her more desperate. Force her to make a mistake if she goes forward.

By unspoken agreement, they stop. Lyndsey feels the tension in the air as she carries the glasses to the sink while Theresa goes upstairs to get her son ready for bed. She's set the trap: now to see if Theresa walks into it.

She listens to the sound of their voices, mother and son, without being able to make out the words. The gentle negotiation of bedtime. There's something reassuring about those two tones together, Brian's voice high and singsong, like he's reciting nursery rhymes, Theresa's even and slightly melodic. It makes her feel slightly guilty for what she's done. If things go as planned—as hoped—she'll be putting Theresa away in jail. Brian will be without either of his parents. What will happen to him? Theresa's mentioned that her mother is still living—could she take care of a young grandson?

Lyndsey shakes her head, as though it can rid her of these unpleasant thoughts. Whatever happens to Brian, it's not her fault. That was Theresa's decision. It's all been Theresa's decision.

It's tense and unpleasant when Theresa sees her to the front door, hugging herself against the cold as Lyndsey slips on her raincoat. It's a few hours to midnight and tomorrow is a workday. They smile grimly at each other, and Lyndsey fancies it's an acknowledgment of what they both know. Where they stand.

The battle lines are drawn, the end is near. There's only one question left to answer: who will prevail?

"Thanks for a lovely evening." The words slip from Lyndsey with a crisp edge.

"See you in the office tomorrow," Theresa says as she closes the door.

TWENTY-NINE

Lyndsey sits in a cocoon of darkness.

It's completely still in the office. So quiet, you can hear the tick of the minute hand on the big office clock. She didn't go home after dinner but went back to work. Maybe she's not as hard as she'd like to think. The evening with Theresa has shaken her. She can't help but worry that she's wrong, that she's made a mistake. Was Theresa acting guilty? In the moment, she'd wanted to believe that, but now . . . She's not so sure.

According to the FBI transcript, the Russians will make contact with Theresa shortly. If Lyndsey's missed anything, she needs to know.

She pores over her notes one more time, looking for some overlooked tidbit that will exonerate the accused. Lyndsey wants to be wrong about Theresa. It would be a relief to be wrong. And there are so many pieces to this puzzle that it's entirely possible that she could've missed or misunderstood something. It's her duty to double- and triple-check.

She's not wrong. There is the serial number of Theresa's computer trying to access the restricted files for Lighthouse, Skipjack, and Genghis.

Though the way she tried to access Genghis's file looks a little different.

Check. We've identified this already. One of the reports officers confirmed that Theresa chatted her up.

Still, something niggles at Lyndsey. She bats it away.

There's nothing to debate. She's been caught dead to rights. Surveillance has Theresa being contacted by a suspected Russian agent. *We'll catch her red-handed and it'll be all over. It's almost over.*

She's a traitor.

Lyndsey flicks a page of an old report, a paper copy. Her eyes are tired. She debates calling it a night.

Her eye falls on a cover term, Razorbill. It's the first time she's seen it. The memo seems to refer to some horrible op that ended in disaster, ended so badly that it's been hidden under a complete blackout of secrecy. She's pretty sure this is the cover term that's been redacted on a few of the reports she's seen associated with Richard Warner's disastrous mission. They've been very careful to keep this one out of the records but here it is slipped out. Fat black ink covers up the most tantalizing pieces of text.

She flips to the front of the folder. THERESA WARNER, it reads in block letters. Why is this report in Theresa's file?

Razorbill has something to do with Theresa. She sits back, her thoughts starting to race. It's only right that Lyndsey knows what it is. The woman's future depends on it.

Why wasn't she told about the compartment earlier? It's not out of the realm of possibility that it's so obscure and so restricted that the very few people who were involved have forgotten about it or moved on and would certainly not know of Lyndsey's task. She's not ready to ascribe ill intent on anyone's part—yet.

Tomorrow, she can contact Raymond Murphy and set him to run this down. Find out what Razorbill is, get her access if it's warranted.

But . . . things don't always move quickly in this bureaucracy. Sometimes it feels like the more people who get involved, the worse it is.

The Russians could make contact with Theresa at any minute and they have no idea what form this contact will take, or what might happen. If things bog down, it might be too late. Razorbill might be nothing, and it'd be a disaster to pull the plug at this late date. It certainly would upset some people, sour senior management. *Do you know what you're doing or don't you?*

She needs someone very high in management to grant her immediate access to the compartment. Her gaze drifts down to the chat window tucked in the corner of her monitor. It's nearly empty, just the names of one or two of her die-hard friends still burning the midnight oil.

But there's one particular name with a blinking green square next to it. Patrick Pfeifer. Patrick is very high up now, the Director's Chief of Staff. He had been interested in her research when she was first hired—just doing his job, maybe, encouraging new hires, but they'd stayed in touch over the years. A word of congratulations when she'd gotten the Moscow posting, that sort of thing. He seems like a nice guy, one of the good ones—or is she being naïve?

She hesitates again. If she's wrong, or wrong to ask this man so directly, at this hour, she could burn this bridge forever.

She clicks on Pfeifer's name. A little window pops up. *Good evening, Patrick,* she types.

Before she can finish, a response pops up. *You're working late tonight, Lyndsey. What can I do for you?*

Now she doesn't hesitate. *I need your help.*

F ive minutes later, she's sitting in Pfeifer's office.

In some ways, he looks much like the man she met over a decade ago in the alumni center at Penn, asking questions about her studies. His hair at the time was the palest blond she'd ever seen and so she can't even tell if he's starting to go white. There are unmistakably more lines on his face, particularly around his eyes. He's tall, though the desk and chair swallow most of that height.

She's never been to this office before, let alone at a few minutes to midnight. It's nice, as befits the number-three man at the Agency, but not as luxurious as Lyndsey would've thought. The furniture all looks a little old, like it's been here through several changes of administration. Pfeifer looks worn, too, though the dimness helps to hide that. The lights are low in deference to overworked eyes. His smile is tired and his shoulders slump. But he doesn't seem annoyed in the least to be bothered at this hour.

He listens to her without interrupting, though as she speaks, she becomes aware of how many holes there are in her story. Her heart sinks as she explains, but her mind races: *what was I thinking? I'm making a fool of myself.*

When Lyndsey stops speaking, Pfeifer remains silent. He leans back in his chair, steepling his fingers. "I knew Richard Warner, you know. Good man. I don't know all the particulars of his case . . . and I don't think I was read into Razorbill, or I've forgotten if I ever was . . ." It's understandable; there must be hundreds, if not thousands, of compartments and the top men theoretically have access to all of them. Finally, he shakes his head once as though chasing the thought away. "Theresa Warner . . . The Agency didn't do everything it could've for her. I want to make sure we're right here. If there's even the slightest chance we could be mistaken . . ."

He picks up the phone and punches a few buttons. "Hello—who's on the floor tonight? Put her through." He must be calling the Watch, the round-the-clock center that runs things when the day shift has gone home. The Agency in miniature. Theoretically, it has the power to do anything that could be done by the regular shift, call in the Director if necessary.

"Oh hi, Rosalind. This is Pat. I need you to give Lyndsey Duncan immediate access to everything you have on Razorbill. Can you do that? Thanks." He hangs up. The expression on his face hasn't changed but he's just done something remarkable: he's done in five seconds what could've taken days of phone calls and waiting. "Go down to the vault: they should have the file pulled and ready for you. If not, let me know. I'll be here another hour, at least."

Lyndsey has never liked heading down to the vault.

She's only had to do it a couple times in her career, make the long, twisting trek in the basement to the giant room that holds all the special files. It reminds her of police evidence lockers, which she has only seen on television. But the feeling is the same: a lonely room full of important but forgotten things. A lone figure sitting in the cage like a prisoner, like he's done something wrong and this is his punishment.

She only knows one of the men who man the vault on a twenty-four-hours-a-day basis. Jim Purvis, one of the real old-timers. She thinks it's a little criminal to let someone work at that age, but she's heard a story about Jim, so odd that it can't be true, that he actually threatened to go public with secrets—spill his guts online, post them on Facebook or Twitter, anywhere he could—if they *didn't* give him a job. He hated being away from this world so much that he couldn't stand it, couldn't function outside. Luckily, Jim is not on duty this night. Tonight, it's a bored-looking younger man with a goatee, reading a paperback science fiction novel. As Pfeifer predicted, the file is waiting for her.

Behind the closed door of her office, Lyndsey looks at this thing that was so hard to get. Made of pale green heavy-duty card stock banded with red on the cover. TOP SECRET, it reads, and handwritten underneath, *Razorbill.* The file is thin, holding only a few reports.

The paper smells musty. She looks at the list of records, only about five in all. The first one seems to be notes taken at a closed-door meeting. Judging from the short list of attendees—the Director and Deputy of the Clandestine Service, head of Human Resources, and a few names she doesn't recognize—it had to be about something pretty serious.

MEMORANDUM FOR THE RECORD

August 13, 2016

Subject: RAZORBILL

Meeting with Chief Russia Division (Newman) held at 13:51 when Front Office was informed by COS Moscow of an unauthorized exfiltration attempted today by Agency personnel. Newman felt his authorization alone was sufficient to attempt exfiltration of asset PENNANTRACE. Newman claims he opted to use contract help for exfiltration and did not inform Moscow Station of the operation because imminent threat to PENNANTRACE resulted in an abbreviated timeline.

A creeping sense of foreboding comes over Lyndsey as she rereads that opening. An unauthorized operation on Russian soil? This is against all the rules. First, it's unthinkable for the chief of a division back here in Langley to okay a mission in another country without bringing the Chief of Station in on it. It's a sacred rule of the Clandestine Service. This alone would make the director and his deputy furious. How did Eric manage to hang on to his job?

She continues reading, her pulse accelerating with every word. This *is* about Richard Warner, what really happened when he went to Moscow to try to rescue his asset. What she reads doesn't track with the stories Theresa and Eric have told her.

Time was of the essence, Eric is quoted in the transcript as saying. *Olga Boykova was still at large but the police and the FSB were looking for her. It was only a matter of time before she was caught.*

The logical choice would have been for the Station to send someone to meet her and hide her in a safe house until they could smuggle her out of the country, but that didn't happen—whether it was because Warner didn't trust the Station or knew Boykova would meet with no one besides him, wasn't clear. The Station was kept in the dark. Which is crazy. Heresy.

This is a huge breach of policy, Newman. This from the head of the Clandestine Service. Lyndsey works the dates backward: it would've been Roger Barker, of the legendary temper. *You can be terminated for this.*

In the stories she's heard Eric tell, the exfiltration was *both* their idea, his and Richard's. But according to the transcript Eric says, *Richard insisted. We were peers, I didn't feel I could override him. Boykova was his biggest case. His star asset. I felt it was Richard's call. I didn't think I could take this away from him. He said he would take the blame if things went wrong.*

The transcript doesn't track with the legend. Of course, the transcript contains only Eric's side. Maybe, after it blew up in his face, he lost his nerve and put the blame on the man who wasn't there. It's easy to imagine the scene, Barker's face getting redder and redder as he yells and rants.

The transcript gets worse and worse. *We put together a team of independent contractors—*mercenaries—*willing to go to Moscow.* Lyndsey had worked with guys who fell in this category, former military and security services who'd served in lawless places like Somalia, Afghanistan, Sudan. It's not clear from the report whether Eric has used these men in previous operations or if they were unknown, but that would be another red flag, another indication of how rushed and desperate Richard and Eric were in throwing this fiasco together.

Too bad we can't interview them, Barker is recorded as saying. *Moscow Station says they're all dead. It was suicide, and that's why you didn't tell anyone else what you were doing.*

Boykova had betrayed Putin himself; worked in his house, lived under his roof. In passing secrets to the CIA, she made the FSB look like fools. It doesn't get any more personal than that. The FSB was not going to let her get away, it would've meant their heads, not to mention their balls.

We flew everyone in under cover. They rendezvoused at 2300 local time to go over the extraction plan and then deployed along the route. This is all from Eric.

Richard went in alone to meet Boykova. She was hiding in the boiler room of an apartment building in Tverskaya, hadn't stuck her head out in three days, likely starving and dehydrated. Richard got her close to the safe house—a street in the neighborhood of Arbat is given—*when the Russians closed in. Apparently, they'd been tracking them all along.*

How did the Russians find out about the op? the head of Special Operations demands. The transcript shows that Eric has no answer.

It appears to have been a slaughter. Station picked up police chatter about a shootout in the area of the safe house. Seven dead, specifically. One alive. We assume the one still living was Boykova.

That makes sense: they'd want to take her alive, to eventually suffer something painful and drawn out before her eventual death. At this point, there is no word on Richard, but he is presumed dead. If he is lucky, he will have died on the scene.

This is a colossal clusterfuck. Barker again.

Has the ambassador been notified? Westinghouse is an asshole. He's going to go ballistic. He'll throw us out of country for sure. Deputy Director of Operations.

Eric is dismissed from the meeting, but the record shows he was spoken of harshly. Barker talks about going to the Director of CIA to demand Eric be fired. He has exceeded his authority. He's responsible for the loss of one officer and the death of British and American contractors.

But what is he guilty of, exactly, the director of Special Operations asks.

Fucking terrible judgment, the deputy director of Operations says.

He didn't order Richard Warner to go on this suicide mission. Warner asked for it. And if a few mercenaries get killed, what of it? That's why we hire them, because they're expendable and because no one will hear about it.

The transcript ends inconclusively.

Hands trembling, Lyndsey turns to the next one. It's a cable from Moscow Station, two days later, sent in a special channel that's for the Director, CIA. She can see that it was later turned around to a handful of seniors in what is now the Razorbill compartment.

She runs a finger under each line as she reads, reading it a second time to be sure. The report starts out by saying Ambassador Westinghouse is furious with the Station. There is radio silence from the Russian foreign ministry. It's like being in the eye of a storm. They know that something may happen at any moment, but they don't know what. All operations have been placed on lockdown in the meanwhile, sure that the Russians will use any excuse to roll up their officers.

But in the meanwhile, the Station comes in with a bombshell: Carousel, a reliable asset, has reported that the FSB is holding an American spy, a CIA officer. He was captured in a firefight, trying to smuggle a traitor out of the country.

Richard Warner. They have no name, but who else could it be?

Station reports that they are trying to corroborate the asset's story as well as obtain additional information, but their assets have scurried for cover, afraid to pop their heads up from the foxholes, afraid the FSB is waiting for them. There is nothing to do but sit and wait. Someone has hand-scribbled in a corner of the page, *Russian demands?*

Lyndsey leans back in her chair. Her chest is tight, her head swirling. She realizes she has been holding her breath.

Richard Warner was alive. At one point, anyway.

Funny. She notices a small red smudge on the upper-right-hand side of the page. Blood? No, too bright for that. Strange.

But she dismisses it. This isn't the last report, after all. There are a few sheets of paper to go. Taking a deep breath, she starts the last one.

Another memorandum for the record recording another meeting. Two flimsy sheets of paper. This is where they find out Richard is dead, Lyndsey reckons. This is where they learn he was killed by the FSB, dying in a Russian prison hospital, and that the vindictive Russians refuse to return the body.

Except it's not.

For a formal memorandum, the words are hot and visceral and jump off the page. The meeting starts in outrage, but at least Eric has managed to hold on to his position, if only by his fingertips. He tells the assembled group of furious, fuming Agency seniors that the Russians have refused to acknowledge that anything ever happened, their silence deafening. Moscow Station has speculated it's because Putin cannot have the truth get out, that one of his housekeepers had the temerity to spy on him, to ferry secrets out from under his nose. It would embolden a whole class of Russians—the serfs—to rise up against the oligarchs. It would be the start of the French Revolution on the banks of the Moskva River.

The FSB has made no demands? No offer to trade Richard Warner for one of their traitors? Not even for Aldrich Ames or Robert Hanssen, their most successful recruits? CIA seniors are clearly flummoxed.

And, surely, they mean a trade for Richard Warner's body. The man is dead.

The language is clear: there's no reference to Richard in the past tense. The understanding is that the man is alive.

What can we do? Barker asks. *We can't leave him to rot in a Russian prison. We owe Richard more than that.*

Richard didn't go through proper channels, the Deputy Director says. *He knew the risk he was taking. He didn't expect to be bailed out if things got out of hand.*

There's nothing we can do, Moscow Chief of Station weighs in. The Russians refuse to even acknowledge anything happened. *They will deny that they have Richard Warner, and if we press the point, we risk exposing CAROUSEL. I'm not going to lose this asset—we've lost enough of them because of this fiasco.*

Fiasco. The word must've dripped like acid onto Eric's skin. He was already in water hot enough to boil him alive. All his years on the Russia target, his reputation, going up in smoke.

Risk big or go home—wasn't that always Eric's motto?

But not Richard's. Yes, there's something here that niggles at Lyndsey, like a buzzing gnat.

Finally, the Director weighs in. *Our hands are tied. There's nothing we can do for Richard, poor bastard. Maybe the Russians will change their mind one day. For now, we let it go. Seal the records.*

No one speaks up, according to the report.

And Theresa? The Deputy Director asks the question.

Tell her nothing. Let her think that her husband is dead.

Who could be so heartless to keep this from Theresa? Lyndsey wonders. That director, the political appointee, the one before Chester-field? Some outsider, oblivious to the Agency's obligation to its people.

It's right there on the page, who said it.

Eric Newman.

Eric Newman told them to keep this information from her.

It went on: *We don't know that we'll ever get him back. Let her get on with her life. There's no reason for her to suffer for his mistake. Isn't it better for her this way?*

No one objects. Not the Director, not the Deputy Director. No one speaks up for Theresa.

I swear she'll never know, Eric goes on. *It remains on the seventh floor. We'll be the only ones to know.*

And it's done.

Lyndsey pushes away from her desk, her heart pounding in her chest like she's just run a marathon at a sprinter's pace.

This is unbelievable—and yet it is completely plausible. In the clandestine service, you hear rumors of assets captured by foreign security services and left to rot in jail for years and years. It's the risk they all acknowledge and accept.

But it only happens to assets, foreigners who decide to give away their country's secrets. This doesn't happen to CIA officers. There are always secret negotiations, trades for an adversary's agent languishing in a U.S. prison. Right? That's what the Clandestine Service would have its new hires believe.

Two years in a Russian prison. Lyndsey can only imagine what it must be like for Richard.

And Theresa . . . They decided she would never be told. *Eric* made the suggestion, the men in suits backed him up. Left his friend to rot in a Russian prison, to be tortured, maybe even killed, and leave the wife thinking he was gone forever. And all the stories Eric's told, over and over, making him look like the good guy, the hero who fought for her . . . Lyndsey feels a stab in her chest like a cold dagger plunged deep.

There is no indication that Theresa ever found out the truth, but if she did . . .

There is her motivation for working with Russia. To get back at CIA for their betrayal.

Lyndsey's stomach drops, like being pushed off a cliff.

This is a tangled, tangled web of deceit. And at the heart of it, The Widow, bruised and battered.

THIRTY

First thing in the morning, Lyndsey marches into Eric Newman's office. It's seven thirty. She's barely slept, thanks to the Razorbill reports she read hours earlier, still percolating like a narcotic in her veins. Luckily, at this hour Russia Division is nearly empty, just the same early birds hunched over their monitors, the same blue light flickering in the dimness. None of them pay attention to her as she heads straight to Eric's office and closes the door.

His head jerks up at the sudden intrusion. "I'm getting ready for the eight thirty stand-up. Can this wait?" No smile, no "good morning." It's like he was expecting her. Perhaps there was an email in his inbox from the Watch, letting him know someone was given access to the Razorbill compartment last night.

She folds her arms across her chest. "Were you going to tell me about Richard Warner?"

The energy seems to go right out of him. Then he stiffens. He pushes back from his desk but remains in the chair, looking up at her. "So, you know—"

"About Razorbill, yes. A mention slipped through sanitization. I was read into the compartment last night," she says, not wanting Eric to cut her off before she can ask all her questions.

He almost seems relieved that she knows, as though he's wanted to say something all along. "You don't know the half of it." He rises to his feet and starts to pace, full of a wild energy. "It was *hell*. I thought I was going to get brought up on charges. I *would've*, if Roger Barker had his way."

Few people survive a clash with Barker, head of the Clandestine Service. He looks like your sweet old grandfather but is rumored to play as rough as legally possible. *What big teeth you have, Grandfather. The better to eat you up with, my dear.*

"You let Theresa think her husband was dead."

"It wasn't my idea."

"That's not what the transcript said."

An expression passes over his face, angry, then gone. Tamped down. "I don't know what's in this transcript you're talking about . . . It's a mistake, then. Maybe done on purpose, to make those snakes in the room look better. You know I'd never do that to Theresa. You've heard me defend Richard—and try to protect Theresa."

Yes, she has. "Does Theresa know Richard is alive?"

"What difference does it make?" He sounds miserable.

"Motive, Eric. It gives her a motive to go to the Russians."

His face reads *pain*. His brows furrow and the corners of his mouth collapse. "She knows. Jack Clemens made a deathbed confession. I guess he wanted to clear his conscience."

She heard about Clemens's death. He had been Eric's deputy for a long time, even though he was much older than Eric and that he was past the time to be running things. Some grumbled that Eric made him deputy precisely because he wasn't very good. He got a cushy position and plenty of time to play golf and in return, stayed out of Eric's hair and never made him look bad. Why else would Eric carry him all these years? the skeptics asked. Others swore there was nothing nefarious in it, that Eric was just doing a favor for an old man and helping preserve his dignity.

There were two sides to everything. What mattered, and what was almost impossible to find out, which was the truth? "And when was that?" she asks.

There's that frown again. There's definitely something wrong with Eric's frown, a complexity that defies classification. *An indicator that's being repressed.* "Jack died in early May."

Lyndsey works through the months in her head: if Theresa had acted on Clemens's information right away, the timing fits. "Did she come to you? Did she ask for your help?"

"Does it matter? I told her there was nothing I could do, because there wasn't. The seventh floor wasn't going to change their minds. I didn't think she'd go to the Russians, for god's sake. I would've reported her if I thought she was a danger." He stands up. "Look, what you saw in that file made you mad, I get it. It certainly doesn't paint me in a flattering light."

"Eric, I *want* to believe you. I want to be on your side. Be straight with me: why didn't you tell me about Richard? *You* put me in charge of this investigation—I should've known."

He turns on his heel and starts pacing. "It was highly compartmented, one of the Agency's most closely held secrets . . . I didn't think they would give it to you. Because of what happened in Beirut."

That stings.

He continues, not stopping for air, rolling over her. "What does it matter, anyway? You figured it out for yourself. I didn't have to tell you. You got to the truth on your own. And—how did that happen, exactly? How were you able to see this transcript?"

"I saw the cover term in a report in one of the old files. I went to Patrick Pfeifer in the middle of the night—"

Eric switches from controlled to ballistic in the blink of an eye. "You went to the Chief of Staff, behind my back?"

There's a nasty edge in his voice. "Not behind your back—he was available, we know each other . . . slightly. I saw there was a compartment and asked him to get me access. It took five minutes." Then, she thinks to add, "We didn't discuss the case."

Eric is quiet. Lyndsey knows there's more to this investigation than meets the eye. There's more she's not seeing—yet. Like most everything at the Agency. A long hall of smoke and mirrors.

Then suddenly, he's across the room, standing right in front of her. "What happened with Richard was one of the worst moments of my life, personally and professionally, and I'm willing to talk to you about it—just not now, okay? I have to get ready for the stand-up and I don't want to be thinking about all this while I'm standing in front of the Director." He's searching her eyes, trying to read her. He wants to know if she believes him. "You can trust me, Lyndsey. I brought you into this, didn't I? Made your problem go away?"

What's going on? She feels as though she's a step behind, that she's missing something. Eric hasn't answered her question, not really: why didn't he tell her that Richard Warner was still alive? Was it nothing more than an honest lapse in judgment, as he says?

He turns his back to her, gathering the things he needs from his desk. Portfolio, pen. "Don't let this rattle you. We're almost there, Lyndsey. Keep your eye on the ball: Theresa is the bad guy here. This could be the biggest catch for Russia Division since—since you brought in Yaromir Popov. Keep working it—but come to me first, if you learn anything more, understand?" And then he's gone, leaving Lyndsey alone under the harsh glare of office lights, wondering what just happened.

THIRTY-ONE

W ell, well, well.

A few weeks ago, from across the office, Theresa watched Lyndsey in conversation with Jan Westerling.

As everyone in the office knew, her asset was just found dead. Westerling was young, so this may well have been the first person she has known, personally, to die. And to die so horribly, so violently. She was shaken so badly that she burst into tears in the office, not a good place to display emotions, especially the weak, "female" kind. Someday she'll rue it, realize it set her back in ways she couldn't know.

Theresa remembers the incident now, and tries to tamp down the accompanying wave of panic. Who else might Lyndsey have spoken to? Theresa should've thought of this earlier, done something about it. What else is she forgetting?

It's exhausting being on high alert all the time. When was the last time Theresa did her actual job? She should be going over the reports coming in from Moscow Station but it's nothing but low-level assets, handled by bored case officers who have been going through the motions for years. She's supposed to read these reports and put the pieces together, to see the bigger picture. Occasionally she is asked to translate, her Russian that good fifteen years after college. She hasn't done any real work for days, maybe weeks, but it would be easy to catch up before anyone asks.

If something else doesn't happen first.

All she can think about now is keeping two steps ahead of Lyndsey and the investigation. She listens for footsteps behind her, waits for the hand of an officer from Security to fall on her shoulder. *You're coming with us, ma'am.*

But this hasn't happened.

After a minute—checking her watch, pretending to be thinking of some important thing, a reason to be standing in the aisle like this—Theresa turns around and scoots through a little-used back door into the hall. Once outside the vault, she feels better. It's less likely that she'll be observed out here. People come and go up and down the hall, and no one takes note. She joins them, walking with just enough purpose to give the impression she's on her way to a meeting.

Lyndsey was talking to Jan Westerling. It could be coincidence: maybe Lyndsey saw Westerling crying and wanted to comfort her, but Theresa senses that wasn't it. Lyndsey isn't integrated into the office yet. She's not part of the team. She doesn't know Westerling, and isn't the den mother type. Lyndsey was talking to Westerling for a reason.

It's obvious what she's doing: she's talking to the reports officers for the three Russian assets. She's trying to put the pieces together. Theresa listens to the sound of her own heels echo off the walls. Loud and sharp and insistent, drawing attention to her. *You'd better run away. They're coming for you.*

Don't look guilty. Whatever you do, don't look guilty.

Theresa is going to have to find out who else Lyndsey has spoken to.

Without conscious thought, her feet have brought her to Kyle Kincaid's office. To this domain of former military with their telltale clipped haircuts and their self-consciously unfashionable manner of dress, as though they're not quite used to picking out shirts and ties. Wrong colors, cheapish synthetic fabrics. They joke with each other loudly, and their desks are messier than over in Russia Division, as though there is no one to tell them that appearances matter.

Kyle Kincaid sits at his desk with his back to her, unaware of her approach, even though the boyish chatter dies down as she walks into the bullpen, as the men stop and stare at her. They don't know she's The Widow; they only see an attractive woman.

She hasn't thought of what to say to Kincaid but she's not worried; it will come to her. It always does. She's a cat who always lands on her velvet paws. He looks up when she stands beside him, and his face lights up. "I was in the neighborhood and thought I'd drop by," she says. She hopes her smile looks genuine.

They leave the vault and meander to the end of the hall, walls of glass with a view of the parking lots. It is dead space where no one ventures unless they have come for the vending machines. They have privacy.

He seems at a loss. He sneaks glances in her direction like a schoolboy afraid to ask her to the dance. Like all popular girls, cheerleaders and prom queens, it will be Theresa who will have to do the leading, carefully shepherding him along to get him to say what she wants him to say.

"You heard what happened to the other missing asset?" she asks in a low voice. There are few secrets in the Agency. "I wasn't sure if the news got out of Russia Division yet."

"What? No," he answers, quickly masking his surprise. He doesn't want to look out of touch. She tells him about Kulakov's messy end while at the same time tamping down her guilt. She's almost managed to erase the pictures from her mind. It's amazing how well she's learned to compartmentalize. It's survival: concentrate on putting one step after the other. "And your asset—any word on him yet?"

He shakes his head.

She wants to ask about Lyndsey. She wants to know if Kincaid has spoken to her yet, what Lyndsey may have told him, how much she knows. If she mentioned Theresa's name. The problem is she can't think how to do this without making Kincaid suspicious.

Before she can think of a way, however, Kincaid surprises her. He steps in closer than is proper in the workplace, so close that he can practically see down her cleavage. She can smell the dying scent of his deodorant and faint traces of the last thing he ate. Too intimate too fast.

"Would you like to go out to dinner with me? It's hard to talk here at work, don't you think? Someone always listening. It would be easier to speak freely out of the building." This is a funny thing to say under the circumstances. There's something about his tone and the hard glint in his frankly untrustworthy eyes that make her think there's something he hasn't told her.

She's losing control. Like with Tarasenko and Morozov. Someone she thought was a pussycat might turn out to be a tiger.

She feels the knife edge of panic, but it's not enough to keep her from accepting. After all, she has to know what he may have said to Lyndsey and he's right, it will be easier to talk outside of work. She doesn't want to have anything to do with Kyle Kincaid, socially or otherwise—but she has no choice. It's a risk she has to take.

"Why Kyle, I thought you'd never ask."

Theresa pulls into the parking lot of the restaurant and turns off her Volvo's engine. She sits behind the wheel, not looking to see if she is being watched. A voice in her head tells her to turn around, that it's not too late. She can send the sitter home early, wipe the makeup off her face, curl up on the couch to watch a Disney movie with Brian, and leave Kyle Kincaid sitting at his table alone, wondering what happened to her.

Her hands rest on the steering wheel, seemingly too heavy to lift. She didn't want Kincaid to come to her house, for Brian to see her leave with a strange man. On this point, she is adamant: Brian will not know of Kyle Kincaid. Their lives will never intersect, not at any point.

Kincaid has chosen a nondescript restaurant a few towns over, one—she senses—that isn't frequented by Agency employees. He doesn't want them to be seen together, and while that's fine with her, it also raises a faint alarm. He's trying to hide what they're doing. Why?

He hasn't arrived yet, so she waits at the bar with a glass of wine, again fighting her desire to leave. A sinister air seems to hang overhead: nothing good can come of this evening. It's like she's deliberating courting disaster but can't stop herself.

Finally, Kincaid shows up. He's changed into a sports jacket and open-collared shirt. He seems more nervous than when she last saw him.

He compliments her on her appearance, even though she made sure to dress conservatively: a high neckline, low hem. He asks the maître d' for a table in the back. Theresa doesn't like it—it implies a certain intimacy—but she figures he wants it for privacy. She slides into the banquette, giving herself the best view of the restaurant. In case she needs to make a hasty exit.

"Let me get you another wine," he says, lifting his hand for a waiter.

"I'm fine," she says coolly, but his grin is cocky.

"Oh, you're going to want another drink," he assures her. And then he tells her about his conversation with Lyndsey. "She came to see me. Asking questions." Kincaid has a whole new tone now. More confident. Mean, like a schoolyard bully's voice. He slides closer, just a degree, but deliberately. He is trying to intimidate her. "It means you're in trouble. The investigation."

She wouldn't think Kincaid capable of putting it together. He seems the kind of guy who needs problems explained to him by the smarter guys, the ones who figured it all out. She wonders, for a few fleeting seconds, how much he really knows. If there's a way out of this.

"I don't know what you're talking about," she says, her face frozen.

"I don't believe that for a minute." He toys with a tumbler of Scotch. "I didn't tell her about you. I gave her another name. But I could always tell her I was mistaken. That I got confused."

Cold sweat starts to trickle down her sides. She can't ask him what he wants: it would be an admission of guilt. And she doesn't doubt for a minute that he'd take it to Lyndsey, like he threatened. He'd like to be the hero.

How ridiculous is it that—of all the brilliant minds at CIA—she was caught by Kyle Kincaid? There must be a way to discourage him from making good on his threat. She racks her brain, trying to think how.

Meanwhile, Kincaid is still talking. "Look, I don't know why you did it and I don't care. That's your business. But if you don't want to go to jail, you've got to give me something. You got money—everybody knows it. That sports car, the house in McLean. So, you're going to pay me to keep my mouth shut." He smiles so broadly his face might crack. He puffs out his chest and leans back, arms over the banquette like a mobster. She'd like to pick up that slender, sturdy fork and drive the tines right in his chest.

He has no idea what she's thinking. He looks at her like she's a Popsicle and his eyes are licking her up and down. Revolting. He ducks his head close so he can whisper in her ear. "And there's one more thing you're going to give me. You're coming with me to a hotel. Tonight." His hand hovers close to her breast. "You're a widow, right? Been alone for a while now? So, this will be as much a treat for you as it is for me. It's a shame a pretty thing like you has been sitting on a shelf. What you been saving it for?"

He's just been upgraded to the dinner knife. She'd plunge its dull blade deep into his heart and not feel the slightest glimmer of regret. It's all she can do to keep her hands in her lap, to keep from reaching for it.

Oblivious, he takes a lock of her hair, fiddles it between his fingers, savoring the silkiness. "Ready to ditch this place?" he asks.

Somehow, she doesn't scream. She manages to maintain control. Gives him a tight, icy smile. Smooths the hair he's just mussed so not a strand is out of place. "Sure. Just give me a minute to get ready." She rises from the banquette and walks deliberately to the restroom, feeling his eyes on her ass.

Thankfully, it's empty. She staggers to the granite counter, which she hangs on to like a life preserver, and avoids looking into the mirror. She doesn't want to see the face of defeat.

No, not defeat. Not by the likes of Kyle Kincaid, not when she's come so far.

She reaches for her purse on the counter. She digs through it, looking for something buried beneath the tissues and loose breath mints and package of crushed Oreos that she carries for Brian. Considering what it is, she really should keep better track of it. It's not the kind of thing you want to fall into the wrong hands . . .

Yes, it's still there, a small battered Altoids tin ("curiously strong") held closed with a rubber band doubled, tripled over. She opens it with trembling hands. There it is, one lone pill, large, white, chalky to the touch. A present from her Russian handler, totally unrequested. *You'll never need this, Kanareyka—but just in case. For your peace of mind.* For *their* peace of mind, she's no fool. They'd rather not have any loose ends if things go south, would rather not leave behind a CIA officer capable of telling them things. An officer with names, places, tradecraft.

She rolls the pill between her fingers. Not for herself, of course—she has Brian to think about. She's not going to leave her son on his own, not when they're so close to being a family again.

It's for Kyle Kincaid. She can hardly believe her thoughts, they're so hard, so calculating. But she can be hard because he's a solitary man, with no one dependent on him. No one would miss him if something happened to him.

She looks down at the pill: how would she give it to him? It's not like he's going to take it voluntarily. He's just threatened her: he'll be on his guard. He won't take a drink from her that he hasn't watched her mix himself. And how else could she give it to him?

Her mind blanks, then blurs. It's impossible. It can't be done.

Impossible is not the answer. She'll have to find a way.

She puts the pill back in the tin. She doesn't know what's in it, but you have to respect a Russian poison pill. Those Russians know their stuff. She rinses her hands, just in case.

For every second she's away, Kincaid will grow more anxious. She doesn't have all the time in the world. She doesn't want to give him too much time to think. She dries her hands, reapplies her lipstick, and goes to face the music.

The hotel Kincaid has picked is not stylish, but neither is it a flea-ridden dump. It's merely suburban and nondescript, stucco walls and garish, multicolored carpeting in the lobby to hide wear and tear. The clerk at the desk doesn't raise an eyebrow as they wait without luggage, Kincaid tapping his credit card against the counter as the clerk works the keyboard.

Theresa keeps her eyes trained on that horrible carpet, wishing she could disappear.

The room itself is smallish. She slips off her coat and sits on the bed, fighting claustrophobia. She insisted they pick up a bottle of whiskey on the way and he didn't argue, sensing perhaps that she'll need to get good and drunk to go through with what he wants. He pours shots into two thick, ugly hotel glasses.

She takes a sip, savoring the burn, before heading to the bathroom. It smells of cleanser in there, though not enough to mask the mildew. She runs the taps to cover noise as she takes the Altoids tin from her purse. She snaps the big, awkward pill in half and then, feeling a pang of conscience, breaks off a little more. The crumbs she brushes into the sink, letting the running water wash them away. She doesn't want to kill Kyle Kincaid, she just wants to send him a message. *Don't mess with me.* All she needs is to make him hesitate; it won't be long before the Russians help her leave the country.

She tucks the remaining piece into her bra, where it sits like a rock pressed against her sternum.

When she comes out, Kincaid is sitting on the edge of the bed with his legs splayed wide like a careless man on the subway, already a little drunk and not caring what she thinks. His glass sits empty on a nearby dresser.

She sets her glass next to his. She reaches to her waist for the ties that hold her wrap dress closed and with one quick, deliberate motion—before she can think about it—she yanks the knot undone, so her dress falls open. She lets it slide over her shoulders and fall to the floor in a silky flutter. Kincaid smiles, a happy schoolboy. She stands before him in bra and panties and heels, a gold chain at her throat. She can practically feel Kincaid's throat go dry.

Before he can say or do anything, she climbs onto the bed, straddling his lap. She peels off his jacket first, pulling it down over his shoulders. He watches, amazed. Maybe it plays into a fantasy he has, that a woman could want him so much she'd tear off his clothes. In any case, he lets her. He runs his hands over her body, and she tries not to think about the way he kneads her ass through the lace panties. She loosens his tie—his throat shouldn't be constricted in any way—and unbuttons his shirt. He throws his head back, loving it, giving her full access, giving her whatever she wants.

"I knew you'd enjoy it, if you gave yourself a chance," he says. Does he really believe this? His erection rises beneath her, pushes clumsily at her crotch as she undoes the buttons of his shirt.

"I want you to use your mouth," he whispers in her ear.

She'd rather die first.

It's now or never.

She pushes his shoulders back on the mattress. He doesn't fight—why should he? It's all going his way, his wildest dreams fulfilled. She turns, reaching for her glass on the dresser. And in that moment, he can't see what she's doing.

In the flurry of hands undoing his buttons and her twisting and gyrations, she has managed to slip the nugget of poison from her bra into her mouth. She doesn't want to keep it there for long. Not for one second more than is necessary.

She leans over Kincaid, their faces so close that his five o'clock shadow grazes her cheek, and kisses him full on the lips. She anticipates the open mouth and the tongue rising up to meet hers.

In that instant, she uses her tongue to shove the poison into his mouth. Then follows with the glass, rim crashing into his teeth, and empties the whiskey down his throat.

He knows something is up and flounders beneath her, trying to sit upright, but she wills herself to be as heavy as an anchor. She sits like a banshee on his chest, a succubus. Her fingers pinch his nose closed, clamp his mouth shut. She doesn't want him to be able to breathe. She waits for him to gulp for air. *Swallow, you motherfucker. Swallow.*

He's thrashing, he's flailing, but she only has to hold on a few seconds more. His face turns red. Tears well in his eyes. A little whiskey seeps at the corners of his mouth, but he's on his back and gravity is on her side.

Finally, his Adam's apple moves.

It's done.

She springs off his chest like a cat and scrambles backward. Standing a safe distance away, she watches, anxious for what will happen next.

Russian poisons work quickly. Once the deed is done, you want it to be fast. The last thing the Russians want is for someone to have the time to tell a few secrets before they expire.

With the weight gone from his chest, Kincaid sits bolt upright, a strained expression on his face. His first thought is not of revenge. It's pure self-preservation. He knows something terrible has happened. He knows he has been poisoned. Could he be feeling the effects already? What will she do if he yells for help, or tries to run away? She watches for the slightest twitch, any indication of what he'll do next.

His hands search around him, as though he's gone blind and needs his hands. He rifles his jacket, then stops: his cell phone. He pulls it out of a pocket and starts to jab desperately at the keyboard. She slaps it out of his hand, sending it spinning across the room.

He tries to yell but nothing comes out, only the hiss of air and a long, foamy string of bubbles, like a washing machine run amok. His eyes search her face—*what have you done to me?* He's frightened as the truth starts to dawn on him. Frightened as a little boy.

Then his expression changes. *Help me.*

"Don't worry. You're not going to die," she tells him as she reaches for the bottle of Scotch. She takes a big swig, swishing it around in her mouth, rinsing vigorously, while sprinting to the bathroom. Spits it all into the sink. Has she been quick enough, or could a minute amount of poison have gotten into her system?

Wiping her mouth on the back of her hand, she stands over him and starts to dress hurriedly. "I didn't give you the full dose. It'll just make you sick—really sick. Something for you to think about."

But Kincaid isn't listening. He's fallen backward onto the bed. Pink-tinged foam pumps out of his mouth now like a bubble machine. He's gone pasty white, except for his face, which is turning blue. His eyes are wide open and stark. She leans over and slaps his cheeks. Unresponsive. Feels his throat for a pulse and it's wild, all over the place. He starts to vomit dribbles of yellow liquid.

She steps back from the bed, her heart going like a jackhammer. This is not what she expected. A quarter of the pill is apparently enough to kill him. She'll call for an ambulance from the first pay phone she sees but from the looks of things, he's going to die. The realization turns her ice-cold, makes her want to double over puking.

And she held that pill in her mouth for one, two seconds.

And now her thoughts turn to self-preservation. Brian. He's her only concern.

Can she be linked to this room, to him? There was, undoubtedly, a camera in the lobby and she hung back when they were checking in, but there's a chance it may have caught her face.

Well, it's a chance she has to take. She puts on her coat, snatches up her handbag. With wadded up tissues, she wipes down every surface she remembers touching in the bedroom and the bathroom. Wipes the rim of her glass.

Taking one last look at the body convulsing on the bed, she averts her eyes and wipes the door handle as she leaves.

———————

There's a lone light burning in the rear of the house as Theresa pulls into the driveway. She collects herself before heading in, wishes there was a way to erase the smell of Scotch that seems to exude from her pores.

She gives the babysitter—an older woman who lives a few doors down—forty dollars and locks the door after ushering her out. A quick check on Brian—so trusting and innocent in his sleep, she almost bursts into tears—before heading to the bedroom. Pulling the codebook out of the shoebox.

Writing, with shaking hands, the numbers for the message she formed in her head on the drive home.

SITUATION DIRE. CANNOT REMAIN IN PLACE. TAKE ME OUT NOW.

THIRTY-TWO

Outside it's raining, but if Lyndsey had not gone to the vending machine for coffee, she would not have known, not in her small, windowless office. She stands in the cul-de-sac at the end of the hall, the bit of space given over to vending machines. The walls are gray-tinted glass, ceiling to floor. She takes a minute to sip at the steaming hot coffee and watch fat drops of water slide down the glass in streams. She tries to predict which way the stream will break as gravity pulls it down—as though it matters. Anything to stop thoughts running through her head.

Masha needs you. Time is running out.

Don't let Popov down. He trusted you.

Theresa is a traitor. Theresa is your friend.

No sooner does she return to her office than the phone rings. "Lyndsey, do you have a minute? It's Dwayne." Dwayne Molina is a peace offering from Raymond Murphy in CI, a computer tech offered up to help sift through the copious amounts of data associated with the case. She was about to give up on CI completely, but Murphy has redeemed himself with Molina. The tech is a shy young man, recently out of the military, far more willing to be helpful than Murphy, thankfully. He's had the data for all of twenty-four hours and already she's talked to him more than Raymond. The previous calls from Molina were all explanatory, providing background and generally bringing him up to speed, but the man has proven a quick learner. "Sure. Got something for me?"

"Maybe. I don't want to get your hopes up," he says. There is a faint tap-tap in the background. Molina never seems to stop typing. He's always buzzing like a bee. "I was going through the forum data and noticed something weird." Tap-tap-tap. "Yeah. After we isolated the serial number of the computer Theresa's been using, I ran it against all the activity on the forum. There wasn't a whole lot, barely anything before June and then—bam—she starts using it three, four times a day."

"Is that unusual?" It seems people usually are active when they first start using a new app, judging from her own experience. You stop using it once the novelty has worn off.

"Not by itself. It does track with your hypothesis, though." More tapping. "Then I took a look at the activity around those three cases you told me about. Lighthouse, Skipjack, and Genghis."

"Right."

"I found her computer serial connecting on threads that have to do with Lighthouse, the scientist, and Skipjack, the cyber dude, all right. She drops in on every thread dealing with those two cases."

The first part makes sense. Lyndsey has already confirmed with Jan Westerling that Theresa made personal contact. Molina's work just provides more evidence. But this part about Skipjack is significant.

"What about Evelyn Wang?"

"No joy," Molina says flatly. "I mean, she connected a few times with both Westerling and Kincaid, but nothing sustained. I think she's just trying to be seen as part of the gang, you know?"

That doesn't track with what Kincaid said. "One more thing, and I don't know if you can do it"—not without higher authority—"but is there any way you can see if there were communications between Theresa Warner and Kyle Kincaid?"

A tense silence. "You mean, like, read their emails? Users sign consent to be monitored in order to get an account on the system, but I'd have to get permission to get records."

She bites her lip. "Do it. I'll go to Eric for authorization, if I need to."

"Raymond can take care of it. I'll let you know when we got something." He hangs up.

Lyndsey lowers the phone. As she starts to put the pieces together, she feels a familiar buzz of excitement in the back of her skull. Why didn't Kyle Kincaid tell her about Theresa? Obviously, she'd been in contact about Skipjack. If Molina finds emails between the two, they might prove interesting.

Molina's revelations sit badly with her, like spoiled meat. There's nothing to be done for it but to continue digging.

Lyndsey is turning the facts over in her mind when she looks up to find Maggie Kimball standing at her door. Her arms are full of binders and manila folders but her dark eyes sparkle as usual. "Eric wants to see you."

He sits behind his desk, staring glassy-eyed at the monitor. When she walks in, he looks visibly relieved. "Close the door, please."

He waits until she takes the seat opposite his desk. "We might have a little complication. I got a call from the NSC." National Security Council. "They've seen the medical examiner's report on Popov and feel they need to issue some kind of statement. To publicly call out the Russians."

This is expected. Sovereign states don't take kindly to other nations poisoning people on their territory. Since the exact time of death hasn't been determined, there might be some issue over sovereignty, but there is no denying that whoever is behind the killing brought a deadly poison to American soil, capriciously endangering American lives.

She can see why Eric's upset. That means going public about Popov's death. So far, it's been kept out of the papers. As far as anyone knows, it was nothing more than a personal tragedy. A Russian diplomat had a heart attack.

An official U.S. statement would be a complication, to say the least.

Eric swivels in his chair. "I don't want the NSC mucking around in this. There are still too many unknowns. It's too early to tip our hand to the Russians. I want you to talk to the NSC. Make them understand we have an important investigation going on and we can't have it jeopardized. See if you can get them to hold off."

Why isn't Eric going? It would be more effective if the request came from the Chief of Russia Division. When she hesitates, he steps in. "I'd go but I'm too busy. I've got a full schedule of meetings for the next three days and this can't wait."

"Okay. I'll see what I can find out."

"One more thing," he adds as she's almost out the door. "Tom Cassidy is coming into town, in case you need to talk to him. It's for that other op I told you about. But as long as he's here, if he can be of any use to your investigation . . ."

Tom Cassidy, the man who failed Yaromir Popov. He's been stonewalling her, not responding to emails and not returning her calls, using the thousands of miles between them as a barrier. Yeah, she has a few things she'd like to ask him about.

A t one point in Lyndsey's career, a trip to the NSC would have been thrilling. It is housed in the Eisenhower Executive Office Building, next door to the White House, after all. The West Wing and the Oval Office are mere steps away across the manicured lawn. The building stands behind an iron fence. It's formal and spooky looking, with a vaguely Victorian mansard roof and embellishments that make it look like an overly decorated wedding cake. The floors inside are a dizzying black-and-white-checkerboard pattern that makes the long corridors seem like optical illusions and always remind her of Alice in Wonderland. She climbs the staircase to the second floor and makes her way to the offices of the Senior Director for Russia.

She's not meeting with the Senior Director, Anthony Olcott. She has heard Olcott speak on several occasions—a former professor at Georgetown University who started his federal career at State Department, ending as ambassador to Russia before moving to the NSC—and wouldn't mind seeing him again. He impressed her with his encyclopedic knowledge not only of Russia but of U.S. policy, past and present. It will have to wait for another day because she's not senior enough to meet with Olcott. Eric would be, yes, but not a mere case officer like her. Instead, she's meeting with two of the staffers, Renee Dentley and Bruce Cavanaugh. NSC staffers are often on loan from other federal agencies, careerists familiar with policy in the subject area. Sometimes they come from outside the government, academics or researchers with a background on the topic whose outlook is in line with the administration's position. Lyndsey has met Renee, a political officer at State Department, several times before, but Bruce Cavanaugh is new to her.

Lyndsey is ushered into a small office shared by the two. "Thanks for coming down." Renee Dentley has always struck Lyndsey as a typical State Department officer, smart and composed but recklessly overworked. She looks exhausted, too worn out to care much about her appearance. Cavanaugh, on the other hand, is nattily dressed. He must've risen at five a.m. to look this good. She heard that he came from a university in the Midwest and so he's not had much experience dealing with intelligence types. He watches Lyndsey as though he fears she might try to set the office on fire.

"We've been told you're working on the Popov murder," Dentley continues. "We saw a report on the poison. It's definitely Russian?"

Apparently, Randy Detwiler has already released a report on his findings. Lyndsey can't blame him—it's his job, and it's important to get this information on record—but the timing could be better. Maybe he didn't imagine the NSC would pick up on it so quickly.

"It appears to be, but—"

Cavanaugh leans forward, eager to use his prerogative as an NSC staffer to interrupt. "I thought it was strange that they didn't use Novichok. If it really were the Russians behind the hit, they would've used Novichok, wouldn't they?"

Novichok is the poison du jour, it seems. It was used in the spring of 2018 to poison Sergei Skripal, a Russian military officer who had been spying for the British, and the case seems to have made everyone a Russian poisons expert overnight. That's Lyndsey's sum total knowledge on the subject, however. If she had known they wanted to talk poisons, she would have brought Detwiler with her.

Lyndsey levels a cool eye at Cavanaugh, hoping to take the edge off his aggressiveness. "I'll ask our poison expert for his opinion, but my guess is that the Russians wouldn't use it on Popov if they didn't want to tip their hand. It doesn't mimic a heart attack or look like natural causes—it doesn't provide plausible cover, in other words. And don't forget: Novichok is far from a sure thing. Skripal and his daughter survived."

Cavanaugh nods. "So, you don't think the Russians want us to know it was them?"

"Their thinking is unclear."

"But CIA believes it was murder?" Dentley adds.

"Popov was definitely murdered. But we'd also like to ask you not to take any action against Russia at this time."

The two exchange worried glances before Cavanaugh starts up again. "Ms. Duncan, you've just told us that the Russians committed a murder on U.S. soil—"

"It was aggressive, no doubt about it. But hear me out, please. We have reasons for asking you to sit on this—for now," she says. Cavanaugh fumes and avoids Dentley's attempts to catch his eye, but to his credit he lets her speak. "We think there might be a mole on the U.S. side giving the Russians information. We're guessing that's why Popov was killed."

"Guessing?" Dentley asks, raising an eyebrow.

But Cavanaugh is cowed. "Criminy," he says, his voice about an octave higher now.

"We think they found out he was a CIA asset and had him executed." She's just given them a field promotion since neither was cleared for Genghis's compartment; Lyndsey makes a mental note to have the pair read in later. "We're making good progress on the investigation, but we haven't found the mole yet. It's too soon to let the Russians know that we know what they did."

She braces for the pair to blow up: *how could you not know anything about this, an asset blown, a mole in the ranks?* She may get her chance to have face time with the NSC senior director after all.

The two staffers are so dazed that they sit stunned. Finally, Dentley says, "The Brits have been pressing us on this. They're still smarting after

Skripal's assassination attempt. They want us to accuse the Russians, and use the incident as the basis for another round of sanctions."

"But that's out of the question now," Cavanaugh hastens to add. "We'll tell them the medical results were inconclusive and that we have to run more tests. That will buy us time. When do you think you'll have this investigation wrapped up?"

Lyndsey sends up a silent prayer of thanks. "I'm not sure. We're moving quickly, but you know how these things can drag out . . . A month?"

Dentley is about to respond—probably to give her two weeks, max—when Cavanaugh taps his watch. "I'm sorry—we have another meeting. We'll have to wrap this up." The place runs on meetings. Every hour on the hour. Can they ever do anything more than scratch the surface? It's a miracle any decisions get made.

Dentley reaches for her leather portfolio, a signal that it's time to leave. Cavanaugh has already bolted out the door, as though he can't get away from the spook fast enough. It's a good reminder to Lyndsey that outside of the Washington bubble, most of America is leery of who she is and what she does.

Lyndsey stands and follows Dentley into the hall. Dentley leans in close to Lyndsey. "Look, I'll give you a break this time because we've worked together before. We'll stall the Brits for now, but they won't be patient forever. This whole thing sounds a little half-baked to me, but I'm trusting you. Keep us in the loop. Let us know when you're close." She furrows her brow, searching Lyndsey's face. "If I find out you're hiding something from us, there'll be trouble."

Where is this hostility coming from? Has she ever broken a promise to the NSC? Ah, but it's not just her track record being questioned here. It's everything Russia Division has ever done to Olcott's team, every promise made and broken, every assessment that was wrong, every shady trick they found out about after the fact. "I'll talk to Eric about this as soon as I get back to the office."

"Eric—that's Eric Newman, right? You work for him," Dentley says like she's just putting two plus two together. "You know, there's a rumor he's coming to the NSC."

This is a first heard for Lyndsey. "What?"

"As senior director." Uncertainty flits across her face. "You didn't know? Tony is going to retire in a couple months. He says four years is long enough. He's going to go back to Michigan and dote on his grandkids. I heard Eric's name is on the long list for Tony's replacement."

Lyndsey is at a loss for words. Eric Newman plays his cards very close to the vest indeed. Has he been getting ready to bolt for new pastures? Senior Director for Russian Affairs would be a plum position, indeed. Finding the mole who eliminated CIA's top Russian asset would be certain to clinch the nomination. The revelation doesn't sit well with Lyndsey but she's not sure why. It doesn't change anything, not really. Yet she can't help feeling like there's a veil over her eyes obscuring her view.

B ack at headquarters, Eric is overjoyed to hear how the meeting went. "Thanks, Lyndsey. Sounds like you handled it perfectly. That's a load off my mind."

He seems relieved, though Lyndsey can't figure out why. It wouldn't be impossible to bring the NSC into the investigation, and they'll have to do it at some point anyway. Of course, some managers don't like to have outsiders looking over their shoulders. Things would get complicated once the NSC stepped in.

"Something wrong?" He's studying her.

"Renee Dentley mentioned that Tony Olcott is retiring in a few months. Did you know?"

She doesn't fool him. Eric smiles as he leans back in his chair. "Oh, someone let the cat out of the bag while you were there, didn't they? Yes, I heard a rumor that my name might be on the list of replacements . . ."

"Why didn't you say anything?"

He shrugs. "They'll probably pick someone else, someone with more policy experience. I didn't want to rattle the team here, have them think I'm leaving."

His expression says he's not telling the truth. He's so pleased that he's like the cat that ate the canary, but she won't call him on it. "And if you *are* selected? Would you go?"

A mask descends, and she can't read him. He's trying to read her, too, though: the slightest narrowing of his eyes, tension around the mouth. "I've been in this position for some time . . . Most men would've moved on by now, wouldn't you say?"

That's his ambition showing itself. "So, you're saying you'd take it?"

He laughs lightly, eyes crinkling at the corners. "Let's just say I'm comfortable here."

It could be he's afraid of jinxing it by talking about it—or that he doesn't want to make himself vulnerable by admitting that he wants it. She decides to let it drop. "There was one other thing. Cavanaugh asked why Popov's killer didn't use Novichok. You know, the poison from the Skripal case."

"And what did you tell him?"

Now it's her turn to shrug. "I can see reasons why they might not . . . but I'll talk to the poison expert and see what he has to say."

Eric has gone a bit glassy-eyed, lost in thought. He tugs at his lower lip. "Interesting. Yeah, let me know what he says."

The unanswered questions nag as she walks back to her office. Why would the Russians be subtle? If they knew Popov was a traitor, why didn't they want everyone to know they'd killed him? Playing it subtle would be uncharacteristic, to say the least.

And yet, that's what happened.

For today, she has no answers.

THIRTY-THREE

Back at her desk, Lyndsey checks her IM and sees a little green box by Detwiler's name. He's at his desk.

She types, *Heard you put out a report on the Genghis toxicology report.*

His reply is almost instantaneous. *I did. But I found out something since that report. I did a little more research on the variant of gelsemium used on Genghis. Turns out it's slightly different from the compound the Russians have used in the past. Chemical makeup suggests the variant found in Genghis's body was gelsemium rankinii and not gelsemium elegans . . .*

Lyndsey types furiously. *In English, please.*

A pause. *It's not the kind found in previous Russian killings, which is actually Chinese in origin . . .*

The conversation with the NSC directors, Dentley and Cavanaugh, flashes through her mind. They were right to be suspicious about the poison. *What are you telling me?* she types. *Was it the Russians or wasn't it?*

It's not that simple.

She resists the urge to slam her hands on the keyboard. It's never a simple answer with these analysts. It's always messy and complicated. *Let me ask you something. If it was the Russians, why didn't they use Novichok? Isn't that their poison of choice lately?*

There is a long pause, the cursor blinking at her like some kind of electronic eye. Finally, he replies, *Granted, Novichok is what they tend to use these days. But it's not their only poison and it depends on a lot of things. Availability, for one . . .*

She types, cutting him off. She is going to force the issue. *If they kill someone today, which poison is most likely?*

Blink, blink. Assessing, weighing. Figuring the odds. The wait seems maddeningly long. *Probably Novichok.*

She stares up at the ceiling. The ground is crumbling beneath her feet. Or, at least, it feels like it. Until the meeting with Dentley and Cavanaugh, Popov's death seemed like a slam dunk. It was the Russians. They had found out about Popov and killed him. Then they found out about Kulakov and Nesterov and killed or detained them, too.

Now Lyndsey is not sure.

And Theresa being the one behind it all? She feels a glimmer of a doubt.

She types her thanks to Detwiler and closes the window.

A minute later, there's a message from Molina. *Got what you wanted. Only there weren't emails between them, so I looked for chat. I'm sending you the instant messaging records.*

In another few seconds, an email appears in her queue from Molina. The attachment isn't long, but it is damning.

13 august 2018 2322Z WARNER, THERESA: *Saw you sparring with Wilson in the teleconference over the Milan hack. That report you cited, is it Skipjack?*

13 august 2018 2322Z KINCAID, KYLE: *Yes. All the best stuff is.*

13 august 2018 2323Z WARNER, THERESA: *I really should get read into the compartment. I need a little more info, though, to convince my manager.*

13 august 2018 2323Z KINCAID, KYLE: *Sure, whatever you need. How about we meet for coffee*

The last chat session was from a few days ago.

7 december 2018 1805Z KINCAID, KYLE: *How about Wildfire, on Foster Drive? 8?*

7 december 2018 1805Z WARNER, THERESA: *Sure. I'll meet you at the restaurant*

You don't meet for work at a restaurant. Had they gone on a date?

Lyndsey looks up Kincaid's phone number, then reaches for the phone. He has some explaining to do, such as why he hadn't told her about Theresa's interest.

But there is no answer. It goes to voicemail.

She slams the phone down. She can't wait for him to get in touch with her and besides, he'll only continue to be evasive.

She goes to the online white pages to pull up Kincaid's record. It takes only a minute more to track down Kincaid's supervisor. She exhales slowly in an effort to calm down, and is surprised when the phone is answered quickly.

She explains that she's running an investigation and needs to speak to Kincaid. Can he tell her how to get in touch with him, please?

There is a strained silence on the other end. Finally, the man says, "You haven't heard? I guess you don't know . . . Kyle is in the hospital. He's in a coma."

THIRTY-FOUR

Theresa stands outside Lyndsey's office, listening. She has always been as quiet as a nun. Able to hide from her parents, sneak up on her husband.

She overheard all of Lyndsey's conversation with Kincaid's supervisor. There can only be one reason Lyndsey is looking for Kincaid: Lyndsey is onto her. Once she finds out Kincaid is in the hospital and starts tracing Theresa's steps, it will be over.

She will lose everything. Her son. Her one chance to get Richard out of prison.

Which means all these terrible things she's done will be for nothing. Betrayed her country, caused one man's death, probably responsible for a second (though not Yaromir Popov, she had nothing to do with that).

All for nothing if the Russians don't pull her out in time.

Tick tock, tick tock. With every minute, she feels Lyndsey closing in on her.

Tarasenko is a sadist, keeping her on tenterhooks.

She feels helpless. She doesn't like to feel helpless.

She tiptoes away from Lyndsey's office, silent as a swan gliding across a lake. She needs a minute alone. She grabs her purse and heads to the ladies' room. Standing in front of the full-length mirror, she plucks nervously at her hair. Reapplies her lipstick, moisturizes her hands.

What she needs is a plan, a way to buy time if everything goes to hell.

She's pretty sure Lyndsey hasn't put it all together yet, or else they'd have arrested her already.

All she has to do is keep Lyndsey from putting the last pieces together. There's still time.

As she returns the moisturizer bottle to her purse, her hand falls on the tiny Altoids tin. She picks it up, gives it a shake. Is rewarded with a tinny little rattle.

There's still half a pill inside.

THIRTY-FIVE

The details surrounding Kincaid's hospitalization, when Lyndsey finally hears them, are gruesome. Found alone in a hotel room, half-undressed, unresponsive.

No one knows why he was at the hotel. His apartment is fifteen minutes away.

The clerk told police that a woman was with him, but he couldn't provide much of a description. He didn't recognize her, which means she wasn't one of the prostitutes who came through the hotel regularly.

The Agency's Security department was working with the police, of course. They always did when an Agency employee was injured or died under suspicious circumstances. But so far, there was maddeningly little. After Lyndsey reads the medical report, she contacts Randy Detwiler. "I'm no poisoning expert, but it looks like one to me. And this is the second poisoning related to this case, which seems like too much of a coincidence to be one." He promises to look into it.

She must turn back to the case, as little as she has the stomach for it:

Detwiler's finding on the gelsemium and Molina's findings mean another late night for Lyndsey. Outside the closed door, she listens as one by one, the others leave for the day. The rattle of cabinets being shut and locked, doors opening and closing. Finally, it is completely quiet, so quiet that she can hear the handler cycle on and off. The air in her tight little office grows stale as she pulls out her files and rereads every report, looking for more clues. Something she's overlooked. The list on the yellow legal pad grows longer slowly, line by line.

She puts down the pen and pushes the legal pad away. She wishes there was more face-to-face. She's better at that, understanding what is meant by every flick of the eyes and shift of weight in a chair. There's more certainty in the tilt of someone's head than in their words, at least to Lyndsey. She wants to study Theresa from across a room or behind one-way glass.

Near midnight, she finds something that was overlooked before. The manifest from Popov's flight was attached to the toxicology report, at the very back, which may account for the oversight. Somehow the medical examiner's office was able to get Delta to cough it up. Perhaps the office was afraid of contagion, and thought it might need to track down the passengers if the cause of death was airborne.

Given what Detwiler told her about the effectiveness of the poison, time of death, and duration of the flight, it's very likely that Popov's killer is one of these people.

Delta flies an Airbus A330 on this route, 335 seats: she knows this because she looked it up already. She eyes the list. According to the manifest, it was fairly empty. Inwardly, she groans: that's still over a hundred people to check, when you take pilots and crew into consideration.

There is nothing to do but start searching in Agency databases. If nothing shakes out, if there are no matches, first thing in the morning she will ask FBI to run the names through their files. There's a good chance FBI will have information CIA doesn't, information germane to law enforcement, access to U.S. Customs and Border Protection, not to mention arrest records.

By this point, the office is empty. The last person to leave, Evert Northrop, stopped by her office to tell her so she could lock the door behind him, standard protocol. It's now one a.m., and Lyndsey pauses in her work. Her eyes are so tired, she's unable to focus on the words on the monitor. She's halfway down the list and questioning the usefulness of this approach. So far, she's gotten a big fat goose egg: not one passenger has appeared in the Agency's databases, meaning the person has no connection to intelligence, was never an asset or informant, never worked for the Agency, or their name never came up in a report, ever.

She decides to switch tactics and begins to search on the open internet. What she sees quickly confirms her suspicions: the passengers were mostly Russian businessmen, or if they're spies, they've built a plausible cover. And the vast majority of names are Russian. The few Americans are mostly businessmen, too. There's a smattering of students, and retirees on a packaged holiday tour. No one on the list jumps out at her yet, and that makes her nervous. The two pilots are former military, and it seems unlikely that one of them would be a secret assassin for the FSB.

Then she finds something. One of the passengers is former Special Operations—only he's American, not Russian. Navy SEAL, then Blackwater, then a few years at other private security firms before disappearing into the ether like a ghost. The downward spiral through the industry, frequently switching between employers, is a bad sign. Or maybe he's fine and not screwed-up in the least and there are other reasons he can't hold a job. She's met enough of these guys and heard enough stories to know that some—a minority, but still some—drink the Kool-Aid and get lost, drawn to the use of violence, finding they like being in places where there are few rules and even fewer people to enforce them.

Their resumes read like this one.

Still, he's American. The FSB would never hire an American to kill Popov. They have more than enough men to handle it in-house. Nothing to see here.

Except . . . the name seems familiar. Claude Simon is just uncommon enough of a name not to be something she'd picked up from a celebrity news rag or overheard on television. Could he have been coming home from a private security job in Russia? The odds are long that a job like that would be completely innocent. There are plenty of Russian mercenaries in the country already—why would a Russian company hire foreign mercenaries—and an American at that?

She goes back to the classified files and starts searching on the name. She tries every kind of database open to her, logs, personnel databases, anything and everything. Nothing, nothing, nothing.

She is jotting the name on the list going to FBI—maybe they'll have something on him—when one of the open windows beeps at her: she's got a hit on one of her searches. It's a reporting database, another internal memo for the record. She leans closer to the screen. It's late and she's tired and her eyesight is failing, and she knows the odds of this having anything to do with Popov are slim to none. She's not even sure why she's bothering with this level of diligence . . .

Except it is germane. Or it seems to be . . . She fights exhaustion to make sense of what she's reading. The report has to do with the planning of an operation in theater a couple years ago, an exfiltration, and there is Claude Simon's name. Freelance security. Lyndsey reads through his list of qualifications, which all have to do with weapons, the terrible places where he's willing to work, the terrible things he's willing to do.

What was he doing on that flight?

His business is making bad things happen.

And a man died on that flight. Could it be nothing more than a coincidence?

She goes back to the old report, scanning quickly through the next part, anxious to see if the report says who brought up his name. Who knew of Claude Simon. Who wanted to hire him for the extraction team, so long ago.

Lyndsey's heart stops for one long beat.

It was Eric Newman.

Somehow, Lyndsey manages to leave her office. Locks up her notes in the safe—she's not going to take chances leaving it in a simple locked cabinet *now*. She drives home through the quiet streets of Tysons Corner even though her mind is racing in a million directions at once.

Don't jump to any conclusions now. Get some sleep. Things will look different in the morning.

They'd better. Because everything she can think of is crazy, crazy, crazy. Not only the link she's found between Popov's killer and Eric Newman but Theresa's connection to Kincaid. And the fact that Kincaid is in the hospital, near death. The truth is still in shadow, though she feels as though she's getting closer to it. Almost close enough to grasp.

In bed, she twists and turns, wrapping cool sheets around her overheated body. She is desperate to fall asleep but can't stop thinking about what it means that Eric once hired the man who may have killed Yaromir Popov. Eric *knew* him, knew what kind of work the man did. And the man did bad deeds. He was in the bad deeds business.

It is plausible that someone at CIA hired him to kill Yaromir Popov.

It is plausible that Eric Newman was that man.

That thought causes her stomach to clench.

Why would Eric Newman want Popov dead? More important: even if there was a reason, a valid reason, how could Eric do that to someone he knew and to whom he owed so much?

The late hour and her disorientation make it easier to free associate. Her thoughts are liquid, slippery. There was a photo of Simon in the file. Forties, a big fit man with a heavy beard. Dark eyes, dark hair. Nothing about him would make you think he has any qualms about what he does. There is a remorselessness about him. He is the kind of man you cut a wide berth should your paths cross. A man who could hunt another man through an airport with a needle hidden in his palm, looking for an opening. Slipping in behind his victim as they queue to board. A quick brush pass, a scratch or needle so light that it's unnoticeable.

Yes, she can picture Simon doing it, but why? Why would Eric New- man want Yaromir Popov dead? He had been, at one time, the Division's top asset. Lauded as a crown jewel by no less than Roger Barker, the hard-to-impress head of the Clandestine Service. Of course, that was a few years ago, when Lyndsey was his handler, but something catastrophic has happened in those scant few years. Apparently, he'd decided not to cooperate since then. To know why, she'll have to talk to Tom Cassidy. For some reason, Yaromir Popov became expendable. To be completely cold- blooded about it, it was better to eliminate your former assets than to leave them like unexploded bombs.

But that wasn't how CIA operated. That's what they chose to believe about the enemy. That's why they were the bad guys. You don't hand your assets over to the enemy. That would be the consummate betrayal. *You'd be no better than the Russians.* How many times had she heard that from her colleagues?

Except Eric didn't tell the Russians that Popov had betrayed them. No: he may have had him killed himself.

That means the Russians didn't know Popov had been a spy. The secret would be safe for a little while, until the FSB figured out what was going on.

Could that be why Eric doesn't want the NSC to open an investigation? Why was it important for him to keep Russia in the dark a little while longer?

And if Theresa *had* turned those names over to them—Lighthouse and Skipjack, and everything points that she had—it won't take them long to figure out. Two assets are uncovered, a Russian officer makes an unscheduled midnight flight to Washington . . . The FSB will jump to conclusions, it's the cautious thing to do. This confirms for Lyndsey that Masha and Polina are in danger.

Unable to sleep, Lyndsey gets out of bed. She sits in the dark in the front room with a glass of cold water, listening to the hushed sound of traffic on Route 7 beyond the apartment complex. Tysons Corner never sleeps, even at three a.m.. A handful of lights are on in one of the new high-rises across the highway; Lyndsey takes a little comfort in the fact that she's not alone.

Could Eric be involved in this somehow? She takes another gulp of water, hoping it will jolt her out of this dreamlike state. *I must be half-asleep. I'm overlooking something.* Why would Eric push an investigation, bring her in, and put her in charge, if he were involved?

This. Is. Maddening.

Is Eric the kind of man who could condemn Yaromir Popov to death? The answer is yes—of course. It comes with the job. But there would have to be a good reason, one that she can't see.

Some men would resign before carrying out that order. Lyndsey would've quit. Why didn't Eric?

What she needs is someone to talk to. But the only one she has is Raymond Murphy and she can't go to him with a half-baked suspicion about Eric. Raymond is not up to being entrusted with such an explosive secret. There's no way it wouldn't get back to Eric and, if he's innocent, he'd never forgive her.

If he's innocent. Her subconscious knows there's a shadow of a doubt.

There are other ways it could've gone down. Yaromir Popov might've been poisoned before he got on the plane. A Russian agent could've gotten to him on the way to Sheremetyevo or inside the terminal. The timing would probably work. She'll have to see if Detwiler can tell from the toxicology report.

Claude Simon could've been on the plane for personal reasons. He could be innocent, this could all be an unfortunate coincidence.

A huge, crazy, unlikely coincidence.

But she's never been one to believe in coincidence.

There's only one remedy for it. She'll talk to the FBI tomorrow, see if they can't find out what Simon was doing in Moscow. That would help put her mind at ease.

Three a.m. She can catch a few hours' sleep, if she's lucky. She carries the glass to the kitchen, then shuffles to the bedroom.

THIRTY-SIX

In the morning, Lyndsey tries to clear her head with a run. Six o'clock and the neighborhood is blanketed in a gray haze, a mix of fog and frost. She starts out at a slow jog past neighbors armed with briefcases and backpacks, heading for their sedans and SUVs, the early-morning shift at one of the many corporations with nearby offices. After a mile, she feels better physically—her heart pumping, sweat trickling down her face—but her thoughts still skitter all over like spilled marbles, no better than the night before. To make it all worse, time is ticking. There's only a handful of days before Theresa's Russian handler comes to town and too many questions left to be answered.

The main thing, however, is that she needs to call Sally Herbert at FBI. It won't do any good to go in to work right now: she has to wait for normal office hours. Eventually, when she can't stand it any longer, she swings wide on an empty stretch of road and heads back to the apartment. *By the time I take a shower and get into the office, it will be eight a.m., a reasonable time to call.*

Overnight, Lyndsey compiled a wish list for FBI longer than her arm, but she knows she has to pare it back. Like CIA, FBI has limited resources and she can hardly demand that they stop whatever they're doing to help her out. There is only one favor she is going to ask for today: find out everything they can about Claude Simon's trip. Why was he on the same flight as Yaromir Popov? And she needs them to find out as quickly as possible. Simon's trip may be innocent, a simple coincidence, but if that's the case, Lyndsey wants to eliminate this poisonous suspicion of Eric Newman.

The eight a.m. call finds Sally Herbert at her desk. "I didn't have you pegged as an early bird," Herbert jokes. "I thought you guys in the clandestine service all kept late hours."

"I'm not sleeping much since I got this assignment," Lyndsey answers truthfully, before explaining what she needs. She gives Herbert everything she has on Simon.

"I'll see what I can do." It helps that Herbert has the authority as squad supervisor and that she's sympathetic. "I'm glad you called. There is another thing we need to discuss, though. FBI needs to stand up an interagency task force. It's part of our protocol for cases like this. We're going to pull in a couple agencies to do the work that falls outside our mandate, like the U.S. Attorneys office and State Department. I know CIA is concerned about possible leaks, but we do this all the time. We know how to manage it."

Lyndsey had been hoping it keep this tightly held for as long as possible, but she knew this day was coming. It's going to accelerate now, like a train barreling down the track. "I understand."

Herbert hesitates before continuing. "The other thing you should be prepared for is that this is going to be out of CIA's control very soon. We're talking about arresting a U.S. citizen and charging her with espionage. Once you bring in other agencies, you can't put the genie back in the lamp."

She thinks of the seventh floor, how they hate to be blindsided. But there's no doubt in her mind that, if she tells anyone at that level of her suspicions about Eric, he'll know about it within an hour. He is king of Russia Division. Inside the building, loyalties can run deep.

"I understand." Inwardly, Lyndsey roots for Herbert to find something to put her fears to rest.

"And your boss? He seems to have control issues."

Lyndsey swallows. "Don't worry about him. I'll handle him." She prays that she can.

"Okay. Sit tight. I'll be in touch."

Lyndsey is mulling over her call with Herbert when there's a knock at her door. Randy Detwiler stands with a folder in his hand.

"I hope it's not too early in the morning to talk poison," he says with a smile. He takes the chair opposite her desk; the space is barely able to accommodate his tall frame.

He slides the folder to her. "The police's medical examiner shared a blood sample from Kyle Kincaid."

Lyndsey flips to the report. "And what did they find?"

"It looks to be Novichok-7, an experimental agent. Really powerful. He's lucky to be alive."

"And you're sure of this?"

"Definitely a trademark Russian poison. Though it's usually administered through contact, through an aerosol spray, or put on a surface that the victim touches, say on a doorknob."

"It wasn't this time?"

Detwiler shakes his head, then pushes his eyeglasses up the bridge of his nose. "As far as the examiner can tell, it was ingested. That's his guess, anyway."

"He took it willingly?"

Detweler shrugs. "It does raise the possibility that Kincaid was a Russian agent, and he was given the poison to take in case he was discovered."

Kincaid doesn't strike Lyndsey as the type to sacrifice himself. If he was a Russian mole, and had been found out, Kincaid seems the type to offer to sing like a bird in exchange for leniency. Besides, why would he go to a motel fifteen minutes from his home and get half-undressed before attempting to kill himself?

"I don't think that's what happened."

Detwiler rises to leave. "If he ever comes out of that coma, you can ask him yourself."

Lyndsey glances back at the report. FAIRFAX COUNTY POLICE, OFFICE OF THE MEDICAL EXAMINER. At the very top, it reads, *Victim was found unconscious in room 207 of the Tysons Inn on Westwood Avenue. Police and ambulance arrived on the scene at 10:14 p.m. on December 7, 2018 . . .*

Her heart begins to race. Kincaid was found unconscious on the nineteenth. She's seen that date, in conjunction with Kyle Kincaid, before. The chat messages Molina sent to her.

That was the night Kyle Kincaid was meeting Theresa Warner for a date.

A date with Theresa ends with being found in a coma on a hotel bed. Could Theresa really do something like this? Lyndsey turns cold when she realizes, *yes, she could.* The woman Lyndsey knows absolutely could.

Before Lyndsey has time to ponder the implications, Maggie Kimball stands at her door. The office manager has her arms full, as usual. A stop on her way. She tilts her head toward the office. "Eric would like to see you. And between you and me, he's not in a good mood."

He has no reason to be, as far as Lyndsey can tell.

As she hurries the few steps to Eric's office, she weighs whether to tell him about Kyle Kincaid and the likelihood that Theresa is responsible. But then there's her uncertainty over Eric's involvement in Yaromir Popov's death. She needs to hear what the FBI finds out, but if Kincaid should die . . . She may run out of time.

"You want to see me?" She steps into Eric's office.

"Close the door." Maggie was right: Eric is tense. He points to the couch and steps around his desk to join her. "Any update from the FBI?"

For a moment, she is confused: he can't know about the call to Herbert, can he? If that were the case, he'd be bawling her out for taking Agency business to the FBI. She scans his face for telltale tics that he's hiding something, for anger bubbling under the surface, but either there's none or he's so good at hiding his true feelings that it no longer makes a difference. What he truly feels, what he truly believes, and what he wants others to believe. "FBI?"

But he doesn't seem to notice her confusion. "The next time you speak to them, I want you to let that squad supervisor know that we're going to have a team on the ground at the time of the arrest. It's going to be a joint operation. Tell her I'm not going to take 'no' for an answer."

Is this normal procedure? Eric isn't in the mood to be argued with. "Okay, I'll bring it up to her. But—"

He is too impatient and interrupts. "We're not going to let them hog all the glory, do you understand? This is our investigation—you're the one who figured out it was Theresa Warner. This will be a huge deal and we can't lose the limelight to the FBI. Do we know when the Russians are coming to get her?"

"The FBI thinks it could be any day now."

A huge sigh of relief escapes from Eric. Finally, his shoulders relax, his body unclenches. "Good. We're close now—so close. Keep a close watch on this, Lyndsey. We can't afford to make one mistake. We've got to bring Theresa Warner to justice."

The call Lyndsey is waiting for doesn't come until the afternoon. Lyndsey picks up the secure phone on the second ring.

"It's Sally Herbert. I thought this was going to be a simple job. I forgot that nothing with you CIA guys is ever simple."

It started off well, Herbert explains. The name is unusual enough to narrow the field. She played a hunch that, with his prior work for CIA and in security, he might be ex-military. Once she concentrated on military records, Simon proved easy to track down. She found him in the Northern Neck of Virginia. The area is old, home to the birthplace of George Washington, rich in Colonial history, now a slow southern graceland, a patchwork of working farms and marinas filled with expensive weekend toys owned by retired executives. "Simon probably lives there because he is an outdoorsman," Herbert says. According to his records, he's into hunting and fishing. A member of the NRA, owner of at least a half dozen firearms. Being an independent security specialist makes it possible to live the lifestyle that he does, out in the woods in the Northern Neck with his pickup truck and rifles and his bloodhound. It's the kind of work that takes him away for weeks and months at a time and pays well enough to afford him the opportunity to stay home and disappear into the woods for long, luxurious spells.

"I sent a couple agents out to talk to him. It's the kind of job done better in person rather than on the phone. You need to read the body language. The Norfolk office sent two ex-military. They'd have the best chance of connecting with him."

The FBI agents reported that Simon's reaction was—interesting. "He seemed alarmed that two FBI agents came all the way out to his little hunting shack just to ask him a few questions. That set the agents' radar off. They figured he was hiding something for sure. The more they pressed, the more nervous he became. We knew he had been to Russia, our database confirmed that, but when they asked what he'd been doing there, he got belligerent. He asked if it was a crime to go to Russia, then told them to get a subpoena. That's never a good sign." Herbert gives another dark chuckle. "Then he changed tactics. Decided to be a bit more cooperative. He told them he had gone on business, but he couldn't give them the name of his employer. Wasn't allowed to. The more they pressed, the more evasive he got."

Eventually, Simon admitted to them that he had been on official government business—"You know, playing the 'national security' card. He said that if it were up to him, he'd tell them, but they didn't have need-to-know. I guess he hoped that would be the end of it but of course, it wasn't. They said they needed a point of contact who could corroborate his story."

"Did he give them a name?"

"He sure did. Tony Schaffer." She rattles off a phone number. "Know him?"

It is the name Lyndsey's been dreading, though she doesn't want to admit it to Herbert. Tony Schaffer manages classified contracts for Russia Division, handling everything that couldn't be overtly tied to CIA. She is sure that if she finds the contract from the last time Simon had been hired, Schaffer's signature will be on it, too.

"I take it you know this Schaffer guy?" Herbert asks after the silence.

It feels like she's been punched in the gut. Any doubt about Eric's involvement has been erased. Worse yet is having to admit this to Herbert. It means she's been hoodwinked. Something nefarious had been going on and she failed to see it. "Yeah. I do."

Silence. "Look, you didn't explain Claude Simon's relevance to the

Warner case, but if there's a connection you need to let me know. Does that mean he was working for you guys?"

Herbert made it clear at the kickoff with Eric that Theresa's case belonged to FBI. She'd crossed a line and it was a federal matter now. But Yaromir Popov's murder—now that Lyndsey doubts it is connected to Kulakov and Nesterov, it doesn't belong to FBI, does it? The weight of the evidence is that Eric Newman arranged it. She can't go to FBI with that, not until she knows why.

"I'm not sure what it means," Lyndsey says. That much felt fair to say. "I'll talk to Tony and find out if we sent Simon to Russia." What she doesn't say, because she doesn't need to, is that the case just got turned on its head.

Herbert waits a beat. "Look, Lyndsey, I'll give you space to work this through, but are you sure this isn't something I need to know? It'll only slow down the investigation if you don't tell us everything."

"You and I know this could have serious implications at the Agency. I don't want to be wrong. I just need a little more time to be sure of what I'm seeing."

"Uh-huh."

"Twenty-four hours. Then I'll tell you everything I know."

"I'll hold you to it." Herbert hangs up.

Alone, the realization hits Lyndsey like a baseball bat. She doesn't have a doubt, not a whisper, not a glimmer. Eric Newman was behind Yaromir Popov's death.

THIRTY-SEVEN

There's a courtyard outside the Agency cafeteria. It's got a handful of tables, and benches under the scant trees. A huge sculpture stands in a corner, strips of metal with letters of the alphabet punched out in seemingly random placement, inviting further inspection. It's meant to represent cryptography, and those letters encase a hidden message.

Lyndsey sits on a bench staring at the statue. The sun is filtered by trees but still glints brightly off the metal, making her squint. She left her desk because she couldn't risk running into Eric in her current frame of mind.

What game is he playing? No matter how she twists and turns the facts, she can't think of one scenario that makes sense. Why would Eric Newman bring her in to solve the case—or *not* solve the case—if he's the one who had Popov killed?

He says he is on her side.

She looks at the metal sculpture, but her gaze goes right through it. The letters are a tangle. Like everything else, it seems.

She goes back to her own puzzle, trying to lace the pieces together in a way that tells a logical story. Eric hired Simon to kill Popov. No one knows why Popov was rushing to Washington, but the circumstances imply he had something to tell CIA but didn't trust Moscow Station. What did he know?

That's where she comes up blank. He had something to tell her, according to Masha. Something he didn't think he could share with Moscow Station. Which could mean he didn't trust his handler, Tom Cassidy, or didn't trust the entire station.

All she can do is think about Eric. Why this charade when Popov was killed, when he was behind it all along? It couldn't have been sanctioned, then.

He authorized it on his own.

She's afraid of the emotions running through her right now like a raging river. At CIA, you're trained to be wary of emotions. Emotions cloud your judgment and trick your mind, leave you susceptible to manipulation and error. So right now, she's fighting with everything she has. She wants to go into Eric's office and push him up against the wall and demand to know what he's doing, damn the secrets within secrets, *tell me*. Why—of all the assets available to him, all the deadbeats and liars and drunks who've strung CIA along for years—he chose to sacrifice Yaromir Popov. But you don't ask the fox to explain why he went into the henhouse when all the chickens are lying dead on the ground.

She feels eyes on her. She's sure it's paranoia, nothing more than an old friend who didn't know she was back from Beirut, ready to walk over with a big "hello." Lyndsey looks over her shoulder, expecting to find nothing there, no one—but it's Theresa. Lyndsey would recognize her trademark red lipstick anywhere.

Theresa is looking at her quizzically. They haven't been seeing as much of each other in the office of late, not like at first. Lyndsey realizes, cynically, that was because Theresa was looking for information about the investigation, not out of real friendship. This realization comes with a sting.

Yet, their friendship felt real.

Don't be a chump: it's all smoke and mirrors. And has been since day one.

*L*yndsey *suddenly remembers her first date with Davis. He brought her to Bourj Hammoud, the Armenian neighborhood in the city, for a dinner of sujuk shawarma. After dinner, they strolled back down Armenia Street and Davis told her stories from his various assignments, the safe stuff, no secrets, no names. The more she enjoyed herself, the more she worried because it couldn't be. It wasn't allowed. If she were smart, she would nip it in the bud, stop it before it began.*

Davis picked up on her silence, and tucked her arm over his, drawing her close. "I know what you're thinking—and don't. Don't listen to them. Don't let them think for you, Lyndsey."

"But, the rules—"

"Fuck their rules—no, really. If you follow their rules, you're going to miss the important things. The things that are worth fighting for. You and I know we're not doing anything wrong, so why should we give up the good thing we could have, just to obey some pointless rule? The thing is, they wouldn't want you to, if they knew. They need rule breakers. You just need to know which rules to break."

Theresa is still waiting across the courtyard. Lyndsey has only a second to decide what to do. She's angry with Theresa and more than a little wary—she probably put a man in the hospital—but those dangerous emotions tell her to talk to her. It's not too late to save her. And Theresa has the answer. She knows what's really going on.

Yet, too, she knows what Raymond Murphy and the Counterintelligence guys and the people on the seventh floor would think: she's lost her mind. Theresa Warner is a traitor. She's crossed over.

Lyndsey's heart squeezes. But *they* did this to her. The seventh floor, Eric, all the people who let her down. They made Theresa Warner into a bad guy.

At the heart of all this is a greater evil, she suspects. But she has to be able to prove it.

And Theresa Warner might be the only one who can do that.

Lyndsey rises from the bench and starts to walk to Theresa.

Theresa looks happy to see her. She holds something up as Lyndsey approaches: a cup of coffee.

Theresa laughs. "You look like you could use this. Two pumps of caramel, just like you like it."

Lyndsey stares at the paper cup. Theresa's hand is trembling ever so slightly. Confident Theresa, who would never let anyone see her sweat.

Lyndsey takes the cup to be friendly. But she doesn't feel neighborly toward Theresa at this very moment. "There's something we have to discuss. Where we won't be overheard. Come with me."

They sit in Lyndsey's car in the parking lot. The seats smell strongly of vinyl baking in the sun, and of cleaner with a fruity perfume.

Theresa's perfect eyebrow arches. Her breathing is shallow, a fox run to ground. She sips at her coffee, hands still trembling. It's disconcerting. "What's this about, Lyndsey? Why are we sitting in your car?"

Now or never. Once said, it can never be taken back. Theresa could run. The case could blow up, and the truth—the delicate truth, hidden deep within a tangle of conflicting clues—could be trampled in the ensuing investigation.

The Widow may be too hardened, too bitter, to agree to cooperate. Lyndsey senses that she isn't.

But there's only one way to find out. Only one way to save Theresa Warner.

She takes a deep breath. "I *know,* Theresa. I know what you've been up to with the Russians."

The Widow tries to fake surprise and indignation. Her eyebrows shoot up, her mouth drops open in a perfect red O. But it only lasts a fraction of a second. "That's insane. How can you accuse me of such a thing? My husband—"

"You can play it that way if you like, Theresa, but it won't do you any good. I'm trying to help you. I know—*we* know, the FBI is involved now—the Russians are coming for you in a few days. We know that you're planning to run." Theresa takes a breath to speak, then stops. She presses her lips together. *She wants to speak but she's stopping herself.* "I know everything—most everything," Lyndsey corrects. "I know why you're doing this. Eric lied to you and hid things from you. You made a deal with the Russians for Richard. It's not too late, though. Think about what will happen if you go through with this. CIA knows, FBI knows. They're not going to let you leave with the Russians. They have a dragnet set up and they'll catch you. And then what happens? You'll be disgraced. You'll lose everything: your house, your bank accounts, your family, your friends. Your son. Everything."

In the passenger seat, Theresa turns away from her. Her chin drops, and she closes her eyes. *Doesn't want to see the truth.*

"There's no turning back now. If you warn the Russians that we know, the FBI will still track you down and arrest you. We've got enough to do that, but we want your Russian handlers, too. I'm giving you a chance to help yourself," Lyndsey continues. "Think about Brian. What will happen to him? Who will take care of him? The disgrace will ruin his life, haunt him forever. And Richard—"

Theresa laughs bitterly. "If I'm arrested, at least Richard's story will come out. They'll be forced to do something."

"Is that what you were hoping for all along? To help Richard? You're not a traitor."

Another rueful chuckle, then a sigh. The resistance crumbles like a sand castle under the tide. "Of course not. The plan was to get him out of prison and for the three of us to find a quiet place to start a new life." She brushes at the corners of her eyes. "I wasn't asking so much. A normal life. That's what other people get."

For a moment, it's not clear what Theresa will do next. The air between them is charged, electric. Anything is possible, even violence. Lyndsey is pretty sure she could physically stop Theresa from harming her—or herself. She seems so fragile at this moment.

"Were you out to get me all along?" Theresa asks. She is sad in that moment. Her mouth is grim. "Our friendship—was it an act, from the beginning?"

"I could ask the same of you."

Theresa looks wounded. She stares out the windshield, something ticking in the back of her mind. "You might as well let me go. The damage is done. They have Nesterov . . . and you know what they did to Kulakov. There's no taking it back. But Richard would be freed. Doesn't he deserve that?"

This woman is not about to accept the fact that she's lost. Sweat trickles down the back of Lyndsey's neck. "It's over, Theresa. I'm saying help me fix this, and I'll help you."

Theresa stares at her hands. "You don't understand. I've done things . . . things you can't help me with."

"You mean Kyle Kincaid?"

A curt nod.

"You're right—I can't make any promises there. You better pray he doesn't die."

"He wanted to blackmail me." That laugh again, brittle. "They're wolves on the seventh floor, you know. They'll never forgive me. They'll never let me go."

There is a flicker in Theresa's eyes: *she wants to trust me.* "I'm asking you, Theresa, *as your friend:* don't do this. Trust me. We'll find a way."

The seconds stretch long. There is no choice, not really. Theresa is taking a long time, Lyndsey knows, because it means admitting she will never see Richard again. It means giving up on him. She has to choose between her husband and her son.

Finally, she asks in a whisper, "What do you need me to do?"

"Let's go somewhere else to talk. I don't feel safe—even in the parking lot." She turns the key in the ignition, puts the transmission in reverse.

And then, Theresa does a strange thing. She lowers the window, then grabs Lyndsey's untouched coffee and throws it out. The cup hits the car parked next to it, coating the driver's door in a wash of brown liquid.

"What was that about?" Lyndsey asks as she pulls away.

"Don't doubt that I was ever your friend," is all Theresa will say.

They drive into McLean, to a tiny coffee shop in a quiet shopping center. It is the middle of a weekday and Lyndsey is certain that they won't be seen together by anyone from work. They sit in the back of a small, bright shop. It's just the two of them and a middle-aged waitress in jeans.

As they settle at a table, Lyndsey thinks she sees a crack in Theresa's flawless façade. She looks tired, like she's been running for months.

"I'd like you to clear up a few things for me," Lyndsey says. They both have their hands wrapped around thick ceramic mugs. "You had nothing to do with Yaromir Popov's death, did you?"

Theresa's head jerks up like a spooked horse. "No. I didn't even know he was one of ours until the incident on the plane."

Her expression and body language support that she's telling the truth. Taking into account the data trail and what Evert Northrop said, Lyndsey is inclined to believe her.

"Nesterov and Kulakov—you gave the FSB those names."

Theresa drops her chin. She can't look at Lyndsey. "Yes." Unsaid between them is that Kulakov's death is on her head. Nesterov is still missing, and she'll be responsible for whatever happens to this man, too. "But those were the only two."

Lyndsey knows what Raymond Murphy would ask: *how do I know you're not lying? Prove it.* All that will come soon enough, the interrogation, interviews, Theresa showing them every step she took, every file she touched.

It's time for Lyndsey to share her real concern with Theresa and it's impossible to predict how she'll react. "I have a suspicion—with no way to prove it, at least not yet—that Eric is involved in this."

For a moment, this seems to amuse Theresa. But if it's true, she's afraid to trust it. Theresa smiles sadly. "As much as I'd like to believe that, Eric had nothing to do with this. I—I let my anger get the best of me. I did it to myself."

Lyndsey lets Theresa's remorse play out before she lays out all the facts. Theresa is an experienced reports officer—she has a stellar reputation, as a matter of fact—and Lyndsey could use her perspective. If she'll tell the truth.

Theresa listens as Lyndsey tells her about the poison, Simon, and—without going into too much detail—the strange digital fingerprints left all over Popov's files. "It appears that Eric has something to do with

Popov's death, I agree with you on that. But all the things I've done . . . He has nothing to do with it. I went to Eric when I found out Richard was still alive. He was as surprised as I was by the news . . . I begged Eric to help me, but he refused. He told me to make my peace with it, that the seventh floor would never reopen the case . . ." Theresa shakes her head.

Lyndsey goes cold, like being plunged in an ice bath. "Eric told you he didn't know about Richard? You're sure of it?" *She doesn't know. She's never seen the transcript . . . the damning transcript in the Razorbill file . . .*

Lyndsey has to stop herself from grabbing Theresa by the shoulders and shaking her. "He lied to you, Theresa—"

"I don't follow you. Lied about what?"

"Eric knew Richard was alive. He knew and never told you. He was the one who proposed it to the seventh floor. That you not be told . . ."

Theresa draws back, her face curdling like she's bitten a poisoned apple. "What are you talking about? How do you know?"

Lyndsey can barely keep her eyes on Theresa's face as she recounts the transcript for her. Sadness, hurt, anger pass over Theresa's face in quick succession. Solidifying into anger, blind fury.

"So he did it to save himself. He insisted the seventh floor had already made up its mind. He swore they'd squash me like a bug if I tried to go to my congressman or the press. I had Brian to think about . . . He—he told me to trust him, that he would take care of me. It's been an act, all this time. That he was Richard's friend, that he cared for me . . . An act."

She stops, silent. The two women exchange a knowing look. They're in this together now. They will both succeed—or both fail. Together.

THIRTY-EIGHT

Tarasenko finds himself back in the city he hates most.

He takes an Uber from National airport to his hotel. Settled into the back seat of the Honda Accord (very clean by Russian standards, and the driver even offered him a bottle of water), he watches the cityscape roll by. George Washington Parkway, past exits for the Pentagon and Arlington National Cemetery, and now plunged into woods as dark and lonely as any Russian folktale. And he's heard just as many stories about the parks of Washington as he has about the woods outside Moscow. Who knows what goes on in these woods at night? Murders, drug deals, assaults . . . It is not what it pretends to be—to the world, to itself.

The main reason he doesn't like D.C. is that it tries too hard to be liked. So many pretty monuments, too many trendy shops. Too many expensive, fancy cars on the roads. It's all too neat, too clean for his tastes. The capital of a great power should be like a heavyweight prizefighter, in his opinion. Washington lacks the spine of steel that a true superpower needs to let other countries know that it's not fucking around. It should inspire fear. Washington, D.C., lost its spine a few presidents back and it's only gotten worse with time. Now it's overrun with lobbyists and lawyers telling the government what to do, corporations backing politicians like it's a horse race. They may be in it for the money in Moscow, too, but no one forgets who is in charge. It's not a crazy land grab, everyone out to get what they can. Under the Hard Man, there is harmony. He keeps everyone in line.

In the Uber, he keeps an eye out for an FBI tail but he's pretty sure he's clean. He's traveling under a new identity and it looks like they haven't picked up on it yet. More proof that Washington isn't the superpower it once was. There was a time when the FBI would be on them from the second they got off the plane. In Beijing, you have to worry about facial recognition everywhere you go. Again, a superpower that doesn't fuck around. Younger Russian intelligence officers prefer to be posted to Singapore and Hong Kong and mainland China for the challenge. The technology in these places keeps you on your toes. Keeps you from getting complacent. It's no fun when your adversary doesn't give a fuck.

As he drinks that evening in the hotel bar, he is overcome with an ill-advised recklessness, a child whose parents have gone out for the first time without getting a babysitter. Should he stick a fork in an electrical outlet, leap from the roof of the garage into the bushes, play pranks on the neighbors? He orders up a rental car—no Uber for what he's about to do—and drives out to northern Virginia, to the neighborhood where Kanareyka lives. He loops through the dark streets for over an hour just in case there is a tail following him, then parks within easy view of the gray-and-white house, lights a cigarette, and watches.

The Rezidentura has been circumspect about bugging the house of a CIA officer. For most assets, it would be a given, the price of doing business. They would sneak in under the guise of an electrician or other serviceman and place recording devices in the house. But the housekeeper doesn't let anyone in when Kanareyka is away, and they know better than to try this with Kanareyka herself. The Rezidentura has to make do with men watching her house from fake service vans, risky in a neighborhood of former spies who think nothing of knocking on your window and demanding to see identification or, worse yet, calling the police.

Kanareyka's Volvo is in the driveway. At one point, he sees Kanareyka through an upstairs window, her angular face in profile, arms crossed over her chest, looking down as though she is talking to someone who is very short. It has to be Kanareyka's son, the one mentioned in the reports. There is a blue glow cast on Kanareyka's cheek from a television or computer monitor. Is her son begging for a few more minutes to play his video games, like boys in Russia? Like boys everywhere. They talk for a few more minutes and then the light clicks off and the room goes black.

Everything looks normal, and that is good. Again, in this neighborhood of spies, you don't want to raise suspicions that the family is about to leave. On the other hand, everything looks too normal, and that makes him nervous. Could Kanareyka be trying to trick them? Maybe she is not planning to flee after all. Maybe she's going to *defy* them. He studies the quiet house—no signs of packing, no trash piled on the curb waiting for pickup, nothing out of place—and puffs on his cigarette. What does this utterly placid house tell him about Kanareyka's state of mind? He needs to know more. After all, he's the one walking into that house in a day's time. It's not too much to want assurances, to know he's not heading into a trap. He needs to look inside.

Dropping the cigarette butt out the car window, he zips up the front of his dark jacket to cover the light-colored shirt beneath it, which glows like it's radioactive in the dark. Like the seasoned case officer that he is, Tarasenko walks casually down the street, like he lives there, a homeowner taking in the night air. He doesn't cross onto her property until he gets to a spot behind a huge tree, hidden completely in shadow. If anyone had been watching, it would've looked like he simply disappeared, but no, he is making his way behind the garage to the back of the house, where he can get close to the windows. For a big man, he is surprisingly quiet on his feet. He sidles around the shrubs and close to the window without snapping twigs or rustling old, forgotten leaves.

He finds one where the blinds are not all the way down, and he can use the gap of a few inches to peer in. The room is dark, but he can see through into the next room, where a light is on. It is very still. No television, no radio or stereo. It doesn't appear that anyone is on the lower level.

He figures out a way to get to the second story. He pulls himself onto the roof over the enclosed patio and then crawls on his belly to the gable that looks over the backyard. There's a faint glow from one of the windows so he heads toward that. It's tricky, because the roof here is steep and the ledge under the window is narrow, mere inches. There is nothing to stop him if he should fall. It's only about fifteen feet to the ground; he wouldn't injure himself but there's no way he wouldn't be heard.

He makes his way cautiously, gripping the trim under the bank of windows to steady himself, then peers around the sill. Theresa left the curtain partly open, perhaps because she is a fan of moonlight, or because a row of tall trees gives her privacy from the neighbors. Tarasenko holds his breath and inches forward, until his face is close to the glass. Carefully, he peers through the gap in the curtains. Kanareyka wouldn't like it if she found out he'd been spying on her but really, what can spies expect if not surveillance?

There is Kanareyka, her pale skin luminous in the low light. She reminds Tarasenko of a ballerina: elegant and graceful, but also cold and aloof. Not his kind of woman. The room she is in is spare, nearly empty. It's not a room anyone has been living in, it's too sad. She is sorting clothing in a cardboard box. Some pieces she drops in a careless pile by her feet, others she puts in a second, smaller box. She moves slowly, deliberating. These are a man's clothes, Tarasenko figures out. *Must be her husband's. She's packing clothing for him.*

She pauses at one piece, a rather worn and rumpled plaid shirt. It is very American, like something you'd see on a lumberjack in an old drawing. As a case officer, Tarasenko has been schooled in American folklore and history. The stories Americans tell themselves about their country, bedtime stories meant to comfort frightened children. She buries her face in the shirt. He watches for a moment, mesmerized. There is something special about it, her husband's favorite perhaps, and she hasn't seen it for years. She *wallows* in it. He thinks he sees her shoulders heave; is she crying? She has never cried in front of him, though she has had plenty of reason to, and it occurs to him that he had come to assume she did not cry. That something inside her had hardened over the years, because of these bad circumstances. But perhaps she is not completely ruined, yet. Perhaps there is still a vulnerable part deep inside.

They have not told Richard Warner what has happened or what is coming. After hundreds of days in captivity, Richard Warner has given up nothing, not one scrap of information to make it go easier on him, though no one at Langley would blame him if he had. There is no way a man like this will approve of what his wife has done. Morozov had wanted to tell him, because Tarasenko's boss is a sick fuck. He had come to resent Warner—just as he resents being trapped inside Russia's borders, CIA as patient as a remorseless mother-in-law—and thought it would be fun to torture him, letting him see that they had gotten forbidden knowledge at his expense. Morozov left it up to Tarasenko, however, and Tarasenko did not see the advantage in tipping his hand. He hated to admit it—he liked to think his operations were airtight—but anything could still happen. Kanareyka could get cold feet, she might be discovered, the Hard Man could catch wind of their plans and put a stop to it. The prospect of the latter, especially, made him nervous, turned his guts to ice water. It was his ass on the line, not Morozov's, and he had only the wily old general's word that he would protect him.

Seeing Kanareyka cry shames him. She really does love her husband, to be willing to go to such lengths for him. He thinks of the women in his life and cannot imagine any one of them capable of the same devotion for him. Quite the opposite: they'd applaud his jailers and encourage them to throw away the key. What Kanareyka is doing for her husband takes tremendous courage. He cannot despise her. If anything, he comes to respect her a bit more.

In any case, it looks as if she is proceeding as planned. Satisfied, he scrabbles back the way he came, inching carefully across the roof before dropping down to the covered porch, and then to the ground, stealing back the way he came like the shadow he aspires to be.

There is one more thing he needs to do tonight.

He drives a few miles down the highway, following the bright streetlamps. The address he looked up after getting the name from Kanareyka. He wants to know more about his adversary, this Lyndsey Duncan.

The parking lot outside her apartment building is completely still. It is what the Americans call a garden apartment, the buildings only a couple stories tall with open stairwells connecting them. It's not so late that there aren't lights on in some of the windows. He pulls a pair of binoculars out of the bag in the passenger's seat.

The curtains looking into Lyndsey Duncan's apartment are half-drawn, enough to afford Tarasenko a glimpse inside. It's tantalizing, like peeking through a keyhole. A figure moves back and forth in the room and for a long time is nothing more than a shadow. Like watching a ghost.

But then she stops right in front of the divide and he can see her clearly. Tall, lithe, strong. Long legs, which he has always liked on a woman. As a matter of fact, he likes everything about her: her confidence, which he can tell by the way she stands. The intelligent expression on her face. Her reddish hair, which falls over her shoulders. He can picture himself twisting that hair around his fist. He can picture himself doing a lot of things with this woman. A familiar, not-unpleasant longing comes over him. It's all he can do not to charge up those stairs and force his way into the apartment.

He could act on his impulses now, but that would ruin everything. Better to play the long game. He stows the binoculars and starts the engine, heading back to his hotel.

Kukla. That will be his name for Lyndsey Duncan. Doll.

THIRTY-NINE

"We've had eyes on Cassidy since he landed at National."

Lyndsey sits inside a humongous black SUV, an FBI agent at the wheel, a second in the passenger seat. Sally Herbert sits next to Lyndsey in the back seat, not nervous in the least. They're streaking down the George Washington Parkway. A cloak of indigo has fallen over the city. D.C. is not a party town at night: the road traffic is thin and the sidewalks empty. The SUV glides through darkness decorated by red brake lights, streetlights, and the occasional distant glow from spotlights trained on a skyscraper or monument.

They're going to the Hilton in Tysons Corner. Cassidy is staying there while he's in-country; they know this from the itinerary he filed with Russia Division, which Lyndsey got from Maggie. According to his itinerary, he'll spend a few days helping Eric with the side operation and then take a week of home leave in Ocean City, Maryland. He has no idea of the welcome he's about to get.

The driver pulls up in front of the hotel. Lyndsey remembers the reception area from previous visits. It looks something like a futuristic ski lodge, roughhewn wood and stone finishes and modern furniture. There is little activity, thanks to the late hour. A couple strolls through the lobby from the bar, and in the far corner a small party is camped in a comfortable seating area finishing their drinks, light from the flames twinkling off martini glasses.

At reception, Herbert flashes her credentials at the clerk and the poor man's face freezes as he tries not to betray alarm. "The man who just checked in—what's the room number?"

On the elevator ride to the sixth floor, Lyndsey tries to calm the pounding of her heart. She's done a lot of things in her career—shaking surveillance tails while feeling eyes on her back, following adversaries on their way to meet their assets in a crowded shopping district—but leading a team of FBI agents to a colleague's room isn't one of them. She hopes she'll never have to do it again.

Cassidy answers the door and it's obvious he had no idea what was waiting for him on the other side. He looks like he didn't get a wink of sleep on the fifteen-hour journey. He's in the same clothes he wore on the plane, jeans and a sports jacket, rumpled and wrinkled. A faintly sour, stale cloud hangs around him.

"Lyndsey? What are you doing here?" He seems to ignore the credentials Herbert holds up as she pushes her way into the room, less interested in the FBI than in her. They leave an FBI agent on station in the hall as Herbert closes the door.

"I'm Special Agent Sally Herbert of the FBI Counterintelligence Division." She uses her height to her advantage with Cassidy, who is short, forcing him back a couple steps. With Lyndsey on the other side, Cassidy is boxed against the wall. He cringes as he backs away. *He knows he did something wrong.*

"We have your management's permission to speak with you. Why don't you take a seat?"

He turns away instead, rubbing the back of his neck. *He doesn't want to face us.* "Now is not a good time. My flight just got in and I'm beat. Can't it wait till the morning?"

"I'm afraid not."

Reluctantly, he sits on the edge of the bed.

"We're conducting an investigation into one of your colleagues"— Cassidy doesn't look surprised, but then, Eric would've told him about Theresa—"and need to ask you a few questions."

He runs a hand through his sticky hair, giving him a harried, disheveled look. "Whoever it is, they're not going anywhere tonight. Look, I'm beat. The Moscow to D.C. route is a bitch. Can't it wait till morning?" he asks again testily.

Herbert presses on. "New information has come to light concerning Genghis. He believed his cooperation with CIA had been revealed to the FSB, and that's why he was headed to Washington."

It's a bluff Lyndsey fed Herbert, bait to see how Cassidy will react. He shrugs as though it's common knowledge. "Why else would he be going to Washington?"

"You were the one who told him, right? But I couldn't find any reporting to the fact—like there *should* be, right?—so perhaps you can tell us who gave you this information."

Cassidy's eyes dart momentarily to Lyndsey, an uncontrollable tell. The unmistakable look of a rat who feels the trap closing on him. "Why do you think it was me?"

This is the missing part, the piece that will bring everything together. Cassidy has got to be involved—he was Popov's handler, after all—the trigger that sent the old Russian spy running to find Lyndsey.

All they have to do is get him to admit it.

"Masha told me," Lyndsey blurts. The thought comes to her out of thin air. "Yaromir shared everything with Masha. He shared this, too."

The color drains from Cassidy's face. It doesn't dawn on him to question her, probably because of the immediacy of the situation, the FBI agents hemming him in. "That's right. I haven't had time to write it up yet, so much going on. The information came from another of my assets. He told me Genghis was blown, so I passed it on to Genghis. Told him not to panic and to sit tight. We were in the process of deciding what to do for him when he bolted. It wasn't my fault."

Cassidy's gaze shifts left and high, like he's plucking thoughts from midair, another common tell. It could be that he and Eric didn't work this part through, or that he's exhausted and scared, and can't remember the story they'd come up with. In all likelihood, though, they didn't bother to tidy up this loose end, confident they wouldn't be questioned. Popov *was* a double agent and if Russia found out, they would assassinate him. It happened with unfortunate regularity. No one would think to question it.

Herbert leans forward, using all her height. "Who is this other source, Tom? And why did you talk to Genghis before Station had a plan in hand to deal with it?"

She has rattled him. He looks at Herbert, and then around the hotel room at the dark gray walls and the curtains rippling over the big glass window. "I'm not going to discuss this here. These are highly classified sources and we're in a hotel, for god's sake."

Herbert is unbothered. They'd hoped he'd make this very objection. "I was just about to say the same thing. Let's go down to FBI headquarters. We'll use the classified SCIF there, and then you'll feel like you can speak freely."

It was Herbert's plan to take him to the forbidding FBI headquarters building all along. Now Cassidy is on Herbert's territory. He was shaken up by the unexpected visit to his hotel room, but now he's been whisked away, flanked by a pair of strapping federal agents and escorted through the deserted halls of this concrete fortress to a vault deep in the earth. It must feel like he's being taken to prison. The overhead lights here are harsh and carve deep circles under Cassidy's eyes. He looks like a convict. He's left in an interrogation room by himself for a few minutes while Herbert and Lyndsey watch from behind a one-way mirror.

"It's good to give them time to think," Herbert says. "Our job tonight is to get him to tell us what his role was." On the other side of the smoky glass, Cassidy sits with a forced look of blankness. He tries to seem dazed and overwhelmed and above all innocent, but Lyndsey suspects it's an act. "This isn't a typical case, and I'm not exactly sure what we should be looking for. I'll know it when I hear it. But you should be prepared for bad news, Lyndsey. Whatever he did, we might not be able to bring a case against him. A lot of intelligence work falls outside of U.S. domestic law. There's a good chance that whatever Cassidy did, it was under the direction of his supervisor. Even if it was illegal, and resulted in an unwarranted death, his culpability will be mitigated."

Lyndsey tries hard to tamp down her anger, to stop thinking of Yaromir Popov. It's all she can do not to burst into the interrogation room and shake Cassidy hard. *How could you do this to him,* she wants to ask. *He depended on you.* What could be worth that man's life?

Before she can do anything, Herbert gives her a stern look. "I know how you must feel, Lyndsey, but stay with me. We need him to talk. Follow my lead."

They go into the interview room together. The room is dingy and the sour smell has gotten worse. It's the smell of fear. How many people have they interrogated here? It must've seen all manner of suspects: presumed terrorists and armed robbers and serial killers, yes, also federal types gone bad. FBI agents who cooperated with drug cartels and organized crime, CIA officers who sold their souls to the other side. Aldrich Ames or

Robert Hanssen may have sat in that chair. Greed, ambition, bloodlust: these emotions hover in the air like poltergeists, impossible to banish.

Herbert sits in the chair opposite Cassidy, resting her forearms on the table. "You're in a SCIF, Mr. Cassidy. Authorization for us to talk to you came from the highest levels of your organization. And you should know that I've been read into all Moscow Station's compartments. There isn't one aspect of your work that you can't discuss with me. Is that clear?"

Cassidy gives a halfhearted smirk. He may be nervous but he's not ready to throw in the towel.

Herbert takes in his smirk and nods. "Let's get right to it, then, shall we? We know you told Yaromir Popov that the FSB knew of his relationship with the CIA. How had you learned this?"

"I told you: one of my assets."

"You'll give us his name. And he'll corroborate this?" Herbert jabs a finger into the tabletop. "Look, we're pretty sure the FSB *didn't* know about Yaromir Popov. So you just told me a lie. Lying to the FBI is a federal offense."

"It's not my fault if an asset gave me the wrong information," Cassidy blurts, shooting upright. "I was trying to protect him." The reaction is right, but the tone of voice is all wrong: whiny and high. A liar's voice.

Herbert doesn't change. She's a stone wall. "Look, we know something funny's going on and we know you're not behind it. You're a bit player— you're being used. Be smart. This is your chance to clear yourself, to give us your side of the story."

A furrow deepens between Cassidy's eyes. A man having an argument with himself. "You're right. I was just following orders."

"So, tell us what those orders were." More internal struggle. Herbert tries again. "Who gave you the orders to talk to Genghis? Was it the Chief of Station?"

This should worry Cassidy. He doesn't want to implicate someone wrongly. His frown is twisted; he's conflicted.

Lyndsey decides to build on that. "You don't have to say anything, Tom. We'll take your silence to mean it was Hank Bremer. Just nod if that's correct."

From what she's heard, Cassidy is tight with Bremer. The Station Chief seems to have been supportive of Cassidy, giving him good assets to run despite his questionable record. Cassidy wouldn't want to burn that bridge. From where he's sitting, he's going to need all the help he can get.

He glares at her murderously. "You'd like that, wouldn't you? You have it in for Hank, don't you?" A good try, but Lyndsey is not going to let him push her buttons.

Maybe it's the hours and hours of grueling travel, or being surrounded by FBI agents in this dark, airless space, but after another minute of silent struggle, something breaks inside Cassidy. "It wasn't Hank. Don't drag him into this—he wasn't involved. It was Eric Newman. He told me to tell Popov he'd been blown."

Lyndsey has to force herself not to react. Even with everything she knows and suspects, this is still hard to hear. A man she trusted ordered the death of a man she adored.

Herbert leans forward. "But it wasn't true?"

Cassidy won't look in Lyndsey's direction. "Not to my knowledge, no."

"Why?" Lyndsey checks herself before she can lunge at Cassidy. *How could you betray him? You were his last line of protection.*

Cassidy leans back in his chair like a schoolboy caught red-handed. "It was some plan of Newman's. Look, he told me to do it. That's what we do, we follow orders."

"You don't know what's behind all this?"

"Oh no, I know what Newman was trying to do." Cassidy turns to Herbert, his expression perfectly calm. Smug, even. "It's a trap for Evgeni Morozov."

His words fall on Lyndsey like a landslide. For a moment, nothing makes sense.

Morozov. Tarasenko's boss. Tarasenko, Theresa's handler. But there's been no connection to Yaromir Popov . . .

Except for Eric. Eric is the only connection.

"Morozov's been on CIA's most wanted list for years now. This was a plan to shake him loose, to dangle something he wanted in front of his nose in order to get him to come out. And Morozov took the bait. To snare a CIA officer, someone from the inner sanctum . . . And Richard Warner's wife, no less. The man Putin hated above nearly all others."

Stars dance before Lyndsey's eyes like she's been hit with a baseball bat. It had been right in front of her, pieces of a puzzle begging to be put together. She sees Eric's plan now, devastatingly cunning and breathtakingly selfish.

We're nothing but pawns to him. Popov, Theresa, Richard . . . even me.

Lyndsey opens her mouth to speak but Herbert holds up a hand. "And who is the bait, Tom? Who is Eric Newman using to draw out this Russian?"

Cassidy blinks as though woken from a dream. "I—I'm not sure. I thought it was Popov."

"He's dead, so it can't be him, can it?" Lyndsey slams her hands on the table. "*Theresa Warner* is the bait. A fellow officer."

Only then does Cassidy acknowledge her. He turns his head slowly and smiles, the smile of a mortal enemy. Why would he hate her? She's younger, and a woman; she's done nothing to him, except be a better case officer. But that's the only excuse some people need. "No one put a gun to her head to make her hand classified information to the Russians. She chose to do this herself."

"You don't know what you're talking about." Lyndsey wants to tell him that he was tricked. He thinks he is clever, but he was played by a master. A soulless man with no conscience.

Herbert catches her eye. *Don't say another word. Let him talk.*

"You think you know everything, Duncan, but you're still a rookie. Where would you be without your protectors? Without Reese Munroe looking out for you, or Yaromir Popov? You think no one knows why Popov was so good to you—and for me there was nothing? It doesn't take a genius to figure it out. The old man was worthless since you left— worthless. If we lost him, it was no big deal." He looks back to Herbert. "You can't possibly understand. Morozov has been thumbing his nose at CIA for ten years. Killing one of our COS in broad daylight, in front of his own home. The guys who got Morozov would be heroes. We'd get any-thing we wanted. We'd be set for the rest of our careers."

Lyndsey wonders what she would find in Cassidy's personnel folder: botched operations, personal arguments with colleagues, pettiness and intrigues. Probably a bad marriage, estranged kids, maybe bankruptcies. Not one or two bad choices but a string of them, a chain of mistakes held together by self-pity. Bad people make bad decisions. Weak minds are easily led. It's obvious that this wasn't Cassidy's idea: it was Eric's. Cassidy is malleable, just what Eric needed.

She feels exhausted, suddenly. She aches all over, like she's been dragged behind a truck. Days and weeks of searching, searching, searching—and this was under her nose all along.

Tricked. It was all a trick.

Cassidy is mad and red-faced, like a crying infant. He's been waiting to say these things for a long time and now it's his chance to show them—

Herbert, the uninformed, and Lyndsey, the misguided—who really is the better man. "Here's the other thing you don't know, either of you: what Eric did, that's the way it is at CIA. We're supposed to be bold. We're supposed to do the things nobody else can. You want to be all high and mighty and make us out to be the bad guys, but it only goes to show that you don't get it. We didn't do anything wrong here. The ends justify the means—you've heard that before, haven't you, Lyndsey? Well, this is what it looks like." He stares hard at her. "If you think what Eric Newman did was wrong, you don't belong and you never will."

Cold shivers run down Lyndsey's body. So, assets like Yaromir Popov and officers like Theresa Warner can be toyed with so casually, because they don't matter. The irony—lost on Cassidy—is that if Cassidy thinks Eric will be loyal to him and protect him now that the whole thing is unraveling, he's delusional. There is no honor among spies, apparently.

"If you don't think big, you're not doing your job," he says belligerently. "The only crime is getting caught."

Where has Lyndsey heard that before?

They slip into a nearby room to confer, leaving Cassidy alone.

Herbert has an assistant fetch water, coffee, to give Lyndsey time to recover. Herbert excuses herself to check her cell phone while Lyndsey takes in everything she has heard. How she wishes she could leave the building, get into her car and drive. To look at something—anything—that will take her away from where she is. She feels the need to purge the deceit and lying from her head.

Lyndsey has to hand it to Herbert: she has a great poker face. She has no idea what the FBI squad supervisor is thinking at this moment.

"Well, now you know what I was working on," Lyndsey says. "Eric

Newman ordered Yaromir Popov's death, and pushed Theresa into going to the Russians. Theresa was bait to lure Morozov out of the country. But Popov—I'm still not sure why he had him killed."

Now that she's said the words out loud and feels the truth of them in her heart, it only takes a second for Lyndsey to push that last puzzle piece into place.

It was for *her*.

Eric killed Popov to entice her to do the investigation. It wasn't that Eric had faith in her: no, it was the opposite. To lead the investigation, he needed someone he could dupe and manipulate. To make sure they came to the right conclusion: that Theresa Warner was a double agent for Russia and that she'd done so out of spite and malice.

Lyndsey was nothing more than a pawn. In a way, she is responsible for Popov's death.

For a moment, she can barely breathe. *The human lie detector—I missed every sign.*

She opens her mouth to tell Herbert—but stops. It is too embarrassing to admit. Too shameful.

It doesn't matter: Herbert doesn't give her more than a moment to recover—or maybe she can't feel the depths of Lyndsey's distress. She runs a hand impatiently through her short hair. "I have to hand it to you: FBI has its share of ambitious pricks, but you guys are in a league of your own."

Lyndsey isn't about to argue the point. "What are we going to do with Cassidy? He knows we're onto Eric. What's to stop him from telling Eric before the takedown?"

"FBI can't detain him. There's no evidence that he committed a crime. I'll tell Cassidy he'd better keep his mouth shut. If he leaks word of our investigation to Newman, he'll face federal charges. But maybe it would be better if CIA handles this one. Can you get your folks to take care of Cassidy? I have a feeling if the orders come from Langley, he'll listen."

Herbert looks Lyndsey square in the face. She's sizing her up, that's plain, taking her measure. "But we've got something bigger to worry about right now. This is where you and I figure out how we're going to trap Eric Newman. If you're right, he has a lot to take responsibility for . . . But you and I both know that he can try to deflect the blame, to wiggle out of it. Sometimes hiding behind clearances and policies, rules and regulations. If Eric Newman had your asset killed and provoked Theresa Warner into spying for the Russians, how are we going to prove it?"

It's now the moment of truth. Her real fear, she realizes, is that she's afraid everything Cassidy said is true and they'll side with Eric. That they, too, will want Morozov so badly that they'd be willing to sweep it under the rug, look the other way.

She almost loses her nerve. Eric is not stupid; he will have covered his tracks well. They'll need conclusive evidence of what Eric has done—does that even exist?

Then she thinks of it: somebody paid Claude Simon, and she is sure it didn't come out of Eric's pocket. Simon gave Tony Schaffer's name to the FBI agents in Norfolk, which means he handled the contract that paid Simon. Eric's signature would be on the contract, too.

"You're going to have to subpoena the Agency to show you a classified contract," Lyndsey says. Shakily at first but then with more confidence. "But yeah, I think we can prove it."

She calls to set up an appointment with Patrick Pfeifer as soon as she gets into the office the next morning. She hasn't been able to shake the suspicion that Tom Cassidy telephoned Eric as soon as he was released, but that was a risk they had to take.

Turns out Pfeifer is juggling a lot of duties as Director Chesterfield is on vacation, Lyndsey is informed rather grumpily by the secretary who answers the phone. "It's of the utmost importance. I need to prepare him for a call from FBI," Lyndsey says.

"You can have fifteen minutes," the woman says curtly, and Lyndsey gratefully accepts.

She practices what she will say in her head over and over, but it dissolves like salt in warm water on the long walk to the seventh floor. She perches on one of the chairs in the anteroom, the secretaries explicitly ignoring her as they fall into the morning's rhythms. Attendees arrive for the first morning meetings, prep for the President's Daily Brief. Women and men walk by busily, throwing curious glances in Lyndsey's direction. Voices drift in from the private offices in the back but Lyndsey deliberately tries to ignore them so that she can focus on the task at hand.

The investigation has come to a dangerous junction. She can only see one way to succeed, but once Pfeifer hears what's going on, he may take it all out of her hands.

And what will she do if he looks her right in the eye and tells her she's being naïve? That Eric is in the right and she in the wrong, just as Cassidy said.

One of the secretaries lifts her head in Lyndsey's direction. Salt-and-pepper hair cut short, piercing blue eyes. "You can go in now."

Pfeifer sits behind his desk, flanked by stacks of papers. This morning he seems more harried than usual. Is that a look of annoyance she sees flit across his face? Lyndsey is hypervigilant for any sign of impatience, and she wouldn't blame him if he told her to stop these drop-bys. The Chief of Staff owes her nothing, after all. He's just a kind man who paid attention to her years ago when she was a new hire. CIA has thousands of employees and he has a responsibility to each one. The strained smile on his face could be her tenuous connection to him going up in flames.

"Hi, Lyndsey. I have a teleconference with State Department in a few minutes, so we'll have to keep this brief. Now, what can I do for you?"

Deep breath and it all comes out. She tells him everything, including her research, all the evidence she's compiled. She almost stumbles when she gets to what happened last night, Tom Cassidy's poisonous admission . . . Eric's plan, it sounds so preposterous now, said aloud in the Director's office, even if there is a contract with Eric's signature on it that will bear her out . . . She wonders in the back of her mind if she's hallucinating. She runs over her allotted fifteen minutes—the salt-and-pepper-haired secretary knocks at the door and, when there is no response, clears her throat, but Pfeifer asks her to get one of his executive assistants to cover the teleconference. State Department will have to understand.

As Lyndsey wraps up, Pfeifer's face goes ashen—for which she is grateful. She wasn't wrong to take this insane risk. To follow her gut. "This is incredible," he says when she has finished.

She's laid quite the problem at his feet. She wishes she were wrong, hopes there's something she's overlooked that Pfeifer, with his experience, will see. Her stomach roils while waiting for him to say something.

He sits back. "I don't know Eric Newman all that well. We never worked in the same office, and that's how you get to know a person. I've heard stories—but that's all they were, stories, and I never knew how much stock to give any of them. I wish I'd paid more attention then. This is bad, Lyndsey. Bad."

He doesn't qualify his statement with "if it's true." He believes her, for which she is immeasurably grateful.

"What I should do is call Newman into my office, with Roger Barker, his boss. Give them a chance to explain themselves. That would be standard operating procedure." For a moment, Lyndsey's stomach is in free fall. "But I'm not sure what that will get me. Newman will deny it, of course, and things will drag on, and from what you tell me, we don't have a lot of time. The meeting with this Russian agent is due to happen any day, you say?"

She nods.

Pfeifer rubs his chin. "And FBI is witting? They know the extraction is set to happen?" She nods again. He's silent as he thinks. Lyndsey lets her gaze skitter over the piles of papers on his desk. There must be dozens of crises demanding his attention, secrets that could cause the rise or fall of a foreign leader, unrest that could boil over to violence. CIA serves the president, not itself. This is one of many things Pfeifer must juggle at this moment, but she fears it must be the most personal to the Agency.

At length, Pfeifer lets out a sigh. "Okay—let's let this play out and see where it goes. It sounds like we have safeguards in place—FBI is witting, Newman's planning to pounce on the Russian agent?" She's explained that it's not *any* Russian agent but Evgeni Morozov, one of CIA's most wanted.

Even though this is what Lyndsey hoped for, she's surprised at Pfeifer's decision. She doesn't know why it's such a big surprise: the Agency takes risks every day. Some are moonshots. After a moment's thought, Lyndsey realizes that going against protocol seems out of place for Pfeifer, that's why it bothers her. He isn't talking about replacing her. She expected that, after this meeting, she would be ushered to the side and someone more experienced would be put at the helm.

She thinks she knows why, though. Eric Newman has been Chief of Russia Division for a while now. A senior executive. He has his allies, people who know him and will find it hard to believe that he's capable of this. Things could still blow up, even at this juncture. But Pfeifer has chosen to place his trust in her.

She almost wants to ask him—*are you sure? I'm not a human lie detector. I almost didn't see this. Eric nearly got away with it.*

And yet, she did figure it out. By some miracle.

Pfeifer nods his head with finality. "We'll let it proceed. I'll inform the General Counsel's office."

As his hand goes for the telephone, Lyndsey brings up two more things. First, someone needs to pay a visit to Tom Cassidy. "If his loyalty is to Eric, he may have already told him what's happened."

Pfeifer grunts. "Considering I haven't gotten a phone call from Newman yet, I doubt that's the case. We'll get the General Counsel's office to handle this one. Remind him of his legal obligation." It's the best he can do under the circumstances, and she'll just have to accept it.

The second ask is harder: Masha and Polina Popov need CIA's help. "They're in danger because of what Eric did. No one in the FSB suspected Popov was spying for us. He was safe. Now it's only a matter of time before the Russians figure it out." Help for Masha will be hard to keep from Eric. As long as he's Chief of the Division, there's a chance that he can find out about any operation that involves Russia. It could be an inadvertent slip by someone working logistical issues or the contracts office, pushing through the purchase of plane tickets or hotel rooms. There are a thousand little details that need to be taken care of in order to get someone out of hostile territory and set up a new life for them in America. To do it under intense time constraints increases the risk of discovery that much more.

"I'll talk to Roger Barker and ask him to take care of it. I can't make any promises until I talk to him, but . . . It sounds like we owe them at least that much."

Her gratitude is so great she cannot find words.

"Keep me posted," he says as she leaves, already turning back to the pile of paperwork on his desk, the next crisis beckoning.

FORTY

Lyndsey has barely returned to her office when Theresa appears at the door.

Lyndsey cannot help but notice that she looks so different from when Lyndsey returned to the office a few scant weeks ago. She's aged twenty years. She is exhausted. There is strain around the eyes, a tightness to the mouth. This is a woman ready for her trials to be over. But under the weariness and anxiety, there is a glimmer of resolve, of determination. A glint of steel. She is ready to set things right.

No doubt, the same could be said of Lyndsey. She feels like she aged twenty years between Cassidy's questioning and Pfeifer's office.

Theresa won't linger. They are both highly aware that Eric will notice, and become nervous, if there's any change in their behavior of the past few weeks.

Lyndsey locks eyes with Theresa but keeps her voice low. "We know what Eric's after. Cassidy spilled everything under questioning. He wants Evgeni Morozov. That was his plan all along. You're the bait."

Theresa can't believe what she's just heard. "I'm the bait?"

"There was intelligence that Morozov would come to Washington to bring you in personally. Eric was banking on that."

Theresa bites her lip. "The Russians haven't told me much . . . They never give me much detail, it's all in code . . . But Morozov's not coming to the meeting: it's Tarasenko, Dmitri Tarasenko. That's what I came to tell you. They contacted me last night. It's on for tonight. Ten o'clock. I don't know for sure who's coming. I was only told to be ready." She glances over her shoulder in the direction of Eric's office. "I'd better go. He'll be back any minute." Then she's gone, as suddenly and completely as a ghost.

It's go time. A familiar feeling, part anxiety and part anticipation, rises inside her. Equal parts dread and eagerness to have this over.

At least there's one bit of poetic justice in all this: Eric is going to be destroyed. After all this plotting and scheming, he isn't going to get Morozov anyway. He would've ruined lives only to end up with nothing.

Lyndsey reaches for the secure phone, punches in Herbert's number.

Theresa's house is ready. Herbert's team has fitted it with microphones and cameras. It was done stealthily, in case the Russians are watching the house—which they undoubtedly are. The FBI found an agent who looked uncannily like the woman who watches Brian in the afternoons, and she was sent in, backpack slung casually over one arm, to set up the equipment. A technician was sent in later to finish the work and test the connection to the command post, posing as a repairman come to fix the refrigerator. Herbert shows Lyndsey and Theresa on a map where the FBI teams have been posted, hours in advance. The house is covered; she and her son will not be in danger at any time, she assures Theresa, but of course she can't know that, not for certain. That's just what they tell you. What they want you to believe.

"I wish Brian didn't have to be there," Theresa says, fist pressed against her mouth. Rouge Rebelle smears across one knuckle.

Herbert gives her a tense smile. "Don't worry—my agents know his safety is our number one priority."

It's six o'clock, and they're in a van parked just outside Theresa's immediate neighborhood. She is ostensibly getting dinner and must rush back to her son so the sitter can leave. A bag of Chinese food, picked up earlier by one of the FBI agents, sits at her feet. It fills the van with spicy and savory aromas. Lyndsey's stomach growls to remind her that she hasn't eaten all day.

Theresa sighs. "At one point, months ago, I almost told Brian he was going to see his father again. I'm glad I didn't."

That must be the hardest part of what she is doing: knowing that Richard is alive but accepting that she is never going to see him again. In agreeing to take the safe course, she has chosen her son over her husband. Would she ever forgive herself for it?

She picks up the white plastic bag, the weight of the containers within shifting. It crinkles softly in her hands. "I'd better get home. Brian will be waiting."

Lyndsey will spend the hours leading up to the event with Herbert and her agents. She and Herbert sit with another agent in the command post, made to look like a delivery van on the outside but fitted with equipment inside. An agent with headphones sits at a station next to her, listening to what comes in from the microphones in Theresa's house. He also listens to a police scanner. Herbert is at a monitor, tapping away at emails. Lyndsey feels out of her element. She's not given anything to do and listens to bursts of chatter between the FBI teams, reporting potential activity, picking out recurring vehicles and pedestrians lingering in improbable spots, probable Russian surveillance. The good news is that there doesn't seem to be too many, about four total units spotted so far.

Somewhere, not far away, Eric's team is setting up. As decided in advance with Lyndsey, Herbert's team told Eric they'd intercepted a call that gave the final date and time, setting the trap. Lyndsey tries to picture what Eric will do—this is his big night, after all. The payoff for all his cunning. How many officers and contractors has he got on his team? He told Lyndsey, in passing, that he will lead them himself. She'd assumed he wouldn't let someone else steal the limelight. He will want to nab his prize.

So many teams converging on one target in such a confined, busy area, it's a miracle they haven't tripped over each other yet. In a more well-coordinated operation, Herbert explains to Lyndsey, CIA would let FBI handle it or a few officers would be invited to participate as part of the team. The fact that there are two separate teams should've tipped Eric that something unusual is going on—but he was so close to his prize, perhaps he decided not to fight it.

At one point, there's a crackle over the radio and one of the FBI units says they believe they've spotted the CIA team in a large SUV parked down the street. It has a clear line-of-sight to Theresa's house. Thinking of all these agents, armed and converging on the small Cape Cod, worries Lyndsey. Maybe Theresa was right, maybe this is too dangerous for Brian to be there. But it would've been risky to sneak him out. Someone might have seen him leave. Anyway, it's too late to change the plan now.

"If things go well, we'll catch our Russian handler. We'll also take Newman into custody. And Cassidy, for questioning. Your Agency hasn't turned over the contract yet, so we don't know if Newman's signature is on it," Herbert says, a little coolly on the last part. There's a rivalry between the agencies, and for some people, their natural instinct isn't to be cooperative, no matter what the orders say. One more thing to follow up on later, Lyndsey notes, maybe with Patrick Pfeifer.

It's right around ten o'clock. Outside the van, there's still traffic, car and foot. This part of the neighborhood is commercial, with small restaurants and coffee shops, a gift store, and a dentist's office. One block away, it all becomes residential, a mix of the original small houses and McMansions sprouted up from teardowns. It's a densely settled neighborhood and to think of the activity that will go down before long . . . It would be easy for a civilian to be hurt. Too, she thinks of Theresa, not far away, and how she must feel, alone in her house with her son, knowing that all hell is about to break loose. Earlier, they overheard a conversation picked up by the microphone, a disagreement between mother and son over bedtime. Theresa had ended up snapping at Brian in a way that made him burst into tears, which probably hurt Theresa to the quick. She couldn't explain why it was so important tonight, of all nights, that he listen to his mother.

The radio crackles to life behind her. "Black Escalade approaching target. Slowing down."

"We saw that car earlier," another unit chimes in. "Circled the block fifteen minutes ago. Same license plate."

"Just the one car?" Herbert asks into a microphone. "No tails?"

"None spotted—yet."

"Three inside. Possibly more—it's hard to tell with tinted windows."

"They're stopping. They've pulled into the target's driveway."

Lyndsey checks her watch. It's five minutes after ten.

"Two men have exited the vehicle. They're approaching the front door." Pause. "They've gone inside."

Herbert nods to the other agent, who gets up and heads to the driver's seat. "We're getting into position," she says into the microphone. The engine roars to life and the vehicle lurches out into traffic. It only takes a minute to swing around the corner and slide into an empty spot in front of a neighbor's house, just out of sight from the driveway.

They can see Theresa's house, albeit not completely. Shadows move on the curtains in the front room but rapidly disappear. Lyndsey remembers the layout of the house: they're going toward the back, to the family room and kitchen.

"Thomas, cover the man in the SUV," Herbert says in the microphone as she draws her weapon and heads for the van door. "Let's move on my mark—"

But they're interrupted by the appearance of black figures approaching Theresa's house. Bulky shadows suddenly glide between the trees like phantoms. They move down the street, past the FBI van, cross to Theresa's side of the street, and then, with raptor-like swiftness, fall on the SUV in the driveway.

"What the hell?" Herbert mutters into the mic.

Five, no, six. Six men move toward Theresa's house.

"That's got to be Newman's team. What the hell—Move, move!" Herbert says as she bursts out of the van.

Lyndsey sprints after her. She knows she's supposed to stay in the van until the site has been secured but she can't help it. Surely the Russian driver has seen the CIA team and notified his people inside. Theresa and her son could be in danger. At that moment, FBI agent Thomas drags the driver out of the van and presses him up against the vehicle, cheek ground into the glass window. But if the driver was quick and attentive, it could be too late.

Lyndsey holds her breath. Gunfire should break out at any moment. How could it not when the FBI teams explode out of nowhere, descending on the CIA team? It's going to be a debacle, a clusterfuck, as the two teams engage each other. Lyndsey can picture the seventh floor's reaction. But

Herbert is holding up her credentials for the nearest member of the CIA team to see and gestures broadly for silence, so that no one mistakes the other team for Russian. It settles as quickly as it started, nearly noiselessly. Thank goodness Theresa and the two Russians are deep in the back of the house, away from all this.

Herbert continues to the house, her men following her, and the CIA team falls in behind them. In total, there's a swarm of about a dozen men, weapons drawn.

Herbert tries the front door: it's open. Clever Theresa. Herbert points a finger to the hall, where shadows fall on an ochre wall, the advancing men darting like mice. Herbert heads down the hall, shouting, "FBI! Freeze!" The team hustles to follow her back, where the Russians will be, and sure enough, there stands Theresa with two men. Brian hides behind Theresa, face buried in her skirt.

The two men's faces are dark and dour with an unmistakable detachment, as though watching this unfold from far away. They are large physical specimens like linebackers, and dressed for travel, in coats and hats. They take in the FBI agents without saying a word, their eyes doing all the talking, searching left and right for a way to escape. Practicing a story that should get them out of here quickly.

One is clearly the leader. He carries himself with importance. He stands up and puffs out his chest, even though the circumstances call for him to make himself small and unobtrusive. He's not the type to go down without a fight, then. He's well dressed, looking like he plans to board an international flight shortly. But his face is pure malevolence. His square jaw clenched. And the scar at his temple, white and puckered, seems to pulse.

"He's not here. Goddammit, he's not here." That's how Lyndsey knows Eric has arrived: his voice. It rises up from the gathering of men. Anger seasoned with fear. The sound of failure. "Where the fuck is Morozov?"

Pushing his way through, Eric marches up to the man with the scar and goes nose-to-nose with him. "Is he waiting to meet you somewhere?"

A slow smile breaks out over the scarred man's face. "Is that what this is about?" He cannot disguise his Muscovite accent. Then there's that smile. He is clearly enjoying himself.

Herbert steps forward with enough power and authority to make Eric turn and stalk away. She flashes her credentials at the scarred man. "My name is Special Agent Sally Herbert and I'm with the Counterintelligence Division of the FBI. Dmitri Tarasenko, I'm arresting you and your accomplices for espionage against the government of the United States."

There's only one way they would know his name and he's figured it out in a flash. He turns in Theresa's direction; his face is a frenzy of anger. He bares his teeth in a nanosecond of animal impulse. She steps more fully in front of her son so that he can't see the hatred directed against her. *"Izmennick,"* he hisses. Traitor.

Then he turns back to Herbert, struggling to get his anger under control. His hand reaches for his breast pocket.

"Hands where we can see them," one of the FBI agents says, lifting his weapon.

The fingers gingerly pluck a document from the pocket. "I don't know what you're talking about. I am with the foreign ministry. Let me show you my passport. I have diplomatic immunity—"

The rest of the FBI team has surrounded the other Russian, who has raised his hands. "We'll contact your embassy, but in the meantime, I've got a witness willing to testify that you attempted to suborn her to commit treason," Herbert says. "We're taking you to FBI headquarters." Hands fall on Tarasenko's shoulders as they pivot him toward the door.

He jerks hard, trying to shake them off. "This is absurd! I demand you contact my embassy immediately . . ." This is an act; he was trained long ago in what to expect and how to act if he was ever caught.

"As soon as we get you to headquarters," she says. "But if you don't come quietly, we're going to have to cuff you." At that, he stops resisting. She nods toward the door for the agents to hustle him out. Now that the scarred man is no longer fighting them, the second man follows easily with no need for manhandling, which is good because he's as big as a refrigerator.

As soon as Tarasenko is out the door, Eric wheels around, jabbing a finger in Theresa's direction. He's going to try to salvage some victory. "What about her? Shouldn't you arrest her, too? After all, she committed treason. She passed classified information to the Russians. We have proof. That's still a violation of the law, isn't it? That's what I've always been led to believe."

Theresa seethes but doesn't react. She knows better. They're not going to get into a shouting match here, in front of the FBI or her son. She reaches down and lifts Brian, letting him press his face into her shoulder. "I'm taking Brian upstairs. I don't want him here for this."

Herbert nods as she holsters her weapon. She stands between Eric and the staircase, nearly as tall as he. "Ms. Warner is cooperating with us, Mr. Newman. The provisions of that cooperation have already been approved by the district attorney handling the case. Ms. Warner is free on her own recognizance until a judge decides otherwise."

The news almost knocks Eric backward off his feet. His face is nearly white with fury. He throws his hands in the air. "Why wasn't I informed of this? It's *my* office. The secrets she stole are *my* responsibility. That woman is a traitor, and you've made a deal with her?" He seems to remember in that moment that there is someone else he can pivot to, someone else to deflect the attention, and he looks for Lyndsey. "Why didn't you tell me about this? You knew, didn't you?"

As angry as she is with Eric, and as guilty as she knows he is, Lyndsey knows not to confront Eric. She must trust that there will be an investigation. She doesn't want to mess it up with an errant word, not when they're so close.

Herbert proves she has ice water in her veins. She looks past Eric to nod at a pair of agents, who step up to Eric, flanking him like sentries. "You're going to have to come with us, too, Mr. Newman, for questioning in regard to your role—"

"What?" Eric jerks away from the hand that falls on his shoulder, and skitters backward out of their grasp. If Tarasenko's fury was an act, Eric's is not. "My role? You must be joking! This is ridiculous—"

"You're Ms. Warner's supervisor, aren't you?" Herbert asks. "I'd think you'd want to cooperate."

"Of course, but . . . This is CIA business. I'll answer to an internal investigation but there's nothing I can say to you. It's classified . . ."

"Let me assure you, Mr. Newman, that I've been read into all the compartments germane to this investigation. We've briefed your seventh floor. Patrick Pfeifer authorized everything we've done. Now, you can come with us voluntarily or I can take you into custody."

That's the moment when Eric realizes it's all over. Everything he's schemed for, everything he wanted. The men in the ivory tower know what he's done. Those traitors, they talked to the FBI behind his back, without doing him the courtesy of talking to him first. This would never happen to guys at the top. Or to Richard. But Eric is not one of them and now, he never will be, and it was a colossal mistake to think he was. There's nothing more to say.

He quiets, perhaps realizing that it wouldn't look good to resist. He lets the agents lead him away, though not before giving Lyndsey a piercing glare. She figured out his secret but, unlike Cassidy, refused to keep it. *You were in on this, weren't you? Even you. I can't trust anyone.*

Herbert watches Eric leave with her men. To Lyndsey, she says, "You did the right thing. Though I know it was really difficult."

What will people at CIA say when this comes out? How many will side with her and how many will decide she's a traitor for not circling the wagons to protect her fellow officers? She might never be trusted again with a special operation because she didn't cover up what Eric had done. She may have torpedoed what was left of her career.

Herbert is looking at her cell phone and frowning. "My director wants me to brief him in person. Now. I'm going to need to head off." Lyndsey nods. "It'll take a few hours before we're ready to question Tarasenko. You should join us. Call my office when you arrive and I'll send someone to escort you."

There's nothing left to do but to check on Theresa.

The trip to the second floor of Theresa's house is longer and steeper than she remembers, or maybe it's because she is suddenly exhausted. The adrenaline high has worn off. The stress of the past twenty-four hours has caught up to her. At the top, a wedge of dim light from Brian's room spills across the hall. She catches the murmur of low voices, mother and child.

She gives a two-knuckle rap on the door before she steps in. Theresa sits on the bed holding Brian, her chin resting on the top of his head. He looks much younger than his seven years. They hold each other: they are all the other has.

Theresa looks up at her.

"I'm going now. There will be a police unit in front to watch the house tonight." Lyndsey is merely reminding her. Herbert went through this beforehand, how they don't think Theresa has anything to fear from the Russians, not right away in any case, but they would leave police protection in place until they have a sense of how the Russians are going to react. Right now, there's a jumble of vehicles in front of the house and they'll likely remain there for hours gathering evidence.

Theresa nods as she strokes her son's head.

"The FBI took Eric in. They have . . . questions."

Theresa's eyebrows shoot up, but she keeps mum in front of Brian. The boy knows him, after all. He's been in their house. Daddy's friend.

"Try to get some sleep. I'll be in touch tomorrow."

Lyndsey has one hand on the bannister when Theresa calls out. "Wait a minute—I want to thank you. This could've ended differently, a lot worse, and . . ." She looks down at her son.

"You don't have to thank me, not after what you've been through." And she has been through so much more than anyone will ever know. Because of what she did tonight, her husband may remain in a Russian prison for the rest of his life. Brian doesn't know that yet, but he may one day. What then?

"You did the right thing," Lyndsey says. Theresa deserves to hear it, too. Even if Lyndsey is the only person who will ever say it to her.

FORTY-ONE

The next morning, Lyndsey is sluggish. In the end, she only gets a couple hours of sleep before daylight and traffic noise force her out of bed. Even a hot shower does little to revive her.

For one thing, she had to take a late phone call from Pfeifer. He'd spoken to the attorney general and wanted to warn her that the FBI had decided not to hold Eric overnight. "Barker called someone and threatened hell to pay if they did," he had told her, an uncharacteristic grittiness in his tone. "I'll talk to Barker about it in the morning. And Lyndsey, there's something else. I've spoken to a few people about Eric, people whose judgment I trust, and they had some unsettling things to say about him. Clearly, we missed the signs on this one. Obviously there's something we should've caught sooner. We'll be watching him of course, but his ego is bruised, and that's the worst thing you can do to a guy like him. Be careful. Keep your distance. At least he doesn't know where you live," Pfeifer said in parting. She's not sure that's not the case. She remembers mentioning where she was staying to him once, but surely Eric hadn't been paying attention at the time.

That morning, she spends the gridlocked drive into D.C. wondering if Herbert was able to get much of anything out of Newman before he was released. Will he be fired? Pfeifer had warned her it was unlikely that Eric will face any disciplinary action. Strictly speaking, he broke no CIA regulations or U.S. law. The only offense he's guilty of is recklessness, which is viewed at Langley as a blessing and a curse. Pfeifer has made it clear that Eric has committed enough wrongs so that his career, if not over, will be ruined. That's a catastrophe when your career is all that matters. Barker has been particularly outspoken, Pfeifer confided. Apparently, it's one thing to let a case officer sit in an FBI holding cell but quite another thing to ignore Clandestine Service protocol and bypass proper vetting.

Merely losing his job doesn't seem like punishment enough. Yaromir Popov is dead. Theresa Warner was tricked into committing a crime and very nearly ruined her life. The unfairness eats at Lyndsey as her car creeps down Route 66.

By some miracle—the capricious D.C. commuting gods smiling on her this morning—Lyndsey finds space in a garage not far from FBI and is able to make good time. A young woman from Herbert's office escorts Lyndsey, chirping brightly over her shoulder as she leads the way. "I heard about the takedown last night. It sounds like you had an exciting evening."

You don't know the half of it.

The young woman works a keypad at the front door of the SCIF, leading Lyndsey inside. Herbert is talking to a couple men. She introduces them to Lyndsey: Steven Riley from the U.S. Attorneys office, and Jonah Rhee, from State Department. "Steve will participate in the questioning. Joe here delivered the bad news to the Russians this morning."

Rhee smiles sheepishly. "We're trying to slow roll them for you, but they're pretty anxious to get their men out of jail. They're claiming diplomatic immunity, of course. We told them we IDed one of their men as FSB. That's where we're at, at the moment."

They step into the interview room, the same one where Tom Cassidy was questioned less than two days ago. Was it only a day ago? The past twenty-four hours feel like an eternity.

She'd seen the man at the table just a few hours earlier, but now he looks completely different. He was like an enraged bull in Theresa's house, defensive, dangerous, looking for a way to free himself. Here, he sits—not calm exactly, but not on edge. He sizes up his three visitors, but his gaze lingers on Lyndsey. She's seen a lot of Russian intelligence and military from her time in Moscow. Men like Dmitri Tarasenko tailed her wherever she went in the city. They would give her the same little smirk to try to intimidate her. It enrages her, and then she remembers the reports she read on Tarasenko's military service and a shiver runs up her spine. He is not a man to engage lightly.

Sally drops a folder on the table. "Dmitri Tarasenko. Major Tarasenko, of the FSB. We've been in touch with your embassy and informed them of the charges against you. They denied them, of course, and demanded your release."

Riley takes over. "I'm with the U.S. Attorney's Office for the Eastern District of Virginia. We handle all criminal prosecutions for violations of federal law. We're preparing the court papers. We'll be charging you with espionage against the United States of America, and you should be aware that you could face a number of years in a U.S. prison—"

"An idle threat, no?" Tarasenko lifts one shoulder in a lazy shrug. He doesn't come across as nervous or afraid. To the contrary: he's not threatened in the least. "We both know you will not prosecute me. You don't want to give away secrets in court. You will trade me for your spies in Russia, the people we caught working for you."

Richard. This could be how they get Richard back. The FSB won't be able to deny they're holding him any longer, not when they were trying to entice his wife to work for them. This could be the opening they were hoping for. Lyndsey will have to talk to Patrick Pfeifer to see if the seniors will agree to offer a swap.

Tarasenko sinks back in his chair. He looks down at the Formica tabletop, at two worn patches where countless people have rested their elbows, exhausted by the weight of their duplicity. "There is one other possibility. One you haven't considered, perhaps, but is much more beneficial to you." He locks onto Lyndsey with those cold-as-creek-water eyes. "You are with CIA, yes? Do not bother to deny it: I know your name from your time in Moscow. I would like to make a deal with you. I want to become a double agent for the CIA."

It is pandemonium. They have to clear the room, unsure who needs to take part in this discussion. This is above Lyndsey's pay grade. Ideally, someone much more senior would handle this negotiation, but Lyndsey is here. It seems as though Tarasenko is counting on this.

Standing in the hall with Riley and Rhee, Herbert is relieved. "You know he's right," she says to Lyndsey. "He'll never be prosecuted. His people are going to fight like hell to get him released. The best we could hope for is a prisoner swap."

She needs to bring this back to Langley. Logically, the decision would be made by the Director of Russia Division, but Eric has been removed from his position. Kim Claiborne has been Eric's deputy since Jack Clemens went into the hospital. But Claiborne has been on a long-term assignment out of the office. Lyndsey hasn't met her since her return from Beirut and is pretty sure Claiborne hasn't been kept in the loop on any of this. Eric is known for eschewing deputies. He has them because he has to, it's part of the management structure, but they quickly find out Eric considers them about as useful as a knitted condom.

She'll call Pfeifer's office. He has more important things to do, but she's pretty sure he'll want to hear this. And hopefully, Claiborne is already on recall and winging her way back to Virginia.

"I need a secure line. I have to make a phone call—but then I'm going back in there."

N ow it's just the two of them in the interview room. Tarasenko leans far back in the chair, defying gravity. The Russian is cockier now. He's happy he's gotten the attention he needs. He likes to be in the driver's seat, this one. Lyndsey assesses him as quickly as she can from across the table.

They've given him a cup of coffee and cigarettes, letting him smoke in a federal building. The cigarette burns lazily between his fingers. He's watching her, too, deliberately letting his gaze wander away from her face over her body. He's just trying to intimidate her. She learned a lot about old KGB tactics from Popov. This man would've been happy under either the Soviet regime or the oligarchs. A bully and an opportunist, he's tailor-made to be a foot soldier in Putin's Russia.

"You've had quite a change of heart," Lyndsey says.

He taps ash into the paper cup they've given him to use as an ashtray. "How do you know? Maybe I've always wanted to help the CIA."

Or maybe you just want to play us. "We'll see. You'll need to talk to some people who will evaluate you. They'll decide whether you can be trusted."

His smile is reptilian. "Ours is a funny business, no? We deal in deceit but in the end, there is no magic formula to let us see into a man's heart. It comes down to gut and need. Do you feel you can trust me? Do you need me enough to override your distrust?"

She's been through this before, of course. She went through the whole drill with Popov; even though she never doubted his sincerity, she understood the need for polygraphs and interviews and evaluations.

Those things take time, however. The clock is ticking with Tarasenko. Every day he's detained will add to the FSB's suspicions. After a certain point, they will assume he's been turned.

"Do you think you can see what's in my heart?" He narrows his eyes at her.

The human lie detector. Does he know about her, her reputation? It wouldn't surprise her: she'd been stationed in Moscow, after all. Theresa may have told Moscow she was the person running the investigation for the mole. Tarasenko may be trying to keep her off-balance. Baiting her.

"That's up to other people, and we'll see soon enough. In the meantime, I need to ask a few questions. But mainly I want to know why? Why flip?"

He closes his eyes as he takes a drag on the cigarette. *Avoiding her.* "I can see what will happen. The Hard Man will be displeased by this . . . miscalculation. Morozov will be in trouble. This is not good for me. His enemies will use this to their advantage, and he has many enemies." He crushes the cigarette in the paper cup. "I can tell you are disgusted. What kind of person in our profession would do this, offer to turn on his country? I am looking to survive, that is all. A man must look out for himself. CIA wants Evgeni Morozov. I can help you."

Russia could've handed him over to the UN for what he did in South Ossetia, but it didn't. There is no honor among thieves.

Tarasenko is not stupid; he's being practical. He's been caught by the enemy. His mentor's stock will be dropping back in Moscow. He must cut his losses and find a way to land on his feet. He has one card to play—and he knows this offer will quicken the pulse of every official back at CIA headquarters. But Lyndsey finds his treachery breathtaking. "You were Morozov's protégé, weren't you?"

He tilts his head. "He helped me, yes, but I did not ask for this. This is how it is in the FSB; the ones at the top surround themselves with men who are indebted to them. We are an insurance policy. It is like with parents: you do not choose your father. What do you do if your father is a bad man? What do you owe him?" She feels a sting—does he know about her father, too? Is he trying to manipulate her?

"Look"—he leans forward, a tiger constrained only by his cage—"I know you don't like me. That is fine. Do we *like* any of the people who spy for us? Of course not. But that does not stop us from using them. It is like an arranged marriage, no?"

There are certainly case officers who disdain every asset who works for them—and many assets are damaged people, weak and narcissistic, desperate for approval, for love. Hard to like. But she also thinks of Yaromir Popov, whom she admired. She thinks of other case officers who tried to protect and care for their assets, even to advise them against their worst selves.

She doesn't think she will be able to like this one, though. He is doing this to save himself and that will be good enough for the evaluators.

"How will you deliver Morozov, if he never leaves the country?"

He flips a lighter in his hand end over end with the dexterity of a magician. "I will help you get him. I cannot say how, at this point. We must assess. It is true, he doesn't leave the city often, but he has a secret place he goes when he needs to get away from the Hard Man. A country dacha. Something *might* be possible there—maybe."

Is this true, or is he making it up? Tarasenko would know this is exactly what CIA would want to hear. She studies him for tics and tells but the vault is closed. He's good.

Lyndsey stands. She knows what she needs to do. There was no question that they will take him up on his offer, but she wanted to satisfy herself. "I'll recommend we proceed. You know what comes next. Evaluations. Interviews. A polygraph. We'll want to make sure you're telling us the truth."

He snickers. "I expect as much."

"And the expression you were looking for is 'a marriage of convenience.'" Yes, this is a marriage of convenience, slightly better than an arranged marriage. She can't help but have the feeling, however, that Tarasenko is a bad bargain at any price.

As she turns for the door, she hears him whisper. Almost too softly to be heard.

Kukla. Doll.

But he wanted her to hear. She turns back to face him and doesn't like the smile on his face.

FORTY-TWO

Lyndsey stands in the observation room, looking through a one-way mirror. On the other side, Tarasenko sits in an armchair, chatting easily with a CIA tech ops officer as though they were old friends. He snorts cigarette smoke through his nose like a cartoon bull while they go over a piece of covert equipment Tarasenko will use once he's back in Russia.

They're in a safe house in the verdant Virginia countryside, not far from a covert CIA facility. They're not going to bring Tarasenko into the facility, where he would get the opportunity to see the faces of CIA employees and learn more about the workings under the cover. Not yet. Such privilege only comes with trust. He has to prove his trustworthiness.

The safe house is small, an old farmhouse surrounded by acres of overgrown fruit trees, gone half-wild and impenetrable. Tarasenko sleeps upstairs, and there's someone on duty in the house—half housekeeper, half truant officer—around the clock. Outside, a security team patrols the grounds to make sure no unwelcome visitors come at night but it's unlikely the Russians have made up their mind about him yet, let alone know where the safe house is. Tarasenko has been here for three days. The first two, he was evaluated by psychologists. By the end of the second day, they concluded that he was probably making the offer in good faith. "He's not motivated by ideology—obviously," one of the psychologists said when she presented the team's decision to Lyndsey and Kim Claiborne, now returned from overseas. "He's an egoist, so he'll respond well to flattery. That will only go so far, however. Our best chance to control him is through incentives."

That evening, there had been a tense negotiation with Tarasenko. Claiborne, Lyndsey, and a few old Russia hands, guys who had worked the target their entire lives. They sat around the dining room table, intent on making a deal.

Claiborne is with Lyndsey now, watching Tarasenko recite the tech ops officer's instructions back to him. It was clear from Claiborne's behavior and the way she led the meetings last night that she'd been appointed acting Chief of Russia Division. Whether or not she'd keep the top post remained to be seen.

"He's a smooth one," Claiborne says. She'd come to the deputy position after tours in Iraq. She'd worked the Russia target early in her career but then took assignments in other offices—it was clear, at that point, that she was looking at upper management one day, and needed to broaden her experience. There would be others vying for Eric Newman's old job, now that he'd been forced out. Men who'd been eyeing the plum position, biding their time. "Can we trust him?"

He'd asked for a lot of money: a hefty down payment, deposited in an offshore account, and the balance to be paid after Morozov was delivered. He didn't want to stay in place, working for CIA: he would give them one thing, and one thing only: Evgeni Morozov. Once Morozov was captured, his future in the FSB was over. It wouldn't take them long to figure out who had helped the Americans. There'd been some debate whether it was better to keep an asset in place this high in the FSB versus getting a juicy but ultimately symbolic target like Morozov, but they'd decided to get Morozov. With a snake as slippery as Tarasenko, there was no telling when he'd turn on them. It was only a matter of time and the right circumstance.

The dollar signs lit up in Tarasenko's eyes as CIA made its offer: the payment, plus resettlement in the U.S., and more money as an "advisor" to CIA. Teaching Langley all about FSB techniques, recalling as much as he could about Russia's spies in the U.S. It was lucrative, but he would have to look over his shoulder for the rest of his life, or at least as long as Putin remained in power which, at this point, is looking like a lifetime appointment.

They are being careful with Tarasenko, not exposing him to too much of their tradecraft and methods. Still, it is hard to predict what will happen once he's back in Moscow, especially when he returns to work. A technical team is in Tarasenko's apartment right now, not far from Lubyanka Square. Tarasenko knows, of course. CIA's strategically placed microphones and cameras will pick up his every conversation, see who's coming to his door, who passes outside his windows. It's part of the dark bargain. If he wants to burn his American handlers, it will happen when he passes through the doors of FSB headquarters.

"We'll see if he passes his first test," Lyndsey replies, arms crossed over her chest. There's always a first test, low-hanging fruit. A sign that he's willing to do what's needed. He's been given initial requirements: Morozov's schedule for the next three months. The address of this secret hideaway Tarasenko alluded to, which he swears he doesn't know—yet.

Claiborne lifts an eyebrow. "I'm glad to hear you say that. It sounds like you're emotionally invested in this case—"

"Of course I am."

"Then I hope you'll consider what I'm about to say next: Tarasenko wants you to be his handler."

It's a great opportunity and she should be elated; she's anything but. The whispered word—*kukla*—echoes in her mind.

Lyndsey looks through the glass at the Russian. The relationship between handler and asset is close and often tempestuous. It demands clear thinking and emotions kept under control. Tarasenko seems to push others emotionally, hoping they'll make a mistake that he can capitalize on. Plus, she knows his background: he is violent, highly dangerous. It would be a challenge. And she has always liked a challenge.

But then there's the look he gave her at FBI headquarters. Chilling.

"You're probably sick of this case and want nothing more than to step away. I get it. But, Lyndsey—he's asking for you," Claiborne says.

"He wants me as his handler because he thinks he can play me."

"Maybe. There could be other reasons. Maybe he's attracted to you. Maybe he doesn't see young women as a threat. I don't mean to belittle you or your abilities—you're obviously very capable." Claiborne begins pacing, eyes directed at the floor. *Something she doesn't want me to see.* "You won't have to go it alone. We'll pull together a team of the best Russia hands to work this case. They'll be there to advise you. And at least you wouldn't be looking at an open-ended assignment: Tarasenko is going to help us get Morozov and then it's over. In the confusion after the snatch, we help Tarasenko slip out of the country. We give him his money and his new identity and then you're done."

Claiborne makes it sound so easy. Then why does she look so worried? What is she hiding?

There's one other thing bothering Lyndsey. She runs a hand along an empty shelf. "I can't work in Russia Division if Eric comes back."

"I don't want to misspeak, Lyndsey. Eric's situation isn't settled, not definitively, but . . . I think it's safe to say he's not coming back. He's going to be fired. It's not just what he did here—though you'd think that would be enough—but there have been other cases. Just not as egregious. I think they've finally come to see that Eric shouldn't have been put in a position of such high trust." She hesitates. "I wish I could say that he'll be punished for what he's done, but that's up to the Justice Department. It's out of our hands."

If Eric returns, there's no way she can continue at CIA. He'll hound her for the rest of her career, no matter where she goes or what she does. Still, she doesn't want to be responsible for ending a man's career. He's certainly done good along with the questionable. Undoubtedly, there are people walking the halls at Langley who would swear Eric Newman was the best manager they ever had. Those people will come to resent Lyndsey, too. Her enemies list grows by the hour.

Staying means reporting to this woman, but Lyndsey thinks it might work. She can tell already that Kim Claiborne is not Eric Newman. That much is clear from the careful way she speaks. Though Lyndsey feels guilty here, too: does Claiborne know about Beirut? Maybe she won't want Lyndsey to stay on the case after she finds out.

Lyndsey walks slowly across the small room, gaze directed at the tips of her shoes. "There's something else you need to know. I was recalled from my last assignment. There's an investigation—"

Claiborne waves her hand. "Davis Ranford, MI6?"

"Don't tell me you know him, too."

"Oh, I know him. So, I know there's nothing for Security to worry about. Besides, after what you've done here—it's water under the bridge. If you tell me it's over, I believe you."

Lyndsey hesitates. Does it have to be over? Is there a chance they will allow her to see him? It seems an impossible thing to ask . . . and she doesn't know how Davis feels. Maybe he's relieved it's over. Those were the unspoken rules when they started.

But Claiborne is already moving on. "You'll be happy to know that we've convinced State Department to offer to swap Tarasenko for Richard Warner."

It takes a moment for the words to process. All the heartache and treachery of the past two years might have been avoided if this had been done in the first place—or maybe that's not true, maybe nothing could've been done then to persuade the Russians to listen.

"The seventh floor changed its mind?"

"This is a different director. Chesterfield wants to do the right thing. What's more, they have someone to trade who's important to the Russians. And it will get our new asset back to Moscow at the same time. What's not to like?" Claiborne's shrug is playful. "So, let's not look a gift horse in the mouth. We'll see if it works."

"What about Theresa? Has anyone told her?"

Claiborne shakes her head. "Not yet. They thought it was better not to get her hopes up until it's official."

There it is again, the paternal attitude that rubs the wrong way. As though Theresa Warner doesn't know how capricious these things can be. Like Richard's return should be a gift. You don't want to spoil the surprise. "Wouldn't it be better if she knew the Agency was trying to free her husband, rather than to keep her in the dark?"

Claiborne suppresses a grimace. "I see what you mean . . . Let's put it this way: if someone were to tell her *informally* I don't think that would be a problem. Understood?"

She will drive out there to deliver the news in person. "Thank you."

"So . . . Should I take this to mean you'll stay? You know, if you're going to be Tarasenko's handler, you might need to be stationed overseas.

Maybe we can arrange for you to live in London. Would you like that?" Is that a wink Claiborne gives her? Her informal permission to see Davis.

Lyndsey looks back through the one-way glass. There sits the Butcher of Tskhinvali, laughing amicably with the tech ops officer, pretending that we're all friends, that he is just another guy. Doesn't think twice about all the blood on his hands.

He won't be anything like Yaromir Popov. Not at all. He will be a test of all her abilities as a case officer.

But after everything she's gone through with this case, she feels a powerful urge to see it through to the end.

She nods.

FORTY-THREE

Lyndsey opens a bottle of prosecco. Maybe she should've sprung for champagne, but she feels superstitious and is afraid it might jinx things.

The plan had been to go over to Theresa's house tonight, but Theresa called that afternoon and asked if they could meet at Lyndsey's apartment instead. She was on her way back from her aunt's vacation cottage at Lake Anna, where she'd just dropped off Brian. He would get away from the house and the neighbors' stares for a few days, and Theresa would be free for the inevitable meetings with Justice Department and CIA Security. "Is it okay if I come over? I'd rather not face an empty house right now."

Lyndsey putters around the apartment but, unsurprisingly, there is little tidying up to do. The apartment still shows few signs of occupancy. Sorting through the clothes she's tossed onto the bedroom floor, she resolves to get her life together. She'll find a new place to live, a real place. She'll buy furniture and a car.

Because pretty soon, she'll have a whole new life, too. She's getting her career back which, despite her misgivings, is a huge relief. It's like she's getting her old life back, but different. She'll be back in Russia Division, true, but if things go well with Tarasenko, she could move overseas again to be closer to him. In any case, it means returning to a target she understands, having familiar ground under her feet. Not being left to fend for herself the way she was in Lebanon.

Then there's Kim Claiborne. It may be too early to come to any conclusions, but she seems like a good leader. It's hard to know; it might just be wishful thinking, self-deception as an act of self-preservation. But each interaction with her has felt right and at this stage, at least, Lyndsey is willing to give it a chance.

There's a sharp knock at the door. Theresa stands in a red trench coat, cinched tightly at the waist, a bottle in her hand. Prosecco. Lyndsey accepts it with a smile: they've even come to think alike.

Lyndsey leads the way to the living room. "How is Brian?"

Theresa kicks off her shoes and sinks into the sofa. "Hopefully, a few days at the lake will bring him around. He's shaken up, of course. I can only hope he won't be scarred for life."

"He'll be fine. He's strong. At least he's not going to live in a different country."

Theresa hides her face in her hands and groans. "I can hardly believe I was going to go through with it! The things we do when we're desperate . . . I hope to never be that desperate again in my life."

Lyndsey hands her a glass of prosecco. "What's next? Have they given you any idea . . . ?"

"They have to file charges, but the U.S. Attorneys office is going to recommend that the charges be dropped. My clearance has been pulled, of course," she says with a sigh, leaning back into the cushions. "At the moment, I'm on administrative leave while they decide what they're going to do, but if they just fire me and there are no other repercussions, I'll consider myself lucky."

They do not discuss Kyle Kincaid. He came out of the coma and is undergoing tests. It is too soon to tell what the consequences will be for Theresa, whether Kincaid will tell the police what happened. He's not entirely innocent, either. The Agency's investigators have not been able to speak with him, however.

"What will you do?" What does a disgraced spy do for work? Will Theresa be able to get another job? You'd think it would be a big black mark on your permanent record, like a dishonorable discharge from the military.

"We could move away from here. I can't help but think this won't seem as bad if I can just get away from D.C." Lyndsey also feels this way, that all this cloak and dagger stuff becomes less and less important the more miles you put between yourself and Washington. "My house is worth a lot, thanks to the location. We could live quite nicely off that in another part of the country. Then there's Richard's car. Did you know a man chastised me once for driving it to work? He said it was downright reckless of me. I could sell it. That's Brian's college fund, right there."

It seems a good opportunity to break the news to Theresa. Lyndsey has to be careful: she doesn't want to get Theresa's hopes up prematurely. The seventh floor has blessed the prisoner exchange but it's far from a done deal. It could still be derailed.

Lyndsey pours more prosecco into Theresa's glass, smiling. "Oh, I don't know about that—Richard might just want it back."

It takes a minute for Theresa to put it together, but once she does, her eyes cloud with tears. "Are you saying there's a chance?"

"Chesterfield gave the okay. I think they've got it all lined up on the U.S. side. Now it's up to the Russians. I can't imagine they won't agree. They must want to put this debacle behind them."

For a long moment, Theresa cannot move. She seems to be paralyzed with hope and fear. Then she shakes her head, brushing aside tears. They clink glasses.

She tells Theresa, too, that she will become Tarasenko's handler. "You know him best. What advice do you have for me?"

Theresa puts down her glass. "I wouldn't say I know him well at all. We only met a few times. Still . . . I wouldn't trust him, Lyndsey. Be careful."

"It's meant to be a limited relationship. He's going to help us get Morozov—that's it."

A scowl ruins Theresa's lovely face. "Morozov. Look at everything CIA has done to try to get him. They paid informants, they've gone through all the 'official' channels . . . All the people who've died, and it's all been for nothing. And if they do get him, what then? Will it be worth it?" Theresa is bitter and Lyndsey doesn't blame her: Eric was willing to sacrifice her and turn her whole world upside down in order to bring him in. Is it worth going to such extremes for revenge?

Then, too, there's the question of whether an asset like Tarasenko couldn't be put to better use. A well-placed spy like Dmitri Tarasenko could be used to save, potentially, hundreds of lives. The thought nags at Lyndsey, though she knows the deal has been made. This is what Tarasenko offered, and CIA accepted.

There's an unexpected knock at the door, definitely an uncommon experience at this hour of the evening. Lyndsey's first instinct is to assume someone has mistakenly come to the wrong door and to ignore it, but no: it could be a neighbor with a problem or a mishap in the parking lot, someone swiping her car. She gets to her feet and answers it.

Eric Newman. He's the last person she ever expected to see at her door, so his presence seems like a mirage. He's all wrong, his expression, his stance, even what he wears, Burberry raincoat over jeans and anorak, running shoes on his feet, no socks. It's something you'd throw on to run down to the drugstore for cigarettes and lottery tickets.

He pushes his way inside. "I want to have a word with you," he says a little too loudly. The smell of alcohol is strong on his breath.

In two steps, he sees Theresa on the couch. His face falls. "I came because I thought you'd be alone. But I see you two couldn't wait to celebrate my downfall. You've got champagne and everything."

Lyndsey wasn't worried when she first saw him at the door. He was obviously in a bad way. She actually felt sorry for him. Now that he's pushed his way into the house and is obviously drunk, reeking of self-pity, and a little out of control, it's a different story. Pfeifer's warning comes back to her. Just one day ago, Eric suffered the worst indignities of his life. He was taken to FBI headquarters. He was fired from his job. He is under investigation. He probably gave the slip to a surveillance team to make it here.

She touches his shoulder, meaning to steer him back to the door. "Eric, you shouldn't be here. And you're drunk."

He shakes her hand off violently. "So, now I'm not welcome. You were pretty friendly when I invited you to run the investigation. You were only too happy for my help then. For me to make that bad thing you did in Lebanon go away—"

"'Bad thing'? There's no comparison between what I did in Lebanon and what you've done."

"Your friend has questionable judgment, did you know that?" he says over his shoulder to Theresa. His tone is mocking and gleeful. If he's going down, he's going to take everyone with him. "Do you know why she was recalled from Beirut? She was caught sleeping with a foreign intelligence officer. She's either self-destructive or incredibly stupid, you decide."

"What I did is none of your business." Lyndsey knows he's trying to make her lose her temper, but that doesn't make it any easier to keep from getting angry. She never guessed Eric could be like this. He hid his ugly side so well.

Theresa is on her feet, cell phone out. "Eric, you shouldn't be here. I bet you were told not to contact either of us. If you don't leave right now, I'm calling the police. Do you understand?"

As he spins on Theresa, his face softens. His anger evaporates. "It's your fault, you know. If you hadn't—If we . . ." He stops, catching the words in mid-flight. "Things could have been different. In another world, we could've been happy and none of this would've happened."

Strangely, Theresa doesn't snap back at him. She doesn't speak. She drops her head, avoiding his eyes.

What is going on here? Lyndsey is confused but she doesn't say a word. The air prickles like an electrical storm has just passed by.

Eric stuffs his hands in the pockets of his raincoat and shuffles his feet. "I just wanted you to know—it's your fault. Both of you," he says, turning back to Lyndsey like she's an afterthought now. "You remember that, when they ask. You'll have only yourselves to blame." And then he pushes past her again, only this time she has no desire to stop him. He leaves the door wide open to the night.

Stunned, Lyndsey stands at the open door. Theresa walks up beside her. "What was *that* about?" They both look at the spot where Eric had last stood. There is a weight to the emptiness. That moment with Eric is dissolving by the second. It is hard to say what they saw, let alone believe what it might mean.

Lyndsey turns from the door, reaching for her cell phone. "It almost sounds like—I don't know—like he's going to do something drastic."

"Do you think he might try to kill himself?" Theresa asks, dubious.

It would be easy to say, *He's just drunk. He's upset. It will pass.* That they heard wrong. They misunderstood. To avoid the embarrassment of Eric being found in two hours waiting to board a plane for Minnesota to visit his family and lick his wounds.

But that's not what's happening. There was another kind of threat in Eric Newman's demeanor. Lyndsey calls the Watch and gets the same officer who called her in the night Yaromir Popov died. Sergeant Mitchell.

"You're right, ma'am. It sounds like he evaded the surveillance team.

We'll alert them right away. It's doubtful that Mr. Newman will try to contact you again tonight, but if he returns to your apartment, try to detain him."

The two women return to the couch, rattled. Theresa is already getting her things together, readying to go. But there is one thing bothering Lyndsey. She heard what Eric said and this moment, right now, might be her only chance for an explanation. In an hour, a day, the moment will be lost. Deniable. It must've been important for Eric to say it to her, under the circumstances. Lyndsey wants to know. "What was that he said to you? That the two of you could've been happy?"

The sigh that comes from Theresa is long and low and pained. She turns away, crossing her arms over her chest. "It's nothing. A long time ago, before Richard. But it was nothing."

Suddenly, Lyndsey understands. Eric had been in love with Theresa all this time. Maybe it was the reason he'd kept the secret of Richard's survival from Theresa two years ago. Maybe he'd hoped things would be different this time. "It was something to Eric, apparently."

Theresa turns her head. Her hair sweeps over her eyes, and she reaches up to brush it away. Even this tiny gesture is elegant and perfect, and she can see why Eric would fall in love with her. "He should've known better. And he was never in love with me. He was in love with what Richard and I had. With what *Richard* had. Respect, love. I might've been young and inexperienced, but I could see that he didn't want me—he wanted to be Richard. And he proved it in the end, didn't he? Whatever love he had turned to hate. He was willing to burn me and let Richard die in prison."

Now Lyndsey feels a slight afterburn of embarrassment. Because she recognizes that this is what she has wanted, too. Once she came back to Russia Division and became friends with The Widow: to have a piece of what she didn't have a decade ago, when she was on the outside looking in.

And yet . . . That seems like a lifetime ago, the desire for acceptance a holdover from her first uncertain days at the Agency. That self-doubting young woman is gone, Lyndsey's eyes opened by the events of the past weeks. She understands Davis better, how one becomes toughened in this business. Cynical.

She deserves that relationship with Davis now, she decides. It's been hard-won.

Just like her friendship with Theresa.

FORTY-FOUR

I t is a rainy and cold afternoon. Lyndsey stands inside an old concrete building, next to a wall of windows.

Outside, the air base looks like any airport the world over. Huge runways. Planes touching down in the background with languid regularity. Ground crews in camouflage and reflective vests scurrying about. Huge transport vehicles parked on the periphery, painted olive drab. Rainwater runs down the glass in streaks, the grayness lending an air of weariness and ennui.

Closer to the doors leading to the tarmac are Theresa and Brian. They are more animated than everyone else in the terminal, and certainly more than the last time Lyndsey saw them. Theresa is pointing out ground equipment to Brian, who seems to know the name of each one. Brian, who has barely said two words in the entire time Lyndsey has known him and perpetually hid behind his mother's legs, can't stop talking. He's pressed against the windows, straining to see the landing of the aircraft carrying his father.

There isn't a big crowd waiting in the terminal for Richard Warner's return. Spy swaps tend to be done on the hush-hush, even for a man who has been declared dead. There are a couple Agency representatives to handle all the administrative work, the paperwork, and to explain what happens next. What the government is prepared to do to make amends. Once they're back in Virginia, there will be debriefings. Eventually, he will be brought back into the headquarters building. There are a lot of people who want to see him, to hear his stories, to cry over his return.

The two representatives stand back, conferring with each other in a waiting area. This is the family's time, Theresa's and Brian's.

She and Theresa have barely spoken since they heard the news that Eric Newman has disappeared. That night, right after Lyndsey's call, the Watch sent an officer to Eric's apartment to check on him, only to find certain key things missing, such as his suitcases. Then they found out that he'd withdrawn most of his savings from his bank account the day before, just walked in and took what he could in cash. They were trying to track him down, but it wasn't hard to disappear when you know how. When you've been trained for it.

A woman in an air force uniform walks up to Theresa, their liaison since arriving on the base yesterday. "Your husband's plane should be touching down any minute. If you go over here"—she starts to lead them along the wall of windows—"you'll have a better view." Theresa and Brian follow, hand in hand. Lyndsey hangs back a little.

The plane, a military transport, comes into view shortly. It's so big, it's like watching an aircraft carrier descend from the clouds, then touch down on earth, the ground rumbling beneath it. You hold your breath as it wheels toward the terminal. It looks impossibly big, like it could roll over this building.

The officer escorts Theresa and Brian through the doors and onto the tarmac. An ambulance has pulled up, its red lights flashing. They've already been told the ambulance is just a precaution; Richard Warner has been seen by medical personnel at the U.S. embassy in Moscow and he's in reasonably good health for a man who's been imprisoned for two years. But that's why he's been flown to Ramstein and not directly to the United States: he's getting a complete checkup. It seems that's the protocol for prisoners and hostages, a trip to the army's Landstuhl Regional Medical Center. He'll stay for a couple days, at the least, before flying to Virginia. A psychiatric evaluation before he touches down on U.S. soil is a big part of the reason he is at Landstuhl.

Lyndsey remains inside and watches. The terminal is cold; perhaps it's just too hard to heat this old building. So much glass. A damp German chill seems to emanate off the walls. She watches as they roll a set of metal steps out to the aircraft, Spartan and old-school. No jet bridges here.

A couple of other passengers disembark first. None are Richard, she guesses, because they're wearing military uniforms. Did they know that man at the back of the plane, the quiet man in civilian clothing, has just been released from a Russian prison? That he's a hero? He'll never be a famous one, though; his story won't even be well known in the halls of CIA. The real story will be kept secret. Not for the first time, she wonders what will become of Richard Warner. What do you do with your life after something like this? She tries to imagine him back at CIA, working for men who left him to rot in prison, but that can't be possible. He will have been changed forever by the experience. He must be ready to close the book on his life in the intelligence business.

Eventually, Lyndsey catches sight of him as he steps onto the top of the portable stairs. He's so far away that she can't see him very well but it's close enough. A wisp of a man, his hair gone completely gray. He's wearing a tan jacket they probably bought for him in Moscow, and a plaid shirt like something a lumberjack would wear. It seems incongruous and a tad fanciful until she realizes Richard used to be an outdoorsman, loved his hiking and fishing, and he wore plaid flannel all the time.

Brian jumps up and down on the tarmac, but waits until his father gets all the way to the bottom to launch himself at him, wrapping his arms around his father's legs. Richard leans over to rub his back, a comforting gesture, but doesn't try to pick him up—is he too weak?

This whole time, Theresa hangs back. She can't take her eyes off him, but she doesn't throw herself at him the way Brian did. Moscow Station must've told Richard what happened, the reason why the U.S. was finally able to arrange his release. He knows that she made a deal with the Russians. That she gave up names of assets and is responsible for the death or disappearance of two men. She broke the law—but for him, all for him. He should be flattered, logic would seem to dictate. Only someone who loved you very, very much would go to such lengths—right?

But Richard is—or was—a Boy Scout, with unshakable loyalty to the Agency and everything it stood for. After two years in prison, is he still? Will he be able to forgive his wife for what she did?

Lyndsey wishes it weren't so complicated, for Theresa's sake. The woman did her best for him. She stands riveted, her face almost pressed against the cold glass.

They look into each other's eyes, Richard and Theresa, for what seems to be a long time. Maybe they're thinking about what lies ahead. Both of them have changed in ways the other can't begin to know. They'll have to get to know each other once again, and most important, to trust each other. If they're going to stay together, that is.

The same challenge, sort of, waits for Lyndsey. She doesn't know if she should stay with the Agency. She knows what she told Claiborne, but she's had time to think about it. Russia Division is in complete turmoil: for better and worse, it's losing the man who has been running it for years, who knew it inside and out, knew every man and woman who worked there, knew every asset they'd ever run, knew every operation backward and forward, knew its twisted, wicked history like his own. It's been rocked by this scandal, made people shaky and timid. People are talking about leaving, finding new positions elsewhere or quitting altogether. The scandal has to be a sign of deeper rot, right? How can you trust this place to do right by you after what happened to Richard and Theresa, two of the Agency's anointed?

Oh, but there's more to the story than the rank and file will ever be allowed to know. Yet another deep, dark secret hidden away in its deepest, darkest vaults.

Lyndsey, hands shoved in pockets, pushes through the double doors and meanders out onto the tarmac. She has the same question before her: can she trust the Agency? Patrick Pfeifer has done the right thing, and that gives her hope, but how many men like him are there, and how many more are like Eric Newman, lying in wait? She's agreed to run Tarasenko, yes, but it feels like she hasn't fully committed. That she's still looking over her shoulder, wondering if she's doing the right thing. Kim Claiborne seems trustworthy. She's no Eric Newman. But these managers all seem rock solid—at first. You must be confident to be a manager in the Directorate of Operations: people have to be willing to do some pretty dangerous things on your say-so, after all.

She looks at Richard and Theresa, still observing each other at arm's length. This is what it can do to you: make you doubt the very ground beneath your feet.

Then, Richard stirs.

He stretches out his arm to Theresa.

She tumbles into him, pressing her face to his chest. His right arm wraps around her back, drawing her closer. They cling to each as tightly as possible.

Lyndsey edges closer to the family as they make their way to the ambulance. Richard is about to climb into the back when Theresa waves her over. Her eyes glisten with tears as she takes Lyndsey's arm and pulls her into their circle.

"Richard, I want you to meet Lyndsey Duncan. We owe her so much . . . We owe her everything. If it weren't for her, you wouldn't be here today."

He squints through his eyeglasses. She can tell he is searching his memory, perhaps remembering something about her face. Lyndsey is shocked to see how he's aged. He could easily be fifteen years older. His clothes hang off his lean frame. His face is creased with wrinkles, the skin rough, as though he's been left in bad weather for a long time. There seems to be an involuntary tremor in his hands—but Brian clings to them nonetheless.

But there's the same intelligent twinkle in his eyes that she remembers from her earliest days in Russia Division. Despite what they did to him in prison, they didn't manage to destroy the man. To break his spirit.

She's glad to see, after everything he has been through, that sometimes the best endures.

"Hello, Richard. It's good to see you." She extends her hand. "Welcome home."

ACKNOWLEDGMENTS

For those who know of me through my novels, it may come as a bit of a surprise to learn that before I started writing, I had a long career in intelligence, which I drew on to write *Red Widow*. I always wanted to write a spy novel because I felt there were things about working in this field that people didn't understand, especially if what they did know came from popular movies, TV shows, and books. I am grateful for my career: as I've told many people, through it, I was able to do many things I would otherwise never have experienced. But it has its dark side, too, and it's that trade-off and the personal toll it can take that I wanted to capture in *Red Widow*.

I can't reveal the names of all the colleagues who helped, befriended, and challenged me over the years but know that I think of you and appreciate your kindnesses. I would like to drop the first names of a few special friends here (you know who you are): Andrea and David; Bev; Charlotte; Jen; Jan; Jay; Kathy; Peter, Simona, Jim, Gary, and everyone at the Center. Also, thank you to the patient folks in the Pre-Publication Review office and a special thanks to Larry P. for letting me base a character on him.

Thanks also to John Nason for his help understanding what happens when a foreign national is arrested by the FBI for spying. Thanks, too, to former colleague and friend Ed Mickolus for the introduction to John.

ACKNOWLEDGMENTS

There would be no *Red Widow* without my editor at Putnam, Sally Kim. I had pretty much given up on writing a spy novel and I didn't take it up again until she challenged me to come up with an idea that eventually blossomed into this book. She went through countless revisions to get me to the version you hold in your hands. I am grateful for her vision and patience.

Deep thanks to the entire Putnam team for all their support and enthusiasm: president Ivan Held; director of marketing Ashley McClay; director of publicity Alexis Welby; the tireless Gabriella Mongelli; Katie Grinch, Sydney Cohen, Emily Mlynek, and Nishtha Patel.

Many thanks, as always, to my literary agents Richard Pine and Eliza Rothstein, who make everything better. Thanks, too, to my film agent Angela Cheng Caplan. And last but far from least, thank you to my husband for letting me disappear behind the door of my study to write, after thirty-four years of letting me disappear behind the gates and barbed-wire fences of work.